STUNNING REVIEWS FOR KAT MARTIN:

Bold Angel:

"Kat Martin has superbly captured the essence that is the medieval period. Fans will most assuredly ask for more from this talented author."

—Linda Abel,
The Mediaeval Chronicle

Gypsy Lord:

"Kat Martin has a winner...A page-turner from beginning to end." —Johanna Lindsay

"Kat Martin dishes up sizzling passions and true love, then she serves it with savoir faire. Bon appetit!"
—*Los Angeles Daily News*

Sweet Vengeance:

"Kat Martin gives readers enormous pleasure with this deftly plotted, stunning romance." —*Romantic Times*

"A rich read, memorable characters, a romance that fulfills every woman's fantasy." —Deana James

His mouth came down hard over hers and the world spun away. The strength of Ral's need made Caryn grow flush and damp. In seconds, he was stripping off her tunic and the chainse she wore beneath, carrying her naked to the edge of the bed.

"I have longed for this moment." Ral tore the spun gold snood from Caryn's head, drove his hands through the heavy mass of her hair, and spread it around her shoulders. When he pulled her against him, shivers raced through her body and a fever roared through her blood.

"As always, you are ready," he said in a voice gone rough.

Waves of heat washed over her, rippling eddies that tore a whimper of desire from her throat. Her body trembled and flames roared deep inside her.

"Ral . . . sweet God . . . Ral."

Caryn's hair trailed onto his powerful shoulders. He took her mouth savagely. The world became blurred and distant, then it faded completely away. Fire engulfed her, and waves of mounting desire, until she finally succumbed to the mind-numbing fury. She was bathed in sweetness, awash against a blazing crimson sand. She cried out Ral's name . . .

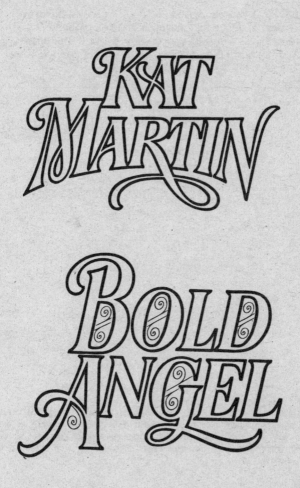

KAT MARTIN

BOLD ANGEL

St. Martin's Paperbacks

BOLD ANGEL

Copyright © 1994 by Kat Martin.
Teaser for *Devil's Prize* copyright © 1994 by Kat Martin.

All rights reserved. No part of this book may be used or reproduced in any manner whatsoever without written permission except in the case of brief quotations embodied in critical articles or reviews. For information address St. Martin's Press, 175 Fifth Avenue, New York, N.Y. 10010.

ISBN: 0-312-95303-8

Printed in the United States of America

St. Martin's Paperbacks edition/September 1994

10 9 8 7 6 5 4 3

For the family I rarely see—my uncles and aunts and cousins. Though we are scattered like seeds on the wind, I think of you warmly and often.

John Crowder and Owen Moore; Bonnie and Ted Hawthorne; Marilyn and Lionel Oliveira, Kris, Jerry, and Adrianna; Rob Crowder, Rebecca and Matthew; Rocky and Arlene Loop, Jason and Dawn; Rick and Debbie Loop; Sheila and Sherri; Betty Pugh, Bob, Bobbie, Carol and Marla, Lollie and Al Short; Geri Wilson; Ross and Sandra Kelly; Mary Ruth Ledbetter, Joannie and Megan. I wish you love, luck, and happiness—each and every one.

A special thanks to my great and good friend Wanda Handley for her help on this and other of my books.

Chapter One

S he should have been afraid. A goodly number of Saxon warriors had fled the sight of him in full battle dress, yet Ral saw no fear in the bright blue eyes that searched his face. From beneath his conical helmet, he watched her walk toward him, her small hand offering him a bright bouquet of flowers. She smiled, heedless of the dried blood darkening his chain mail hauberk or the fierce black dragon on his shield.

She should have been afraid, yet she only came closer, curious but strangely serene, interested, almost eager, as if she had found a new friend.

Ral shifted in his saddle, uneasy at her regard. The huge black destrier beneath him stomped and blew, then perked its ears and turned its head toward the lovely black-haired maid who stood no higher than the horse's massive withers.

Raolfe de Gere would have sworn he had never seen a more beautiful woman or a smile more winsome than the one that brightened the young woman's face. She looked no more than eighteen summers, with a body ripe for a man and a radiance in her cheeks that said she might welcome one. Yet surprisingly the feelings she stirred were of a different sort entirely. Feelings of hearth and home and an end to the blood and the fighting.

She said nothing, just lifted her small bouquet. Ral reached out a gauntleted hand and took it. When his fingers brushed hers, her smile grew broader, and he gave her a weary smile in return. He waited for her to speak, curious to hear the sound of her voice but reluctant to break the spell she had woven. He wondered where she had come from and what could be her name.

Where could her sister have gone? Caryn of Ivesham rounded the large granite boulder and searched among the oak trees off to the right. Sweet Mary, she had only been gone for a moment; Gweneth could not have gotten far.

Caryn scanned the meadow then the knoll at the opposite end. The pale blue tunic rippling softly in the breeze could only be Gweneth's, but beside her—Holy Mother of God—Caryn's breath caught in her throat. The Dark Knight! A black dragon on a field of bloodred. Raolfe the Relentless! And there stood Gweneth, painfully unaware, offering him a cluster of posies.

Lifting the hem of her forest green tunic, her heart slamming hard against her ribs, Caryn raced across the meadow.

"Gweneth!" she shouted. *By all that's holy.* "Gweneth!" But her sister did not turn and Caryn didn't stop running. Not until she reached the girl's side and stared into the hard dark features of the huge Norman knight astride his big black horse. Ral the Relentless, the man who had been sweeping across the country, harrying the north in King William's name, determined to squelch the rebellion.

"Let her go!" Caryn cried, the words a bit irrational since the man merely sat upon his steed. The huge knight said nothing, just kept staring at Gweneth as if she were some fey creature from another world, which in a way she was.

"I pray thee," Caryn said, "my sister means no harm.

'Tis not her way to be wary. She does not understand. She is not . . ." What could she say about Gweneth? About the world in which she lived, about her sweetness, her gentleness? But looking at the Dark Knight's face, it seemed there was no need.

"She is lovely," he said with soft reverence, as if he joined her in that place faraway. Then he straightened in his saddle, so tall he blocked the sun. Black hair shone beneath his helmet, worn longer than most of the Normans she had seen, his jaw strong, his skin swarthy. For the first time, his attention turned to Caryn and any hint of softness in his manner swiftly fled.

"You should not be out here. There are men in these woods, knights and men-at-arms fresh from battle who would do you grave harm. Surely you know 'tis not safe to be about in these times." He spoke to her in Saxon, not fluently, but well enough to be understood.

"We were on our way home from the village," Caryn lied, for in truth they had merely been escaping a dreary day in the hall. "We mistook our way but we have found it now. We will return home at once."

"You are no peasant. From the looks of your clothes, you are highborn, both of you. You should be better tended."

Caryn stiffened. " 'Tis no concern of yours. I tend my sister well enough—better than anyone else. I can take care of us both!" She grabbed Gweneth's arm, but her sister pulled free. Smiling, Gweneth reached a hand to the tall knight above her. Caryn's eyes went wide when the huge knight reached down and grasped it, giving it a gentle squeeze.

"Go," he said, looking back at Caryn, his voice once more harsh and rough. "Return to your home before trouble finds you. The next man you cross may seek far more than friendship. Go!"

Caryn swallowed and backed away. With a sharp tug on her sister's arm, she hauled Gweneth away toward a

copse of trees. She was shaking by the time they
reached the forest, though Gweneth merely strolled
along beside her, picking up more spring flowers, the
towering dark man on the knoll already forgotten.

Thinking of their narrow escape, Caryn leaned against
a boxwood tree and released a breath of relief. He was
so big! One blow of his massive fist could end the life of
a man. It was said he'd slain dozens of Saxon warriors,
that he had raped and pillaged all the way from the
coast. The image she saw instead was one of the huge
dark Norman holding the small bouquet of posies, of
him gently squeezing her sister's hand.

Caryn frowned, unable to puzzle it out. They should't
have come out today. She had known that from the
start, but the Normans were rumored to be miles away
and she had been cooped up in the hall far too long.

She thought of the Dark Knight's words, that she and
Gweneth should be better tended. In truth, her uncle
rarely knew where she was and, she suspected, was
most times relieved when she and Gweneth were not
underfoot. Besides, Ivesham wasn't in danger. Though
her uncle's sympathies lay with his Saxon brothers, he
had staunchly pretended loyalty to the king.

None knew of his rebel sympathies. Not even Caryn,
until she had overheard him one night in the hall.

She let go of her sister's hand and leaned down to
pluck a perky yellow marigold. The day was so perfect,
so sunny and warm. She glanced at the cloudless blue
sky with yearning. There was little to do in the hall, save
for the usual women's work which she hated. Caryn
kicked a pebble with the toe of her cloth shoe then
heard it alight in a nearby pond.

She should return to Ivesham—and she would—but
what harm could there be in an hour or two delay? The
Dark Knight was gone, they would take better care, and
no other would come upon them. They could enjoy the

pond, spend a bit more time in the sun, then she and Gweneth would go home.

Ral stared at the trees where the girls had disappeared, torn between his worry for the beautiful black-haired maid and his need to return to his men. So far the rebels had been routed, but there was always the chance they might return. If that happened, his men would need him.

Beneath his helm and heavy chain mail, the sun beat down unmercifully, making him uncomfortably warm. Satan, his big black destrier, pawed the earth with growing irritation, yet Ral's thoughts remained on the lovely young girl who had tried to befriend him, who for a few short moments had blotted out the horrors of war. Surely the little maids would do as he bade and return to the safety of their home. But recalling the saucy auburn-haired girl who had faced him with such defiance, he wasn't so sure.

He smiled to think of it, then swore an oath at her foolishness in wandering the fields alone. She was hardly the beauty her sister was, yet in time she might come into her own. Both of the women were tiny and fair, the auburn-haired maid far thinner, still at the gawky stage before womanhood. He wondered what she would look like when she was a woman grown.

He glanced their way one last time. 'Twas needless to worry. He had seen the younger girl tremble at the roughness in his voice. Even she would not be foolish enough to disobey his command. He looked down at the flowers in his hand and their fragrance stirred a memory of clear blue eyes and incredible sweetness. Reluctantly, he tossed the flowers away and rode back toward his men.

"Ral! 'Tis good you've returned. I had begun to wonder at your absence." This from Odo, his most trusted knight and longtime friend, who rode up beside him, lance in hand.

"What news?" Ral asked. "Have our scouts returned?"

The red-haired knight merely nodded. "They bring tales of a rebel force fleeing toward de Montreale's men. T'would serve us well should we reach them first." The rivalry between Ral and Stephen de Montreale, Lord of Malvern Castle, was legend, an enmity carried down even through the ranks of the men in their command.

"Which way do they ride?"

Odo pointed in the direction Ral had just come. He thought of the two little maids and an uneasy shiver slid down his spine. "Gather the men. Warn them to be on guard and let us be off."

Two hours later the small rebel force had been discovered, met, and routed. Twenty Saxon men had been taken, another twenty lay dead or dying on the field of battle. Still, the rebellion was far from ended. Soon word would come from the king revealing the treachery of other Saxon thegns. It would be Ral's task to end that treachery. William wanted peace once more in his war-torn land.

And Ral wanted land of his own.

"The men have done a good day's work," he said, surveying his defeated foe and his battle-weary soldiers. "There's a meadow not far from here. 'Twill be a good place for us to make camp."

Bone-tired, he rode beside Odo through a thick grove of alder toward the place where he had seen the two young girls. They were nowhere in sight and for a moment he felt relieved. Then a noise drew his attention and he paused. Off to his right, he heard the trickle of running water mingled with boisterous men's voices, speaking Norman French.

"Hold!" he shouted to the line of armored troops

mounted or marching behind him. "Odo, you and Geoffrey, Hugh, and Lambert come with me." *Stephen's men —it had to be.* They were not his concern, yet he would know what they were about.

They rode silently through the trees, listening to the men's coarse laughter, then Ral heard a woman's high-pitched scream. He spurred the big black and the animal leapt forward. In minutes, he reached the clearing where the sound had come from and saw to his horror what some sixth sense had been warning him about all day. Swinging down from his horse, he drew his broadsword from the scabbard at his waist.

"You men—hold up there!"

Their laughter died at the hard note in his voice. A group of Stephen's men, bloodstained and weary from battle, swiveled their heads to face him.

"Malvern may say naught against rapine and murder, but I will not abide it. If you wish to live, you will leave the women and back away."

A thickset knight stepped forward, "The wenches are ours by right of war! What right have you to gainsay us?"

"This right." Ral hefted his sword, the broad blade glinting in the fading sun's rays. His kite-shaped shield hung over one shoulder, the fierce black dragon glaring at them with warning.

" 'Tis him," one of the five men whispered. "Have a care, Bernart, 'tis the Dark Knight you confront. Surely you have heard of him." He swallowed so hard Ral saw the knot in his throat move up and down.

"There are five of them and five of us—I say we take them!"

"Let him have the wenches," cried another. "Why be greedy—we have already had our fill."

The other men laughed at that, though a thread of nervousness tinged the sound. Drawing back from the women they surrounded, they straightened their tunics and retied the drawstrings holding up their chausses.

Ral looked at the two girls lying on the ground. Both of them were naked. The black-haired maid sprawled in the grass, staring sightlessly up at the heavens. Her thighs were bloody, her heavy dark hair a tangled mass around her pale shoulders. Beside her a few feet away, the auburn-haired girl lifted her head, struggling in and out of consciousness. She was battered and bruised, one eye puffed nearly closed, her lip cut and swollen. Blood trickled from a corner of her mouth.

His fingers tightened on the hilt of his sword. "I warn you again, back off from the women!"

A thickset knight with dirty brown hair was the first to move away. "Consider the skinny one a gift from Lord Stephen," he sneered. "Her maidenhead remains intact. You may do with her as you wish."

"The lush little wench was the plum," said another. "We took her—one after another. God's truth, the wench loved it more than the lustiest scullery maid!"

Ral's quick movement caught him unawares. With a gauntleted hand, he gripped the man's throat, cutting off his air supply and lifting him clear off the ground. Kicking and squirming, the man lashed out, gasping for breath, but Ral's hold only grew tighter. When the knight wheezed one last time and went limp, Ral grumbled a low-muttered curse and tossed him aside like a piece of rotten offal.

"Take him and be gone!" Ral commanded.

Muttering among themselves, dragging the unconscious man away, his comrades gathered their horses and arms and began to slip quietly into the forest.

"Fetch another blanket," Ral said to Odo as he pulled his own from the back of his saddle and the last of Malvern's men disappeared. Kneeling beside the black-haired maid, he gently wrapped it around her then lifted her into Odo's outstretched arms. When he knelt to cover the auburn-haired girl, she struggled and began to fight him, swinging her fists with more force than he had expected.

"Leave her!" she cried, a balled hand connecting with his jaw. "You must not hurt her!"

He captured her wrists and gently subdued her.

"Rest easy, *ma petite*. You and your sister are safe." She fought a moment more, her small body straining, then went limp in his arms. Ral lifted her and carried her toward the horses.

" 'Tis good we arrived when we did," Odo said. "The maids would both have been dead."

Ral nodded.

" 'Tis a shame." Odo shifted his light burden. "The black-haired wench is uncommonly pretty, and the young one is a tiger."

"She fought bravely, I think."

"What shall we do with them?"

Ral hesitated only a moment. "We know not where they live. Should their kinsmen be among the Saxon rebels, they would not be safe even within the walls of their home." He handed his bundle to Geoffrey, the youngest of his knights, a blond boy of seventeen years who had served as squire to Odo.

"Take them to the Convent of the Holy Cross. The sisters can discover where they belong and send word to their family to claim them."

"Aye, 'tis a wise choice, considering what may yet lie ahead."

Ral merely nodded. He couldn't rid himself of the image of the beautiful black-haired maid torn asunder by Stephen's ruthless men. Or the battered face of the younger girl who had fought so hard to protect her.

Ral clamped his jaw. He should have seen them to safety. They were so young, so innocent. So trusting. He knew the dangers they might face. He had just been so used to command he hadn't believed they would dare disobey him.

Damn, but he felt guilty.

It was a burden that weighed heavy on his heart as they rode past in the arms of his men.

Chapter Two

England, 1072

Bells tolled the hour of matins, the sound an eerie echo in the deserted halls of the convent. In a chapel in the far east wing, rows of black-garbed nuns rested on their knees on the hard stone floor, readying themselves for prayer.

"Where has the girl gone this time?" the abbess asked, surveying the nuns and a small group of novices kneeling off to her left.

Sister Agnes stood beside her, equally incensed, a righteous curl to her lips. "I have not seen her." A woman in her thirties, she was thin as a stick and just as unbending. "She did not break her fast with the rest of us this morning, and two days in a row she has fallen asleep during afternoon prayers."

"Find her," said the stern-faced abbess, "I wish to speak with her at once."

Two hours later, Caryn of Ivesham, wearing a coarse brown tunic and stiff white camise, her hair pulled into a single long auburn braid, stood before Mother Terese, the tall formidable Abbess of the Convent of the Holy Cross. Caryn laced her fingers tightly together and tried to look demure.

The abbess sighed, breaking into the silence between them. "You must learn obedience," she said, continuing the tirade she had begun some time ago. " 'Tis certainly not something that comes easily to you. Still, you must endeavor to achieve the lesson."

"Yes, Mother Terese."

"You must learn humility and piety," she droned on. "Your family is dead, Caryn. Ivesham Hall lies in ruin. Your blood sister, Gweneth, and your sisters here in the convent are your only family now. Gweneth is happy here. You must learn to accept your life here, too."

Caryn caught only the last remark, her attention having drifted to the flock of birds chirping outside the window. *Accept this dreary life?* she thought. *Never!* But she didn't dare to say it.

"You must resign yourself to becoming one of us," the abbess continued. "If it takes strict discipline to accomplish that end, then that is what shall be done."

Caryn dragged her eyes up from the floor where she had been studying the intricate movements of a long-legged spider.

"Did you hear me, Caryn?"

"Yes, Mother." Sweet Jesu, what had the old woman said?

"Good, then you will repeat it for me."

"Wh-What?"

"Repeat what I have just said."

Caryn figeted nervously, twisting the folds of her ugly brown tunic. "Humility and piety, that is what I must learn." As good a guess as any. That was what the abbess usually said.

"What else?"

"What else?"

"I believe you heard the question."

"Discipline. You said I needed discipline." The frown on Mother Terese's face might have meant Caryn was guessing well, or not well at all.

"Thank you for reminding me. For falling asleep during prayers, you will repeat sixty psalms while lying in a pool of water. 'Tis possible the next time you feel sleepy, you will remember the lesson you learned in watchfulness."

Caryn shivered just to think of it. The convent was cold and drafty. Warm fires were rare, the floors hard and damp. No doubt she would be stripped to her camise, then later, since it would be wet, forced to wear her scratchy woolen tunic without one.

"Sister Agnes will see to your penance. Good day."

Caryn sighed as she walked out the door. Mayhap it wouldn't be so bad. Surely it couldn't be worse than scrubbing the floors in front of the altar with a twig, or missing her meager fare of fat mixed with peas for two or three nights in a row.

"Await me in the hall," said Sister Agnes with a satisfied smirk. It seemed to Caryn that the skinny little woman could well use some penance herself. "I shall fetch a pitcher of water and join you forthwith."

"Thank you, dear sister," Caryn said with a sarcastic smile.

In no hurry to accomplish her unpleasant task, she went to check on Gweneth and found her quietly embroidering in her cell. When Caryn spoke to her, Gweneth smiled warmly but continued to shove her needle with infinite care through the fabric she held in her lap.

In her strange state of mind, life was easy for Gweneth, peaceful and full of joy. Caryn sighed. For her, life had always been a quest of sorts, a search for something, though as yet she wasn't sure what it was. She would find it one day, she was certain. Then she would enjoy the same peace her sister did.

Caryn waved good-bye to Gweneth, resigned to the ordeal ahead. By the time she returned to the hall, Sister Agnes had doused the floor with water, darkening the stone in an inch-deep circle, and stood waiting impatiently for Caryn to appear.

"Remove your tunic," she commanded.

Caryn did so grudgingly, trying not to think hateful thoughts about the nun.

"Mayhap the next time you feel like shirking your duties, you will remember the consequences of such behavior."

" 'Tis certain, Sister Agnes, that I will." Shivering against the cold, Caryn lowered herself facedown onto the rough stone floor. Her camise was instantly soaked and her shivering increased. Dutifully she began to repeat the psalms the abbess required, saying them as rapidly as she could, knowing Sister Agnes would be counting every one.

Before she had finished, her skin was blue and she was shaking all over. She climbed to her feet, forced herself to smile at Sister Agnes, turned and stiffly walked back to her barren room.

"Are you all right?"

Caryn looked across her cell to see Sister Beatrice standing in the doorway. Beatrice was her best friend, a slight girl with big green eyes that occasionally glinted with the same sort of mischief her own too often did.

Sitting on her corn husk mattress, Caryn pulled the itchy woolen blanket more closely around her. "Just cold is all."

"Where were you this morning?"

She shrugged her shoulders. " 'Twas the first sunny day we have had in weeks, and the flowers have started to bloom." She smiled. "I wanted to pick some for Gweneth."

Beatrice smiled, too. "She does so love them. But then 'tis a gift she has, finding joy in the smallest of things."

"Aye. There are times I wish I could be as content as she."

Beatrice walked toward her. "You will learn. One day you will be able to accept things as they are."

"One day I will leave, Beatrice. You will see. One day I will strike out on my own."

"For now you had better strike out for the chapel. They will be watching you closely for a while."

Caryn sighed. "I suppose you are right." She climbed up from the floor. "Sister Agnes seems to find a secret joy in my failings." Tossing off the blanket, she pulled on her coarse woolen tunic, trying to ignore the scratchy feel against her skin.

They started down the hall, but the sound of someone banging on the oaken door in the entry stayed their movements. Curiosity turned Caryn in that direction. "Who do you suppose it could be?"

" 'Tis not our concern. Come. We will be late."

But Caryn started walking toward the door, forcing Beatrice along in her wake. Even before the tiny nun hurrying to answer the knock could pull the door open, armored men poured into the entry.

" 'Tis the Lord of Malvern Castle—Stephen de Montreale," Beatrice whispered with a gasp of surprise, recognizing the tall blond man richly clothed in crimson who strode in at the head of his men. "My father spoke of him often, usually with loathing."

Malvern. Caryn knew of him—what Saxon did not? She knew he'd made a bloody raid on Beatrice's village, and that fear of Norman swine like him was part of the reason Beatrice was there. Malvern was hated, Caryn knew, by most of her Saxon kinsmen, and his ruthlessness was legend.

"I have come for your novices," he said to the abbess, who stood angrily before him. "The women who have not yet spoken the vows. You will bring them forth at once."

"What do you want with them?" The abbess eyed him warily.

"There is work to be done at Malvern. I am in need of extra hands and you have more than enough." He was tall and lithe yet muscular and solidly built. His shoulders were broad, his hips lean, his face almost perfect. Had it not been for his slightly too-pointed nose and hard male mouth, he might have looked pretty. As it was, he merely looked handsome, yet there was a cruel air about him.

"These girls are under the protection of the church," the abbess countered.

"They will soon be under my protection."

"But—"

"You will do as I say." When she still didn't move, he added, "Now!"

Caryn turned as Sister Agnes walked up with a cluster of nuns.

"What goes on?" Agnes asked. "Why is Lord Stephen here?"

"He has come for the novices."

"The novices? What does he want with them? By what authority—"

"He is Malvern," Caryn said. "He needs no authority but his own." She turned to Sister Beatrice. "Whatever happens, you must keep Gweneth away. She is still in her cell. You must see her hidden safely away."

Beatrice glanced at the men, nodded and turned to leave, but Caryn caught her arm. "If anything goes awry, promise me you will see to her safety."

"What could—"

"Promise me!"

"You have my word." As the men began to move through the halls, Beatrice hurried toward the rear of the convent. The women who wore no veils were roughly rounded up and hauled toward the front, Caryn among them. She nervously glanced to the rear of the convent, but neither Beatrice nor Gweneth appeared.

"These are the only ones," the abbess said to Malvern, obviously distraught. "Just these six girls." That

she intended to spare Gweneth made Caryn regret some
of the harsh thoughts she'd had about the older woman.

"Six will be enough for our needs." Malvern surveyed
the young women, none beyond eighteen years. A
knight near the great oaken door eyed them with relish
and chuckled gruffly.

"How am I to explain this?" the abbess asked. "What
will their parents say?"

Malvern's face turned hard, his nose suddenly looking
beaklike and pointed. "Explain to the Saxon swine that
we are well aware of what goes on inside these walls.
These so-called convents are havens for the daughters of
the very Saxon landlords whose treachery continues to
plague us. Places like this breed unrest and discontent.
They harbor cults of sedition, and shelter the king's enemies. You are lucky William is a man of God, else he
would likely order this place and its like burned to the
ground."

The abbess had begun to tremble.

"Take them outside," Stephen ordered and the men
dragged the women out the door.

Some of them were weeping, struggling to get away.
As uncertain as she was, all Caryn could think of was
that she was leaving. Even the drudgery of Malvern Castle couldn't be as bad as the years ahead she faced in the
convent.

Then she heard Malvern's knights begin to mutter
among themselves, speaking the Norman French she
had been learning for years. They were talking about the
women, speaking crudely of what lay under the young
girls' tunics, how they would make short work of the
dreary fabric once they were away.

Malvern cautioned them that they would have to wait
until they reached shelter. At Braxston Keep the de-
bauchery could begin.

Caryn started to tremble. Sweet God in heaven, the
men meant to make the women their whores! Fighting

back a wave of fear, she felt a thick male arm slide around her waist. She was hoisted up in the saddle in front of a sallow-faced knight with stringy brown hair.

"Do not fear, *demoiselle*," he said, trying to make himself understood. "I will not let you fall." The arm beneath her breast gave a too familiar squeeze then he set his spurs to the sides of his horse.

"Trust in God," the abbess called out as they thundered away. "You will all be in our prayers."

For the first time in a long time, Caryn gave up a fervent prayer of her own.

Raolfe de Gere forded the icy stream toward home then awaited his men and retainers on the opposite side. The day had been a long one, the final leg of a journey from Pontefact, where he had met with several other barons concerned with the problem of the outlaws plaguing the nearby hills.

Odo rode beside him. They had been friends since boyhood, when they had both been fostered to Ral's uncle. They had free-lanced together as knights, gaining experience in battle, then returned to Normandy to serve Duke William before he became the king.

"What say you, Ral, do we make camp here or ride for home? 'Twould make for a long day's journey, but the comfort of a fire and a good hot meal would well be worth it."

"Aye," Ral said, "I too crave the sight of home." Braxston Keep. He was Lord of Braxston now, a token of William's esteem for his long years of service.

Like his father before him and his father before that, Ral had ridden beside his liege lord, sworn to fealty and determined to honor that vow even at the cost of his life. So long had his family been known for their knights' service, they had come to be called de Gere. Men of war. He prayed his own son's life would not be spent fighting those same bloody battles.

"Then we ride?" Odo pressed.

"Aye." Ral grinned. "Mayhap Lynette will still be about. Then the journey would be rewarded by a pair of soft thighs and a ride far more pleasant than this one."

Odo smiled. "God's truth, Ral, whether the maid be abed or not, there is little doubt she'll be well ridden this eve."

Ral chuckled good-naturedly. "Let the men water their horses and rest for a time, then we'll make ready and be off for the castle."

He found himself eager to return. In the three years since William's grant of the lands near Braxston Gap, once belonging to Harold of Ivesham, and Ral's construction of the keep and its surrounding walls, he had come to think of the place as home.

In truth, the first he had known since his boyhood. The lands his father had amassed through the years had gone to Alain, his older brother. He could have had his share but there wasn't really enough for the two of them and he believed he could garner lands of his own. William had obliged after Senlac, giving him the demesme that had been wrested from the plotting old Saxon thegn.

"I may find a willing wench of my own this night," Odo said as they rode along. "The kitchen maid, Bretta, appears willing enough to spread her thighs for a silver coin or two."

"I've little fear you will go untended."

"Nay, 'tis truth, yet a wife would be more to my liking." He smiled, his freckled face looking a little younger than his thirty years, a single year older than Ral. " 'Twould be better to be greeted by a comely maid who would warm my bed and bear me lusty sons. I vow I shall set about finding one before the winter settles in. You should give thought to the same."

In truth, he already had. Now that he owned a castle and lands, was overlord to a large number of churls and villeins, and was one of William's most trusted barons, he could use a helping hand. And stout sons who would inherit the lands and fortune he intended to amass.

He thought of his mother, gentle and caring, seeing to his father's every command, making the hall run smoothly. Loving mother, wife . . . woman. His sisters were equally devoted to the men they had married. They were skillful in the kitchen, adept at embroidery, at tending their children, the sick, and the needs of their men.

William would approve and assist with the match, and with the king's aid, the woman would no doubt be well dowered. *Marriage . . . aye.* A faint smile curved his lips. He would see to it, Ral decided. Lynette would be angry, but she had known from the start one day he would wed. Besides, what difference would a marriage make between them? She would still be his leman, would still warm his bed.

Ral smiled even more broadly and rode on.

Caryn knew well the path through the forest they now traveled. It took them through marshland overgrown with bracken, then higher into the mountains. The path led to Ivesham Hall—or at least what had once been the place of her childhood. Now that great wooden structure with its timber palisade lay in ruins, her uncle as dead as her mother and father, a victim of his own rebellion against King William's rule.

Caryn never saw him after the day she was taken to the convent. During the period of her recovery, she had learned of the attack on the hall, of her uncle Harold's death, and the surrender of his small valiant group of defenders. Someone had mentioned the Dark Knight's name, but it was said another powerful knight had actually lain waste to the hall. A short time later, work began on Braxston Keep, which now rose up in its stead, though Caryn had never seen it.

She guessed this night she would and something unwelcome tightened inside her.

" 'Tis not far now," said the gruff knight who held her. "You will soon be in out of the cold."

Out of the cold and into the hot lecherous hands of one of Malvern's men. Sweet Mary, she knew what that would be like. She would never forget her sister's pitiful moans as a brutal Norman thrust between her legs. Caryn had fought them, done her best to stop them. She would fight them again if she had to, but first she would try to outwit them.

She feigned sleep as they rode along, but beneath her half-closed lids, her eyes remained watchful, and just as the gruff knight had said, it wasn't long before the gray stone walls of Braxston Keep rose up before them, a tall stark fortress against the backdrop of a glowing moon.

Lord Stephen and two of his knights rode forward, speaking to the wardcorne, the watchman at the gate, seeking shelter for the eve while the other men, no longer tired but eager now for what lay ahead, restlessly awaited the lowering of the drawbridge. When word finally came, the horses' hooves thudded eerily against the heavy oaken planks, their exhaustion as apparent as Caryn's own.

It was the numbness, her sense of disbelief combined with the chilling cold, that allowed her to keep her senses. It was no secret now, the fate about to befall them. Too many groping hands, too many lewd remarks that in any language foretold the Normans' awful intent. While the other girls sobbed and begged for mercy, receiving no end of rough warnings and brutal slaps, Caryn remained silent, determined somehow that she would not fall victim to such a fate.

Outside the tall stone tower a hundred feet square, its walls at the base nearly twenty feet thick, they climbed the wooden stairs to the first floor entrance to the keep and made their way into the great hall. It stood two stories high with a vaulted ceiling open at one end to let out smoke from the fire pit. A second floor gallery wrapped around it, and great stone stairs spiraled steeply upward until they disappeared.

" 'Tis unfortunate Lord Raolfe has not returned," someone said to de Montreale in French with heavy Saxon overtones. Caryn twisted in the arms of the knight who held her, then sucked in a great breath of air at the sight of Richard of Pembroke, a sandy-haired man in his middle twenties who had once been steward to her uncle.

"You must send him our thanks for the use of his hall." Lord Stephen smiled, making him look deceptively handsome. "My men are weary. They require food and drink. We shall be off again once they are rested."

"Mayhap you could advise us how long your stay might be," Richard said a bit unkindly. Caryn didn't miss his unconcealed dislike of Stephen de Montreale.

"Two days, three at most. Now, food and drink—and hurry. Braxston's no pauper. I would see my men well fed."

"And the women?" Richard flashed them a shrewd assessing glance.

"They are none of your concern. My men are in need of diversion. These will serve the purpose well enough."

Richard scowled but said nothing more. He started to walk away then paused, his eyes going wide at Caryn's familiar face, which surely looked bloodless and wan. Then his indifferent manner returned and he continued toward the kitchen. There was little the man could do, yet it gave her fresh hope and the courage not to falter.

"Assemble the trestle tables," a serving maid called out. "We've hungry men to feed."

In minutes, the hall was transformed from a place of sleeping servants to a raucous assembly of Lord Stephen's men. Horns of ale were filled to overflowing and trenchers of meat brought out. A leg of mutton, loaves of buckwheat bread, hunks of cheese, platters of cold boiled peahen.

The gruff knight dragged Caryn to one of the tables and forced her to sit on a bench.

"Eat, wench, you will need your strength before this night is done—that I can promise." He chuckled crudely and roughly squeezed her breast.

Caryn jerked free but said nothing, just eased away as far as she could. Pretending to pick at the food he urged upon her, she surveyed the great hall, looking for a means of escape. Instead she saw another familiar face, one that warmed her insides and brought a second shot of hope. Though the woman was bent a little more than when last Caryn had seen her, there was no doubt that it was Marta, the woman who had suckled her, who at times had been more a mother to her than her own. Caryn had long believed her dead.

"Marta," she whispered, barely forming the word as she realized the woman had already seen her. A warning finger came up to the old woman's lips. Mayhap there was help here after all, in this castle of her enemy, on the very spot she had once called home.

She turned to the thin gruff knight beside her. "If you please . . . I am in need of the garderobe. Might I not be allowed—"

"You will be allowed to warm my pallet, that is all."

" 'Twas a long ride, sir. Your needs were met along the way. May I not now see to my own?"

He grumbled something crude, then jerked her up from the bench. "If you would go, then I will go with you." He grinned and she noticed a missing tooth. "In truth it might be best we leave the others. Mayhap a little privacy would better suit for your first time."

Sweet Mother Mary, what have I done? Before she could think how to dissuade him, he was leading her off through a passage behind the wall, Caryn stumbling along in his wake. Behind her the men's coarse laughter and the women's tearful pleading made her stomach clench into a hard tight ball.

Sweet God in heaven. It wasn't until they had rounded a corner out of sight that she heard a muffled thump and the grip on her arm grew slack.

"Come, my pet," came Marta's soothing voice, "we must find a way to hide you." She stepped from the shadows and Caryn went tearfully into her arms.

"I thought you were dead," Caryn told her. " 'Tis a blessing from God I have found you again."

" 'Twill be a blessing indeed shall you keep your virtue this night. Hurry, we must away." Down one passage and along another, Marta led her unerringly. Behind a curtain in the kitchen, she crouched down on a coarse heather-filled pallet and Caryn did the same. "You must stay hidden. Do not venture forth no matter what disturbance you might hear."

"What about the others?"

"There is naught you can do but pray for Lord Raolf's return."

"You speak of Braxston? You believe he would help us?"

"He is not like the others. He would not see innocent young women come to harm."

"But he is Norman!"

"I pray thee, do as I say this once." The old woman's hard look softened. "Hear me this night, my pet, as you never have before. In this, I beg you, do not disobey."

Caryn only nodded. Too often she had ignored the old woman's wishes. Freedom from tedious women's work, or mischief-making held far greater appeal. It had been so that day she had left the hall for the meadow, though had she stayed home, her fate would have been much the same.

Caryn shivered. This night she would heed old Marta's warning. She would stay where she was, pray that the gruff knight would not be missed and that the lord of the manor might return. She chewed her bottom lip. If only there were some way to help the others. Though she steepled her hands and crouched on bended knee, prayer seemed not nearly enough.

Ral caught sight of the signal flag near the wardcorne atop the stone tower at the gate. Visitors in residence. He would know who they were before he led his men inside the castle.

Riding ahead of the others, he approached warily, but naught seemed amiss. The guards at the gate warned him of the baron's presence—Stephen de Montreale— but said he traveled without his usual vast number of retainers and only several dozen armored men.

Ral breathed easier as he returned to Odo and his other knights and men-at-arms.

" 'Tis de Montreale. Richard has granted him shelter, though had he any other choice 'tis certain he would not have."

" 'Tis only a three-day ride to Malvern. With your return, 'tis unlikely he will stay overlong."

Ral merely grunted. An hour in Stephen's presence was more than enough.

"Signal the men. I would have us enter as quietly as we can." He would see what Malvern was about before the others came into the hall.

Odo nodded and moved off through the ranks of the men. In minutes they reached the drawbridge and crossed into the bailey, where the stables, barns, storehouses, and living quarters for a number of his troops had been built. Several sleepy pages rushed to the aid of the men-at-arms while squires saw to their knights, then the animals and harness.

As the men finished their labors, Ral made his way toward the hall, inwardly glad he still wore his hauberk, the fifty pounds of chain mail growing heavy in these hours not long before dawn.

Inside the hall, the snores of sleeping knights he had only half expected were instead the raucous laughter and lecherous grunting of drunken men. As Ral stood silently in the shadows, he could hear a woman weeping. In the rushlights that flickered against the walls, he saw naked pale thighs spread wide beneath the pumping hairy buttocks of one of Malvern's men. The woman's face was not known to him. Even Stephen would not risk Ral's fury by harming the maids in the hall.

Stephen had seen to his men's amusement, curse the man to the flames of hell.

"My lord, 'tis I . . . Marta." The old woman slipped from the darkness. It unnerved him the way she could move with such stealth. "I would speak to you, my lord."

"What is it, old woman? Can you not see I have problems enough with Malvern in the hall?"

"It is of him I wish to speak." Her thin lips curled in disapproval. "The man is a jackal."

"The women—they are not from the village?"

"No. Malvern brought them with him. The maids are little more than children. Novices from the convent. Malvern stole them away."

Ral's hand balled into a fist. It was a deed he might have expected from a man the likes of Stephen. "Would that I could help them, but there is naught I can do. Malvern holds the king's ear. He has far greater power than I. At least with my return, 'tis certain he will soon be gone."

"But, my lord—"

Scuffling in the hall drew their attention. "So, at last you have found her!" Thick with drink, Stephen's voice echoed loudly across the hall. "Bring her here!"

"She was hiding in the passage. The bitch was

dressed in the garb of a scullery maid, but 'tis hard to mistake those big brown eyes and rich auburn hair. She's the comeliest of the lot, to be sure.''

When the tall knight dragged the girl into the light Marta gasped. '' 'Tis the Lady Caryn,'' she whispered from her place in the shadows beside him.

Malvern laughed as he gripped the maid's arm. ''So you thought to escape us, did you?''

''She was helping the others,'' the knight said, dragging her closer. ''Two of them have come up missing, my lord.''

Stephen chuckled. ''The little wench has courage, but in this she has outfoxed herself.'' He pulled the tie on his chausses as he stood up. ''I shall initiate this one myself.'' He reached for the neck of the little maid's tunic, grabbed hold of the fabric, and ripped it to her waist.

''Let me go!'' the maid cried, struggling to pull away. Stephen slid an arm around her waist and brought her hard against his body. He rent her camise and stripped it off her shoulders.

Standing in the shadows, Marta gripped Ral's arm. ''I beg you, my lord! Lady Caryn is the old thegn's daughter.''

''Harold?''

''No, Harold's brother Edmund. He was lord before.''

Ral barely heard the old woman's words. Instead his eyes remained on the maid. She was tiny, but not fragile, a woman fully grown. He couldn't quite recall what it was but there was something familiar about her.

''Rest easy,'' Stephen was saying, forcing her chin up with his hand. ''I am not unskilled at bedding an unbroken wench. Give yourself into my care and I will go slowly.'' He smiled with cold malice. ''Fight me, and I will tear you apart.'' Holding her immobile, he pulled the string binding her thick auburn braid, then sifted his fingers through the shiny mass and spread it about her shoulders.

The moment he did, the hazy images Ral had been seeing came together, colliding with a force that caused a roaring in his ears.

"Sweet Christ," he said, " 'tis her." It was a face he remembered all too well, one of two that had haunted him for the past three years. Stepping from his place in the shadows, he strode forward into the hall. Behind him the heavy oaken door swung wide and in walked a group of his men.

Near a bench in front of the fire, Malvern laughed at the girl's useless struggles, bent her back over his arm, and began to fondle her breasts. They were lush and high, Ral saw, feeling a tightness in his groin. Nothing like the tiny plums he had seen that day in the meadow. And her features looked different, her cheeks soft and full, her mouth a rich burnished crimson. She was not the gawky maid he remembered, but nothing could erase the image he carried of her face, nor that of her beautiful raven-haired sister.

"Hold, Stephen!" Ral strode toward him, his mail and spurs clanking as he moved.

"Well . . . Braxston. Home at last. I might say 'tis good to see you, but we would both know the words for a lie."

"You've been offered the comfort of my hall. 'Tis nothing less than I would expect of you. You've women enough to ease your men's needs. I ask your leave of this one."

Stephen's mauling ceased, but his pale blue eyes turned hard. "These women give succor to the enemy. I have claimed them in the name of the king." The little maid pulled her coarse brown tunic up over her breasts with a trembling hand. "This one will warm my bed 'ere this night is done. She belongs to me and we both know I keep what is mine."

"You have others to amuse you."

"This one has fire." He twisted his fingers in her hair, dark shades of crimson and gold, and pulled her head back. "I would see her spread beneath me. She is mine."

"Nay!" said the girl, pulling away. "I belong to no man."

Ral clenched his jaw. He glanced from the maid's stricken face back to Stephen, whose men had begun to gather round him, their hands resting uneasily on the hilts of their swords. Behind him, Ral's own men fanned out across the hall.

"You are both wrong," he said. "The girl belongs to me."

Malvern set her roughly away. "You dare to gainsay me in this?" Feet splayed, he rested his hand on his blade.

"The girl is mine. She is the daughter of the old Saxon thegn." He flashed her a hard look of warning. "Caryn of Ivesham is my betrothed." He smiled at her but it didn't reach his eyes. "Is that not so, my love?"

Chapter Three

C aryn reeled as if she had been struck. The Dark Knight her betrothed? Never! She had not forgotten him, would never forget those cool blue-gray eyes, that unforgiving jaw and thick black hair. The heavy strands were even longer now, not shorn in the way of most Norman men, but curling softly against the neck of his chain mail hauberk. Sweet Mary he must be mad!

She studied him more closely, trying to battle down her fears and read his fierce look of warning. He was handsome, she saw as she hadn't before, in a hard, forbidding way far different from Lord Stephen. His nose was straight, his lips well-formed but his jaw was a little too square, his cheekbones a little too severe. He was a massive man, broad of chest, neck thick, arms corded with heavy muscle, and his legs long.

"Is that not so?" he repeated, the glint of warning more pronounced, a reminder that should she deny him, Lord Stephen and his men would ravish her as they had done the others.

She swallowed hard and stared at the tall dark knight who towered above her. She hadn't forgotten what he and his men had done to her sister. She could still see his face among the others, though the memory was hazy and illusive, mixed with the terror, the anger, and the pain. She did not know the part he had played, but she knew for certain he had been there.

He was just as bad as Malvern.

Still, time was what she needed. She really had no choice. She tried not to tremble beneath his close regard. "Aye, my lord, that is so."

Malvern's sleek blond brows drew together over eyes that glinted with fury. He knew the Dark Knight had lied but the lie had effectively stayed his purpose. Angry heat tinged his cheekbones. Then he smiled with such venom his skin drew back from his teeth, making him look like the deadly predator he was.

His hand fell away from his blade. "Had I but known, I would have left her at the convent. As it is, mayhap 'tis a blessing in disguise." Another vicious smile. "Knowing in the past how reluctant you have been to take a bride, how could I be less than glad to see that you intend to do so now. What say you, Ral? Have you yet made plans for the wedding?"

"I wait to hear from William. Once I receive his blessing and the banns have been posted, the deed will be accomplished." He turned in Caryn's direction. "What of your sister?" he asked in a voice she alone could hear. "Is she also in the hall?"

"Gweneth is safe at the convent." *Away from you and the rest of the carrion—thank the Blessed Virgin.*

The huge knight started to say something more, but a stirring on the stairs turned his look in that direction. From the top of the landing leading down to the hall, a woman in a lavender tunic stared boldly down at the men.

"What is this you say, my lord? Have my poor ears heard correctly?" She was blond and fair, willowy and graceful, yet her lips were hard-edged and her green eyes held no hint of softness. "Surely my ears have deceived me."

The Dark Knight's jaw went tense. " 'Tis none of your concern, Lynette. Get back to your chamber."

"Ah, the fair Lynette," said Stephen. "I hadn't thought to see you."

"I will not allow it, Ral. 'Tis truth, you've made no pledge to me, yet I say that I will not let it happen!"

"And I say get thee gone! Another such outburst and you will feel the back of my hand!"

For a moment it appeared she might argue. Then the rage left her face and a stiff smile curved her lips. "Forgive me, my lord. 'Tis only that I've missed you these long days past. I shall await your pleasure in my chamber."

Caryn looked from the Dark Knight to the tall fair maid. His leman, no doubt. But if that were so, Caryn wondered, what could he possibly want with her?

"So—at last—the lord of Braxston takes a bride." Malvern's lips curled sardonically. "I shall pen William myself, telling him how urgently you wish to wed. With the king's permission, mayhap the vows could be spoken within the fortnight. What say you, Ral? Would you not be well pleased?"

Whoreson, Ral inwardly swore, cursing the position he found himself in, knowing Stephen enjoyed every moment of his discomfort. Guilt had been his motive. He had failed the black-haired maid. One so sweet and innocent had deserved his protection and yet he had not kept her safe. He meant to right the wrong he had done in the only way he knew how, by protecting the girl's younger sister.

"It pleases me well enough." He could fight de Montreale of course. Outnumbered as his rival was, Ral was certain to win. But good men's blood would be spilled, and the king would make him pay dearly. Stephen's father was William's closest friend. Ral would be stripped of his lands and title, left with naught of what he had worked so hard to build.

"William will approve the match," Ral said. "He wants this land in the north subdued. With the children of Norman-Saxon unions, he believes 'twill happen all the sooner." Ral forced himself to smile. "Bedding a maid as fair as this is a duty I look forward to."

And marriage the only answer to his dilemma. He had known that from the moment he had interfered on her behalf. Once Stephen learned Ral sought to protect her, the girl would not be safe outside the castle walls.

Malvern's eyes raked the maid as if he still owned her. "The pleasure may yet be mine," he warned, "should your words prove less than true." He walked past her, his hand brushing a breast one last time. Ral stiffened at the insult.

"Leave off, Stephen. Even the king will not back you in this." Assuming he did indeed approve.

Malvern smiled at the girl. "Beg pardon, my lady, for any insult I may have given. 'Twas the rags that had me fooled." He looked at Ral. "I would advise that you clothe her befitting her station. There are others who might make the same mistake as I."

Ral ignored the barb. "My men are weary. I would have them fed and rested before this night is through." He reached for Caryn's arm, felt her tense, tightened his hold, and drew her along with him. "Till the morrow, Stephen."

Caryn resisted the urge to pull away and instead let the tall Norman guide her toward the stairs. Once they reached the solar, he led her inside and closed the door. Caryn whirled on him in an instant.

"Are you mad?"

The huge man turned to face her, his expression distant and inscrutable. Rushlight glistened off his glossy jet black hair and the gray of his eyes seemed to glitter. "In this moment, 'twould seem as if indeed that might be true."

"Why have you done this? What do you hope to gain? Do you really believe I will wed with you?"

The Dark Knight stiffened. "I believe you will do whatever it takes to save your skin."

"I will never wed a Norman. Especially not one as vile as you. You are murderers—all of you—robbing and killing, burning our homes and fields."

"There is truth in what you say. Foul deeds were committed by both sides. 'Twas done in the name of war. There is much that has happened that is better left in the past."

"You are Norman. Time will not lessen the hatred I feel for you. Think you I did not see what happened here this eve? My friends were beaten, assaulted. Sweet Virgin Mary, they were taken from the sanctity of the church!"

"You speak of Malvern's deeds not mine. Could I have helped them, I would have. I could not."

"Why? Because you fear him?"

"I fear the king. William is my liege lord. I have vowed to do as he bids. Stephen is the king's man."

"And you are not?"

"Malvern controls vast fortunes. His father is one of William's closest friends. I have not the power to gainsay him."

"Then you are a coward as well as a cur."

He took an ominous step in her direction. "I have given you leave to speak your mind this eve, for the circumstances have been unsettling. But I warn you, lady, you had better learn when to curb your wayward tongue. No man would dare speak to me thus. I will not tolerate it from you."

He meant it. His thick black brows had drawn into a frown and his mouth looked thin and grim.

"Had you planned to take your vows," he said, referring to her status as a novice, " 'tis far too late for that. Your marriage will be to me and not to the church.

Should you refuse, Stephen will take you the moment you set foot outside these walls."

"I never meant to live the life of a nun. In truth, I can think of nothing more loathsome than whiling away the years within some cold damp cell." She lifted her chin. "Except, mayhap, being married to you."

"Marriage to you is hardly what I had planned. You're naught but a girl. I would wed with a woman—a full-sized one at that." Caryn bristled. "You are not dowered. You bring naught to this union but the rags on your back. Still, 'tis too late to change things now."

" 'Tis not too late. You cannot force me and I will not consent." She turned her back to him and walked to the small arrow hole that served as a window.

She hadn't liked the way his eyes found the rent in her garment, the way her stomach tightened when they did. He was hard and tough, his look even fiercer than Lord Stephen's . . . and far more intimate. As if he yet sized her up for the duties she would perform in the marriage bed.

"Should you refuse me," he said, "Malvern would make you his leman. When he tires of you, he would share you with his men. You have seen enough here this night to know what will happen when he does."

She would be beaten and brutalized, a victim of rapine, mayhap even murder. Caryn shivered beneath those stormy eyes. "Why? If I am such a poor choice for wife, why do you want me?"

He shrugged his massive shoulders, rippling the muscles along his arms. "I owe you. What happened that day in the meadow . . . it never should have occurred. I would change things if I could. Since I cannot, this time I would see you safe."

So the big brute had a conscience. As much as she loathed what he and the others had done, Caryn found the thought strangely comforting. And equally strange, she found she did not fear him. At least not in the same way she feared Malvern.

"Why should I believe I am better off with you?"

"You will be my wife."

Wife. It was a word she had scarcely considered during her years in the convent. Certainly 'twas not a state she looked forward to. She wanted her freedom. She craved it now, as she had every day for the last three years. Mayhap even before that. She wanted to be on her own, beholden to no man, experiencing the world and all its wonder. It would not be easy, yet she had always believed she would find a way to make it happen.

Time was what she needed. Time enough to make plans to escape. She forced herself to smile, an idea already forming at the edges of her mind.

"Mayhap you are right, my lord. The past has no place in the present. Besides, it would seem I have no choice. Should you wish to wed with me, I will agree." Mother of God, the words nearly stuck in her throat.

"My name is Ral."

Ral the Relentless. The Dark Knight. Never would she have guessed he was the Lord of Braxston Keep. "I am called Caryn."

"So your tiering woman, Marta, has said. She has served you well this eve and will remain in your service from this day forward." He strode to the door and yanked it open, bellowed for servants, and Marta appeared.

"Show your lady to a chamber." Though he spoke to Marta, he turned in Caryn's direction, those cool blue-gray eyes looking not nearly cool enough as he assessed her. "There is a peddler in the village. We passed him on the road. Send a messenger on the morrow. Ask that he bring his wares. I would see the lady clothed as one."

Caryn started to protest, to tell him she wanted nothing from the Norman scum, but caught herself just in time. Instead she glanced at the wall where a weathered shield hung beside a leather quiver filled with arrows. A huge black dragon on a field of bloodred. Caryn shivered.

When she looked at the Dark Knight's face, she found him watching her, his eyes fixed on the rise and fall of her breasts. It was almost as if he touched her, not the rough brutal touch of Malvern's hand, but a soft caress that slid over her like the wisp of a feather.

"Do not return downstairs until Lord Stephen has gone," he warned as she forced her legs to move toward the door.

Caryn paused, turning to look into his handsome face. "Surely I am no longer in danger."

"Do not gainsay me in this, *ma petite*. Should you wish to reach my bed with your maidenhead still intact you will do exactly as I say."

Caryn flushed crimson. She didn't wish to reach his bed at all, but she didn't dare tell him that. "As you wish, my lord." She fell in behind Marta, who shuffled hurriedly from the room.

Ral watched them go, the maid's small hands gripping the remnants of her tunic, her thick dark auburn hair rippling nearly to her waist. She wasn't the blue-eyed beauty her sister was, but she was comely to be sure. She'd blossomed into a vibrant young woman. With her slim straight nose, finely arched brows, and lush ruby lips, she would stir the loins of any stout-blooded man. And there was a fire in her warm brown, thickly lashed eyes that the older maid had lacked.

He heard a heavy oaken door close down the hall, seeing her safely inside her chamber. She had fought Stephen without a tear, done a fair job of standing up to Ral himself, then accepted her fate with her head held high. She would obey him; she had proven that already.

And bring some of that fire to his bed.

Ral's loins grew hard at the thought, yet he was also disturbed. He had never bedded a wench so small, had taken pains to avoid it. He was a big man, more than twice her size. He was a man of lusty appetites; he meant to spawn big lusty sons. Would she be able to take him inside her tiny woman's body? Would she be able to bear his children?

Whatever the truth, his course was set. Soon they would be wed and she would find herself beneath him. His arousal strengthened, becoming thick and heavy at the notion of thrusting inside her, her pale thighs spread, her burnished hair glistening like soft fire beneath her.

Ral shook his head, fighting to dispel the image. Damn, he had been too long without a woman. He grumbled a curse. Lynette would be vile-tempered after what she had heard in the hall. 'Twould not soothe his mood to seek her out this eve. The morrow would be soon enough to face her, to tell her she must leave until after the wedding yet convince her that once the deed was done nothing need change between them.

Mayhap that was the answer to his problem with the tiny auburn-haired maid. Being careful not to hurt her, he would take her to his bed until she conceived a son then set her away and return his attentions to his leman. He liked his bed sport as lusty as his women. This one might be fiery, but each time he took her, he would worry for her care.

Ral sighed and began to pace the floor of the solar. The maid was hardly the wife he would have chosen, but he would not go back on his word. The girl would be protected by his name, and through him so would her sister. Besides he needed a woman's help in the hall. This one would do as well as any, and she would soon learn her place.

Ral felt the stirrings of a smile. Calling for his squire to assist him in removing his heavy chain mail, he left the solar and strode off toward his chamber.

Stephen de Montreale left Braxston Keep two days hence, vowing to return for Lord Raolf's wedding. For once, Caryn did as she was bade and stayed within her bedchamber. She was fearful of Malvern's intentions and needed the time to plan her escape.

By the end of the week, she was garbed once more as a lady, as she hadn't been since the day she left Ivesham Hall. Braxston had insisted on a wardrobe of expensive clothing. To gainsay him would have been to admit she never intended to wear them, that she would soon be gone.

Choosing a green velvet tunic over a white linen chainse belted with a corded golden girdle, she left her room for the first time in days and made her way downstairs.

"Lady Caryn," Ral said, rising as she approached the dais at the far end of the hall. " 'Tis high time you joined us." Garbed in a tunic of dark blue velvet that emphasized the width of his shoulders, he rose from his highbacked carved wooden chair and motioned for her to take the seat beside him.

" 'Tis a pleasure, my lord." She nearly choked on the words. She hoped Braxston didn't notice. "I've looked forward to the occasion." When she glanced at him again, she saw he watched her with a hint of suspicion.

"When last we spoke," he said, "it did not seem 'twas such a pleasure to be in my company. I am glad your mood has changed."

Hardly, she thought, but merely smiled. "What choice have I, a simple maid? Soon I will be wed to a great Norman knight. 'Twas foolish of me to resist your kind offer. I will try my best to be worthy of it."

Lord Raolfe said nothing. Just stared at her with those shrewd gray eyes. "So now you are eager to please me."

"Of course, my lord."

" 'Tis good I have chosen such a sweet, docile woman for my wife." He smiled but it looked more wolfish than friendly. "Since you are so willing to please me this day, I would ask a boon of you."

"A boon? What boon, my lord?"

"I would have a kiss."

"What!"

"A kiss from my betrothed. A kiss to seal our bargain. Surely 'tis not too much to ask of such a grateful maid."

"You may kiss my—" *arse, you Norman swine* "—hand, Lord Ral. Till we are wed, twill have to be enough."

"Your hand, is it?" He clasped her small fingers in his big ones and brought them to his lips. His mouth felt firm and surprisingly warm, yet soft and appealing in a way she hadn't expected. Standing, she tried to pull her fingers free, but he jerked unexpectedly and she tumbled into his lap.

"A real kiss, my lady, would far better suit the occasion." She opened her mouth to protest, but he caught her jaw between his fingers and covered her mouth with his.

Soft-hard lips. Warm male breath tinged with the flavor of wine. Odd sensations bombarded her senses and heat swirled through her belly. His tongue slid into her mouth, invading her and fueling her anger, yet the heat grew more intense, and a small sound came from her throat.

Caryn jerked free, trembling and strangely off balance, her hand drawing back to slap his face. He caught it midswing, stilling the motion, and she saw he was nearly as angry as she.

"What game is this you play?" He shoved back his chair and came to his feet, setting her firmly on her own. "Do you think I cannot hear the venom dripping from each of your honeyed words? I would have you resigned to this marriage, but that you are not is apparent by your face. Do not play me for a fool, *cherie*. I am not a man who deals well with deceit."

So, black-hearted devil that he was, he had seen through her pleasant facade. She never had been much of a liar and he was a man not easily duped.

"If 'tis truth you wish to hear, then know that indeed I do not wish this marriage. Now that Malvern is gone, I ask that you release me from my pledge."

"A messenger has already been sent to William. I am certain to receive his approval any day. Your request comes too late, even would I concede to your wishes—which I would not."

"You cannot force me to wed you."

"Can I not?" Anger flared his nostrils, making him look even more fierce. "You believe a maid no bigger than a child can gainsay me in this?"

"I-I believe that you will see the error in your thinking. Surely I am not the woman you wish for a wife. You have said as much yourself. Marry the blonde you call Lynette. She would be more to your liking."

"You, my fiery little shrew, are enough to my liking."

"I will not wed you."

He dragged her against him. "You will wed me. Should you continue to refuse, I will carry you up to my bed and dispense with your maidenhead. I will plant my seed so deep it is bound to take root and you will have no choice but to accept your role as my wife."

"Curse you! You are an ogre! Have you not dealt me enough pain already? Must you continue to inflict more and more?"

At her words, the Norman's hard look softened. He tipped her chin with his hand. "Hear me well, *cherie*. I do what is best for you and your sister. Without my name as protection, Malvern will not rest until he beds you—and worse. There is nowhere for you to go, no place where you would be safe."

"I ask for my freedom. It is all I have wanted since the day I entered the convent. All I have ever really wanted."

"A woman can never have such a thing. You belong to the man you call lord. As a child it was your father. Should it not now be me, it would be William or some other. You will do as I tell you. Resign yourself and accept your fate."

"Rot in hell."

Ral gripped her arm. "I have been patient with you, Caryn. But should you speak to me that way again, you will feel the weight of my hand." He jerked her down into her chair and shoved his half-full trencher before her. "Eat. You will need your strength."

Caryn stared mutely down at her plate, at the dry, dark brown bread moistened with broth and a chunk of roast mutton. A page filled a goblet with wine and Caryn took a calming sip. The Dark Knight cast her a last warning glance then ignored her. For a moment, she found herself oddly irritated that her presence should mean so little, then she went back to eating the meal put before her.

Beside her, Lord Raolfe was engaged in conversation with several of his men, a heated discussion about a group of outlaws who appeared to be hiding in the forest.

Caryn suddenly grew more alert. Saxon rebels—they had to be. And the Norman and his men were planning to attack them. On the morrow they would ride out, he said, headed for Baylorn, where word had come down that the band had for sometime been camped. These men were her people. If only she could help them.

Caryn ate a few more bites of food, her mind spinning with ways she might warn them.

It shouldn't be too hard. The hall was filled with Saxon servants. If one of the kitchen maids could be sent to the village, someone there would know how to contact the rebels. She thought of speaking to Marta, then caste the notion away. The old woman felt a certain loyalty to the Norman lord. Besides, she might not approve. Caryn would do it without her. She was a Saxon by birth. She would do what she had to.

She ate a bit more food then asked Lord Raolfe for permission to leave. One battle with him for the day was enough. Besides, she had more important matters to attend. Caryn forced herself not to hurry from the hall.

Ral sat astride his big black destrier, his leather-gloved hands balled fiercely into fists. Around him the remnants of the outlaw camp lay scattered carelessly about, the embers of their fire just recently grown cold.

" 'Tis certain they left in all haste," Odo said. "Should they have learned of our arrival well beforehand, we would not have found a trace. It has been their way to leave little in the way of clues."

"Send Geoffrey along with ten of our best outriders. I would see if their trail is still warm enough to follow."

"They will leave no trail, but scatter with the wind. You know that as well as I. It has been their method from the start."

"Curse the brigands. They murder and rob, yet still some Saxon fool sets out to warn them."

"Most of the villeins wish them dead. Besides, none knew our plan. Only those in the hall could have known and except for Richard and your betrothed none speak our language."

Ral had been careful to speak Norman French as they planned the attack. Richard had been nowhere near and he hated the brigands nearly as much as Ral, but the maid . . . Surely her enmity would not lead her to this. Surely she would fear his wrath—would tremble in terror at what would occur should he discover she played a part in the outlaw's escape.

He tried to imagine the saucy wench cowering in

fear, saw instead her spitting her defiance like a tiny cornered kitten, and knew in an instant who the Saxon traitor had been.

" 'Twas the wench," he growled, jerking Satan's rein as he spun the big horse around. "Leave off the search. The whoresons will be long gone by now. We will rout them another day."

In the meantime, he would see to the maid. The bitch would soon learn the price of her folly.

Chapter Four

Caryn saw the huge Norman's rage even as he crossed the hall toward the steep stone stairs. Lord Raolfe had stripped off his mail but still wore his heavy leather jerkin. His face was a mask of fury, his strides long and powerful, the muscles in his arms tensing as his hands balled into fists.

Sweet Blessed Virgin! How had he discovered her role so quickly? From her place on the landing, she saw him give terse instructions to Richard that he not be disturbed then continue toward the stairs. Caryn turned away and made a quick dash for her chamber, but if she thought to reach it before he caught her, she had underestimated him sorely.

"Let me go!" she cried out as a hard arm went around her waist and he lifted her off the floor. Instead he kicked open the door and dragged her in, then slammed the heavy oaken planking behind them. Roughly, he set her on her feet before him.

"It was you, was it not? You who warned our quarry?"

"I-I do not know what you mean."

"Do you not? Art a terrible liar."

Caryn's chin went up. She waited for him to go on, her heart hammering hard against her ribs. Sweet Mary, what would he do? She tried to sound calm, but her hands were shaking. She buried them in the folds of her tunic.

"I am sorry, my lord, if I have done something to displease you."

Anger swept his features, making his eyes turn the color of the gray stone walls around them. He gripped her shoulders and dragged her up on her toes, his jaw clenched so hard he could barely speak.

"You have more than displeased me—as you too well know! Why did you do it? Why!"

Caryn swallowed hard. There was no way around it and she would not cower. She forced her chin up a notch and faced him squarely.

"Because I am a Saxon. Because I owe them some measure of loyalty. They are my people. They are only fighting back."

"You little fool!" When Ral released her, she stumbled and would have fallen if he had not caught her. "These men are not rebels. They are murderers and cutthroats. Brigands cast out from towns far and wide. They have killed as many Saxons as they have Normans—probably more."

"What!"

"You did not know that? But then I suppose that you would not, locked away as you have been these three years past."

"Nay, 'tis not the truth."

"No? Ask the people in the village. They have come to me for protection. 'Tis for their sake as much as my own that I seek these vermin out."

"These men are not rebels? You are telling me the truth?"

Ral's eyes searched her own. He must have seen how troubled they had grown, for some of his anger seemed to fade.

"Their leader is a man they call the Ferret. A murderer and thief, a brigand more ruthless than any I have known. 'Tis a name that strikes terror in Norman and Saxon alike.''

Caryn's bottom lip trembled. Sweet God, what had she done? "I-I did not think . . . I never would have . . ." She straightened her spine. " 'Tis not enough to say that I am sorry. If only I had known 'twould not have happened.''

"If only you had known . . ." he repeated, raking a hand through his wavy jet black hair. "Were you not afraid that I would beat you? Had you no care for yourself?''

Surprised at the tone he had taken, Caryn searched his face. "The consequences were unimportant. I believed they were my kinsmen. I felt that I should help them." She met his hard look squarely. "In truth, I did not think that you would find out.''

"There is only you and Richard who speak my language.''

Caryn gripped his arm. "You did naught to Richard? He is innocent of any crime. Your seneschal had no part in this.''

"So you worry for Richard, but not for yourself.'' He made a harsh sound in his throat. "Richard of Pembroke has sworn his allegiance to me. I did not believe him guilty. You are the one who accomplished the deed, the one who deserves to be punished. What would you have me do?''

"You . . . you're asking me?''

One corner of his mouth curved up. "Should the punishment you choose not be fitting, you may be certain that I will choose another.''

Caryn chewed her bottom lip. A beating, she had expected, savagery and cruelty—certainly she had not expected this. "In the convent, the abbess made me scrub the floors with a twig." She glanced up at him from beneath her lashes. "I had missed the Mass, you see. It was such a lovely day and—"

" 'Tis clear what must have occurred. From what I have seen thus far, 'tis not your wont to follow orders."

"I would not enjoy a beating, my lord."

"No, I do not suppose that you would. Though you may not yet believe it, I would not enjoy giving you one."

"Mayhap I could go for a time without sustenance. 'Twould be fitting, since the outlaws rob others of theirs."

He shook his head. "I would see a little more meat on your bones. I like my women soft beneath me."

Caryn flushed to the roots of her hair. She studied a crack between the boards in the floor. "I could work in the kitchens."

"You will soon be my wife. I would not have it said I have married a scullery maid."

Ignoring that unwelcome reminder, she started to suggest something else, but he raised his hand to stop her.

"You will remain in your chamber for the balance of the week, inside the keep for a fortnight." She looked stricken. "Knowing you as I am beginning to, and considering you did not know the truth of the brigands, I believe the punishment severe enough for the crime."

She glanced around at the drab gray walls, noticing for the first time how dreary the bedchamber was, the castle itself was in fact. "Sweet Jesu," she grumbled, "I would rather have had the beating."

Ral's mouth twitched. "Mayhap you will think next time before you act. You are new here. Your punishment in this has been light, but I will not abide your disloyalty. Remember that, Caryn." With that he strode from the room.

"Did you beat her?" Odo approached as Ral strode toward the dais. " 'Tis a pity, since she is so small. I pray you did her no permanent damage."

"She thought they were rebels. She has been shel-

tered these past three years. I have ordered her confined
to her chamber.''

Odo's mouth dropped open. "I was worried you
might kill her. Instead you command her to stay in her
room? 'Tis not like you, Ral.''

" 'Tis not like me to injure a woman—particularly one
who is yet no more than a child.''

"A child? Is that what you see when you look at her? I
see a woman fully grown. I see a fiery little minx who
needs a strong man's guidance. What your Caryn needs
is a good hard taking. Someone to ride her long and well
and teach her her place. Should she not belong to you, I
would be happy to see it done myself.''

Ral felt a prickle of anger he hadn't expected. He and
Odo had been friends these long years past. The man
would not trespass, yet even the notion goaded Ral's
temper. "The woman belongs to me. I will see she
learns to obey.''

"And I will take care not to trust her, just as you
should do.''

Ral nodded. "You may be certain that I will.'' He
shrugged. "Once she is wedded and bedded, her loyalty
will belong to me. Until then, she is still a Saxon. It is
difficult to fault where her loyalties lay.''

Odo scoffed. "Methinks the girl has caught your
fancy. I do not believe you would have spared Lynette
the beating.''

"Lynette would have acted out of spite. Her concern
is always for herself, her needs always selfish. She
pleases me in bed or she would not be here.''

"Do not let the little one into your heart, *mon ami*. It
is dangerous for a woman to wield that kind of power.''

Ral bristled. "You speak like a fool,'' he snapped.
"There is not a woman on earth who could tempt me to
that. I have seen what harm can come of it. I have seen
men driven to lengths no sane man would consider.''

Ral thought of Stephen de Montreale and a talon of ice slid down his spine.

"I am certain you are right," Odo said. But his eyes said his friend should beware, and Ral would well heed his warning.

"Do not fret so, my pet. Tomorrow you will be free to roam the hall." Marta crossed the barren chamber to where her young charge sat fidgeting on the end of the bed.

Except for a heavy iron-banded trunk, an oaken table where a half-spent candle sat beside a pewter bowl filled with the sodden remnants of hare stew, and a brazier black with dead coals from the eventide's fire, the room was empty.

" 'Tis a prison, still. I would see the sun, hear the singing of the birds."

"You are lucky he did not beat you."

" 'Tis worse than a beating."

Marta smiled, warmed by the young girl's presence once more in the hall. "You could work on your embroidery. 'Tis certain you could use some improvement." The child had always been a handful. Three years in a convent had not changed her. She was flighty and irresponsible and too much of a dreamer, yet there was sweetness in her, and always there was caring.

"You know well how much I hate it."

"I know well you prefer to roam the fields, watching the insects or studying the patterns of bark on a tree. I know you would waste away the hours in some cottar's hut, learning how he plants his crops or how he would burn off the harrow. 'Tis useless information, I vow. 'Twould be far better should your interests lie in how to please your husband."

"I want no husband."

Marta harrumphed her disgust. "You would rather have stayed in the convent?"

"You know that I would not."

Marta shook her head. It had been hard on poor Lady Anne, protecting a daughter who constantly displeased her father. After the lady was gone, dead of a plague, Caryn not yet seven summers, instead of the beatings her mother had feared her daughter would receive, Caryn's father merely ignored her. She grew restless and even more disobedient—independent her dear mother always called it—yet ever was the child kind and loving, seeking always to be helpful, mostly seeking to learn.

" 'Tis as I once told you, Lord Ral is different from the rest." Marta eyed the little maid now, assessing the beauty she had become. Not as lovely as Gweneth, at least not in that same ethereal way. That one was a raven-haired, fey creature who captured the hearts of all who knew her. But Caryn, with her fiery auburn curls, big brown gold-rimmed eyes, and lush woman's body could turn any man's mind to bed sport, and a yearning to render his claim.

"He is no different," Caryn said. "He is a Norman."

"He takes you to wife—what Norman would do that? He does it to protect you."

"He does it to salve his conscience."

"You have told me what happened in the meadow. You have told me of the soldiers' brutal treatment . . . of the rapine of your sister. I would tell you there is a time men are not themselves. 'Tis the bloodlust that comes over them . . . the fighting and the killing . . . the nearness they feel toward death. I have seen it among our own kinsman. It should not have happened but it did. You should not have been there, but you were. If the lord wishes to make amends, then 'tis your Christian duty to let him."

Caryn's mouth thinned. "By rutting with him in his bed?"

"By the honor of becoming his bride. If you choose not to think of yourself, think of the good you could do for your people. As a Saxon and the wife of a Norman lord, you could intercede on their behalf. In time, mayhap you could make things better.''

Caryn pondered that. It hadn't occurred to her that she might somehow make a difference. Being wife to one of William's barons would be a grave responsibility. There was the castle to see to, the harvest and food stores, clothing, medicines, supplies—to say nothing of the people in the village. Caryn winced just to think of it.

''I will not wed him.''

''Can you not see that this is your fate? From the moment you first saw him, your paths have been intertwined. Surely you were destined for this.''

''My fate is what *I* intend to make it—not some Norman blackguard.'' Caryn slid down from the bed and walked to the window, setting aside the thin piece of horn that let in the light but served to keep out cold air. ''Leave me, Marta. For a time, I would be alone.''

Marta shuffled toward the door, but paused as she pulled it open. ''Hear me well, my pet. Lord Ral is not a man to trifle with. He will not be thwarted in this. You must not dare to try.''

Caryn said nothing more, just waited till the heavy wooden door slid solidly closed. Tomorrow she could roam the hall, yet that would not serve her purpose. She needed to survey the bailey, secure a horse and supplies. As soon as she had accomplished the task, she could be gone.

She peered with yearning toward the open fields, newly tilled and ready for planting. She could just glimpse the thatched roofs of the cottars' wattle-and-daub huts. Below her in the bailey, great gray hounds that often roamed the hall chased a yellow cat into a haystack.

Oh, to be racing there beside them, or riding the small white palfry she had once owned over meadow and moor. Soon, she vowed. Soon she would again be free.

Caryn left her chamber early the following morning. Lord Raolfe was just stepping out of the chapel, a small room off the great hall with a tiny stained glass window at one end. He was followed by a short, sturdy priest Caryn had never seen.

"Lady Caryn," Ral called out, his voice deep and husky, the unwelcome sound goading her temper. "There is someone I would have you meet." His men-at-arms had finished their early meal—a hunk of bread and a pot of ale—and were heading off toward the bailey for a morning of tilting and swordsmanship.

"As you wish, my lord." She pasted on a smile and moved in his direction. Standing next to the little man, Lord Ral looked even taller than he had storming into her chamber when last she had seen him. Taller, and in a tunic of embroidered dark plum that set off the black of his hair, even more handsome.

Her temper heated a little more that she should notice, when she had firmly vowed that she would not. She felt his piercing gray-blue eyes as she approached in a russet woolen tunic over a soft yellow chainse. His gaze seemed to warm as she drew near, moving over her clothing with approval, then returning to her face.

"You have done well in choosing your garments. I hope you also are pleased." His features were arresting: smooth dark skin, full curving lips, black slashing brows above his unusual eyes. She saw him smile and unwillingly remembered how warm she had grown when he had kissed her.

"The clothes are lovely. I am most grateful, my lord."

"Caryn, this is Father Burton. He is returned from the abbey at St. Marks. Father, this is Caryn of Ivesham, my betrothed."

In a swine's eye, she thought but merely forced another smile. "Good morning, Father."

"Now that Father Burton is back in the castle," Ral said with a slight note of warning, "Mass will be held in the chapel early each day."

Caryn merely nodded. It wasn't that she minded Mass. The church was an important part of life, and in her own way she was devout. It was only that she knew the words by heart, spoke to God whenever she felt the need, and there was so much more she might be learning in that same span of time.

"I had wondered," was all she said.

"Have you broken your fast?" Ral asked. "There is bread and ale, mayhap a chunk of cheese if you are hungry."

"I will wait for the midday meal." At the sound of an opening door, she glanced around and caught a beam of sunlight flooding in with the entry of one of the scullions. She sighed as the heavy oaken door swung shut, once more blotting out the sun.

"Art restless this morning?" Ral asked as the priest bid his farewells and walked away.

"Aye."

" 'Tis just that you should feel so."

Thinking of the outlaws she had unwittingly aided, she could not disagree. "I suppose."

He frowned at her lackluster mood. "Mayhap a breath of air would raise your spirits."

Caryn smiled in earnest, brightened by the thought of a moment out of doors. " 'Aye, my lord. Even a short breath would help."

"I will walk with you for a time, then you will return to the keep as I have commanded."

Caryn's heart plunged. The savage Norman knight would go with her. She groaned to think of spending more time in his company. Then her dark mood brightened. What matter if he should go with her? He could show her the bailey. She could discover the lay of the land, might yet find the means she would need for escape.

If she had to put up with the dark Norman's presence, so be it. 'Twas little enough price to pay.

Ral took the small woman's arm, felt it stiffen beneath his touch, and guided her off toward the heavy front door. The little minx was easy enough to read. She disliked him, blamed him for what had happened to her sister. Yet he would marry her still. In time he would tame her. He would rein in her unruly spirit, gentle her, and bring her willingly to his bed.

He eyed her luscious curves, the fullness of her breasts beneath her tunic. She was small but well formed and far lovelier than he had first noticed. *'Twill be a pleasure, demoiselle*, he thought, feeling a tightness in his groin. *'Twill be a pleasure indeed.*

They descended the wooden stairs to the hard damp ground of the bailey and walked past a gathering of his men. Knights, squires, and pages, men-at-arms assembled in full battle dress trained for war as their lord expected. Ral demanded his soldiers stand at the ready. He wanted his squires well prepared as they approached knighthood. He wanted his pages to make good squires.

"Good day, my lord." Those words from Odo, his chain mail clanking as he doffed his helm and strode forward from the others, his blue eyes bright beneath his fiery red hair. It was cut in the Norman fashion, shaved high up the back of the neck with a long bang in front, a style Ral did not favor.

"My lady." Odo sized up the woman on Ral's arm and cast him a glance berating him for what he saw as weakness in allowing her a respite from her sentence.

Ral inwardly smiled. Odo need not worry—the maid would be returned to the keep soon enough. And she would be grateful for his leniency—another step in his scheme to bring her in hand.

" 'Tis a pleasant day, is it not?" Odo said to Caryn.

"Aye. 'Tis a welcome respite from the cold." She glanced up at the cloud-streaked blue sky. "Though it looks as though it may yet turn to storm."

Ral liked the sound of her voice, liked that it was sweet and light, yet there was something sensual about it. Just as there was in the sway of her hips in the pretty russet tunic, a shade close to that of her long braided hair. It was there in the fullness of her lips when she smiled, the way her lashes swept over those velvet brown eyes when she tried to hide what she was thinking.

"How goes the training?" Ral asked, frowning as he saw his youngest knight, Geoffrey, take a blow to the shoulder, caught off guard as he stared too long in Caryn's direction.

"Well enough. A few have grown overconfident. 'Twould serve them well should you bring them down a peg or two."

"Tomorrow we hunt. The day after that I shall join you in their training. A pouch of silver to any out of ten who succeeds in bringing me low."

"Better to give the coin to the men who try and fail," Odo said chuckling. "They will need it to pay the surgeon."

Ral laughed, too. "As we haven't a proper one here, I will do my best not to injure them too severely."

"You would take on ten men?" Caryn asked, staring at Ral in amazement. "Thou art strong to be sure, but ten—"

"One at a time, *cherie.* 'Tis not so difficult a task."

"Not such a . . . ? I believe, my lord, the sun must be far hotter in Normandy for 'tis certain it has somehow cooked your brain."

Ral's eyebrows shot up and Odo burst out laughing.

"Ten men will be naught to your lord. 'Tis a feat I have witnessed many times, my lady. Mayhap 'twould be permissible for you to watch. What think you, Ral?"

"I think the lady will be spending the day in the keep. The next time she ventures forth, it will be as my wife."

"What!"

"You've received word from the king then?" Odo asked.

"By messenger only this morning. King William sends his blessings and strongly suggests, under the circumstances, the marriage take place in all haste. He has ordered a special license. The wedding is set for six days hence." Acceptance of the marriage had come with the missive, but denial of his request for the lands between Braxston and Malvern. Lands Ral desperately needed.

"He knows Stephen's evil heart as well as you do, though 'twould not serve him well to admit it."

Ral just nodded, his mind still wrestling with the king's unexpected refusal. Why? he wondered, and worried that Malvern was the cause.

Beside him, Caryn stood stiffly, anger seething from every pore. She tossed her thick reddish braid back over her shoulder.

"I would see the rest of what will soon be my home," she bit out, her eyes fixed straight ahead. " 'Twould be fitting to see the farthest walls of what will soon be my prison."

Ral ground his teeth. So the wench remained unresigned. No matter. Their course was set, and no willful, stubborn little maid was going to change it. At this point, not even he could do that. Not even Stephen.

Ral swore a silent oath, suddenly disgruntled the little wench wasn't more grateful. He ground his teeth as he once more took her arm. The girl would show her gratitude soon enough—once he had her lush little body spread beneath him.

"Come," he said gruffly, jerking her along in his

wake, "we are wasting time. As soon as we are finished I would see you returned to the hall."

Walking beside the tall muscular Norman, Caryn worked to control her temper, determined to rein it in, to placate her enemy and restore his good mood. Now was not the time to confront him. She didn't want to raise his ire, didn't want to alert his suspicions—not when time had suddenly grown so short.

Tamping down her own bitter mood, she smiled at him and eventually he returned to good humor. Caryn listened with interest as he guided her through the grainery, stables, bake house, armory, and farriers, speaking of the work he had done and of his intended improvements.

"One day I would have towers installed to command the drawbridge, mayhap a larger chapel out in the bailey. I would like to see a town here one day. Braxston sits at an important crossroad. 'Twould make a fine center for trade."

There was pride in his voice and Caryn could not blame him. Braxston Keep and the wall that enclosed it were a far cry from the ill-kept wooden structure with its crude motte and bailey that had once been Ivesham Hall.

" 'Twould seem you have great ambitions, my lord. I would not have guessed it of you."

"I grow weary of fighting. I would make the most of what is now my home."

It seemed a bold admission coming from a man like him, and Caryn grudgingly admired him for it. Still, she had no intention of becoming a part of the Dark Knight's vast plan.

Instead, as he showed her about, speaking to his men and servants, Caryn worked to discover the lay of the land, where the items she would need might come from, and thankfully, by the time they'd returned to the hall, her plan had at last come together.

'Twas a good thing indeed that is had. For something else had happened in the short span of time they had walked together across the bailey.

Once his disgruntlement had passed and Ral had begun once more to smile, Caryn had found herself smiling back, laughing even, or blushing at some flattering remark he had made. More than once when the lord's mighty hand had brushed her arm or he helped her past some obstruction, goose bumps had feathered across her skin.

Near the workings that brought up the drawbridge, he caught her about the waist to steady her as one of the great hounds raced past, and moth wings fluttered in her stomach.

Blessed Mary, it was dangerous these feelings he stirred. She knew the kind of man he was, knew he'd been a part of what had happened to her sister, and yet . . .

It was time she was away and now she knew how to go about it. With Braxston and his men back in residence, the castle guard was more relaxed. No one seemed aware of the restrictions Lord Ral had set upon her, and tomorrow she had heard him say that he would go hunting.

Her plan was simple: She would clothe herself for riding, have one of the pages saddle the small gray palfry she had spotted in the stable, mention she must needs go into the village and that she would soon return.

Instead she would take the two silver candlesticks she had recognized as plunder from Ivesham Hall and one of the heavy jeweled goblets that had also belonged to her father, and simply ride away. She would head for Willingham, the closest town, sell the booty she had taken —retrieved, she corrected—and go on from there.

A year and a day. That was the time she would need.

For a serf to become a freeman took a year and a day without capture. Surely for a woman, property of the lord just as a serf was, the rule would be the same.

What she would do with her freedom remained uncertain, but the possibilities seemed endless. In the towns, there were ale houses and inns, on the roads, there were traveling bands of players, troubadours, and merchants. Surely someone would have need of a helping hand.

Caryn smiled, her heart speeding up at the thought. Imagine all she could learn, the adventures she might experience. Oh, the places she would see, the wonders of the world beyond the castle walls. On the morrow, she would be ready.

By the morrow's eve, Caryn vowed she would be free.

Chapter Five

Ral shoved open the door to the entry and strode inside, Caesar, his brown speckled hawk, still perched on his shoulder. A blustery wind blew in behind him and clouds blocked the sun, yet he had enjoyed the day with his men.

"Fair hunting, my lord?" Richard approached as he strode through the hall, a man of loyalty and intelligence Ral felt lucky to have in his service. "You've returned far sooner than we had expected."

"Game was plentiful." Ral stroked the huge brown bird. He was training the big male hawk, an oddity among its kind, since females were usually the larger of the species and more suited to hunting. "We'll sup on hare stew and enjoy roast boar on the morrow."

"And the bird? His training goes well?"

Ral ran a leather-gloved hand along its sleek back. Bringing the hawk into the hall among the noisy hum of people was part of the young bird's learning.

"Caesar is the finest hunter I've ever owned. Such swiftness and beauty. 'Tis a pleasure to watch him work."

"I would like to see that, my lord."

"Would you? 'Tis a promise then. When next we hunt, you will join us."

Richard beamed for a moment then frowned. He was

a tall man, lean but firm of muscle, with a pleasant smile and warm hazel eyes. "There is much to do here, my lord. It leaves little time for sport."

Ral nodded. " 'Tis true, but soon you will have helping hands. You forget I take a bride."

"Lady Caryn? Surely you do not mean for her to run the hall?"

"I am in need of a chatelain. At present, you do that work plus your own. I should think you would be grateful."

Richard smoothed his features. "Yes, my lord. Of course. I am sorry, I did not mean to give offense."

"None is taken, my friend." Ral glanced around the hall. "Where is our lady?"

"In her chamber, I think. I have been busy with the books. I have not seen her since this morning."

Ral frowned. "In her chamber? Not likely. The girl is not one to be caged for long." It occurred to him that in a way she was much like the bird perched on his shoulder. In the beginning, the creature had chafed for its freedom. Ral had slowly brought the hawk in hand and with the girl he would do the same.

Ignoring the chatter in the hall, the men who whacked each other on the back and spoke loudly of the day's hunting glory, Ral climbed the stairs. He searched the little maid's quarters, found them empty as he had expected, and went in search of Marta. He found her in the passageway outside the door to the solar.

"Where is your lady? I would have a word with her."

Marta suddenly looked uneasy. "I-I have not seen her, my lord. She is most likely prowling the castle. She gets restless and bored. Even as a child, she often wandered about."

"She is forbidden to leave the keep. Surely she would not disobey me again."

Marta wet her lips. "She never means to disobey, my lord. 'Tis merely that she is ofttimes lured away—like a child tempted by sweets. If you knew her, you would see that she means no harm."

"The girl is not stupid. She must learn to heed the rules the same as the others. Have the servants search her out and bring her to me."

Marta wrung her aged hands. "You said she was free to roam the castle. I pray you, my lord, do not—"

"You worry overmuch, old woman. I only wish a word with the girl about the wedding."

Marta nodded, but did not look relieved. Ral returned downstairs for a goblet of wine, certain his servants would find her, but an hour later, the task was not yet done.

"It seems your lady is not among us, my lord." Bretta, a buxom blond maidservant Ral had often thought of bedding, walked up beside him. Her voice, which had once stirred his blood, merely spawned a wave of irritation.

"Search the bailey. 'Tis as far as she likely would have gone." His fist grew taut around the base of his goblet. If they found her in the bailey, 'twould mean she had once more disobeyed him. Damn the wench, he had warned her. With her blatant disregard of his orders, she had backed him into a corner.

He found himself praying they would find her returned to her room.

Caryn shifted in the ill-fitting saddle, trying to find a more comfortable position. No longer used to riding as she had when she had lived at Ivesham Hall, her legs ached and so did her bottom.

The saddle, the only one available and far too large for her small frame, made matters worse. It belonged to Lynette, but Geoffrey's young squire, Etienne, a gangly youth with deep-set eyes and a vastly engaging smile, had graciously offered it for her use.

She had been careful to choose an unsuspecting Norman to assist her escape, unwilling to call down the mighty lord's wrath on one of her Saxon kinsmen. She felt sorry for the young squire, but she'd had no other choice. And Etienne had made it so easy.

"I must go into the village," she had said, seeing him working in the stable alone. "A child is sick. His mother has asked for my aid."

"Aid, my lady?"

She held up her bag of supplies. "Medicine and blankets. The boy is feverish and gravely in need of assistance."

"But Lord Ral—he has gone hunting. Who will accompany you?"

"Richard of Pembroke has chosen two of the lord's most trusted men. They await me out near the gate. I beg you to hurry. The child lies near death."

"Of course, my lady. I shall see to the task myself." Etienne had returned with the gray. Caryn had smiled at him and let him help her into the saddle.

"Shall I see you to the men?" he asked.

"No! I mean . . . 'twill hardly be necessary. They await me even as we speak." She smiled again, reached down and squeezed his hand. "My thanks, Etienne."

He had returned the smile as she had ridden away, stopping at the bridge where she told the same story to the gatekeeper, except that in this tale Ral's men awaited at the edge of the woods. No one doubted her word. Lord Ral had given them no cause. He had wrongly believed she would meekly sit by and let him drop the marriage noose around her neck.

Sweet Mary, not on her life!

Once the castle lay behind her, Caryn had relaxed and the day had passed swiftly, the little gray's pace steadily eating up the road. A goodly distance along the way, she had allowed them both to rest, then continued on her journey. It would be nightfall before the Norman discovered her missing. Mayhap even morning. She would be miles away by then.

With that thought in mind, Caryn slowed her pace once more, allowing herself to enjoy her surroundings: forested mountains, bracken-covered hills, meadows dense with cattail, cocksfoot, melic and quaking grass. On the ill-kept road, she passed a cheapjack, a sharper by the look of him, selling his numerous wares. Homemade napery traded for goose quills, beeswax for hide, ribbons for a length of cloth.

A salt peddler had passed her by, a friendly sort up from Northwich, doffing his felt hat as if he were a courtier. She had passed several villeins, and had spoken to each of them, certain she was well enough away, eager to soak up any ray of knowledge she might gather as she rode along.

Besides, she would be off for the woods as soon as dusk began to fall. She would find a place to rest, feed and water her horse, then feast on cold mutton, bread, and cheese brought along from the kitchen. She would sleep in her fur-lined cloak and be grateful for the first time that the Dark Knight had bought it.

Only the graying of the sky brought a hint of alarm. Yesterday in the bailey, she had noticed the wispy white clouds. Today they were darker, denser, a harbinger of storm. She had hoped to reach Willingham, to seek out shelter at an inn. Instead, there was every chance the storm would break and she would be left unprotected.

Caryn only smiled. A wet night on the road was little price for one's freedom. Besides, it was part of the adventure.

She nudged the palfry into a trot and continued on.

Troublesome wench. Reckless, willful, and stubborn. Foolish beyond all bounds. Ral's hand grew tighter on the reins, making Satan sidestep and nervously paw the earth. Ral loosened his hold and resumed his search of the tracks the girl's horse had left on the road.

They were easy enough to follow. The little gray palfry was smaller than most, and the road was not heavily traveled. Thank God the hunt had been successful and they had returned home early. He had searched for her in the keep, been amazed—and furious—to find her gone. Once he'd discovered she had fled the castle altogether—he cursed himself for a fool in believing she would not dare—it had been easy to piece together the method of her escape.

"Forgive me, my lord," young Etienne had said, near to tears with remorse, "if I had but known 'twas against your wishes . . ."

" 'Tis not your fault, lad, but my own. Worry not, I will see the lady returned." Damn the wench. He had underestimated her sorely, hadn't believed it necessary to enforce her confinement. He had foolishly imagined his orders would be obeyed.

Ral swore an oath beneath his breath. Curse her treacherous hide. Didn't the little fool know she had put herself in danger? Besides the brigands who roamed these hills and the danger of wild boar and wolf, there was Stephen de Montreale and his men. Stephen would take her without a moment's hesitation. He would use her roughly and discard her. Mayhap even leave her for dead.

Ral's stomach knotted. He hardly knew the girl, yet already he felt protective of her. He didn't want to see her hurt. He amended that. When he found her, he would see she suffered aplenty, but at his hands, not those of de Montreale's men.

Spotting the trail she had taken off the road into the woods, Ral nudged Satan into a gallop. Dusk had begun to fall. Every moment that passed put Caryn more in danger. The willful little wench was as reckless as they came—and more disobedient than his most wayward soldier.

Ral clamped his jaw. She would learn, he vowed. Once he saw her safe, he would see that she well and truly paid.

Caryn glanced around her. She hadn't expected the long thin shadows of the trees to be quite so forbidding. She hadn't thought that every noise would make her jump and turn, make the little horse skitter and sidestep beneath her. She hadn't believed it could turn quite this cold.

"There is naught to be afraid of," she told herself out loud, hearing the snapping of a branch somewhere behind her. " 'Tis only the wind in the trees."

It could not be the huge dark Norman for 'twas his habit, she had learned, to hunt late into the evening. He couldn't have yet found her gone, surely could not have discovered the path she had taken. Of course there were the outlaws, but Caryn did not fear them. If she had to, she could tell them it was she who had warned them. They would be grateful. Certainly they would have no reason to hurt her.

Another noise sounded on the dusty trail behind her. It seemed closer. Hoofbeats, she realized with a sudden shot of fear, yet she was sure it was no more than a single horse and rider.

" 'Tis only a fellow traveler," she whispered to the horse, reining the gray off the path behind the branches of a tree to wait and watch. "There is naught to be afraid of."

"Do not be so sure," came a hard male voice from the forest right beside her. Caryn screamed as the Dark Knight's big black stallion burst through the trees. "You've me to fear—as you should have learned long before this."

Mother of God! Caryn wheeled the little gray, her

heart pounding savagely, and dug her heels into the horse's ribs.

"Pull up!" Lord Raolfe commanded as the animal leapt forward, but she only bent over the horse's neck to urge it faster. The wind rushed past her face, tree branches grabbed at her clothes, but Caryn raced on, riding as she hadn't in years, remembering the skills she had learned as a child and thought long forgotten.

"Hold, damn you!"

But Caryn rode on, driven by her fear of failure as much as that of the huge dark Norman.

Sweet God, how had he found her? What would he do if he caught her? Terror made her daring. She bent over the little gray's neck as they approached a downed tree, cleared it neatly, then took a small stream, spraying a mist as they landed on the bank, Caryn's cloak flying wildly out behind her. The thunder of hoofbeats seemed to drum through the forest, louder even than the frantic beating of her heart.

Ahead the forest grew thicker. Brambles overran the path they now traveled, yet she feared what lay behind her far more than what lay ahead. Taking a breath for courage, she plunged onward, urging the little gray faster. The animal neighed shrilly, Caryn felt it stumble, thought her mount had gone down, then realized the Norman had jerked her from the saddle. With an arm around her waist, he hauled her facedown across his saddle and drew hard on the big stallion's rein.

"Sweet Christ! Do you try to get yourself killed?"

Caryn twisted until she could see his face. Blessed Mary, it looked black as thunder. The stallion danced and pulled at its bridle, but even that great beast knew better than to gainsay its master in such a powerful rage.

"Unhand me!" Caryn shrieked, trying to pull away, but Lord Raolfe merely shoved her back down. A drop of something wet touched her cheek and then another. Caryn realized it was raining. She tried once more to sit up, but the hand at her waist held her firmly in place. The Norman drew her cloak up over her head, and the world fell into darkness.

Caryn rode along in silence, seeing only a blur of the muddy ground beneath them and feeling the hard tense muscles of a thigh pressing into her stomach. Another crushed against her breasts. He was solid as a rock, and every muscle and sinew rippled with anger.

Several times Caryn started to speak, but the tension in his body warned her not to. As the hours crept past, the rain started falling in earnest and Caryn began to shiver. By now her cloak was soaked clear through, so were her chainse and tunic, even her camise. Her arms and legs ached, her stomach was bruised from the pounding it was taking, and the chill damp air gnawed into her very bones.

Still they rode on.

"Might I not at least ride my own horse?" she asked, twisting toward him once more. Had she really come this far since morning? But she knew in her heart she had traveled twice that far.

"You will ride my thigh as you are now. There is a shepherd's hut up ahead. 'Twill do for the night. Cold as you are, I do not think you would survive the trip home."

There was an edge to his voice, and a hard set to his jaw. She prayed the damp night air would cool a little of his temper.

"How . . . how did you know where to find me?"

Ral drew rein on the horse. Apparently they had reached the hut, for he turned her into his arms. Throwing a long, booted leg up over the neck of his horse, he slid to the ground.

"Did you really think to elude me?" He grunted. "There is nowhere you could have gone that I would not have found you." He crossed to the door, kicked it open without knocking, and set her on her feet in the small near-empty room. "God help you should you move an inch from this spot."

Caryn swallowed hard. The Norman merely turned and strode back out the door, his black hair damp and clinging to the back of his thick neck, his eyes more fierce than the storm. Caryn studied her surroundings. There was naught but an empty barrel, a three-legged milking stool, and a rusted empty pail. She kicked it aside then winced as the pain shot into her icy foot.

A few minutes later, Lord Raolfe returned from caring for the horses. He carried her traveling bag, his saddle-bags slung over one wide shoulder, and a load of wood which he tossed down on the earthen floor before the fire pit. Kneeling, he laid out bits of kindling then used a flint and steel to start the wood burning. In minutes he had conjured a rousing blaze and her shivers began to ease.

"There's a blanket in my saddlebag. Get out of those wet clothes then use it to cover yourself."

She blanched a little at the thought, but the chill she felt would not go away until she shed the wet fabric.

"I need nothing from you. I've a blanket of my own." She reached for her bag, but the huge knight pulled it open and dragged out her blanket along with the sack of cold mutton and cheese.

" 'Tis good you raided my kitchen. At least you will not go hungry."

There was something in the way he said *at least* that put her on guard. Turning away from him, she stripped off her tunic with slightly unsteady hands, then pulled her wet linen chainse off over her head. Her camise was drier than she had imagined, the thin white fabric clinging a little too snugly but providing some measure of modesty. Wrapping the blanket around her shoulders, she looked up to see the Norman's cold gray eyes moving from her breasts to her face.

" 'Twas a stupid thing you did. Do you not understand

that you put yourself in danger?" He had stripped off his tunic and faced her naked to the waist in tight-fitting chausses and soft knee-high boots.

"Or I could have been safely away."

He tensed at her words, muscle rippling across his flat stomach as he wrapped the blanket around his hips. She had never seen a man so broad of shoulder, so narrow of waist. Black curly hair roughened the enormous width of his chest and arrowed down his body until it disappeared inside the blanket. 'Twas a sight she had never thought to see yet it held her as if he had cast some sort of spell.

"I commanded you to remain in the keep." The sound of his voice drew her eyes to his face. His thick black brows were drawn together, his lips formed a line as hard as his jaw.

" 'Tis not your place to command me."

"Is it not? I am your overlord. I am also your betrothed. These things alone speak my rights. Soon I will be your husband. Will you continue to disobey me then?"

"I will not wed you. You cannot make me." She raised her chin, defiance clear in her face. The dark Norman's hand clenched into a fist but he forced himself to calm.

"You do not fear me, do you?"

"Of course I do. You are a Norman after all. Why should I not?"

" 'Twould seem a logical assumption. You are half my size, and a female into the bargain . . . yet we both know 'tis not the truth. Had you been afraid, you would not have left the castle. Since you did, then I am forced to believe that you do not fear the consequences."

Caryn swallowed. Her fingers dug into the blanket. "Consequences, my lord?"

"Did you think there would be none?"

"The consequence of my failure is that you have found me. I deem that punishment enough."

A muscle jerked in his cheek. "The consequence of your disobedience is the subject we discuss. You have no fear of me, so you do not heed my words. After tonight you will know exactly what it means to face my wrath."

He jerked the empty barrel toward him, upended it and set it down, then seated his tall frame atop it. "Come here, Caryn."

Caryn's heart speeded up, the blood beginning to pound at her temples. She only shook her head.

"You will learn to obey me. You may start that learning now. I bid you to come here."

Caryn backed away. "I am close enough to hear whatever it is you have to say."

" 'Tis not what I intend to say, but what I intend to do." Caryn screamed as the huge knight came off his perch, his reflexes faster than lightning, grabbing the blanket and dragging her toward him. She spun away, leaving him holding the big square of woolen, anger distorting his face.

"This will only go the harder should you continue your defiance."

"I will not do your bidding, Norman. Not now or ever."

"You will, you little vixen. You will learn that I mean what I say!" With that he moved once more, reaching out as she tried to run past, grabbing her wrist and jerking her against him. A hard arm snaked around her waist, then he half-carried, half-dragged her toward the upended barrel. The huge knight sat down and hauled her across his lap.

"You have ridden my thighs once this day, now you will do so again. I trust this time you will not forget it."

He jerked up her camise, baring her to the waist, and Caryn gasped in horror. Embarrassment heated her blood that he should see her thus, then his palm came down hard on her bottom. Caryn shrieked at the feel of it, at the fire that seared into her flesh. Once, twice, thrice—she soon lost count.

"Let me go!" she cried out, trying to struggle free of his grasp. His hand was so big it covered her bottom and with every fierce blow heat burned into her skin.

"You will marry me," he said, continuing his hot rain of fire. "You will accept me as your lord and you will learn to obey me."

"Never!" But as Ral continued blow after blow, the flat of his hand relentless, Caryn wasn't so sure.

"You little minx," he said, the next several whacks bringing tears to her eyes. "There are few men who would gainsay me as you have. You are lucky your punishment isn't far worse." She squirmed against his hard-muscled thighs but his grip on her waist held her firm.

Whack, whack, whack. The heat of his hand burned brighter. He meant to teach her a lesson and Caryn finally conceded that he had. A sob escaped her throat and then another. She hadn't meant to cry, she hadn't. She couldn't let him win and yet it was certain that he had. She didn't realize he had stopped until she felt him ease her thin white gown down over her hips.

Turning her into his arms, he cradled her gently in his lap. "Do not cry, *cherie*. The worst is past."

He smoothed the hair from her damp cheeks and held her close. To her surprise, Caryn let him, splaying her hands against his chest, turning her face and crying into his shoulder.

"I am sorry, *ma petite*. I would rather not have done it. You left me no choice."

Caryn said nothing as his knuckle grazed her cheek, wiping away the wetness. Kindness was the last thing she expected. She reined in her tears and began to hiccup softly. "N-No choice but to beat me?"

She felt the rumble of his chest. " 'Twas hardly a beating. 'Twas a lesson pure and simple. I would see you safe, Caryn. What I ask of you, I do for your own good."

"You are a b-brute and a bully."

"And you, *ma chere,* are a pigheaded little wench with far more courage than sense."

Caryn looked up at him through her tears. There was something in the way he said the words, something of amusement and maybe a hint of admiration.

"I would have my freedom. 'Tis all I have ever wanted." She turned away from him and came to her feet, her bottom smarting with every step. She crossed the room, bent and retrieved her blanket, then swirled it protectively around her shoulders.

"Your freedom is something I cannot give. Even I do not possess such a thing. I am bound to king and country, just as you will soon be bound to me."

"Think you I have forgotten what happened to my sister? I cannot forget, nor can I ever forgive."

"We are to blame, yes. The Normans conquered your people, taking whatever lay in their path. Your sister was an innocent victim of war. 'Twas a pity she fell prey to its fury, but now that war is past."

"It will never be past for me."

"I would know how she fares," he said, ignoring this last.

Caryn flashed him a look of disdain. That he should care at all amazed her . . . then again, mayhap it shouldn't. From the moment of their first meeting, he had been drawn to Gweneth's ethereal beauty. Caryn felt an unwelcome twinge that it should be so.

"My sister fares well . . . considering. 'Twas lucky, mayhap, that her mind was gone before it happened. She does not remember. She is happy in the convent. She loves the sisters and they love her."

Ral nodded. "I am pleased to hear it. And for no other reason than to see your sister safe I would see the two of us wed."

"You think to ease your conscience by protecting her now when you should have done it then."

Ral sighed. " 'Twas a mistake. I do not deny it."

Caryn eyed him for a moment, surprised at his admission. It was hardly his responsibility to see two Saxon maids safely home, yet he'd been part of what happened after and for that she couldn't forgive him. "I would do anything for Gweneth—except spend time in your bed."

For a moment he made no move, just stood watching her with a dark brooding expression, his thick black brows drawn together in a frown. She shifted beneath his close regard, uneasy at his scrutiny, wondering at his thoughts. When he spoke at last, his voice sounded rough and husky.

"Do you never wish to have children?"

Caryn's head came up. 'Twas a subject she hadn't expected. "I love children. I might have wished for them one day—but not with a man like you."

Eyes that had been cool and appraising now turned dark and inscrutable. "You are certain of this . . . that a marriage in truth is not what you want?"

An odd pang rolled down Caryn's spine. She felt as if she were losing something, but she knew not what it was. "Quite certain, my lord."

Ral turned away and walked toward the door of the hut. Rain clattered on the roof. She could hear his steady breathing. He turned to face her but remained where he stood.

"If that is your wish, then so be it. Even as your husband, I will not force you into my bed. Just remember the words I have spoken. Should you not go through with this marriage, Malvern will claim you as his leman —you *and* your sister. He will use you until he tires of you—in ways you cannot imagine. Then he will share you with his men."

Caryn shivered and not from the cold. "De Montreale would use me, but you—I am supposed to believe—will not force me to endure your lewd attentions."

"Lewd attentions? That is the way you would see it?"

"Aye, why should I not?"

The Norman's sensuous lips grew thin. "What happened here this night could not be helped. Should you gainsay me again, you may count on more of the same, but I will not take you against your will. You have suffered enough already."

"Why should I believe you?"

His cool gaze raked her from head to foot. "Mayhap because your tiny woman's body holds little appeal for a man like me. Mayhap because I do not desire you." Ral expected to be struck down any moment for the lie he'd just told. By Christ, he wanted her more every moment. He had been glad for the blanket disguising his lust when he had seen her beautiful bottom, felt those smooth round curves beneath his hand.

"Should I agree to wed you, you will keep your leman?"

"If you wish to avoid my bed, that is the way it will be."

The girl bit her lush lower lip and watched him from beneath her thick dark lashes. Ral felt an urge to sweep his tongue across her mouth, to thrust it inside and sample the sweetness he had found there once before.

"All right," she said, "then I will agree."

Ral slept fitfully, all too aware of the half-naked woman sleeping across the tiny airless room. In the middle of the night he dreamed of caressing her soft little bottom, of cupping it in his hands as he drove himself inside her.

He had awakened bathed in sweat, his rod high and hard against his belly. Christ's blood, he'd been a fool to agree not to bed her. Yet mayhap it was for the best. She was tiny and fragile—Hardly that, he amended, thinking of her defiance, her escape from the castle, seeing her racing the small gray palfry, handling the horse as well as any of his men. Still, he could too easily imagine the pain he would cause should he drive his heavy shaft between her shapely little legs.

With a groan that betrayed his arousal, Ral turned on his side and forced the image away.

In the morning he dressed quickly, then left the hut while Caryn put on her clothes. As he rounded a corner, he stopped. Camped in a clearing not far away, Odo and several dozen men-at-arms made ready to return to the castle. They had followed his trail, keeping him safe through the night, yet remaining discreetly away.

"We were worried about the brigands—or de Montreale." Odo strode forward to greet him. "By the time we arrived, you had things . . . well in hand."

Ral cocked a brow at the smile that hovered about his friend's lips. "So you weren't so far away after all."

" 'Twas a lesson well deserved. She will not gainsay you again."

Ral only grunted. Not gainsay him? The girl would continue to plague him—of that he had no doubt. "I would see one of the men assigned to watch her. I've enough to do without running after a wayward wench."

"Geoffrey is the youngest. The duty should fall to him."

With his fair-haired good looks and easy smile, Geoffrey de Clare was the last man Ral would have chosen. Yet Odo was right, as the youngest, the unwelcome task should fall to him.

"Give him the news. Remind him of de Montreale's interest. If he believes he protects her, the job may be easier to swallow."

Odo laughed softly. "Better he see himself as her savior than her gaoler."

"Exactly," Ral said.

Chapter Six

Caryn saw little of Ral in the days before the wedding. She'd survived his brutal reprimand with more injury to her pride than to her person. But she had come to believe that was the handsome dark Norman's intent.

He had said his orders were for her protection, that she was in danger outside the castle walls. Now that she'd had time to think things through, she grudgingly admitted it was probably the truth. She knew de Montreale would have made short work of her, had she crossed his path, and even the outlaws she had unwittingly aided might have proved more than she could handle.

Running off by herself had been foolish, just as the Dark Knight had said, yet the chance at escape had seemed worth the risk.

Now she wondered. . . . If it hadn't been for the Norman, might she in truth be injured or dead? Was his harsh treatment a way of ensuring her obedience and thereby her safety? It galled her to think it might be so.

She thought of him now as she sat before the fire pit in the great hall late that eve. In the days since her return, she had worked to avoid him and had succeeded most of the time. When they did chance to meet, he was polite but distant, paying her little attention, though she sometimes thought he watched her when he believed she could not see.

For herself, Caryn found the powerful Norman a difficult man to ignore. Ofttimes just the sight of his tall retreating figure stirred an image of him standing half-naked in the shepherd's hut. She could still see the firelight glistening on his damp black hair, the muscles of his massive chest and shoulders, still feel his powerful thighs as they had pressed against her.

His leman, Lynette de Rouen, had been returned to Braxston Keep, though her quarters were now out in the bailey. Ral spent his nights there, and to Caryn's chagrin the fact that he did so pricked her sorely.

" 'Tis not well done of him to flaunt her before you as he does." Geoffrey, the young knight assigned to protect her—guard her, she was sure—watched the dark Norman speaking with the tall, graceful blonde. " 'Twill end, I vow, once Lord Ral has taken you to his bed."

Caryn felt the heat creep into her cheeks. "He may do as he wishes. It matters naught to me." Still she followed their movements, Lynette laughing softly at something Ral whispered in her ear, Ral's hand sliding boldly up her leg.

"You do not care?" Geoffrey arched a fine blond brow. "Most women would chafe at the notion." He had passed twenty summers, compared to Caryn's eighteen. A handsome young man, lean but strong, with bright green, usually smiling eyes.

"It does a woman no good," he went on, "for 'tis a man's right to bed whom he wishes. Still, I am surprised you would feel that way about one such as him."

"One such as him?" Caryn repeated, coming to her feet. Her hasty movement jarred the edge of the table, knocking over a carved walrus chess piece on the board where they had been playing. "You mean a big hulking brute of a man whose intrigues serve only himself."

" 'Tis not so, my lady." Geoffrey stood up, too, following along at her side as she crossed the room toward the stairs. "Lord Ral's concern is for his men, and for the people in the village. He would see their lot improved—'tis a promise he has made them."

"A promise?" She paused. "What sort of promise?"

"In exchange for the burden of taxes he pressed on them, collections he made in order to build the keep. Their help, he has vowed, will be repaid to each family by a grant of more land."

"And has he kept that vow?"

"He has petitioned King William for the lands between here and Malvern. Unfortunately, 'tis such a choice demesne that Lord Stephen has designs on it for himself."

Caryn turned at the rumble of a deep voice beside her. "You are to guard the lady," Ral said darkly, "not carry tales of my misfortunes."

"N-No, my lord. I am sorry. I meant no harm." Geoffrey stepped away. "When Lady Caryn is ready to retire, I will see her safely to her chamber."

"I will see the lady safe this eve," Ral said, taking her arm. Caryn felt the heat of his hand even through the wide sleeves of her tunic. Geoffrey bowed and hastily backed away.

"Good evening, my lord." There was little warmth in her words, yet the Norman seemed unconcerned. As they walked along, the rushlights brightened his features, making his eyes look more blue than gray, throwing the deeply etched planes of his face into shadow. Why did she suddenly feel short of breath?

" 'Twas a passable evening, ere I discovered young Geoffrey spewing his useless tales."

" 'Twas idle conversation, nothing more." She paused at the foot of the stairs. "Why is the land so important?"

Ral eyed her with speculation. For a moment, she thought he would not answer, then he shrugged and raked a hand through his wavy black hair.

"The building of the castle required a huge investment of labor and supplies. It was necessary for protection of the pass, but the people of Braxston felt the burden. Heavy taxes were assessed, stores depleted, livestock sold off, and a greater number of days required of them in labor away from their own plots of land."

"Which means the winter will be a harsh one for them."

"Aye, and the next year even worse—unless new lands are cleared and planted to make up for what they have lost."

Usually the villeins were expected to pay for the privilege of clearing extra land. Few could afford it and so they lived on small scattered parcels.

" 'Tis a promise I made them," he said, "and I mean to keep it."

"I see. . . ."

"Do you?"

"Aye, though I'm surprised you have confided as much to me."

"You will soon be my wife, *cherie.* Once we are wed, you will belong to Braxston just as I do. Your rights and privileges will be the same as those of the wife of any other Norman lord."

Together they climbed the steep stone stairs, then walked along the passage, stopping just outside her chamber door.

"And my duties?"

Ral's piercing eyes looked suddenly even more blue. "It is not too late, Caryn. Should you wish to be my wife in truth, I can promise you will not find your duties in the marriage bed nearly so loathsome as you might believe."

Caryn bristled. "Do you now break your word?"

"I will not force you into my bed." His finger ran along her cheek and goose bumps feathered along her skin. "But I would have a marriage in truth, if that was your wish, too."

Something squeezed around her heart. She forced herself to think of Gweneth, of the rape and the beating that terrible night in the past. "We have made our bargain."

He smiled but it looked suddenly cold. "So we have. 'Twas a pact conceived by the devil, and a bitter bargain indeed." There was anger in his words, regret, and something more.

In the shadows of the passage, the huge knight hauled her against him and his mouth came down hard over hers. It was a brutal, unforgiving kiss that betrayed his mood, yet Caryn felt the heat of it melting into her bones. His lips took hers fiercely, sliding over the curves, tasting them, then he drove his tongue inside to claim an even more intimate part of her. It was a savage kiss, yet far more compelling than Caryn could have imagined. She found herself clutching the front of his tunic, leaning against his hard-muscled chest and kissing him back.

The hand at her back forced her the length of him. She could feel the sinews in his thighs, feel the washboard contours of his stomach. It was the thick male ridge of his desire that brought a return of her senses, and Caryn jerked away.

"H-Have you forgotten your promise already, my lord?"

Ral's eyes swept down her body. Surprise at her response seemed mixed with his chagrin. "You are lucky our bargain is made, *ma chere*, for had I known the fire you possessed 'twould not have come to pass."

"But you . . . you said you did not desire me."

He grunted. "I like my women stout enough to bear a man's seed and lusty enough to satisfy his passions. It does not mean I do not desire you. I am a man; you are a woman. I would bury myself inside you should you give me the slightest chance." Dragging her back in his arms, he kissed her one last time, then turned on his heel and stalked away.

Caryn watched until he disappeared down the passage, his tall frame nearly filling it. She touched her kiss-swollen lips. Her breasts tingled oddly and she was damp in the place between her legs. Sweet God in heaven, what had he done to her? She felt weak and dizzy, and her heart still pounded whenever she thought of what had occurred. It was frightening this power the huge Norman held.

On unsteady legs Caryn went into her chamber, grateful more than ever for the bargain she had made.

Two days had passed since Caryn's encounter with the huge dark Norman. Early on the morning of the following day, Stephen de Montreale and his vast entourage arrived at the castle—the signal that today was the day of the wedding.

Her stomach clenched at the thought of what she was about to do, yet there was the danger of de Montreale, and the threat to her sister to consider. She wondered how she'd get through it, but she needn't have worried. The hours passed in a mind-numbing blur from the moment she descended the stairs, the stark gray walls of the keep disappearing as she tried to focus her thoughts on the elaborate festivities, the knights and men-at-arms who had crowded into the hall.

In a crimson tunic over a chainse of white silk embroidered in gold, the Lord of Braxston Keep stood waiting at the bottom of the stairs. With his thick black hair brushed back and curling softly above his collar, his strong square jaw, and beautiful dark-fringed eyes, he looked more handsome than Caryn had ever seen him. Yet when she looked up at him, his mouth was set and not a hint of warmth touched his features.

" 'Tis time the deed was done," he said as if the task

were more loathsome to him than it was to her. Still, his
brooding gaze swept over her, taking in her tunic of
royal blue velvet over a spun gold chainse, the beautiful
filigree girdle that had been his wedding gift to her. Her
thick braid of hair laced with gold ribbon formed a
heavy coronet atop her head.

He extended a powerful arm. "My lady."

Forcing a smile to her face, Caryn rested her hand on
the arm he offered, and he led her to a place just outside
of the tiny private chapel. At Father Burton's direction,
they spoke the vows, each of them staring straight
ahead, and in minutes the sturdy little priest had de-
clared them husband and wife.

" 'Tis finished," Ral said, turning toward her at last.
"Now you are safe."

She had known that without his speaking, by the look
of pure hatred that passed their way from Stephen de
Montreale.

" 'Twould seem congratulations are in order," Stephen said, a grim smile twisting his handsome face. In a
silver-trimmed tunic of china blue a shade darker than
his eyes, he strode toward them. Behind him, servants in
the hall made ready for the huge wedding feast, and
food and drink was served to the villeins gathered out in
the bailey. "It appears the lady has escaped my clutches
after all."

" 'Twould seem so," Ral said.

Lord Stephen smiled again, but his eyes betrayed his
displeasure. " 'Tis your bed the lady will warm . . . at
least for a time. . . ." He glanced pointedly toward
Lynette, who had missed the wedding and just now entered the hall. "It remains to be seen if she has made the
wiser choice."

Following the line of his vision, Caryn stiffened.
Lynette moved forward to a place beside Odo, her lovely
green eyes so cold they could have frozen stone. The
two of them had spoken no more than a passing word

since Lynette's return to the hall, yet it was clear the willowy blonde possessed more hatred of Caryn than Ral did of de Montreale.

"We've broken out the wine, my lord." Richard winked at Caryn and smiled his congratulations. "The meal will be ready forthwith."

Ral just nodded, but when he glanced at Stephen, his hold on Caryn's arm unconsciously grew tighter.

They made an appearance to the villeins out in the bailey, then as Richard had promised, the wedding feast was served inside the hall. Beneath snowy white linen, trestle tables bulged with the weight of their bounty: a whole roast boar, a swan and peacock complete with feathers, a giant loaf of bread baked in the shape of the keep, perfect in every detail including the wall and the drawbridge.

There were endless platters of fresh spring vegetables, cheeses, puddings, and sweets; and wine filled goblets and horns until they overflowed.

"You've done a fine job, Richard." Ral clapped his seneschal on the back as he continued toward the dais, Caryn on his arm.

"Thank you, my lord." Richard fairly beamed. He had spent every waking moment preparing for this day since Ral had made the announcement. "Please accept my heartiest congratulations."

Platter after platter of food was served, until there was hardly an empty space on the tables. Soon jugglers filled the hall, musicians played lutes, flutes, horns, and zithers, and dancers twirled in front of the high table.

As the feasting progressed, Caryn shared the trencher Ral offered, but her hand trembled as she nibbled a small piece of meat. She belonged to him now. Would he keep his word—or had it been just a ploy to convince her to do his bidding? More nervous by the moment, she felt Ral's breath on her cheek, warm and tinged with the fragrance of wine as he bent to whisper in her ear.

" 'Twill be over soon. And de Montreale will be gone in the morning."

It wasn't Lord Stephen she feared, but the bedding that would come once the feasting was ended. She grimaced to think of being stripped and tossed into bed with her husband while the whole castle looked on, and afterward—she refused to imagine what would happen should he not hold to his word.

As the long hours wore into evening, they left the dais to stroll among the guests, smiling as if all were well, Caryn wishing to God it were so. Ral left her a moment, then returned to her side. Already she knew his heavy footfall.

"You may rest easy, sweeting, the bedding will be forfeit."

"Forfeit? How did you know I . . . how did you persuade them?" *How had he sensed her fear—and why had he cared enough to ease it?*

"It took little convincing, considering what they know of your past."

Many knew the tale, both of the assault in the meadow, and what had nearly come to pass with Stephen de Montreale. Caryn's cheeks grew warm to think of it, yet should it save her embarrassment this eve, she would be grateful.

"Thank you, my lord."

" 'Tis best we leave the feasting before they change their minds."

"Of course." Leave for where? she thought, suddenly tense. Would he spend the night in her room—in her bed? Sweet Mary she hoped not.

"Your things have been removed to my chamber. From this night forward you will be sleeping in there."

"And you, my lord? Where is it you will sleep?"

He didn't miss the challenge in her words, though he

chose to ignore it. Instead he waited till they had reached his chamber. He dismissed Marta with a wave of his hand and closed the door behind them.

" 'Tis you, my lady, who have set these hellish rules. If you think I mean to break my vow, you are mistaken. Lynette will see to my needs this night, just as she has every other." He opened his hand to reveal a small stoppered vial, held it out to her, then pressed it into her palm.

"W-What is it?"

"Pigeon's blood. 'Twill do to stain the sheets. 'Twould do neither of us good should the servants learn on the morrow that you are still virgin."

Caryn merely nodded. Why did she suddenly feel so forlorn?

"I will stay with you for an hour or two. Time enough to believe the deed accomplished. In the meantime, you will help me remove my finery, as I will help you."

She did as he bade her, lifting off his crimson tunic then turning away as he shed his golden chainse and replaced his fancy chausses with an older more comfortable pair, cross-gartered them, and pulled on his soft leather boots.

Still bare to the waist, he turned in her direction and the firelight in the brazier made the ebony hair on his chest gleam. His skin looked as dark as polished wood and just as smooth. Muscles rippled as he drew a simple woolen tunic over his head and pulled it down his torso.

"If what you see is to your liking," he said, noticing the way she stared, "I would be happy to stay."

Heat shot into her cheeks. " 'Tis only that I have never seen a man the size of you. You are an oddity, nothing more."

His gray eyes raked her, burning into her with scorn. "Were you not such a tiny little wench, I would show you my size in truth. I would ride you long and hard this eve, and tomorrow would see you well broken."

Cheeks flaming, Caryn backed away but Ral merely followed, a cool smile curving his lips. "You've nothing to fear, *cherie*. I only mean to help you with your clothes."

When she started to protest, he sat down on the edge of the bed and trapped her between his legs. "Hold still. 'Tis difficult enough undressing one so small."

With neat, efficient movements, he stripped off her tunic and chainse, but left on her camise. Pulling the pins from the coronet atop her head, he let down her thick auburn braid, unbound the end, and raked his fingers through her hair.

" 'Tis as soft and silky as I had imagined," he said, and the words tugged warm and low in her belly.

Standing, he walked to the side of the bed and drew back the covers. "One of us may as well rest. The day has been a long one. You may sleep late in the morning. I will try to return before the others awaken. Should I fail, do not forget the blood."

"I will not."

He waited until she climbed in, then pulled up the covers, the gesture almost tender. Caryn closed her eyes and pretended to sleep, but watched him as he crossed to the chair beside the brazier and sat himself down, stretching his long legs out in front of him. Mayhap she did sleep after a while for when she awoke, Ral stood at the door.

"Already 'tis time for you to leave?" she asked, the words slipping out before she could stop them.

"Should you wish me to stay, you have but to ask."

Caryn said nothing, but her heart thumped hard within her breast.

"Remember, 'tis you who set the course between us this night. 'Twill be up to you should you ever wish to change it."

Caryn still said nothing, but as Ral strode outside and

closed the door, she suddenly wondered why she had worked so hard to be left alone.

Ral checked the passage, found several drunken men so deeply into their cups he knew they would not awaken, made his way down the back stairs, skirted the hall, and left the keep.

Two of his guards caught his shadowy figure as he moved toward Lynette's sleeping quarters in the bailey. He had hoped no one would know he had left his bride alone this eve, but in his heart he had feared that they would find out.

Ral sighed. There would be gossip. They would say the little maid wasn't woman enough to keep him in her bed. Ral wondered if indeed that were the truth and found himself doubting it. He had tasted her passion that night outside her door. She would have been a fiery little minx once he brought her to fulfillment.

Ral swore an oath into the darkness. He would have spared her this disgrace had he been able, but not at his own expense. She had laid the rules—there was no help for it now.

He knocked on the heavy wooden door and Lynette swung it open.

"So . . . 'twas as you said after all. You pierced her maidenhead and left her alone."

It wasn't the truth, but the girl would not be safe unless the marriage was deemed one in deed as well as fact.

"She hasn't your fire, my sweet. I have come to you in grave need of soothing." That much was true. His blood still raced from the feel of his small wife's near-naked body, the sight of her nestled atop his big bed.

Lynette slid her arms around her neck. "Have no fear. I will see you well-pleased this night as always." She was tall, reaching well above his chin, her blond hair loose to her waist.

"I am certain you will." It wouldn't take much this eve, not in the state he was in. He pulled the tie on her robe and slid it off her shoulders, leaving her naked before the fire.

"You've bathed away her virgin's blood, I trust." Lynette leaned forward, teasing him, brushing her heavy breasts against his chest.

Ral merely nodded, uneasy with the lie but knowing he had no choice. "I told you marriage would change little between us." Sliding an arm around her waist, he dragged her against him, lowered his mouth and kissed her, running his tongue over her cool thin lips. Her long slim fingers were also cool where she slid them beneath his tunic to rub the hair on his chest.

"You said that it would change nothing and 'twould certainly seem that is so." She nibbled his ear and he cupped a breast, wishing he didn't see an image of a high lush pair with dusky nipples. He thought of small warm hands and fiery lips as sweet as berries.

Furious that his tiny wife's image should intrude at such a time, Ral stepped away and began to strip off his clothes. "Get in bed," he said gruffly. "I would have you now—this minute. I would cleanse the feel of the auburn-haired wench from my blood."

"Aye, my lord. 'Twill be my pleasure to see it done." Climbing up on the bed, she opened her arms and her thighs in welcome.

Yet even as Ral drove into her, it was the tiny maid with the fiery dark hair that he wanted. It was the wench who was his wife he took again and again through the long bitter hours of his wedding night.

Chapter Seven

Caryn moved listlessly, stopping in the solar though she knew it would be empty, passing along the narrow, rush-lit halls.

She had never felt lonely in Braxston Keep. There were too many familiar faces. Servants who had once been loyal to her father, Richard and Marta, and new friends she had made. Like the young squire, Etienne, who, on discovering their mutual love of horses, had finally forgiven her for duping him into helping her run away.

She glanced at the people on the floor of the great hall below her. She had never felt lonely, but she felt lonely now, and had since the morning after her wedding. The morning Marta and the others had come into her room, found the bloody sheets but discovered their lord was gone.

His whereabouts had been discovered and word quickly spread. Now there was an uneasy stirring in the hall whenever she was near, a sense of condemnation, as if she had somehow failed them when she had failed their lord.

That was the way they all saw it: The Saxon maid he had taken to wife had fallen so short of the mark he was forced to return to his leman. It angered her they should stand with Ral instead of her, since most of them were

Saxon. How could they side with the savage Norman warlord?

Yet the fault was partly her own. Save for Marta, no one knew of the Dark Knight's presence that night three years past. The night of the rapine of her sister. Though most had heard stories of the soldiers' vicious attack, they knew little about it. In truth, neither did Caryn.

She had been badly beaten that night, had only been conscious part of the time. And she didn't like to remember; at the convent, she had been forbidden even to discuss it.

Still, she would never forget the dark Norman's face above her own battered features, his hard gray eyes piercing as she slid back into the yawning blackness. He hadn't been among the first men-at-arms who had set upon them like feral hounds, but he had been among them at the last.

Mayhap if she told the tale, the others would understand. Mayhap they would turn against their powerful overlord and praise her for denying him her bed.

Mayhap they would, and yet . . .

Caryn sighed, knowing she would never repeat the story. As Marta had said, the war was past, and like the rest of the people at Braxston, her life was now tied to the castle and its lord. Hurting the Norman would only hurt her people and ultimately herself. In time, the others would accept the way it must be between her and the tall dark Norman.

Caryn only hoped she could accept it herself.

Her mind still in turmoil, Caryn made her way toward the door of the keep, anxious for a cleansing breath of air. She was almost there when a soft mewling sound caught her attention. Certain the noise had come from a narrow passage leading to a storeroom, she walked in that direction and stepped inside. In the corner behind a sack of grain, she discovered a litter of yellow-striped kittens, dear little things, so tiny each could have nestled in the palm of her hand. When she crouched beside them to stroke their fluffy fur, one began to suckle the edge of her thumb.

Caryn laughed softly. " 'Twould seem, little ones, that you are hungry. Poor wee babes. Where is your mother?" A noise above her in the corridor drew her attention from the mewling balls of fur. The tall Norman's presence squeezed a tightness in her chest.

"So at last I have found you. I was beginning to worry you had left us again." There was censure in his voice and just a hint of concern. Except for meals and a few brief conversations, this was the first time her husband had sought her out since the wedding.

"The vows have been spoken. The time for running is past." Brushing dust from her tunic, Caryn came to her feet.

"I am glad you understand that." He extended his hand and she noticed he held a heavy ring of keys. "I have been remiss in not bringing these sooner." He pressed the ring into her palm.

"What are they?" Caryn held up the heavy iron loop, inspecting each piece of well-oiled metal.

"Chatelain's keys. They unlock the stores and all of the rooms in the keep. Did your mother not carry such keys?"

"Aye, but—" Caryn stared down at the keys, feeling a growing sense of panic. "I-I thought Richard acted as your chatelain."

"You are my wife. The job is now yours." He looked at her as if she should be pleased. Instead her stomach knotted.

"B-But Richard does such a splendid job. 'Twould surely not please him, should I interfere. 'Twould not be kind to hurt his feelings."

"Richard knows the way of things. The keys are now yours."

It was expected for a wife to manage the hall, even to

act as seneschal—overseer of the lord's affairs—should ever the need arise. But Caryn hadn't the faintest notion how to go about it—nor did she want to learn.

She forced herself to smile. "Thank you, my lord."

Unlike other highborn children, she had never been fostered to the home of a relative for training in wifely duties. After her mother had died, her father had meant to see it done, then he had died and the task was left to her uncle. But there was always Gweneth to see to, then the Normans had come and the war had begun.

And Caryn had never encouraged it. She hated women's work, hated being cooped up indoors. Even now, as she stood beside the man who was her husband, she hoped for a day of riding, mayhap a trip into the village. The people in the castle might think she had somehow failed them, but there were others who would not deem it so. Villeins she had yet to visit, people she had known since her childhood.

"Richard will assist in any way he can," Ral finished, "but the authority now belongs to you."

And the responsibility, Caryn thought with an inward groan. "I will speak to him forthwith." She just prayed that Richard, knowing her as he did, would see the potential for disaster and help her find a way around it.

"I see you are dressed for riding. Might I ask where you are going?"

"To the village. I would visit some of the cottars."

"As long as Geoffrey goes with you."

For the first time she noticed his plum velvet tunic, more elaborate attire than he usually wore. The gray silk chainse beneath it had been embroidered with matching plum thread and his shoes were of soft black kid leather.

"And you, my lord?"

"I hold court this day, though I've a few things to see to before then." He started to leave, but she caught his arm.

"Would you know aught, my lord, of a yellow-striped

cat? 'Twould seem she has misplaced her brood and the little ones grow hungry.''

Ral frowned. He looked past her skirts to the mewling sounds coming from the corner. "The cat is dead. 'Twas injured yesterday morn during the tilting. One of the men seemed to find it amusing to target the cat instead of his squire." The line of his mouth turned hard. "I do not believe he will entertain himself thusly again." His expression said the man had been dealt with and would not soon forget his lord's displeasure.

"What of the kittens, my lord?"

"She must have carried them within from out in the stables." His hard look softened. "They are much too small, *cherie,* to survive long without her. I will see they are dealt with."

"Dealt with? You do not mean to drown them?"

"There is little choice, Cara."

Caryn clutched his hand. "I beg you, my lord, do not order them killed. I will care for the kittens."

"There is naught you can do to save them. They are too small to take food from aught but a nipple."

She flushed at his use of the word but didn't let go of his hand. "I will find a way to feed them."

Ral seemed to ponder her words, and Caryn held her breath. "You may have until the morrow. Should they still be unable to eat, the deed must needs be done. I will not see them suffer."

Caryn let go of his hand, though oddly she found she did not want to. "Thank you, my lord."

His eyes ran over her face, then returned to settle on her lips. There was something intimate in the warm look he gave her, approval mayhap, and something more. Caryn felt herself responding to that look, felt the heat spreading into her cheeks then moving lower down.

With a brief nod of his head, Ral turned and walked

away. In the wake of his leaving, the corridor seemed dark and empty, more so now that he had gone.

Caryn stared at the place he had stood, wondering at the melting sensations she had felt just to look at him, and recalling his compassion. It was difficult to think of this man who was lord as the same brutal knight who had been among the soldiers that terrible day in the woods.

Yet she knew that it was so. Lord Ral had never denied it. More often of late, she wondered exactly what his role had been and whether or not he had taken her sister. More than ever before, it bothered her to think that he had.

At the door to the keep, she saw him pause, stopping to speak to someone entering the castle. Caryn recognized Lynette's throaty voice and the golden bright color of her hair. Ignoring the anger she had no right to feel, she turned away from the pair and went in search of a way to feed the kittens.

Caryn tossed back her hair. If Lynette was the woman he wanted, 'twas only for the best. Still, she could not ignore the dull uncomfortable thudding of her heart, or the feeling of isolation that had just increased tenfold.

"Going riding?" Words from the willowy blonde herself. " 'Tis certainly a poor day for it. 'Tis cloudy outside and a cold wind blows from the north." Lynette strolled into the center of the hall, golden hair gleaming, complexion smooth and elegantly pale, not sun-touched and lightly freckled across the nose as Caryn's was.

" 'Tis brisk, not cold," Caryn said. "Besides, I do not mind the weather. I ride into the village, not that 'tis any concern of yours."

Lynette laughed, though the sound was nothing like the rich throaty purr she shared with Ral. " 'Twould seem the sort of riding you are best at." A perfect blond brow arched up. "I enjoy the ride of a two legged steed myself—the pleasure is by far the greater. But there is little you would know of that. Did you know more, your husband would not have abandoned your bed."

" 'Tis enough, Lynette." Richard moved between them as Caryn took a step in the taller woman's direction. "As the lady has said, 'tis no concern of yours."

Caryn smoothed a blandness into her features. It never crossed her mind she might be jealous of Ral's leman, but she wasn't such a fool she couldn't recognize the emotion for what it was.

"The meal is long finished," Richard told Lynette. "What is it you want?"

" 'Twas boring with naught to do and Ral busy with his men. I seek some sort of diversion." She smiled at him, her eyes moving from his sandy brown hair and hazel eyes down to the width of his chest, which wasn't nearly as wide as Ral's but looked firm and strong just the same. "Mayhap you could find time for a game of chance?"

"I am busy. Lord Ral holds court here this day. I would advise you to take your leave."

Lynette sighed. "Always so serious, Richard. 'Tis a pity you've no woman to take your mind off your work." She ran a slim finger down the front of his tunic and Richard gripped her wrist.

"I do not think Lord Ral would be pleased by your antics. Again I say hie yourself off."

"Lord Ral is more than pleased"—she cast Caryn a meaningful glance—"do not doubt it, Richard." With a satisfied smile, she turned and walked back toward the heavy wooden door leading out to the bailey.

Caryn watched her go, furious at herself for the anger Lynette could stir, wondering what there was about the woman her husband found so alluring. Of course, 'twas obvious just to look at her, and the fact Ral's beautiful leman so pleased him made a bitter taste rise in Caryn's throat.

"Do not let her goad you," Richard said. "She is not worth it."

"I do not believe Lord Ral would agree."

His face turning crimson, Richard looked down at the floor. He was such a kind man, always concerned for others, rarely doing aught for himself.

"I am sorry, Richard. 'Tis not Lynette I would discuss, but my newly assigned duties as Braxston's chatelaine." She held up the keys, which made a soft tinkling sound as they lightly clanked together.

"He has mentioned this to me. I had hoped he might come to his senses." He flushed even redder. "Beg pardon, Lady Caryn. 'Tis not exactly what I meant."

" 'Tis exactly what you meant, and I agree. I know nothing of such a task. I would only make a mess of things. What say you, Richard, we continue as we are?"

The steward looked relieved. "I would say that would be very wise indeed."

In truth, there were things the castle needed: tapestries to warm the walls, bedding that should be aired more often, rushes that might be freshened with herbs. But all in all, the place was well-enough maintained, and Ral and his men seemed content. Caryn smiled and extended a hand. "Then we are agreed?"

Richard smiled back. "Happily, my lady, we are agreed."

Feeling much relieved, Caryn turned to see the young knight, Geoffrey, striding toward her, fair-haired and handsome and very self-assured. He felt strongly about his duty to protect her, though Caryn felt equally certain it was his guardianship the lord truly sought.

"Lord Ral says you are for the village. I have ordered your palfry saddled and ready. We may leave whenever you wish."

Caryn watched the servants scurrying around her, readying the hall for the lord's manorial court about to be held. Tables were being assembled and benches set out. With Richard at his side, the Lord of Braxston Keep would mete out justice from the dais above.

"Save for my mantle, I am ready." She started for the stairs, meaning to retrieve her cloak, but one of the maidservants stepped into her path.

"I beg of you, Lady Caryn. I am Saxon, once a loyal subject of your father. I plead for a moment of your time."

On closer inspection, Caryn saw the woman was a villein and not a servant of the keep. A thin woman dressed in a coarse woolen tunic, she nervously twisted the folds.

"Of course. What is it you need?"

"My name is Nelda, my lady. I am sorry to trouble you but—" She glanced around the hall, her worried gaze darting to the dais then to Geoffrey who stood just a few feet away.

"It might be best if we spoke somewhere quiet," Caryn suggested, sensing the woman's distress. She turned to Geoffrey. "I shall return forthwith and we can go into the village."

"As you wish, my lady. I'll see the horses brought round." Geoffrey left to do her bidding, but something about the thin-faced woman Caryn led down the dimly lit passage told her they would not be going to the village after all.

Weary from the endless cases put before him, Ral rubbed his eyes and leaned back in his carved high-backed chair. Seated atop the dais to his right, Father Burton toyed with the long beaded chain suspended from his neck, while Richard sat on his left making notes on a small wax tablet, to be transcribed later by a clerk. As seneschal, Richard kept track of the proceedings and read from a parchment scroll the nature of each petition.

The case in progress was the swineherd seeking permission for his daughter to marry the beekeeper's son.

"Permission is granted," Ral said, accepting as his merchet, or fee, three succulent young piglets, to be brought to the castle on their maturity. "Convey my good wishes to your daughter."

"Aye, my lord. You have my most humble thanks." The man backed out of the hall with a smile on his face. The old lord would have charged him much more.

"What next, Richard?"

"A tenant seeking grant of an inheritance. The villein Alfred has died. Osrig petitions for the land as his only living son."

"The petition is granted. I'll expect a heriot of one black-faced sheep. Father Burton?"

The sturdy little priest sat up straighter in his chair. In the case of an inheritance, the priest received payment as well. "I would prefer an oxen. Have you more than one, my son?"

"A sheep is the best I can offer you, Father. The oxen died last week."

"A sheep then. Bless you, my son, and may God's bounty be fruitful."

More petitions were read and dispensed, then began cases of men who had broken the law.

Richard cleared his throat as he started to read from the parchment. "The merchant, Gervais, is accused of selling false relics," he said of a middle-aged man, slightly stooped of shoulder, who stood in front of the dais gripping his brown felt hat in his hands. Richard filled in the details of the case and finished by stating, "The man has admitted his crime and now pleads for mercy."

Ral turned to the priest. "Father Burton, I would ask your counsel in this." In certain matters, it was wise to include the church. It represented a different, even higher authority, and lightened some of Ral's burden.

The little priest assessed the man gravely, his bushy gray brows drawn together in a frown. "In this you have sinned against God, my son. Do you not know that you risk the loss of your soul?" Father Burton leaned forward. "To sell some poor wretch one of St. Martin's ribs when in truth 'tis aught but the bone of an oxen—this is blasphemy of the highest degree."

The priest looked at Ral. "Should this man not have admitted his crime, I would see him face an Ordeal By Water." A hand and forearm plunged into boiling water, wrapped and sealed, then examined three days hence to prove a man's guilt or innocence. Only a healed man would go free. Which, of course, never occurred.

The accused man paled, as the priest intended.

"Since you have acknowledged your sin," he said, "it remains for you to repent. Then you must make satisfaction so that you might be absolved." Again the priest looked to Ral. "My lord, I would suggest this man spend time in the pillory reflecting upon his crime. At week's end, he should make restitution to those he has cheated and then report to me. There is work I would have him do in the name of the Lord."

Ral nodded. "So it will be." He motioned toward the brawny knight, Hugh, who acted as guard, and the tall knight stepped forward, his mail clad body clanking with the movement. Though the guilty man was marched from the hall in disgrace, considering what might have occurred, the little man's step was almost lively.

Another hour progressed and for a moment, Ral's attention strayed. In the shadows to his left, he caught a movement then the flash of forest green wool. For the first time, he realized Caryn remained in the hall, had been standing there for some time, watching the proceedings. It made the muscles of his neck grow tense, made his glance tend to wander in that direction. He caught her eyes more than once, saw they looked troubled, and wondered at her purpose.

He wondered if she judged him, even as he judged those brought before him.

"Richard?"

"Aye, my lord." His steward gazed down at the parchment. " 'Twould appear there are just three more."

Ral nodded, thankful the day would soon end. A man who passed counterfeit coins, one of the gravest of crimes, was sentenced to the loss of a hand, as was an old thief who had stolen a poor man's life savings. The law commanded that a thief lose covetous eyes or pilfering hands. Adulterers might lose a testicle, while a runaway villein could have his tongue or ears chopped off.

Ral's title demanded he maintain strict rules of justice: a trip to the stocks, fines, floggings, imprisonment, brandings, amputations, even an occasional execution, though most times those were referred to the traveling royal courts. As a baron and Lord of Braxston Keep, it was his duty to uphold the law, yet there were times he wished someone besides himself might see it done.

Cases such as the one he tried now.

"The boy, Leofric, my lord, is accused of poaching in King William's forest."

In the north country, there was no Verderer's Court to administer forest law and since William had granted Ral use of the lands, the task of protecting them fell to him.

"What say you, lad? Did you poach the king's game?"

The boy looked ragged and dirty, a child of less than ten years with wind-chafed skin and fire-blackened, peat-smudged cheeks.

" 'Twas aught but a hare, milord. Me mother took sick. She couldn't hold aught on her stomach. She grew thin and there was no more food in the larder."

"Where is your father?"

"Dead of a flux, milord, these two years past."

"Why did you not come to me?"

"To you, milord? Why you are a Norman."

"Aye, that I am. I am also your lord." Ral leaned forward. "I would have seen to your needs and those of your mother. Instead you chose to break the law."

The boy said nothing, but his hands began to tremble.

"The penalties for defying your king are grave ones. Poachers are to be hanged or their legs cut off. The law is firm in this. Your mother's illness is no excuse."

The boy seemed to sway on his feet. He reached for the edge of the table to steady himself. "Aye, milord."

"Are you ready, Leofric, to face the consequences of your crime?"

Muscles worked in the young boy's throat but for a moment no sound came forth. "Aye, milord," he finally said. "But if your sentence should leave me a cripple, 'twould be death I would choose instead. I would not be a burden to me mother."

A soft gasp issued from the shadows. From the corner of his eye, Ral saw Caryn step forward while a thin-faced woman, deathly pale, appeared in the corridor behind her. Ral stiffened as he realized his wife intended to approach the dais. Damn the wench, would she never learn her place?

"Beg pardon, my lord."

Ral looked at her and felt his temper rising. "My pardon is not granted. I would have you return to your place at the edge of the hall."

She paused for a moment, her tunic swirling softly about her feet. She glanced back toward the woman, then came forward till she stood between Ral and the lad.

"I beg you, my lord. I know this boy, Leofric. He lived among us when the lands belonged to my uncle. He is a good boy, my lord, and a very hard worker. 'Tis true, he did wrong, but surely the circumstances and the child's tender years should be considered. I would ask—"

Ral's fist slammed down on the heavy wooden table. "You've the right to ask naught!" The color bled from Caryn's cheeks, and Ral felt a shot of satisfaction. A man could strike his wife should she dare to give him counsel. For her to do so here, during such important proceedings, was the gravest of insults. " 'Tis surprising you should once again chance my displeasure. You have suffered my wrath before," he said with cold menace. "Have you forgotten the lesson so soon?"

Her cheeks went from pale to pink as she recalled the humiliating scene. "No, my lord."

"Come here, Caryn."

"Aye, my lord." But instead of climbing the low wooden stairs and appearing at his side, she approached the dais, which still left the high table between them. It was not what he intended and both of them knew it. If he hadn't been so angry, he might have smiled.

"By what right do you dare to give me counsel? Your vastly superior intelligence? The wisdom you have gained in your lengthy number of years? By the fact you were born Saxon? I would know, Caryn, why it is you believe you should guide me in this?"

"I have no such wish, my lord. You have shown your wisdom in the dispensing of justice this day. I only wish to plead the boy's case, since he has said little in his own defense."

"You risk much, Caryn."

She swallowed nervously. "This I know, my lord. In doing so, I hope you will see how much this means to me."

He glanced at the boy, whose breath seemed wedged in his throat. He never meant to mutilate the child, simply to test the lad's mettle. But of course she couldn't know that. And by her interference, she had placed him in a difficult position—curse the little fool to bloody hell.

"Since the boy means so much, I would know if you are willing to suffer a portion of his sentence?"

She chewed her bottom lip. It looked soft and full, the burnished hue of the eventide's sunset. Ral felt a stirring in his groin.

"Aye, my lord, if that is your wish."

"You will await me in my chamber. Justice will be meted out there as well as here."

"But what of the boy, my lord? What—"

"Escort my lady wife from the hall," he said to Hugh through clenched teeth. He fixed a black look on Caryn. "I will join you there forthwith. I would advise you spend the time pondering the consequences of your interference."

A hint of fear darkened her soft brown eyes, then it was gone. "As you wish, my lord." She flashed the boy a look of uncertainty and he returned it, marking his concern for the penalty she must now face. With a nervous obeisance that caused her heavy auburn braid to slide over one shoulder, Caryn lifted her chin and preceded Hugh from the hall.

Bloody Christ, Ral silently swore. Would the woman never cease her aggravation? Cursing her willfulness, he nevertheless conceded a grudging admiration. There wasn't a woman he knew with the courage to speak out as she had. Still, it wasn't her place to do so and he would not stand for it again.

At the closing of her chamber door, Ral returned his attention to the boy.

"Upon this day, Leofric, you have admitted your crime and faced this court with courage," Ral said. "Still, justice must be served. Leofric of Braxston, you will spend the next two months in service to the women of the castle. You will work in the kitchens, scrubbing the floors, skinning the carcasses brought into the hall, helping to prepare the meals and any other tasks you are assigned. After that, should you accomplish your duties well, you will become my page." Ral relaxed against his chair, allowing himself a smile. "There is always room in my service for a young man with courage."

The lad looked so stunned—and so relieved—Ral thought the boy's legs might crumble beneath him. "Marta," he called before that could happen. "Find the lad a place to sleep, send his mother some food, and see he doesn't shirk his duties."

"Oh no, milord," Leo said. "I will do what'ere I'm asked. I give you me word upon that."

Nodding, certain the boy had learned his lesson and would more than earn his keep, Ral waited till the lad was led away, his mother sobbing her gratitude as she hurried along behind him. Then Ral slid back his chair and stood up, signaling an end to the proceedings.

They were over at last.

Near over, he corrected with a dark glance toward the stairs. His jaw set firmly, Ral strode in that direction.

Chapter Eight

Inching the door closed as soundlessly as she could, Caryn scrambled away to the foot of the high carved bed. She had angered him again, but it had been worth it. The boy Leofric was saved!

In the passage behind the great hall, Caryn had heard his mother's story, a broken tale, told between desperate pleas and heart-wrenching sobs. She had asked for Caryn's help, but Caryn had declined, saying her help would be useless, that it would only enrage her husband and might even make matters worse. She had been resigned to sit in silence, hopeful her husband would be just. Then she had heard Ral's words and the sentence the boy might receive, and her feet had moved of their own accord.

Caryn glanced nervously toward the door. In the hall below, she could hear the clatter of men moving about the great room and the sound of the dark Norman's voice as he climbed the steep stone stairs. He'd been as angry as she had ever seen him. Mother of God, what would he do?

Caryn jumped as he lifted the heavy iron latch and strode inside the chamber, the muscles taut in his arms and shoulders, his rich plum mantle sailing out behind him. He didn't stop walking until he stood before her, a black look marring his handsome face.

"So . . . my lady wife . . . you await me as you were told. 'Tis the first time, I'll wager."

Caryn wisely did not respond.

"What have you to say for yourself?"

"Very little, my lord."

"That is a change. 'Twould seem to me that once again you have defied me."

"I-I did not mean to, my lord. I only—"

" 'Tis not enough you should gainsay me in private. Now you must do so in public as well."

"I am sorry, my lord. 'Twas just that the boy's mother was so distraught, so worried you would see the child maimed. She begged me to intercede and—"

"And so you did, though 'twas hardly your place to do so."

"Aye, my lord."

"Did *you* also believe I would order such a sentence?"

Caryn glanced down at her feet. "I was not sure."

"Since 'tis certain you were listening to what went on, I am certain you now know the fate the boy suffered."

Caryn smiled up at him; she could not help it. "Aye, my lord. Thank you."

"I do not believe you should thank me so soon." He unfastened the gold and garnet brooch on his right shoulder, pulled off his cloak, and tossed it onto the bed.

"Wha-What are you doing?"

"I mean to do exactly what I said—see justice done."

Caryn went still. Should he wish to beat her, she knew all too well how easily he could accomplish the deed. Still, she had known the risks before she decided to help; she would not now cower in fear.

"Justice often differs," she said softly. " 'Tis seen quite opposite by the man who prescribes it and the one upon whom it is heaped."

A corner of his mouth curved up. "That is true. But as I recall, 'twas you who agreed to accept a portion of the young lad's sentence."

"You would have me work with him in the kitchen?"

"I told you before, I do not wish it said I am married to a scullery maid."

"Then . . . then what is your wish, my lord?"

"Since your arrival in the castle, too often you have behaved as a man—riding off into danger, speaking out when you should hold your tongue. As the notion holds such an appeal, I will give you the chance to play the part in earnest."

She eyed him warily, but could not read his expression.

"Tomorrow we hunt," he said. "I would have you act as my page."

Caryn just stared at him, certain he was speaking in jest, but there was no hint of amusement on his face. She smiled once more, this time even brighter. "Your page, my lord? Do you mean it? In truth, you would let me go with you?"

Ral's brow went up in amazement. "You would enjoy this? You would be pleased?"

"But of course, my lord."

Ral slammed his fist against the bedpost. "God's wounds!" His scowl could have rivaled the devil himself. "You are like no woman I have ever known. 'Twas supposed to serve as punishment, yet you look at me as though I've gifted you with the moon."

" 'Twould be wonderful, my lord, to ride through the forests in search of game. I am a fair shot with a bow— should you allow me to carry one—though it has been some time since I have drawn one. 'Twas taught me by a bowman who served my father."

"A fair shot with—" Ral swore an oath beneath his breath. During the long uncomfortable moments when he said nothing more, Caryn found herself wishing she had somehow disguised her pleasure.

"I am sorry, my lord. I did not mean to upset you." Still he said nothing. "I am really not all that good a shot. Surely nowhere near as skilled as your archers. The joy came only in the learning."

"And now," he grumbled, "you would enjoy the chance to learn the duties of a page."

"If that is your wish, my lord."

He watched her a moment more, then a hard smile curved his lips. "Since you find the notion so pleasing, 'twould seem needless to wait for the morrow. 'Tis better we begin your duties here."

"Here, my lord?"

"My muscles are tense with the hours I have spent in the hall. I have ordered a bath brought up. As my page, you will tend me in that as well."

"A bath, my lord? That is all?"

His hands balled into fists. "Would you be better served with a beating?"

"N-No, of course not. But you could have commanded that of me even as your wife."

"You are not my wife. Should you be my wife in truth, you would find yourself spread upon my bed, the penalty for your boldness a night of being ridden hard beneath me." Caryn's cheeks flushed crimson. "Since you are naught but a little imposter, you will make amends in the way I've commanded."

Caryn thought no response was the best to make in this. In silence she waited for the servants to arrive. When at last they came and Ral granted them entrance, the door swung wide, and a wooden curvell of water was carried in. The two young pages left them, and Ral sat down on the edge of his wide carved bed.

"You may start with my boots."

Caryn smiled. "As you wish, my lord." She knelt to do his bidding, feeling fortunate she would pay for her brashness in such a small way. At least it seemed so, until he ordered her to strip off his tunic and the chainse he wore beneath. She did so with some reluctance, climbing atop the big bed to accomplish the feat since he was so tall. When she had finished, he stood in front of her nearly naked, looking down at his chausses as if he would have her strip them off, too. She knew her cheeks were flaming, but the sight of his powerful body filled her vision and she could not look away.

"You are staring at me as if you've seen naught of a man before."

"Of-Of course, I have. I have bathed my father and uncle." But never had she seen them fully naked. Even if she had, 'twas certain the men would have looked nothing like the tall powerfully built Norman.

"No other?"

As the daughter of a Saxon lord, the duty might have often been assigned her. Usually she was nowhere near.

"No, my lord." Her eyes ran over his body, magnificent in every detail and beautifully proportioned, from the astonishing width of his shoulders to his deep solid chest to the flat-muscled ridges of his belly. As her glance moved lower, she saw another ridge of muscle, this one jutting forward, straining against his chausses. Caryn gasped before she could stop herself.

"Fetch the soap," Ral said gruffly, relenting to her embarrassment, turning away to strip off the balance of his clothes.

When she returned, she found him seated in the tub —thank the Blessed Virgin—leaning back against the edge with his eyes closed, his black hair plastered wetly to the nape of his neck. Resting on the sides of the tub, his huge arms bulged with muscle, and heavy bands of sinew rippled across his massive chest.

"My back is in need of scrubbing," he said without opening his eyes. He shifted to give her access, forcing water over the edge and onto the planked oaken floor.

"Aye, my lord." Caryn's hand shook as she soaped a rag and began to wash his shoulders. 'Twas like scrubbing well-honed steel.

"Now my chest." He leaned back once more and Caryn bent over him, her fingers moving with purpose, trying not to notice the texture of his skin or the warmth of his breath against her ear.

He captured her wrist and with it her attention. "What you did this day," he said softly, " 'twas unwise of you, *ma chere*. I would have these people's respect. I will allow naught to occur that might undermine that which I have worked so hard to gain."

Caryn's hand trembled where it rested against his chest. " 'Twas never my intention, my lord."

"Had I believed it was, 'twould be a far greater penalty you would pay."

Her eyes searched his face. There was something in his expression, something that told her more than his words. "I fear I may have done you an injustice."

A thick black brow arched up. "How is that?"

"I have come to believe, had I remained in the shadows, your sentence would have been the same. Is that not so, my lord?"

Some of the tension eased from his body. For the first time he smiled. "That is so, Cara."

Caryn smiled, too. "I am glad, my lord."

For a moment they remained that way, Ral's blue-gray eyes on her face, Caryn's fixed on his beautiful lips. It took a strength of will to force her attention away. She started to rise, felt his hand on her arm, felt a sharp tug that threw her off balance.

Caryn shrieked as he tumbled her into the water.

"Sweet Mary, what do you? Have you lost your wits?"

He chuckled, a soft deep rumble in his chest. "Mayhap I have." Her useless struggles made his smile grow even wider. "Since you have once more escaped my wrath, I will assume the next time you find cause to doubt my judgment, you will speak of it when we are alone."

Caryn stopped fighting, her eyes going wide. "You would hear what it is I have to say?"

"You are my wife, Caryn. That alone would grant you a certain amount of respect."

She propped herself up on his chest, regarding him closely. "In truth, my lord, after this day, you have claimed a certain amount of my own."

Ral's eyes turned the blue of the sky outside the narrow slit of a window. She felt his hold on her waist grow tighter, felt the muscles in his arms grow tense. He captured her chin with a hand, bent his head, and his mouth settled gently over hers.

Caryn groaned at the feel of it, at the soft heat melting through her body. His lips were hot and demanding, yet there was tenderness in his touch, too. She opened to his coaxing, let his tongue slide in, felt his hand brush the underside of a breast. Her nipple went hard against the warm, damp fabric of her tunic. Beneath her hips, she felt Ral's throbbing manroot. She should have been afraid of what might happen. Instead the heat grew more fierce and Caryn slid her arms around his neck.

The moment she did, guilt assailed her. Sweet Mother Mary, what was she doing? She knew where this was leading. She knew she had to stop it and she had to stop it now. Pressing her hands against his chest, she broke away.

"Please, my lord, I-I beg you to release me."

He smiled, but the warmth had drained away. " 'Twould seem an odd request, considering . . ." His wet hand smoothed over a breast and she trembled with the fiery sensation.

"Please, my lord. Must I remind you of your pledge?"

"I need no reminder save the vacant place I should be filling in your bed." He rose from the tub, sloshing water all over the floor, Caryn caught up in his arms. "If 'tis your wish, my lady, that I release you"—stepping out of the tub, he turned and dropped her back into the water —"then so be it."

"Curse you!" Sputtering with outrage, furious and oddly disappointed, Caryn wiped away the soapsuds that trickled down her cheeks.

"Mind that tongue of yours, wench." Without a care for his nakedness, Ral strode toward the bed to snatch up a white linen towel. He smiled wolfishly. " 'Tis not nearly as sweet as your kisses."

Her face went hot with color. Cursing him vilely beneath her breath, Caryn turned her back on him and climbed out of the water, her sodden skirts raining a second small ocean upon the floor.

" 'Tis Lynette you should be kissing, not me," she reminded him tartly. " 'Tis certain she awaits you even as we speak."

Ral fixed her with a cool gray stare. "I'm grateful for your timely reminder. I thank thee, my lady *wife.*"

Caryn ignored him as he finished getting dressed and left the room, but her heart throbbed dully, and Caryn feared she knew the cause.

Determined to enjoy the day Ral had promised, Caryn awoke before dawn and made her way out to the stables. The air was brisk but the sky shown with stars; the day should prove to be a warm one.

As noiselessly as she could, she pushed open the stable door and crossed the packed earthen floor, breathing the scent of horses, hay, and leather. She passed several groups of sleeping men and finally found the one she sought. Rousing Etienne from his lumpy fern mattress, she nudged his shoulder and quietly called his name.

"God's wounds, woman!" He gripped his woolen blanket, drawing it up to cover his bony chest as he searched the darkness to see who the vexing female was. "Beg pardon, my lady." He straightened, rubbing the sleep from his eyes. "Is aught amiss? 'Tis practically the middle of the night."

"All is well. 'Tis only that I am in need of your assistance."

The young squire eyed her warily. "You do not think to again run away?"

"Don't be a goose." Kneeling on a pile of straw beside him, Caryn relayed Lord Ral's orders that she should join him today as his page.

Etienne scratched the scalp beneath his sleep-rumpled hair. "By the faith, he must have been angry to demand such a thing of his lady wife."

Caryn smiled. " 'Tis not so bad. 'Twill be a fine adventure, I think. What have you that I might borrow to wear?"

"This is not another of your tricks?"

" 'Tis the lord's command. I swear it."

He nodded. "There is aught I own that would fit you, but there is a page named Osbern who is about your same size. Give me a moment to dress and seek him out. I will see you get the items you need."

Etienne returned not long after, finding her near the stable door, stroking the muzzle of a little sorrel mare. He handed her a bundle of clothes.

"I thank thee, Etienne. I am certain your lord will be pleased." With a grateful smile, she left him, eager to reach her chamber and make ready for the day ahead.

Avoiding the sleeping men and servants in the hall, she returned to her room, changed into her borrowed clothing, and soon stood near the brazier dressed in tight black chausses and a faded gray tunic that ended several inches above the knee.

Her husband arrived not long after, entering as he usually did, without a knock and taking the room by storm. He strode past her without a word, walking to the side of the bed, jerking back the velvet hangings, leaning over the bed to rouse her.

"My lord?"

He turned at the sound of her voice yet still did not see her. Not until she stepped into the light of a flickering candle she had set upon the table near the door.

Ral made a hissing sound as he sucked in air past his teeth. "By all that's holy!"

"I am ready, my lord."

He stared at her in silence, his hard gaze running from the top of her head to the toes of her soft leather boots.

"I have dressed as your page, my lord."

"So I see. . . ." He took a step in her direction then stopped. "I came to . . . to tell you the penance you paid last eve was enough." 'Twas the first time she had ever heard him falter.

"Oh no, my lord. You were more than just in your sentence. 'Tis only fair I serve as you commanded. If there is aught I might do before we leave, it would more than please me to do it."

He settled his hands at his hips as he watched her, his face looking taut and strained. Ral leaned forward. "If you believe for one moment that I will allow you to leave this room wearing those clothes—"

"But you said—"

"I know only too well what I said." Again he surveyed her, taking in the shape of her legs outlined by the tight-fitting hose.

"Please, my lord, I was so looking forward to a day in the forest."

"No."

"I promise I will please you."

Ral pondered this last, caught by her eager expression, knowing full well how much the day must mean. He tried to imagine how he might tactfully avoid the situation he had created, but his eyes kept straying to her shapely legs. Her breasts rose and fell softly and wisps of flame dark hair peeked from beneath the rim of her brown felt hat. When she bent to retrieve her sachel, Ral knew a surge of lust that made the blood pump hotly through his veins.

He wanted to rip off her snug boy's clothes, to pull her down on the floor and drive himself inside her. He wanted to take her there and then, to pound into her again and again. By Christ he'd been a fool when he'd promised not to bed her.

He watched her face in the light of the candle, expectancy adding a glow to her lovely features. " 'Tis not . . . not uncommon for a lady of your station to accompany her lord on the hunt." She looked so hopeful he inwardly groaned. "I will see to the arrangements—while you change your clothes."

"But—"

"Or you may remain here in your chamber. The choice is yours."

Caryn sighed. "Aye, my lord. If it means I may go, I will do as you wish."

"Do not dally. When you are ready, you may join me out in the bailey."

Disgruntled at the change in his plans, Ral strode from his chamber down the passage that led to the stairs. By the time he had reached the great hall, he discovered his dark mood had brightened and he was looking forward to the day ahead. He would order a tentkeeper to accompany them, as well as a cook to see to a proper midday meal. He would make the day a special one, something his little wife wouldn't soon forget.

Besides, they had all been working hard of late; they deserved a day of pleasure.

Within the hour, as the sun rose over the horizon in a fan of orange and gold, Odo, Hugh, Lambert, Geoffrey, and a dozen of Ral's best men rode beside him out of the castle. Dressed in a simple velvet tunic of midnight blue beneath her cloak, Caryn rode the little gray palfry, and even Richard had been convinced to come along.

Ral had also brought his favorite hawk, Caesar. Hooded and regal, it perched atop the leather-covered shoulder of his squire. As they passed through a meadow leading into the mountains, Ral chanced a look at Caryn, whose smile looked even brighter than it had when they'd left the castle.

"Thank you, my lord," she said.

A corner of his mouth curved up. "The day will be a long one. You may yet wish you had stayed behind."

"Never, my lord."

By late that morning, her joy still unfaded, Ral believed she meant it. She might be small, but she was a game little wench with plenty of heart—as he was soon to find out.

'Tis a lovely day, is it not?" With Ral off scouting ahead, Caryn rode beside Odo.

" 'Tis a bit chill and damp," he said sullenly.

Caryn looked around her, seeing naught but the beauty of the forest, recalling the rich black soil of the high fertile valley they had just crossed, hearing the purr of a bog. The wind made a sighing sound as it passed through the tall green grasses alive with squirrels and birds.

"I would spend each of my days like this," she said, "did I have a choice. Surrounded by alder, beech, and yew, the blue sky for my ceiling, fern and heather at my feet."

Odo made a rude sound in his throat.

"Look there"—she pointed toward a shallow babbling stream—"beaver have dammed the brook. They make their home beneath that dome of branches and twigs. See there, one finds its way to the shore."

"They stop the flow of water to the farmlands," Odo

grumbled. "I will send a villein to tear down the dam and let the water resume its flow."

" 'Tis nature's way. Surely there is good that comes of it."

When Odo just scowled, Caryn eyed him thoughtfully. "You do not like me, do you?"

The red-haired knight kept his eyes fixed on the trail. "You are married to my friend and overlord. That is all that matters."

"What is it I have done?"

Odo drew rein on his horse and turned to face her. " 'Tis not my place to say, but since you ask, I will tell you." He shifted in his saddle. " 'Tis not what you have done that I find displeasing, but what you have not done. Think you I do not know how it is between you and Lord Ral?"

"He has a woman who pleases him," she said, the thought more than a little disturbing. "If he is willing to accept the way things are, why is it so hard for you?"

"That you are Saxon and not to be trusted is reason enough. Aside from that, Lord Ral needs sons and heirs. 'Tis your duty to see it done. That you are unwilling to uphold your vows is enough to make me dislike you." Unconsciously, his hands grew taut on the reins. "Were you my woman, I would mount you and plant my seed whether you wished it or not. 'Tis a mistake Ral makes in not seeing the deed accomplished."

Caryn felt the anger rising in her cheeks. " 'Twould be something you know of, Norman, to practice rapine on an unwilling woman. 'Tis something all of you know a good deal about." Wheeling her horse, Caryn nudged the gray into a canter, taking a place beside Geoffrey as she worked to cool her temper.

Was she really remiss in her duties as Ral's wife? She knew without doubt that she was, yet in her heart there was naught she could do. She owed her sister her allegiance. Her marriage to the Norman was betrayal enough—it was the reason she had yet to return to the convent.

She didn't want to look upon Gweneth's beautiful face, didn't want to remember what had happened that night three years past. She didn't want to admit the shameful longings the Dark Knight stirred inside her body.

" 'Tis time we returned to camp." Ral rode up beside her, drawing her attention and making her heart begin to pound. Today he sat a sleek sorrel stallion, fleet of foot, more agile than his powerful black war-horse. "Cook will have readied the midday meal. 'Tis certain the men will be ready as well."

"What found you ahead?"

"We trail a boar. The hounds have lost its scent for the moment, but chances are good we will cross it again. We will pause for a time to refresh ourselves, and water and rest the horses."

They joined the others at the base of the mountain where a stream poured down from a canyon. It looked clear and cool and babbled over rocks worn smooth by the water. Beside it, the tentkeeper had set up camp, providing a place to escape the sun and garner a moment of rest.

They dined on fried bread, cold mutton, and meat pies. Ral shared his wineskin, laughing as a drop of the red liquid trickled down her chin. They ate hot baked crab apples for dessert and Caryn thought it was a fine meal indeed, though it made her a little lethargic.

"You are ready to leave, my lord?" At her husband's approach, Caryn rose from her place on the log.

"My men and I will resume the hunt. I would have you stay here."

"But I thought—"

"Wild boar can be dangerous. We found a trace of blood—which means the beast may be wounded. We won't be gone long. If we don't pick up the scent, we'll go after another stag. I'll come for you then if you wish."

Caryn smiled. "I am content just to be here. Already the day has given me great pleasure."

Ral lifted a hand and trailed a finger along her cheek. "As I have found pleasure in your company."

Caryn said nothing, but her skin tingled where he touched her and a warmth encircled her heart. It was the sound of men eager to be away that disturbed the moment.

"We'll not break camp until my return. Along with the servants and two of my men-at-arms, Girart will also remain. Should there be anything you need, speak to him."

"I am fine."

He studied her a moment more, his eyes searching her face. With a brief nod of his head, he turned and walked away. The rumble of horses and men, of harness and armor and the baying of hounds, carried on the wind as Ral and the others rode higher into the mountains.

Once the quiet settled in, Caryn spoke briefly to Girart, a man in his thirties with dark brown hair and a ready smile who had served Ral for years. As the servants repacked the supplies and Girart sought a yew tree in search of wood for a bow, Caryn wandered away toward the nearby stream.

Needing to relieve herself, she headed deeper into the forest, careful to mark her way with leaves and twigs. When she had finished, she continued a little farther, lured by a patch of bright yellow crocus beckoning from a clearing among the trees.

Once she reached the clearing and knelt among the flowers, she paused. Beneath the thorny branches of a shrub next to a cluster of cocksfoot, a tiny black-nosed fawn, nearly disguised by the small white spots on its rust-colored coat, surveyed her from among the sun-dappled leaves.

"What do you here, little fawn?" Speaking softly, Caryn inched forward to examine the animal more closely. It lifted its head, its big brown eyes intense, fear making it tremble. In an effort to escape, it stuck out its spindly little legs and tried to stand up, only to fall back down.

"Where is your mother, little fawn?" Caryn eased nearer to stroke the animal's fur, which on closer inspection looked patchy and dull. It was obvious the fawn was weak with starvation, that it must have been abandoned. Like the kittens she nursed back at the castle, had the little fawn's mother been killed?

She scratched the animal's neck and it nuzzled her hand, the huge floppy ears folding back beneath her fingers.

" 'Tis good that I have found you. 'Tis obvious you are hungry, so I cannot leave you here." She leaned forward, meaning to scoop the fawn into her arms, but the sound of a low growl coming from the forest snapped her head in that direction. Caryn went still.

A huge gray wolf, its fur standing up in a ruff around its neck, its teeth bared in a vicious snarl, crept toward her into the clearing. Caryn's heart leapt, then set up a pounding in her chest. She grabbed a stone on the ground near her hand, turned and threw it in the big wolf's direction. The animal dodged the stone and continued slinking forward.

"You will not get my fawn," she said, determined to protect her tiny charge, searching frantically for something she might use for a weapon. Her fingers locked on a stout oak branch just as a second wolf crept into the clearing.

"Sweet Jesu . . . there is more than one." More even than two, she saw as a third began to stalk her. With trembling hands, she lifted the heavy barren branch and came to her feet, placing herself between the wolves and the tiny frightened deer. Perspiration trickled between her breasts and dampened her palms, making it difficult to steady her grip on the limb.

Her heart beating fiercely, Caryn glanced back toward the camp. A cry for help welled in her throat, but her instincts said she had wandered too far to be heard, and the noise might set the animals in motion. Instead she picked up another stone, balanced it carefully in her hand, then hurled it at the nearest wolf. The great beast yelped as the rock found its mark, darted a few feet away with its tail tucked low, only to return a few moments later.

A fourth wolf appeared beneath an overhanging alder and Caryn's stomach tightened. She looked back to the fawn, her own life now at stake as well as that of the deer. Even should she turn and run, it was uncertain which of its prey the wolves would follow.

Better to face them, try to kill one of them and hope the others might turn on that one for their feast. She had heard of such things, though without a better weapon chances were slim she could accomplish the task.

Caryn raised the tree limb and steadied it against her shoulder. Behind her the fawn made a whimpering sound of fear. Caryn's own fear made her throat so tight she could barely swallow. Sweet God in heaven, if only she hadn't wandered so far away.

Ral stood in silence among the shadows of the forest, terror slicing into him like an ax of well-honed steel. In the clearing a few feet away, Caryn stood facing him, though she had yet to see him. Between them stood the deadly slashing jaws of four savage gray wolves.

As quietly as he could, Ral pulled his sword from its scabbard, the metal making a slick whir against the sharp-edged blade. His fingers tightened around the leather-wrapped handle as he watched Caryn lift a heavy limb and steady it against her shoulder. Spotting the tiny fawn behind her, he guessed in an instant what had happened: His wife had discovered the fawn and the wolves had discovered her. He damned her to hell for the soft heart that might get both of them killed.

"Ease away from the fawn, *cherie*." Moving toward her a step at a time, Ral's soft command jerked her head in his direction.

"Ral . . ." His name came out on a whisper of air. It was the first time he had heard her say it and it told him how great was her fear.

"Circle around to your left, until you reach the trees."

"But the fawn—"

"Do as I tell you. Keep the limb in front of you. Take each step slowly. Do nothing to alarm them."

She glanced back at the fawn and for a moment he feared she might not obey. Then she eased to the left, and the wolf crept toward the fawn, its ears laid back, its teeth bared, its tongue lolling out. The wolf on the right, a sleek dark female, growled low in its throat, crouched till it nearly touched the earth, then sprang forward, making a rush for the fawn. The animals had chosen their prey, and Caryn might have escaped if she hadn't cried out and swung her makeshift weapon to protect the tiny deer, her blow connecting with the huge wolf's powerful shoulders and knocking it into the dirt.

"Christ's blood!" The wolf was up and running in an instant, and so was Ral, the others rushing forward to join in the kill.

Ral swung his blade toward a tall gray, silver-backed male, severing the head, then turned to catch another in the hindquarters, his blade biting in, blood spraying over his chest as the wolf went down. Two more he hadn't noticed raced forward. He heard Caryn's scream, swung his sword, and steel sank into bone and flesh.

From the corner of his eye, he saw Caryn raise the limb, saw her swing, heard the whine and snarl of a thick-furred male as the wood connected. The blow did little damage. The animal gained its feet, crouched and sprang. Ral leapt forward and swung, slicing into fur and rib, but before he could jerk the blade free, another sprang onto his back.

"Ral!" Caryn screamed as he went down, rolling with the beast in the dirt, turning to grip the savage wolf by the throat, fighting to hold its slashing teeth away. He dodged the snapping jaws, pulled back the head and twisted, breaking the animal's neck. Before he could loose the carcass, a second wolf attacked him. He felt a tearing across his shoulder, grabbed the animal's mouth, and felt the razor-sharp teeth sink into his hands.

"Run!" he commanded Caryn, spotting the dark silhouette of another huge beast. Nausea swept over him at the thought of what the beast would do to her, then he realized the attack was meant for him.

"Ral! Dear God, Ral!"

"Run, dammit!"

But she only raced toward him, swinging the stout oak limb, striking the wolf in the head just as it leapt into the air. With a snarl and then a whimper, it hit the ground at his feet. The limb descended again and again while Ral fought the wolf atop his chest, finally able to cut off its air supply until it went limp and still.

Bleeding from the gash in his shoulder, he dislodged the heavy beast and staggered to his feet, his gaze searching for the animal Caryn had been fighting. He spotted the wolf and realized she had slain it. His gaze swung to the left and he saw her racing toward him. A small cry escaped as she hurled herself into his arms.

"Ral!" Tears streaking her cheeks, she clung to his neck, and he tightened his hold around her.

" 'Tis ended, Cara, 'tis over. There is nothing more to be afraid of."

She only cried harder, repeating his name, her small body shaking with the remnants of fear. He held her and stroked her back, his hands still bleeding and more than a little unsteady.

"The time for tears is past," he soothed. "You are safe and so is your fawn."

Caryn pulled away to look at him, the wetness making tracks down her cheeks. Her braid had come undone and thick dark auburn hair rippled like flame around her shoulders. He brushed loose strands away from her face, felt the silkiness wrap around his fingers. Then she saw the vicious slash across his chest.

"Sweet God, you are injured!"

" 'Tis naught but a scratch."

She scanned his torn and dirty tunic, saw the blood trailing down from his fingers.

"Your hands," she whispered, "your beautiful hands. Look what those terrible beasts have done."

Her words squeezed a tightness into his chest. " 'Tis naught that won't heal. Do not fret so."

But she cradled each hand softly and wiped away the blood with the hem of her skirt. Then she turned her attention to the gash on his shoulder. "I was so frightened," she said. "I thought they would kill you. I couldn't bear it, Ral, I—"

"Cara . . ." Her eyes looked as soft and fearful as the fawn's. Ral tipped her chin with his hand, bent his head and kissed her. It was a soft kiss, meant as thanks for her concern, only a thanks and nothing more. But the moment his lips touched hers, something broke open inside him. His arms went around her and he crushed her against him, his mouth claiming hers full force.

The kiss was no longer gentle. It was fiery demand and a yearning to reclaim the lives they had so very nearly lost. Caryn must have felt the same for there was no holding back, no uncertainty, just a hot wild passion that equalled his own, and a wild fierce joy that they still lived.

With a tiny sound of surrender, Caryn slid her arms

around his neck, her soft lips parting to allow his tongue. She met it with her own and her fingers roamed his chest. Ral jerked open her tunic and slid his hands inside to lift and mold her breasts. Feeling her tremble, he rent the opening wider, lowered his head, and took her nipple into his mouth.

Caryn moaned. *Sweet Blessed Virgin.* Wherever Ral touched, fire swept through her body, and an ache that made the blood throb in her veins. She laced her fingers in his thick black hair, arched her back and swayed against him, giving herself over to the hot sensations.

"Ral . . ." His mouth on her breast made the heat roar through her body. He was laving and tasting, suckling gently, then tugging and setting her aflame. Her legs went weak and buckled beneath her. As she sagged onto the ground, Ral followed her down, pressing her into the soft grassy earth. He kissed her as his hand cupped a breast, kneaded and massaged, then moved lower, tugging up her tunic then sliding up her thigh.

Caryn strained against his fingers, begging him to continue, dimly aware of where they were, caring even less.

He had propped his heavy weight on an elbow, his whole body tense, yet she could feel his hard length and the incredible heat of his body. He shifted his position, she felt his rigid shaft, then he stilled.

"Someone comes," he said, followed by a soft muttered curse. He pulled her tunic back into place with an unsteady hand.

"What . . . what is happening?" She couldn't think clearly. She felt confused and dizzy, yet her body burned with heat. He was leaving her, standing, then pulling her up to her feet.

" 'Tis all right, *cherie.*"

Girart's voice echoed through the foggy haze of her passion.

"I am sorry, my lord. When your lady did not return, I grew worried." For the first time, Girart noticed the wreckage in the clearing, the bloody wolf carcasses, his lord and lady's torn and bloody clothes. "God's wounds, what has happened?"

Ral straightened the cloak around Caryn's shoulders, hiding the rent he had made in her gown. "The lady attempted to rescue a fawn. In the end, she rescued me."

She glanced up at his words. There was a warm light in his eyes and a soft look of approval.

" 'Tis not at all the truth. As you can see, Lord Raolfe is a man of great courage. Were it not for his timely arrival, the wolves would have made short work of me."

Girart dropped to his knees. "I have failed you, my lord. I should have followed sooner. Your lady wife asked for a moment of privacy, but I should not have waited so long."

"Rise, Girart. 'Twas hardly your fault. My wife has a penchant for winding up in trouble." Though the words held censure, there was no anger in his voice.

Girart rose to stand before him. "I did not know you had returned." He shifted uncomfortably, his eyes cast down. "I am grateful that you did."

"The hounds recovered the scent of the boar and ran it to ground. I came back ahead of the others." He had wanted to share the news with Caryn, had discovered that once she was gone, he had missed her bright mood and the smile that seemed to make the day warmer.

" 'Tis good she marked her trail."

Ral nodded. "When I found her gone, I followed. 'Twas easy enough, but I worried she had gone too far. Then I saw the wolves."

Caryn shivered at the memory, then forced herself to smile. "Thank you for coming, my lord." *But not for what happened after.*

Now that she had regained her senses, she felt sick with the knowledge of what she had done. In a moment of weakness, she had let the dark Norman kiss her. She had needed that kiss, craved it as a parched man thirsts for water. The kiss had become far more, and she had craved that, too.

How could she—knowing full well the things he had done? She amended that. She didn't recall what had actually happened that night three years past, and in the days since her marriage, she had been even less willing to find out.

Now she wished she knew every bitter detail, that the memory burned as bright as her passion. Her loyalty belonged to her sister, not some Norman warlord who had brutalized her and her kinsman.

"Cara?"

The softly spoken word drew her from her musings. She forced herself to meet her husband's gaze. He was frowning, aware of the subtle shift in her mood. Sweet Mary, what could she say? "I know there are hours left to hunt but I—"

"We return home at once." His knuckles grazed her cheek. "At least in the castle, I can be sure that you are safe."

Caryn glanced away. Safe? She had just discovered that in her husband's presence she was no more safe than she had been with the wolves.

Chapter Nine

On the route home, Caryn rode in silence. Her lips felt bruised from her husband's passionate kisses, her body still burned from his touch. The tentkeeper had tended his wounds, and for a while he rode beside her, but at her quiet brooding, eventually left and returned to his men.

They had just reached the main road leading back to the castle when Ral called a halt to their journey. Through the men and horses up ahead, Caryn glimpsed the wheel of an overturned wagon. Urging the little gray forward, she saw the road was littered with the debris of the wagon itself and what had once been its contents.

An overturned barrel spilled dried herring into the dust, several broken casks leaked wine, and a bolle of honey had been overturned onto bolts of ruined sailcloth. The merchant had no doubt been carrying a good deal more: butter, ale, pitch, dried herbs, and cheese, pipes of cider, and candles, but those items along with the oxen who pulled the wagon were gone.

At the side of the road, the battered merchant slumped against the base of a tree, cradling his head in his hands, a trickle of blood near his temple.

" 'Twas that blackguard the Ferret," said Geoffrey, riding up beside her. "The merchant is lucky he escaped with his head."

The Ferret. The outlaw she had once so foolishly aided. Caryn's stomach tightened. "What will Lord Raolfe do?"

" 'Tis certain he will give chase, though I'll warrant 'twill do little good. The bloody Ferret knows these woods like his namesake, and every blasted trail leading into the mountains."

Guilt assailed her. If she hadn't interfered, the outlaws might have been captured and this would never have occurred.

"Mayhap this time Lord Ral will catch them." She prayed it was so, though Geoffrey's face seemed to hold little hope.

"Mayhap. Even now our lord gathers the men." They circled around him, listening to his orders, their horses raising dust in the road. When Ral had finished, he rode in her direction.

"Geoffrey, you will see my lady wife returned to the castle. 'Tis not far now and the threat you might meet rides the opposite way."

"But I would ride with you, my lord. Surely there is another who might see her home."

" 'Tis you I trust, no other. Richard will accompany you." He turned as his steward rode up. "Expect our return when the trail grows cold or we've the outlaws in hand."

"Aye, my lord," Richard said.

"You will be safe with them," he said to Caryn, then his hard look softened. "We've much to discuss on my return." He smiled, the angle of his jaw looking less severe, his eyes a lighter gray than she had ever seen them. "For once, try to stay out of trouble."

He leaned forward as if he might kiss her, but when she stiffened and glanced back up the road, he spun the big sorrel, dug in his heels, and urged the stallion away.

In a thunder of dust and hoofbeats, they disappeared

over the distant hill, leaving Richard, Geoffrey, and the servants in their wake.

"Climb up in the tentkeeper's wagon," Geoffrey directed the merchant, a thin-boned, fragile-looking man with watery blue eyes.

"Aye, sir. And I thank ye for your kindness."

They reached the castle not long after, Caryn weary and troubled at all that had happened, but distracted a little by the care she must take of the fawn. A servant saw the tiny deer settled in a corner of the stable near the place where she cared for her kittens.

Using the same method that had kept the kittens alive, she called for a kettle of warm goat's milk and a clean linen rag, twisted the rag into a point to serve as a nipple, dipped it in the milk, and pressed it against the fawn's hungry mouth.

It had taken several hours for the kittens to accept this strange means of nourishment, but the fawn caught on fairly quickly, pulling on the rag and sucking in the life-giving liquid. Soon it lay sated and sleeping atop a fresh pile of straw, Caryn gently stroking its fur.

Satisfied the fawn would survive, and the stable beginning to fall into darkness, she made her way across the bailey and into the keep to search out her own night of sleep.

Instead what little she got remained fitful, disturbed by heated dreams of her husband's fiery kisses, and painful memories of the night three years past when the Normans had brutalized her sister.

She awoke feeling guilty and out of sorts, as angry at herself for responding to his touch as she was at the huge dark Norman. She was grateful when the day came to an end and her husband had not returned. It gave her time to steel herself, to fuel her animosities and garner a protective mantle around her. Even Lynette left her alone, unwilling to bait her in the uncertain mood she had fallen into.

The hours passed and Caryn's ill temper increased. She purposely recalled her bitter memories and every harsh word the Dark Knight had ever said. She reminded herself of his heritage, of the Normans' cruel treatment of the people of her country, of her sister and herself. Again and again, she replayed the scene in the meadow, dredging up painful memories of that awful night in the past.

By the time Ral returned, well after dark several days hence, Caryn's anger had flamed then cooled to a calculated simmer. Though he strode in covered in dirt and weary from his days in the saddle, she greeted him curtly, extending only the barest civility. She inquired of his journey, discovered the men had all returned safe, that the outlaws still roamed free, then asked for permission to leave.

"The day has been a long one," she said as he seated himself beside her atop the dais and food was brought out. "Should there be aught you need, Marta will see to it."

"I had hoped we might share a trencher or at least a goblet of wine." Ral reached for her hand. "I have thought of you much these past few days."

"I am weary." She eased her hand from his. "I would ask your leave."

Ral's expression turned dark. He started to speak, clamped his jaw instead, and finally nodded his permission. Caryn turned and left the dais, the disapproval in his cool gray eyes burning into her back as she crossed the hall and climbed the stairs.

That night she slept more soundly, feeling stronger in her resolve and more determined than ever to rebuild the wall that had once existed between them. When she joined him in the great hall for the midmorning meal, she felt his probing glare and the heat of his displeasure. It was exactly what she wanted.

She finished washing her hands, waited till the page

removed the bowl of water, then dried them on a clean linen towel. She forced herself to smile. "Now that you are home, my lord, will you be staying, or do you resume your hunt for the Ferret?"

A page set a bowl of fermente on the table, along with a dish of calves' foot jelly and a pitcher of buttermilk.

"I've men in place throughout the mountains. Sooner or later, word will come of him. When it does, we will be ready."

"I am certain you will," Caryn said. " 'Tis a shame the brigands continue to elude you. 'Twould appear the blame no longer lies with me but with those of your men who would track them."

If he caught the note of mockery, he let it pass. " 'Tis like following smoke through the woods. Still, you may be certain the day will come the Ferret's head will mount a pike at the crossroads. Travelers will know they may henceforth journey in peace."

"Mayhap they should look to Lord Stephen for deliverance. 'Tis said he seeks the Ferret with even more diligence than you."

Ral turned a hard-eyed stare in her direction. "Do you bait me again today, little wife? I wonder why?"

"I only try to make conversation."

"And what of last eve? Your tongue was as sharp as a war ax. 'Twas clear to one and all you wanted naught of my company. After what happened in the woods, I thought—"

"Whatever you thought, you were wrong. We have an arrangement. I would see that arrangement is kept."

He smiled coldly and speared a bit of meat with the tip of his bone-handled blade. "Lynette was most appreciative. She did her best to soothe the ache you fired, though in truth 'twas you I imagined spread beneath me."

Caryn's face flamed scarlet.

" 'Twas her breasts filling my hands, but 'twas a

rounded pair with dusky nipples I imagined in my dreams."

Anger made her bold. "Mayhap I should tell her. 'Twould be interesting to see how appreciative she then would be."

"Mayhap you should," he countered with a mocking smile, "if you think she will believe you."

She wouldn't. Lynette would only think she was jealous. Caryn shoved back her chair and came to her feet. "There are tasks I would see to. Marta begs my assistance in the wool room."

By sheer force of will, he held her there beside him, then he nodded. "Go. Your absence pleases me far more than your shrewish woman's chatter."

Caryn bristled, wishing she didn't feel the sting, catching herself before she lashed out in return. Off and on throughout the day, she encountered her husband, always with the same result, a sharp-tongued clash that strengthened the wall she worked to build yet left her feeling strangely empty.

By nightfall, her nerves were strung taut and each of Ral's mocking glances tied her insides up in knots. She tried to concentrate on the band of musicians who entertained at supper, at the attempts to converse Richard made as he sat to her right at the high table, but all she could think of was the man who sat in brooding silence on her left.

"I find my appetite wanes, my lord," she said to him at last. "I would prefer to take my leave."

He fixed his eyes on her face. " 'Tis the second time this day you have not eaten. I would know, little wife, why that is?"

"Mayhap the food does not please me. Mayhap 'tis the company."

"That is enough!" Ral shoved back his chair, the grating sound muffled by strains of zither and lute. He gripped Caryn's arm and forced her up too, then hauled her to the edge of the dais.

"I would know what plagues you, lady. I would discover how it is you accept my kisses with such fire then refuse me the simplest of courtesies." He jerked her toward the stairs, knights and servants making way as Caryn hurried to keep up without falling.

Sweet God, she shouldn't have pushed him so far. Mother Mary, what would he do? Trying to calm the wildly beating rhythm of her heart, Caryn clung to him as he dragged her along the passage, opened the door to their chamber, and shoved her into the room.

He followed her in and slammed the door. "You will tell me what this is about."

Caryn straightened, more than a little uneasy. "I do not know what you mean."

"You have been rude and ill-mannered. You have goaded and insulted me at every turn since the moment I returned to the keep. Do you dare to deny it?"

"I am sorry if I have displeased you."

"You ask for trouble, Caryn. I would know why."

Because it is safer to face your anger than your passion. Better to be beaten than seduced. "I told you, I do not know what you mean."

"Do you not? I think you do. I think we both do."

A shiver touched her spine, but she did not speak.

"This is about what happened in the forest, is it not?"

"Nay, of course not."

" 'Tis because I kissed you and you liked it. Because I touched you and you did not push me away."

"Nay, 'tis not so."

Ral stepped closer. " 'Tis truth and you know it. You desired me, just as I did you. Shall I prove it, Cara? Shall I make you desire me again?"

"Nay!" But already he was moving forward, his muscled forearm sliding around her waist as he hauled her against him. He gripped her chin with his hand, forced her head back, and his mouth came down hard over hers.

For a moment Caryn struggled, determined to fight him, to ignore the heat that shimmered through her body. Then his hard kiss gentled, his thumb grazed the side of her jaw, coaxing her lips apart, and his tongue slid warmly into her mouth.

Caryn groaned at the heat of it, at the feel of his powerful body pressing the length of hers, at the muscles that bunched across his shoulders. She found herself kissing him back, gripping the front of his tunic and swaying against him, her blood pumping, her tongue meeting his in a silent plea for more.

It was Ral who ended the kiss, steadying her, kissing her cheek as he gently eased her away. "That you desire me is not a sin, Cara. I am your husband. 'Tis only as it should be."

She looked at him, so tall and strong, felt the pull of his presence and a powerful yearning to press herself against him. Her bottom lip trembled and she had to glance away.

"Is it so hard for you to see? 'Tis not right that I should desire you—not after what you have done." There was pain in her eyes as she looked back at him. "I cannot forget that night three years past." Tears spilled over her lashes and down her cheeks. "I cannot forget—and I cannot forgive." She tried to turn away, but he caught her arm.

"I am sorry about your sister. That night has haunted me just as it has you. Your sister was a rare and beautiful creature. I knew it from the moment I saw her. Had I to do it over, I would take far better care."

"Better care?" she repeated, the horror of that night stabbing at her insides, dredging up the memories as if they had just occurred. "You force rapine upon my sister and you say you would take better care?"

"Rapine?" The hand on her arm grew taut and his

eyes swung to her face. "Is that what you believe? That I was among the men who took your sister?"

"But you were! I was there—I saw you. If I live for a thousand years, I will always remember."

Concern etched his features, his thick black brows drawing together, narrow lines marring his forehead. " 'Tis not a question of what you remember, *cherie,* but of what you may have forgotten."

"Forgotten? I-I do not understand."

"Think you back to that night three years past. Do you remember naught besides your sister's rape and the beating you suffered? Have you no memory of the men who came to your aid, of someone holding you and keeping you safe?"

Caryn wet her lips. There *was* such a memory. Always it lingered at the edge of her mind, but it had never truly surfaced. Until this moment, she believed she had imagined the words of comfort, the strong arms enfolding her battered, pain-racked body.

He touched her cheek with his hand. "Did no one tell you of the soldiers who brought you to the convent?"

"Normans brought me. I thought it was the men who attacked us. The subject was forbidden. 'Twas a topic we never discussed." Nor had she wanted to. In truth, she had worked to forget it.

"Did you not wonder that you were left virgin?"

Caryn shook her head. "Gweneth was so beautiful. I believed the soldiers did not want me."

" 'Twas because we came upon them before they could act. My men were the ones who carried you to the safety of the convent."

"But . . .but how can that be? You said that you were guilty. You've said so more than once."

"Guilty of carelessness. Guilty of letting the duty I felt toward my men outweigh my desire to see you and your sister safe."

Caryn swallowed against the hard lump swelling in

her throat. Looking away from his troubled expression, she walked toward the narrow slit of window. When she reached it she turned to face him.

"You are telling me the truth?"

"I am no liar, Cara."

She faltered a movement, uncertain for a time, then convinced he had spoken the truth. "If that is your only guilt, my lord, then you should suffer no more." She turned to gaze out the window. "I am the one who was careless. I was responsible for my sister's safety, yet I did not see her safe. You told us to return to the hall, but I did not obey. Think you I do not suffer every day of my life for what I have done?"

Fresh tears welled and slipped down her cheeks. Caryn rested her head against the cold rough stone, her body shaking as the tears continued to fall. She felt Ral's hands on her shoulders, kneading them gently.

"We must both accept the blame for what has happened. 'Tis a cross we must bear, though in truth, 'twould be best should we leave it in the past." His hands continued their movements, calming her and lending her some of his strength. " 'Tis true that we both failed your sister, but I would not have this other between us. Of that I am not guilty."

Something opened inside her, blossomed and grew. The guilt she carried lifted and began to fade away, leaving her strangely unburdened. Ral turned her to face him.

"Do you believe me?"

She smiled at him through her tears. "Aye, I believe you. 'Tis the greatest gift you could have given me." Caryn reached for his hand, lifted it and pressed her mouth against the ragged, still-healing wound left by the wolves. "I thank you, my lord."

Ral said nothing, but at the soft brush of her lips, something tightened around his heart. If only he had known, he could have long since eased her worries. He could have set things right and bridged the gap that existed between them. He looked at her now, saw the wetness still shimmering in her soft brown eyes, saw her relief and something more. Her hand looked small and pale against his dark skin, her breasts rose and fell gently, and her neck arched gracefully above the bodice of her gown.

She looked feminine and lovely, and in the time that he had known her, he had never wanted her more.

He tipped her chin with his fingers and kissed her softly on the lips. "Rest easy, Cara, and as you do, I ask that you discover what it is you truly want." With a last lingering glance, he turned and made his way out the door.

Ral sighed as he strode down the stairs, thinking of all that had happened and wondering what his next course should be. Once he reached the great hall, he motioned for a servant to bring him a goblet of wine, carried it to his seat before the fire pit, sat down, and stared into the flames.

"Trouble with your wife, my lord?" Lynette approached from behind him, her slender hand coming to rest on his shoulder. " 'Tis a shame one so small can so displease you."

Ral said nothing.

Lynette ran her fingers through his hair. "Mayhap there is something I could do to ease your mind." She bent over him, allowing a breast to brush his arm, her golden blond hair tickling his cheeek. "Mayhap some chess or a game of chance?"

He hated gaming with Lynette. She had little skill and even were that not so, she would always let him win. "Nay. The hour grows late and I find that I am weary."

Her pink lips parted in a smile. "I too am tired. Mayhap 'tis best we are for bed. What say you, my lord? Do we leave together, or shall I go and await you?"

"You go on. I've a matter to discuss with Richard. It may take some time. 'Tis needless for you to wait up."

"But surely—"

"Take your leave, Lynette."

"As you wish, my lord." She tossed her pretty blond head and thrust out her bottom lip as she reluctantly walked away.

In the past, he had found the gesture feminine and appealing. Twice in the middle of the day, he had followed her back to her chamber, stripped off her clothes, and taken her while he still wore his own. Tonight it would not be so.

"She chafes at the attention you pay your wife." Odo sat down on the bench to his left. " 'Tis good for her. 'Twill ensure she keeps her place."

" 'Tis not Lynette who disturbs me."

"Ah . . . so 'tis true, the story Girart tells of what happened in the woods." Already the tale of the slaying of the wolf pack had been repeated again and again. But it wasn't of wolves Odo spoke and both of them knew it. "He says the little maid may not be as frosty as many believe."

"You may be certain that is so."

"Then take her, *mon ami*. Plant a babe in the wench's belly. A man needs heirs, my friend."

Ral sighed and leaned back in his chair. "That may be so. I will give it some thought." Sweet Christ, he had done little else. Thoughts of the fiery little maid near drove him crazy. Now that he knew why she had denied him, his desire for her had increased tenfold. Still, the choice was hers. He had made a promise—he would not take her unless it was her wish.

He raked a hand through his hair. Mayhap in truth 'twould be best if it did not happen. She was less than half his size and it was certain he would hurt her. Though his own pleasure would be great, she was unschooled in the ways of men and he was unsure he could please her. Most likely he would do ought but give her pain.

Besides, for now it did not matter. He had Lynette to warm his bed. She could give his body ease as well as any, far better than most of the wenches he had known. He glanced toward the door that led to her quarters in the bailey. She would be expecting him and yet . . .

Turning away from the door, he climbed the stairs leading up to the solar and instructed his squire to make him a bed. Once the lad had helped him strip off his garments, he settled himself in for the evening.

Lynette would be angry, but what did it matter? It wasn't Lynette he wanted. Ral frowned into the darkness, thinking of Caryn and wondering how he could possibly consider bedding one so small.

Caryn paced the bedchamber, which now that Ral had gone, seemed empty, barren, and cold. She had never really noticed how large the room was, how wide the big bed, how masculine the objects—bows, shields, and swords—that lined the walls.

This was the lord's room, the huge dark Norman who was her husband. And yet he was not there.

Caryn's stomach twisted. Again this eve, he would spend the night with his leman, driven away from his rightful place in her bed by a promise he had made and, it appeared, even now intended to keep.

Or was that exactly what he wanted? The tall willowy blonde was far more beautiful than Caryn, nearly as lovely as Gweneth. Which of them was the woman Ral wanted? His leman? His wife? Or his wife's far more beautiful sister? Caryn would never forget the look on the Dark Knight's face as he had stared into Gweneth's crystal blue eyes that day in the meadow.

It was because of Gweneth that he had married her in the first place. Because of Gweneth and the guilt he felt for what had happened. Ral knew her sister could never leave the convent, but mayhap his heart still yearned for her. With her elegant beauty, her sweetness and serenity, Gweneth was as different from Caryn as the moon was from the sun.

And if not Gweneth, what of Lynette? Her grace and beauty affected men wherever she passed. Ral had been with her for the past two years, had brought her here from France. Would he be willing to give her up? Caryn did not know and part of her was afraid to find out.

Still, it was she who was his wife, she who was meant to share his nights in the marriage bed.

She thought of him now, of the times he had kissed her, the things he had made her feel. *Do you never want children?* he had once asked. It was a question she had rarely considered. Now it ate at her. Children meant grave responsibilities—and an end to the freedom that she had always longed for. She couldn't imagine herself in the role of mother, yet the thought of a lifetime without a family of her own left her feeling bleak and empty.

Caryn shivered against a sudden chill and walked to the window to pull the thin horn slab back into place. Her husband might not love her, but he desired her. If she asked him, he would share her bed and make her his wife in truth.

Make theirs a marriage in truth.

It was what Caryn wanted, she realized with a sudden jolt of clarity. She wanted Ral to act as husband, but she didn't know quite how to ask. What did a woman say of such things? What should she do? She wasn't Lynette, with her wanton ways and petulant glances. And even if she tried it, she might fail.

What if Ral refused her? She didn't think he would but she wanted more from him than a single night of passion. What if he accepted her overtures, took her to his bed and she did not please him? What if he returned to his leman, as the servants believed had happened the night of their wedding?

It was risky, this course taking shape in her mind, but her happiness, her future, seemed more and more to depend upon it.

For the first time, Caryn smiled. She had always been a willing pupil. She loved to learn and she remembered the lessons she had been taught. She would start with her friend, the kitchen maid, Bretta. The buxom lass was not in the least bit shy about her skills in pleasuring a man; surely she would share that knowledge with Caryn.

Marta would help in whatever way she could. She had been urging Caryn to mend the breach with her husband since the night of the wedding. And there was Isolda, the healing woman in the village. The old woman prided herself on her love philters, charms, and aphrodisiacs. With Isolda's help, Marta's, and the knowledge garnered from Bretta, she would make Ral wild for her.

Caryn left the window and climbed up in bed, her smile now firmly in place. If Lynette could learn to please him, so could she. Tomorrow she would start her lessons. Soon she would bait her trap, settle back, and wait for her tall, dark Norman to take the bait.

Chapter Ten

"You asked to see me?"

"Share a goblet with me, Hugh?" Ral indicated a seat before the fire pit and the brawny knight moved toward it, flashing a crooked-toothed grin.

" 'Twould be a pleasure, my lord." Settling his beefy frame on the stout oak bench across from where Ral sat in his high-backed chair, Hugh stretched his long legs out in front of him. " 'Tis a while since we have sat together like this. Reminds me of our days back in Normandy." A page brought pewter goblets filled with wine and each of them took a hearty swig.

"Normandy . . . aye," Ral said. "We have known each other a good many years."

"That is so, my lord."

"Never have you divulged a confidence."

Hugh eyed him shrewdly. "They could cut out my heart and still your secrets would be safe."

"That is why I ask for your help, old friend." Ral leaned forward and so did Hugh, anticipation plain on his scarred weathered face.

"You've a secret of some import, my lord? As I have said, they may—"

" 'Tis nothing like that, my friend. What I would discuss is more personal in nature." Across from him, the big knight's wooly gray brows shot up, his curiosity piqued even more. "As a man very nearly my size, I thought you might be able to help me. You are older, and 'tis no secret the number of wenches you have bedded."

Hugh laughed. " 'Tis no exaggeration to say I have tupped more than my share. 'Twould be no lie to say the same of you."

Ral grunted. "That is true, but in this I am a novice."

Hugh crossed his arms over his thick barrel chest. "What would you know, my friend?"

"Mayhap I should start at the beginning." Certain his secret was safe with Hugh, Ral told him the truth of his marriage, explaining why he had done what he had and reminding Hugh of the night three years past when they had found the two sisters in the meadow. He told him of Stephen de Montreale and the threat he had posed, explaining that Ral had wed his lady wife in order to keep her safe.

"So you have yet to bed her," the big knight said.

"Nay, I have not, though 'tis a secret that must remain well guarded."

Hugh nodded. "And now that it appears this may soon change, you worry that she is too small."

"The part of me that will fill her is as big in proportion as the rest of me. Surely I will tear her in two."

Hugh chuckled, his green eyes twinkling with mirth. "Your Caryn is far from frail. She is tiny, but solidly built. Have you not noticed how lush are her hips? Why they are broad enough to bear any man fine strong sons."

"Aye, I've noticed." Christ's blood, he had seen the pale sweet curves of her flesh, felt the delicious firmness of her buttocks beneath his fingers.

"And her breasts," Hugh said, "so round and full, ripe enough to fill even a big man's hands. Surely that has not escaped your notice."

"I've already said that I've noticed. For God's sakes, man, I am not blind!"

Hugh grinned. "Blind you've ne'er been, 'tis only concern that gives you pause, and I mean to ease your fears." Hugh leaned forward, his long-boned forearms coming to rest on his knees. "Your little wife is tiny, that is true. But a woman is built to accept a man, no matter how large or small. Your Caryn's body will adjust to yours. She will take all of you inside her—of that you may be sure."

Hugh smiled and stared into the fire pit, reliving some lusty memory of a vixen from his past. "Can you not imagine how small and tight her passage? How easily you could hold her, position her to receive your thrusts? Can you not think of the things you might do with a woman her size?"

Ral's belly clenched. He could imagine, all right. Even now his mind swam with erotic images and his loins felt thick and heavy.

"If you have never thrust into a tiny woman, my friend," Hugh said with a voice gone raspy, "then you have never lived."

Ral's hand shook on the stem of his goblet and several dark drops ran over the edge. "You are certain that I will not hurt her."

"Only the first time. Be easy with her in the beginning, and her body will soon grow accustomed to yours."

Ral nodded, battling the images that Hugh had created, praying the man spoke the truth. "My thanks, Hugh."

Taking his cue that the subject was ended, Hugh set his goblet aside and stood up. "All this talk of women has made me as randy as a rutting boar. Methinks I will search out Bretta. That one has a passage that works like a mare munching oats."

Ral chuckled at the notion as his friend walked away, then grimaced at the ache that throbbed low in his groin. Every muscle felt taut with need, and his blood pumped thick and heavy. He glanced to the oaken door leading out to the bailey. Lynette had already retired. If he went to her now, all would be forgiven and she would welcome him into her bed.

He was tempted. Sorely tempted. But something held him back. Instead, he turned toward the stairs and his bed in the solar. Another night of solitude was hardly what he had in mind, yet something told him the reward he sought would well be worth it.

He was pondering that and had nearly reached the stairs when a disturbance near the door sent several pages running in that direction.

"A messenger has arrived, my lord." Geoffrey strode toward him. "He brings word from the king."

Ral nodded and followed the young blond knight toward the scantily clad runner. Tall and nearly gaunt, the man clutched a long wooden staff he used to vault streams, and a short split cane that carried the message. From the end of the cane, the runner removed a roll of parchment fixed with the king's wax seal. Ral accepted it along with the messenger's greetings and crossed the short distance to Richard.

"See that the man is fed and given a place to rest," Ral commanded one of the servants, handing his steward the scroll. Richard broke the seal and began to read.

"William sends his regards," he said. "He hopes all is well and sends you and your lady wife his wishes for a happy and fruitful marriage."

"Get to the point," Ral said.

"The lands you've requested have once more been denied. De Montreale has also been pressing for the grant. William says he must remain impartial." Richard glanced up from the parchment, his forehead marred by a frown. "The king has offered the land as bounty, my lord, to whichever of you brings him the head of the Ferret."

"Damn!" Ral's fist slammed down on the table, making it shimmy and dance. "William knows how important that land is. Stephen wants it only because I need it to feed the people of Braxston. By Christ, it could mean their very survival."

Richard looked him in the eye. "Then you will merely catch the Ferret before de Montreale." He smiled. "I've no doubt that you will."

Some of Ral's tension eased. "You're a good man, Richard, and in this your words must prove true. Tomorrow, we return to the forest—and the day after that and the day after that—until the Ferret is captured." He clapped his steward on the back. "We won't fail in this —we cannot afford to."

Caryn bent over the mortar resting on the table before her. Plying the heavy stone pedestal against the dried mint and mustard, cloves, rosebud, and leek, she ground the items into a fine dark powder, then emptied the substance into a small stoppered vile.

It was another of Isolda's potions, the making of a powder that fostered lust and acted as a strong aphrodisiac. Caryn had secretly collected strands of Ral's hair, a scrap of fabric worn next to his skin, and dried blood scraped from the shoulder of his jerkin, items the healing woman had fashioned into a figure of clay and buried at the crossroads beneath a waxing moon.

Together the items were meant to form a powerful love philter that Ral could not resist.

Caryn sighed. So far, Isolda's charms and spells had done little to help her cause. Nor had Bretta's lessons in seduction. Marta had forced them together whenever she had the chance, but Ral had been gone from the castle most of the time, in desperate search of the outlaws. When he did return, he was so weary he fell into an exhausted slumber before the fire pit, often too tired to eat.

He had even given up sleeping with his leman, taking

instead a place in the solar. Caryn figured he must be weary indeed and wondered what little chance her untutored seduction could have when even Lynette's vast experience seemed to fail her.

Caryn picked up the vial and walked to the door. Ral had returned that afternoon, disgruntled and depressed that he had once again failed to discover the whereabouts of the outlaws. His dark mood was hardly the one she would have chosen, but finding the brigands might take months. Ral's hunger for a woman would return long before then. If Caryn wanted to be that woman, she couldn't afford to wait.

She headed down the passage toward the stairs, saying a quick word to Marta along the way and receiving a smile of encouragement. Once she reached the dais, she would slip Isolda's potion into Ral's wine, make pleasant conversation during the meal, then attempt to charm him as Bretta had instructed.

Mayhap this time she would succeed in stirring his interest. Mayhap he would carry her upstairs and . . .

Caryn flushed to think of what the buxom kitchen maid had told her would transpire in the marriage bed. She had tried to hide her amazement, but Bretta had seen it and laughed.

"Ye must not worry, milady. 'Tis a woman's lot in life, and 'tis hardly a burden. Ye'll find no more pleasant hours than those ye spend beneath ye brawny lover."

Caryn stiffened. It had never occurred to her that Bretta might have known Ral in that way. "Do you mean that. . . . are you saying—"

"Nay, milady, 'tis not of your man I speak, but of the deed itself." She winked and flashed a bawdy big-toothed grin. "'Tweren't for fear o' me belly growin' round, I'd be tossin' up me skirts far more often."

Caryn felt the heat burning into her cheeks. Focusing her questions on how to attract a man instead of what would happen once she did, she listened as Bretta spoke of smiling and touching, how to walk seductively, and the use of subtle innuendos to signal a man of her interest. Since everyone believed Ral preferred his leman to his wife, Bretta understood Caryn's motives and heartily approved.

"Ye husband belongs in ye bed, milady, not in that o' his coldhearted strumpet."

Still, belonging there and getting him there seemed two far different things.

Ral sat beside Caryn on the dais, hearing her soft feminine laughter, feeling her shoulder brush his as she bantered lightly in his ear. She smiled sweetly, seemingly amused at something he said, working hard to amuse him in return.

Her movements were womanly, seductive, their meaning as unmistakable as they had been throughout the ages. In the past few days, Ral had seen his lady wife use them often, mastering the gestures far too easily to suit him, stirring a response in his body and a desire he could barely contain.

Caryn's breast brushed his arm and the blood pumping hotly through his veins grew thick and sluggish, his heartbeat slowing, throbbing, matching the heavy ache that had settled in his groin. Had Caryn been the woman of experience she pretended, she would have seen through his mask of indifference, seen the hunger for her that he worked so hard to disguise.

"You wear a new gown this eve," he said mildly, wishing the meal would come to an end, wondering if tonight he would give in to his passions and take her. Or if he would wait as he had planned, play the game she had started, let the desire she fostered in him build a fire in her as well.

"Does it please you, my lord?" A dark ruby tunic over a chainse of alabaster silk that brought out the rich red highlights in her hair.

"The color favors your complexion. You have chosen well."

She smiled. "More wine, my lord?" She had seen his goblet refilled several times, and he wondered if her plans included getting him drunk.

"It tastes a little bitter this eve, but 'tis no matter, I've had enough. I face a long day on the morrow." He had no intention of taking her without being sober and firmly in control. He vowed he would not hurt her and to keep that vow, he would needs go slow.

"Since it appears you are finished with your meal," she said, "mayhap you would favor me with a game of chess."

He arched a brow. "I did not know that you played."

"There is much of me you do not know, my lord." She flashed a saucy smile, exposing a row of small white teeth.

Ral's own teeth clamped against a spasm of pain in the hardened flesh beneath the table. He forced himself to relax. "A game before we are for bed might be just the thing to help me sleep." By Christ, what a lie that was! Naught but tossing up the lady's skirts would ensure a night of peace.

He smiled inwardly, enjoying the game in spite of his discomfort, hoping in the end that both of them would win.

They sat down across from each other at the chessboard. Caryn pondered the board and moved a pawn out two spaces. It wouldn't take long to defeat her, he was certain, since the game was one of strategy, much like plotting a great battle. He had yet to meet a woman who could grasp the concept of war well enough to be much of a challenge.

He wasn't saying that several hours later, when the board had been cleared of a goodly number of pieces and his tall black chessmen stood no closer to defeating the white than they had when he had started. Of course, she was no nearer to victory than he was.

"You are a difficult opponent, my lord." She moved her bishop, fashioned from the tusk of a walrus, blocking his move to capture her queen.

He smiled. "You could always let me win."

Caryn glanced up at him, her expression surprised. Then she frowned. "I hadn't thought that you would wish it." She looked as if she had failed in some way and it dawned on him that whoever had been teaching her the art of seduction had failed to mention this particular ploy.

"If you believed that I would not enjoy winning unless it was against a worthy opponent, then you thought correctly. I have enjoyed our playing this eve, more than I ever would have guessed."

She beamed at that, her face looking young and radiant in the glowing embers of the fire. She was lovely beyond belief and growing more so with each passing day.

"I am glad that I have pleased you."

"It would please me more should I defeat you, but not because you let me."

She seemed happy to hear she had guessed right and attacked the board with an even greater fervor. In the end, the game went stalemate. Ral laughed good-naturedly and told her he would best her when next they played. Caryn vowed it would be she who was the victor.

Ral thought that if losing the game to his pretty little wife would see him settled in her bed, he might be tempted to lose on purpose himself.

He glanced toward the stairs. " 'Tis time that we are for bed." He looked at Caryn, careful to keep his expression bland. Something flickered in her eyes, then it was gone.

Say it, he silently commanded. *Tell me I am welcome*

in your bed. He could take her. It was obvious she would let him. But he wanted her committed. He wanted her to admit she was ready for a marriage in truth. He wanted her to desire him with the same hot passion that he desired her.

And he believed his indifference was working.

"You are tired, my lord?"

He shrugged his shoulders. "We've received no news of the outlaws. We will hunt on the morrow to replenish our stores, and I would be well rested." He took her hand and placed it on his arm then guided her up the steep stone stairs.

"You have taken to sleeping in the solar," she said softly. "You are certain your pallet there will suffice?"

Not nearly as well as a place between your shapely little legs. " 'Twill serve well enough for the present." He had never used this particular technique in order to attract a woman, yet with Caryn, instinctively he knew it was his very indifference that would ensure his success. The less he responded, the harder she would work to make him do so.

His Caryn liked to win at whatever game she played.

He stopped in front of her door, turned her into his arms, and kissed her. It was a gentle kiss yet it burned with an underlying heat. It took iron control for him to pull away. In a day or two, he hoped, there would be no need for such restraint.

"Good eventide, my lady."

"G-Good eventide, my lord." Her hand trembled as she lifted the latch, opened the door, and went in.

Smiling to himself, Ral turned and walked down the hall toward the solar. Caryn of Ivesham wasn't the only one who liked to win.

"Milady? Milady, where are you? I bring urgent news from the village."

"In here, Leofric," she called from the corner of the

stable where she sat cradling the fawn in her lap. The little deer grew stronger and bigger every day. "What is it?"

The young boy raced in, his face flushed with exertion, his narrow chest heaving in and out. "News of the brigands, milady. Me mother has been tryin' to discover where they camp. She wishes to repay Lord Raolfe for his kindness."

Caryn gently set the fawn away and climbed to her feet, brushing straw from her tunic and plucking a strand from her heavy braid of hair. "Lord Ral hunts today. He won't return before nightfall."

"I could carry a message."

"I know not where he is. You must tell me, Leofric. I will see he receives the news the moment of his arrival."

"Me mother says they camp near the pass at Chevrey, on a bend of the River Eden. They lie in wait for the king's tax collector. No one knows exactly when he comes, but the Ferret means to raid him and steal King William's coin."

"Surely the money will be well guarded."

"Me mother says the band has grown to near fifty men. They were raidin' to the north, but of late they have returned."

Fifty men! Surely enough to pose a danger to William's men—or her husband and his. Caryn's stomach knotted.

"They're cutthroats, milady. A dozen good knights and men-at-arms have already fallen to the Ferret's blade."

Unconsciously, she trembled. "Mayhap this time Lord Ral will catch him."

"Aye, milady, 'tis certain the lord will bring them in."

Surely a man of her husband's might and skill would be in no danger. Yet Leo's words of warning still echoed in her ears. "I will tell Lord Ral your mother's news the moment he returns to the castle."

"I wish I could go with him."

I am glad that you cannot, Caryn found herself thinking. And with that disturbing thought, worry for her husband suddenly increased.

Caryn paced the hall in front of the fire pit. Ral should have returned by now. Richard had seen to an extra hearty meal and even now it sat steaming in the kitchen. She turned as the door flew open and Girart walked in. Ral never left the castle unguarded. Today he had also left the majority of his men. They were to rest this day and set out in search of the outlaws on the morrow.

Hearing noises in the entry, she hurried in that direction. "Lord Ral?" Caryn asked of Girart.

"Nay, my lady."

Richard strode in behind him, his face looking grim. " 'Tis Stephen de Montreale."

Malvern. "Sweet God in heaven." Lord Stephen was the last man Caryn wished to see—especially with her husband gone from the castle. "Must we allow him entrance?"

" 'Tis only common courtesy. He travels with but a handful of men. We can hardly refuse him a night's food and lodging."

She nodded, knowing it was the truth. "At least there is plenty of food." And plenty of men to guard the keep. "See him in, Richard." She steeled herself to play lady of the manor and suddenly found herself looking forward to the task. "And convey to him my greetings."

Malvern walked in with his usual easy grace, his strides long and supple, though he still wore his chain mail hauberk. His garments were dusty from the hours he had spent on the road, but his blond hair gleamed in the flickering rushlights mounted on the walls behind him.

"My lady." He bent over her hand, brushing his mouth against her fingers, his lips firm and his breath warm. It was all she could do not to jerk the hand away.

"My lord." She made an obeisance and forced herself to smile, noticing as she had when she had first seen him, that except for the cruelty in his eyes and his slightly pointed nose, he was handsome in the extreme.

" 'Twould seem I make a habit of arriving while your husband is away." His pale blue eyes swept over her, taking in her sapphire tunic, golden girdle, and the embroidered silk chainse she wore beneath. "Now that I see the jewel that hid beneath your convent garments, I cannot say I am particularly regretful."

She let that pass, tamping down her loathing. "My husband will soon return. I have seen a chamber readied, should you care to bathe and refresh yourself before the meal."

He nodded. "The day has been a long one. A bath and a goblet of wine would put me in your debt, my lady."

She motioned to one of the servants and turned to leave, but Lord Stephen caught her arm. "Mayhap you would attend me yourself."

She smiled faintly. "Of course." But she hadn't the slightest intention. Accompanied by his squire, Lord Stephen was shown upstairs while the rest of his men filled their horns with ale or sipped a goblet of wine.

Caryn turned toward the kitchen, hoping to seek out a willing maidservant, but resigned to a page should she fail.

"I will tend him, milady." Bretta stopped her in front of the ovens. Fresh-baked barleycorn bread filled the kitchen with a pleasant, yeasty smell.

"You don't have to. I do not know his intentions. I would not force any of the women—"

" 'Tis all right, milady." She grinned. "I fancy the notion o' scrubbin' Lord Stephen's back. He's got a right fine one, I'll warrant."

Caryn smiled. "Just be careful."

"I'll have him purrin' like a kitten in no time a'tall."

Ral still had not arrived by the time Lord Stephen returned to the hall. Dressed in a fine purple tunic over a scarlet chainse, he looked every inch the baron, pleasantly relaxed, and not in the least the brutal man she knew him to be.

"Good eventide, my lord." She smiled as he approached the dais.

"Might I join you?"

"Of course."

He took a place beside her on the platform, his men at the trestle tables readied below them, awaiting the arrival of their lord. They spoke of pleasant subjects, the weather, the crops, events in the village, at Braxston, and at Malvern.

"My sister will soon be arriving," he said. " 'Tis a while since she has come for a visit. Mayhap the two of you will have the chance to meet."

"Mayhap. I would enjoy having another woman to talk to." Assuming she was nothing like her cruel-hearted brother.

"Eliana is a treasure, tall and fair-skinned—quite beautiful, really. Did you know she was once betrothed to your husband?"

Caryn's head came up. "Your sister and Lord Ral?"

" 'Twas long before you. Our fathers arranged it when both of them were children."

"Nay, I did not know."

"I am not surprised . . . since he dishonored her by refusing to go through with the marriage."

Was this then the reason for the two men's hatred? "Surely he had a reason."

The line of his mouth grew taut. "Mayhap he did. I know only that he grievously wronged my sister." He smiled thinly. "Mayhap he will tell you about it sometime."

And mayhap he would not, though she would dearly like to know. "You journey from the south," she said, changing the subject.

"Yes. I return from a visit to my estate at Grennel."

"You travel with very few men. Saw you no sign of the Ferret and his outlaws?"

"Nay. 'Tis said they raid somewhere to the north. 'Tis also said your lord husband has been pursuing them with a vengeance." A corner of his mouth curved up. "Should he discover their whereabouts, I would be happy to lend him a hand."

Caryn leaned forward in her chair, suddenly alert. Much as she loathed Lord Stephen, the danger to Ral would be lessened greatly with the help of Malvern and his men.

"Then again," Stephen said, "I do not believe he would accept it."

Inwardly, she groaned. Nay, he would not. Then a different thought occurred. "If you knew where to find the outlaws, would you seek them out?" Lord Stephen was ruthless, and as fearsome in battle as Ral. What difference, which of the men accomplished the feat, as long as the brigands were captured?

He shifted in his chair, surveying her with renewed interest. "If they camp somewhere to the north as I have heard said, I could send word to my men at Malvern. They are sufficient in number to see the blackguard's days ended."

"Lord Raolfe would not approve of my telling. I would not wish it discovered." But if it would keep him and the other men safe, the risk would be worth it.

"You know where they are?"

"I discovered only this eve. Word came to me from the village."

"Why would you tell me?"

Why indeed? She felt uneasy about it, but the idea of Ral being injured or killed made her feel far worse. "I would see the outlaws' raiding put to an end." *I would see my husband home and safe.* " 'Twould seem the more men seeing it done, the better the chance for success."

He smiled. "As I said, I would be happy to lend my support."

She hesitated only a moment. "They are camped near Chevrey Pass on the River Eden."

"You are certain of this?"

"Word comes from a trusted source, though I cannot say how long the outlaws will remain there."

He surveyed her a moment more, turned in his chair, and called for one of his men. A rawboned knight appeared from the shadows, listened as Stephen whispered in his ear, nodded his understanding, and strode from the hall.

"Durand leaves for Malvern in all haste. He will gather men there and ride for Chevrey. I will leave on the morrow, as I had planned. With any luck, the Ferret and his men will long have been captured by the time I reach Chevrey Pass."

Caryn smiled. "Thank you, my lord."

"Thank *you*, Lady Caryn." His expression looked so smug, Caryn suddenly wished she hadn't told him. Sweet Jesu, she prayed she had done the right thing.

Chapter Eleven

Wearing his chain mail hauberk, his shield close at hand, Ral sat astride his big black destrier on the hill overlooking what had once been the Ferret's camp.

"God's wounds," Odo said, "again we are too late."

A muscle jumped in Ral's cheek. "So it would seem. 'Twould also appear that Malvern was not." He swore a savage oath as he urged the big horse forward, leading his men down the slope into the camp. It was littered with debris: overturned cooking pots, upended wineskins, sleeping pallets, weapons, and clothing. Several plumes of smoke rose up from dying fires—and the bodies of at least thirty men lay sprawled across the clearing.

Ral rode forward, searching for the corpse of the Ferret, his chest taut with bitter disappointment that he had failed the people of his village. If only he had returned from the hunt a few hours early. If only Lord Stephen hadn't been at Braxston when he arrived. If only he had ridden out that night instead of waiting for his hated enemy to leave.

Ral worked a muscle in his jaw. The Ferret would no longer plague them, but there would be no new land to clear and plant, and without it, no way to refill the stores he had depleted in order to build the keep.

Sooner or later, the people of Braxston would suffer. Ral grimaced to think of what lay ahead.

He skirted a group of Malvern's men but still saw no sign of the Ferret—or what remained of him. Picking his way between the knights and men-at-arms who searched for plunder among the fallen bodies, he recognized a big knight named Durand, apparently the leader of Stephen's men, and rode in that direction.

" 'Twould appear you have done a good day's work, Durand."

"Thank you, my lord."

"Does Lord Stephen mean to join you?"

"Even now he rides in this direction."

"What of the Ferrett?" Ral asked. "I did not see his body."

Lifting off his conical helmet, Durant hesitated, then shook his head. "Escaped, my lord, with about twenty men."

Ral released a weary breath. He should have been sorry the whoreson still lived, but his need for the land was so great he felt relieved instead. Then his body tensed with anger. Had he and his men arrived first, the outcome might have been different.

"What happened?" he asked.

"The brigand posted guards in all directions. We had hoped to surprise him, but he had just enough warning to make ready. There were archers in the trees, and in the rocks above us. We felled an ample number, but lost five good men in the bargain."

"How did you know where to find them?"

"Lord Stephen sent word."

Ral frowned. He had supped with Malvern only last eve. Stephen must have known about the outlaws, but been careful to make no mention—but then neither had he.

" 'Tis a shame the whoreson got away. He'll keep to himself for a while, but as soon as he marshals more men, he will return." *And this time, naught on this earth will prevent me from taking his head.*

"Aye, my lord. The bastard don't know when to quit."

Ral said nothing more, just gathered his men and turned them back toward the road. Even Odo said little along the route home, keenly aware of his friend's disappointment.

"You will find him, *mon ami.* The next time you will not fail."

Ral did not answer. His attention was fixed on a point up the road, on the band of armored men who were riding in his direction.

"Malvern," Odo said. "Durand has failed to capture the Ferret. Lord Stephen will not be pleased."

"Durand will have sent word of what has happened. Stephen may not be pleased, but catching the Ferret is of far less consequence to him than it is to me." They rode toward the men and Ral drew rein next to Stephen, the big black destrier dancing nervously alongside Stephen's huge gray.

" 'Tis too soon for congratulations," Ral said, "but I am grateful to be rid of the brigands your men have cut down."

"Travelers will be safer, yet 'twould seem our battle for the Ferret is not done."

" 'Twould seem that is so."

"Mayhap next time you will find him first."

Ral forced himself to smile. "You may count on it, Stephen."

"You almost bested me this time, you know. In fact, 'tis possible you would have—had your pretty little wife not gifted me with the Ferret's location before she saw fit to tell you."

At the look of stunned disbelief Ral could not disguise, Stephen smiled with smug satisfaction. " 'Twas a gift I hardly expected, but a welcome one, I assure you." He smiled again as he signaled his men to move forward, then he rode to the head of the column, leaving Ral to stare after him in fury.

"Give her my regards, will you?" he called back over his shoulder.

Ral watched the men ride past, armor clanking, dust rising up from the road. He fisted a gauntleted hand, fury sweeping through him like an angry wave.

"He may not speak the truth," Odo warned.

" 'Tis truth. I can feel it."

"She is Saxon. I told you she could not be trusted."

"She is my wife." His jaw clamped so tight he could barely speak. Savagely sawing on the reins, he jerked Satan around, making the stallion chafe at the bit and nervously dance beneath him, then he started down the road toward the keep. With a last look at Malvern, he nudged the huge horse into a gallop.

Stephen de Montreale joined the rest of his forces in the clearing that had been the Ferret's campsite, and rode straight for his man, Durand. A big brawny knight with a hard jaw and thinning hair, Durand had earned a place among his most trusted soldiers—as long as he was well rewarded.

"You've captured the Ferret?" Stephen asked.

"Tied up and well guarded. We've kept him out of sight among the trees."

"You are certain that Braxston does not know?"

"Nay, my lord. I have done as you instructed."

"Good. Rest assured you will be well paid."

Durand smiled, exposing slightly yellowed teeth. Stephen left him, making his way to the place where his men-at-arms guarded the Ferret. The outlaw sat with his back against a boulder, his head slumped onto his chest, long black hair falling haphazardly over his forehead. He was a thin man with eyes that darted from one place to another, a man who matched his name, yet it was certain the Ferret was no fool.

"Leave us," Stephen commanded his men.

"Aye, my lord." They backed away from him, melding into the forest and leaving the two of them alone.

Only the Ferret's eyes moved now, watching him closely, judging him, waiting for his words.

Stephen smiled. " 'Tis said that you are the devil himself."

The smaller man grunted. "I have heard the same of you."

Stephen chuckled softly. He circled the smaller man, sizing him up, noticing his whipcord strength. He snapped the end off a branch and flexed it between his fingers. "Are you afraid of me?"

"I am your prisoner."

"That is not what I asked."

"A man would be a fool not to fear you."

Stephen smiled. "That is good. Fear is always a good beginning."

The Ferret raised his head and eyed him warily. "A good beginning for what?"

Stephen chuckled softly, and tossed the branch away. "How would you like to escape?"

Caryn sat at the chessboard across from Richard. The evening grew late, yet she felt only mildly tired.

"Your king is in check to my queen," she said, smiling at her sandy-haired opponent, who looked more than a little perplexed.

"You are a better chess player than most men. Was it Lord Harold who taught you?"

She shook her head. "I saw little of my uncle."

"Your father?"

"Nay. He was never around. 'Twas Edwin of Bedford who taught me. He was a friend of my uncle's."

Richard smiled. "I remember him."

"I heard that he still lives. I wonder what has become of him."

Richard started to answer, but noises in the hall snapped his head toward the entry, then sent him shooting to his feet. "Lord Ral returns."

Caryn stood up, too. "That cannot be. He has only been gone three days. He couldn't be back so soon."

" 'Tis him," Richard said, recognizing Odo and Hugh and several of the others. "He will be weary. I must see to food for him and the men."

Worried at what might have happened, Caryn turned to see Ral standing in the entry, his young squire, Aubrey, stripping off his dusty chain mail. He looked tall and commanding, and the sight of his ruggedly handsome face made her heart begin to pump fiercely. Caryn smiled, thinking as she had a dozen times these past few days, just how much she had missed him.

Aubrey bent to remove Ral's spurs, but before the squire could do so, he strode forward, his shadow looming large on the walls of the keep in the flickering light of the torches. For the first time Caryn noticed the hard set of his jaw, the tautness in his shoulders as he moved. Several day's growth of beard roughened his cheek, and with each of his long determined strides, his hands balled unconsciously into fists.

Sweet God in heaven, he was angry. Furious, it seemed. Caryn's stomach knotted. She forced herself to walk toward him, to greet him with a smile of welcome, praying the anger she sensed was not directed at her.

"You are returned home early, my lord. You are not injured?"

Ral stopped squarely in front of her, his gray eyes steely, anger seething from every pore. "How could I possibly be injured? The Ferret's men were well in hand by the time we reached the camp."

She thought of Stephen, realized her plan had worked, and felt a moment of relief. "Then you and the others are safe."

"Aye, we are safe." Iron gray eyes bored into her.

"You do not ask how that might be. How it was that Lord Stephen's men arrived at the Ferret's camp first."

"I . . . was just so glad to hear all is well. Of course, I would know how it happened."

A cold smile curved his lips, pulling the muscles taut across his cheekbones. "It seems Lord Stephen also discovered the brigands' location. He sent word ahead to his knights at Malvern."

"That is good, is it not? Travelers on our roads at last will be safe."

"You do not ask how it is Lord Stephen found out."

"I-I presume he has informants just as you do."

"Aye, that he does. Men who are loyal to him. And people who would betray me."

"Betray you?" An uneasy feeling swept down her spine. "I cannot see how something that has helped you get rid of the Ferret can possibly be seen as a betrayal."

Around them, men and servants grew silent as a tension settled over the hall. "Is that what you did, Caryn? Helped me?"

"I-I do not know what you mean."

He gripped the top of her arms and hauled her close. "I am tired of playing games. We both know you told Malvern about the Ferret's camp. We both know you have once more betrayed me!"

Caryn gasped. "That is not so!"

" 'Tis the God's truth, Caryn. What I cannot understand is why you would aid a man like Stephen."

"I did not do it to aid him!"

His fingers dug into her shoulders. "By Christ, you are my wife! Your loyalty belongs to me!"

"I am *not* your wife—you said so yourself! Lynette is more wife to you than I am." She hadn't meant to say the words, yet in truth she discovered she meant them.

For the first time, Ral fell silent. Then a bitter smile twisted his lips. "In this you are correct. Speaking the vows does not make a marriage. 'Tis the joining that counts and that has not yet been done. This night that will change."

"But I don't—"

He released his hold on her arms. "Return upstairs to your chamber. Prepare yourself to receive me in your bed."

"What!"

"You heard me. Do as I command."

"But you made a promise."

"Only a fool does nothing to correct his mistakes."

"But—"

"Go, damn you!"

Lifting her skirts up out of the way, Caryn raced across the hall to the stairs, then ran down the passage to her chamber. Slamming the door behind her, she sagged against the thick rough wood, desperate for its support.

Sweet Mary, Mother of God. She glanced at the bed, her limbs quaking, then listened for the sound of Ral's footsteps coming up the stairs. Her chest heaved, her palms felt damp, and her heart slammed so hard against her ribs she could barely hear herself think.

Blessed Virgin, what should I do?

A brief knock sounded, making her jump, and Marta walked in. The older woman looked frail but resigned, not nearly as undone as Caryn. "Lord Ral sent me to attend you."

"Marta—thank God you have come." She went into the small woman's arms and they tightened briefly around her. "I am frightened. I have never seen him so angry."

Marta set her away. "Can you blame him? You have made him look the fool."

"I did not mean to."

Marta harrumphed. "Turn around." Working by habit, she began to strip off Caryn's clothes, removing her tunic and the chainse she wore beneath, leaving on just her linen camise.

" 'Twas a foolish thing you did," Marta said on a sigh. "But at least 'twill put an end to your problem."

Caryn's head came up. "My problem? What do you mean?"

The old woman smiled, deepening the lines at the corners of her mouth. "Has it not been your wish to become Lord Ral's wife in truth?"

"Aye, but—"

"This night your wish will be granted."

She digested that for a while. Indeed, it was what she had wanted. "But he is so angry."

" 'Tis the price you must pay for your foolishness."

It was hard to argue with that. She hadn't thought how Ral would feel, how it would look to his men. Of course, she had hoped he wouldn't find out.

" 'Twill hurt you some," Marta said. "Lord Ral is a very big man."

Caryn felt an uneasy chill. "Bretta told me what must occur."

"Try to sooth his temper. 'Twill go the easier, should he be gentle."

Caryn nodded. Soothing the dark Norman's mood was never an easy task. "I will try."

Marta led her to the table against the wall, picked up the bristle brush and stroked it through Caryn's long auburn hair. It calmed her some, as Marta meant it to, her smooth strokes even as she fanned the heavy mass around her shoulders. Then she set the brush back down on the table.

" 'Twill only increase his ire, should you keep him waiting."

Caryn nodded, more uncertain by the moment. Nervously wetting her lips, she tried not to think what would happen once Marta had gone.

"He is a good man," the old woman said. "No matter

what happens, do not forget that." Marta left the room, her footsteps slowly fading, and Caryn's worry increased.

She started to pace, but in less time than it took to cross the floor, the latch flew up on the door and her tall dark husband strode in. He had bathed, she saw; his thick black hair curled damply at the back of his simple brown tunic. He looked as handsome as he always did, as proud and determined—and not an ounce of his anger had faded.

"I wondered would you try to escape. Had you, I would have dragged you back in here by the hair of your head."

Caryn swallowed hard. "I did not wish to escape."

"Oh?" A bold black brow arched upward. "I should think a wife who betrays her husband would hardly wish to bed him."

A heaviness settled in her chest. "I did not think to betray you."

Ral ignored her words as if she hadn't spoken, but a muscle jumped in his cheek. "Where I am from, we sleep in naught. Remove your garment so that I may see you."

The heaviness grew, becoming a sharp-edged pain. When she just stood there, staring into the handsome face now twisted with malice, Ral stepped forward. His fingers bit into the soft linen fabric and he ripped the gown down the front. "I said remove it!"

She did as he said with trembling fingers, letting the gown pool softly at her feet, leaving her naked, keeping her head held high and willing herself not to weep.

"Turn around. Slowly. I would see what you have kept hidden from me for so long."

She did as he commanded, careful not to look at him, wishing her heart didn't hurt and that this night could be different, that it might be filled with caring and passion as she had imagined.

"I would know why you betrayed me," he said when she faced him once more, his gray eyes hard and probing. "You are not Stephen's whore, are you?"

She should have been angry at his words. Instead her insides felt leaden. "Nay."

"Get in bed and open your legs."

Something clenched inside her. She felt a burning behind her eyes, and though she tried to will it not to, a tear slid down her cheek. "I will do whatever it is that you wish, my lord. But I would have you know that I did not intend to betray you. Leofric said that the Ferret was a cutthroat. He said good knights and men-at-arms had fallen to his blade. I was worried for your safety and for that of your men. I did not think it mattered, which of you put the Ferret's raiding to an end."

Removing his clothes with angry, jerking motions, Ral suddenly went still. He tossed aside his tunic and turned in her direction. "You are saying you know naught of the bounty?"

"What bounty?"

Ral searched her face, her big dark eyes and soft trembling lips. He saw the pain etched in her features, the regret, and the sorrow. The bounty was not common knowledge, though 'twas no secret, either. Still, he had not told her the importance of his mission, had never bothered to explain. The anger in his heart began to ease, allowing the haze of his fury to fade, allowing him to think.

"The king has offered the land," he said, "the demesme between here and Malvern, in return for the head of the Ferret."

Caryn straightened. "The land you promised to the people of the village?"

"Aye."

"Dear God in heaven."

"You are saying you did not know?"

"I meant only to help you," she said softly. "I would

see Malvern's men dead before those of Braxston Keep.''

Ral studied her long and hard. "Why should I believe you?" He wanted to. Christ's blood, he had never wanted anything more. Her eyes came to rest on his face, velvet brown in the light of the candles.

"Because I loathe Stephen de Montreale even more than you do. Because I love the people in my village and I would never wish them harm. Because you are my husband, and I wanted you returned safely home.''

Did she mean it? Did he dare to trust her again? Yet the look in her eyes told him she spoke the truth. Ral took a steadying breath and something eased around his heart.

He reached toward her, ran his knuckles along her jaw, saw her uncertainty and the hope that sprang to life in her face. "Get into bed. What you have said does not change what must happen here this eve." He pulled back the covers. "Only the way it will happen."

Something in the gesture must have helped to ease her fears for some of the tension drained from her shoulders. "Aye, my lord.''

She did as he instructed, climbing up beneath the blankets, then watching as he walked to the door and called for a servant to bring them some wine. A few minutes later, a page appeared, carrying a jug and two tall pewter goblets. Ral waited for the boy to leave, filled the goblets, then strode to the side of the bed.

"Drink this. 'Twill help you to relax.''

She accepted the drink with hands a little unsteady, then did as he instructed, downing a goodly portion while he drank only a sip. Instead he pulled off his chainse, untied the garters on his chausses and removed them, and joined her naked on the bed.

She was staring at the covers, her face turned modestly away. He cupped her chin with his hand and forced her to look at him.

"Again we have suffered misunderstandings. I would not see it happen again." He felt her agreement in the faintest nodding of her head. "From this day forward, you are my wife. Your loyalty belongs to me."

"My loyalty has been yours since the day I learned the truth of what happened to my sister."

"Stephen de Montreale is my sworn enemy. Should you aid him in any way, 'twill serve as a betrayal. I will never allow it again. Do you understand?"

"Aye, my lord."

He bent his head and kissed her, felt her soft lips trembling under his. "I will try not to hurt you."

Another soft kiss and she parted her lips, accepting the invasion of his tongue. She tasted of the rich red wine she had been sipping and smelled of soap and kittens. He wanted to drink in the scent of her, to run his tongue along every sweet, supple inch of her. He wanted to stroke her breasts till her nipples turned hard, then part her legs and drive himself inside her.

Instead he reminded himself that he must go slow, and even then this first time she might not respond to him. In fact even now he could sense her fear in the tremors that coursed through her small woman's body.

He pulled away to look at her. "Are you so afraid I will hurt you?"

She surprised him by shaking her head, her heavy dark auburn hair rippling softly with the movement. "Nay, my lord, 'tis not fear that makes me tremble. 'Tis only that when you touch me, shivers creep over my skin."

Ral chuckled softly, relief flooding through him. " 'Tis only the beginning, *cherie.*"

And it was. Ral kissed her again, long and thoroughly, his warm lips soft yet fiercely possessive. His tongue touched the corners of her mouth, slid over her bottom lip, urging her to open to him and sending a wave of heat through her body. Her own tongue met his, tentatively at first, testing, probing, the taste of him stirring her senses. Shivers crept over her, little tongues of flame that nipped at her flesh until she writhed against him. They fenced and parried, nibbled and tasted, Caryn awash with heat yet determined to learn how to please him.

She felt his hands on her body, strong and agile, lifting a breast, making it feel heavy and achy. His fingers pebbled her nipple, making it hard and distended, and Caryn sucked in a hot breath of air. Then his big hands moved lower, gliding along her skin, pausing at her navel, his finger teasing, tracing, sending currents of flame across her belly.

Hoping to please him, she used her own small hands in much the same manner, ringing his flat copper nipple, running her fingers through the stiff black hair on his chest, feeling the ridges of muscle that rippled across his stomach.

When he groaned, Caryn stopped, afraid she had done something wrong.

" 'Tis all right, *ma chere.* You have always been quick to learn." There was a rough note in his voice as he bent his head and kissed her. "I should have known you would quickly grasp these lessons, too."

She smiled to think she had pleased him, then gasped at the touch of his hand lower down, across the flat spot below her navel and into the patch of auburn curls at the juncture of her legs.

"Easy," he soothed when she stiffened. He kissed her again and she relaxed once more, letting the heat wash over her, letting the fires continue to burn. She bit her lip when his finger slipped inside her, traveling on the slickness of her desire, the heat of his touch like a cinder sparking flame. Instinctively she arched against his hand, urging him onward, then he lowered his head to her breast.

Caryn trembled all over, her body arching up from the

bed, pressing the firm flesh eagerly into his mouth. Warm male lips moved over the hardened crest, Ral's tongue flicking out, circling, laving, tasting. Caryn laced her fingers in his hair, her head spinning, her body afire with the pleasure he stirred.

When he kissed her again, lightning careened through her body and her breath came in tiny, fevered gasps. One hand cupped her bottom while a finger moved inside her. She was wet and slick, she knew, her body responding as Bretta had told her, preparing to accept her husband's hard male length.

"Mon Dieu," she heard him whisper, speaking softly in French as he rarely did, his body as tense as her own. "I have never seen a woman more ready to receive a man than you."

If the way she felt was any indication, she was certain he was right. She tingled from head to foot, her breasts throbbed, and so did the place between her legs. Ral slipped a second finger inside her and she moaned so loud he went still.

"I did not mean to hurt you."

"N-Nay, my lord, 'tis not pain I feel but something . . . something . . ." She wet her lips, but the right word still would not come.

Ral chuckled softly. "You will soon know what it is." He seemed content to leave it at that, returning instead to the pleasure he was giving, using his hands and his kisses, fueling the fires he built inside her.

When she felt so caught up she was certain she would burst into flame, he parted her legs with his knee and rose above her. She could feel his manroot, long and hard against her thigh, then it was probing for entrance, sliding into her slick damp heat. When Ral reached the final thin barrier that was proof of her virginity, he paused.

" 'Tis a rare and wondrous gift you give, and I do not take it lightly." He kissed her then, and Caryn arched upward. At the same moment, he thrust himself deep inside.

His mouth over hers caught her scream. She had known he would be big, had known he would fill her, but she had not expected the tearing, wrenching pain that seared through her body. She lay tense and unmoving beneath him, waiting for the next brutal thrust, the next jolt of agony to consume her. Instead, he held himself above her, strained and tense, propping himself on his elbows.

"I am sorry. I had hoped . . ." Perspiration dotted his brow and his jaw looked taut and rigid. It was obvious the price he paid for his concern.

" 'Tis all right, my lord."

"Ral," he said softly. "I would hear you say my name."

"Even now the pain fades . . . Ral."

He clenched his jaw and she felt a spasm pass through him with his effort at control.

"I cannot last much longer. I have wanted you for too long."

The words stirred something inside her, something womanly and passionate. She took a long deep breath and forced herself to relax. Ral must have felt the movement for he groaned, then he was easing himself out and thrusting himself back in, easing out and thrusting in. Where was the pain? she wondered, but only very dimly. Then she forgot the pain as if it had never existed, forgot all but the feel of him driving himself inside her, all but his long hard powerful thrusts.

Instinctively, her hips moved, arching upward, drawing him deeper, meeting each of his forceful strokes and urging him on.

"Sweet Christ," he whispered, his body growing rigid, her own responding, caught up in the pounding and the fury and the heat.

Then she was soaring, leaving the world behind her,

riding among the stars on a fiery chariot that raced off into a place of sweetness and light. Red bursts of sunlight, tiny pinpricks of pleasure consumed her. She cried out Ral's name as he drove himself on, felt him spilling his seed, and knew in that moment that nothing on this earth could ever be sweeter than this.

Chapter Twelve

Ral shifted onto his side, tightening his hold on the softly curved woman beside him. He saw that she slept and for a while so did he, a peaceful, dreamless sleep more restful than any he had known in weeks. When he awoke, he heard her crying.

"I have hurt you," he said, coming up on an elbow, worry slicing through him at what he might have done. "I feared that this would happen."

Caryn smiled at him through her tears. "You did not hurt me, Ral. 'Twas wondrous and beautiful—like riding a star to the moon."

"Why do you cry, then?"

"I was thinking of the people in the village. Because of me, they will not get their land."

He kissed her gently on the lips. " 'Tis all right, Cara. Your plan was not wholly successful. The Ferret and some of his men got away."

"You mean he escaped?"

He nodded.

"Truly?"

"Truly. But not for long. The next time I find him, 'tis bound to mean his head."

"I will help you," she vowed. "I will discover where he hides and I will—"

"You will do naught—do you hear? You have done enough already."

She fell back against the pillows with a sigh. " 'Tis not completely my fault, you know. Had you confided in me, this never would have happened."

He scowled. " 'Tis not a man's duty to confide in his wife."

"That may be so, but nevertheless, had you done so, the Ferret might now be yours."

He mulled that over in silence, then he sighed. "I will try to inform you of matters of import." Sliding an arm around her waist, he dragged her beneath him, pressing her down on the mattress. "And you will do naught without my approval—is that clear?"

She must have noticed his strengthening arousal for she laughed. "Must I have your approval for a kiss?"

Ral felt the pull of a smile. "Nay, vixen, that you may take whenever you wish."

So she did, sliding her arms around his neck and pulling his head down, pressing her soft lips to his and running her tongue inside his mouth. She was all soft curves and sweet woman scent and he wanted her with a passion that amazed him. His hand found her breast, pebbled her nipple, then moved lower, spreading the petals of her sex and finding her amazingly wet and ready.

God might have made her passage small and tight, but he had compensated by making her woman's place so damp, giving her a different means to accept him. He smiled at the thought, parted her legs with his knee, and slid himself inside with a single steady thrust.

"You are certain this does not hurt?"

"I am filled with you, that is all. 'Tis a most disturbing sensation."

Ral chuckled. "I hope so."

He moved within her and felt her heartbeat quicken beneath his hand. His own pulse beat fiercely, the blood

pumping swiftly through his veins. He forced himself to
go slow, reminding himself that she was new to this, for
all the quickness with which she learned. He kissed her
deeply as he cupped a breast, then lowered his head and
began to suckle her gently. Her nipple budded at the
touch of his tongue, and she trembled beneath him. Her
breast felt heavy and full against his palm, her skin ex-
quisitely smooth. His fingers moved along her body,
which tapered to a tiny waist, then flared to womanly
hips and a taut little round derriere.

His loins clenched as he stroked her there, and the
fire in his blood spread like flames through his body.
With a groan of defeat, the last of his control slipped
away, plunging him headlong into his lusty passions. He
moved faster, deeper, harder. Caryn moaned and
clutched his shoulders, her hips coming up to his, release breaking over her like a wave.

It triggered his own, and his seed spilled hotly inside
her, the sweetness consuming, cooling his blazing need,
if only for a time.

He smiled into the darkness. If ever he had doubted
that a woman her size could please him, he would not
doubt it again.

Caryn propped herself up in bed beside her sleeping
husband. She felt different this day, wiser in the ways of
the world, more feminine. More womanly. She wondered, did it show? Ral's eyes came open and she realized he wasn't asleep, but had been watching her from
beneath his heavy black lashes.

"What are you thinking?" he asked. "What has made
your lovely brows draw together so?"

Caryn tucked a strand of her thick auburn hair behind
an ear. "I would know, Ral, what will happen to the
people should you fail to get your land?"

Ral grimaced and sat up in bed, propping his massive
shoulders against the carved wooden headboard. The

first rays of dawn slanted in through the narrow slit of window. A chill pervaded the room, but it was warm beneath the furs atop the blankets.

"There is money still owed for the building of the keep. Once the crops are in, I must once more levy a burdensome tax. 'Twill leave the villeins with less than enough for the winter and little in the castle stores. I had hoped they could clear and plant new land this spring, but already 'tis too late. We can survive the winter—though 'tis bound to be a lean one. The following year, many of the villeins could starve."

Caryn shivered. "Is there no other land the king might grant?"

"None close by that would be suitable for planting—'tis all too steep and rocky."

"What of another *demesne* somewhere else?"

"The choice ones have all been claimed. Most of the others would require more money to rebuild than could be taken from them."

Caryn fell silent. When she felt Ral's weight leave the bed, she glanced up to see he had drawn on his tunic and now stood staring out the window.

"Had you married a woman of property," she said softly, "you would have all the land you need."

"I married you. That is all that matters."

"You could have married Eliana de Montreale. She has more wealth than—"

"What do you know of Eliana?" he asked, whirling to face her. His look was so fierce, she wished she could call back the words.

"Naught but that she was once your betrothed."

"Who told you?"

She wet her lips. "Her brother, Lord Stephen. He says she will soon come to visit."

"What else did he say?"

She hesitated only a moment. "That you dishonored her by refusing the marriage."

He grunted. "Who is he to speak of honor?"

"You cared naught for her then?"

"I cared for her—once. But even had I not, I would have married her if . . . things had been different."

"What things do you—"

"Enough of this! I will not discuss Eliana. Not here, not now—not ever!"

She forced herself not to glance away. "As you wish, my lord."

Ral's hard look softened and he crossed the room to the bed. "I do not mean to be harsh." He bent and kissed her lips. "Had last night been other than your first night of passion, I would take you again, make you forget your foolish questions." He placed her hand on the long hard ridge beneath his tunic. "Already I want you again."

Caryn felt the heat burning into her cheeks. "As you say, 'tis probably best we wait." She *was* a little sore, yet even as she said the words, her pulse had begun to quicken.

"Tomorrow will be soon enough for you to resume your wifely duties."

"Duties . . . ? It seems a strange word to describe the pleasures you have shown me."

He smiled at her with warmth. " 'Twould not surprise me, Cara, to discover your worth is far greater than that I would have received should I have married another."

As the morning progressed, they bathed and dressed, then returned downstairs. It was quiet in the hall, servants and knights alike waiting, it seemed, to see how fared the lord and his lady.

Though her cheeks were bright with color, Caryn smiled at them warmly and Ral squeezed her hand. He led her down the stairs and across the room to the dais for the midday meal, sitting down to a trencher of meat and a tankard of ale. Speaking in quiet tones, they smiled often and touched each other with an ease that hadn't been there before.

Ral spoke softly to Odo, and she guessed her husband explained about the bounty and that she had only meant to help them. Odo only frowned and walked away.

"Since we are well and truly wed," Ral said, returning his attention to her, "I would grant you a wish. Is there something special that you would like to do?"

Caryn brightened. "I would see my sister, Ral. It has been too long that I have been away. Gweneth will not remember that I am gone, but I remember, and I miss her more each day. I have thought of her much these past few weeks, and I would know how she fares."

"Your sister is welcome to live here, if that is your wish."

Caryn shook her head. "I would wish it, but Gweneth would not. She is happy at the convent. In the years she has lived there, she has found peace. I would not take it from her."

"Then I will take you to see her. We will leave at the end of the week."

In the meantime, they made love. Ofttimes with abandon, other times with tender loving care. Ral was a passionate, considerate lover who seemed to take great joy in the pleasure he brought her. The hours they spent together opened a beautiful new world for Caryn. A time of sensual awakenings, of a closeness unlike anything she had known.

When the day came to leave for the convent, she found herself torn between the excitement of seeing her sister, and missing the hours of passion she had enjoyed in her husband's bed. Thinking of those sweet moments, Caryn smiled as she dressed and made herself ready for the journey then hurriedly went downstairs.

It was an easy trip to the convent. Ral's men made camp outside the great stone building, while he and Caryn were led to a room upstairs. The space was narrow and airless, the cots far too small for Ral's big frame, yet when nightfall came, he slept with her nestled against him. He wanted her; she could see it in his eyes whenever he looked at her, but he did not take her. It was a place of God, and he seemed to sense that memories of her time there did not include him.

Gweneth was just as Caryn had left her, neatly groomed and smiling, her heavy black hair well-brushed and gleaming, hanging several inches below her waist. Caryn's friend, Sister Beatrice, seemed to have taken her place as Gweneth's protector, which in a way made Caryn sad. Still, she had a life of her own now and, so it seemed, did Gweneth.

"She is happy?" Caryn asked.

Sister Beatrice nodded. "She has always been so. And you know how the sisters love her. I think the light would go out of their lives were she to leave." The older girl watched her for a sign that this might happen, but Caryn only smiled.

"She belongs here. I will not take her."

Some of the tension left the thin girl's face. "And what of you, Caryn? Have you found where you belong?"

She glanced at the small, slightly fragile nun who had been her closest friend. "Mayhap, I have. I am not yet certain. But in truth it feels good to be returned home."

"I thought Ivesham lay in ruins."

"The house is gone, but the people in the village remain. Braxston Keep now sits atop the knoll. 'Tis filled with friendly faces from the past." She smiled. "Marta is there, and Richard. 'Tis not often that I feel alone."

"And your husband?" Beatrice asked softly and Caryn flushed.

"I am only just now a new bride, though the vows were spoken some time ago." Her cheeks flamed brighter. " 'Tis clear from what has occurred, that I was never meant for the life of a nun."

Sister Beatrice laughed, making her look less severe in her heavy black robes. "I do not think that was ever in question."

The following day, Ral spoke to Gweneth, and though the black-haired girl remembered naught of who he was or what had happened that day three years past, she greeted him warmly, smiling and offering him a crust of fresh-baked bread. He accepted it with a matching warm smile, but there was no hint of the longing Caryn had feared she would see in his eyes.

On the journey from Braxston Keep, she had tried to prepare herself should her husband still harbor feelings for Gweneth. That he clearly did not was apparent from the moment of their first meeting.

"She has the beauty and grace of a swan," he said. " 'Tis a shame what has happened, but as you said, 'twould seem she is content."

"Aye, my lord. I believe that she is."

"How did it happen?"

"We were traveling to visit my mother's people. Gweneth was ever a poor rider. The animal spooked and she fell off. She hit her head on a rock and for a time we did not think that she would live. When she awakened, she was as she is."

"As I said, 'tis a pity. But that she is happy is all that matters."

"She would have made a man a fine wife," Caryn said, watching him from beneath her lashes.

"A gentler man than I," he said. "I like my women with fire in their veins." He bent his head and kissed her, a lusty kiss that told her what he was thinking. Knowing it was she that Ral wanted and not her more beautiful sister, Caryn breathed a sigh of relief.

It was with a lighter heart and a fresh hope for the future that she said good-bye to Gweneth, and together with her husband and his men, left the convent to return to the castle.

* * *

Rain battered the cold gray stone of Braxston Keep, draughts of chilly air crept in, and the men moved restlessly about the hall. Richard worried that an argument might ensue, should the weather not break soon, but so far there had been only a few ruffled feathers.

The midday meal of mutton and rabbit stew had just ended, yet Lord Ral remained on the dais, speaking with Odo about an upcoming trip the red-haired knight would soon be making to France, about the Ferret and problems that might lie ahead. Richard left them there, intending to return to his duties, knowing he had much to do. Geoffrey stopped him at the edge of the dais, pointing his finger toward a messenger standing in the entry.

Richard followed Geoffrey there, curious and a little uneasy that something grave might be wrong. He greeted the man briefly and accepted the message, then returned to the great hall and headed straight for the platform.

"The king's messenger, my lord." Richard climbed the stairs, capturing the men's attention as he carried the wax-sealed missive to the table. "The man has declined to stay. He remains only long enough to be certain his message is delivered."

"Open it," Ral said.

Richard did as he was bade, scanning the text, his insides growing tighter with every word. "Trouble farther to the north, my lord. William asks that you and as many men as you can spare join him in the field outside Caanan. Even now he lays siege to Caanan Castle."

"Lord Arnaut. 'Twas thought for some time that he could not be trusted." The dark Norman's fist slammed down on the table. "Christ's blood, will this fighting never cease?"

Though the Lord Ral had never shirked his duty or tried to pay the scutage to keep from having to serve,

Richard knew how much he loathed the slaying of men in battle.

" 'Tis the way of men, it seems," Richard said. "Until they learn how bitter the price of war, they are only too willing to pay in blood for the chance at victory."

Lord Ral nodded. " 'Tis an unfortunate truth you speak." He sighed and glanced toward the stairs. "I trust you will keep things well in hand here."

"Of course, my lord." Following the line of the tall Norman's gaze, he smiled. "I believe she will miss you."

A corner of Ral's mouth curved up. It was obvious the notion pleased him. "I will make certain of it." Shoving back his chair, he left the dais, stopping to speak to Odo, who would relay his instructions to the men. Then he strode across the room and climbed the stairs.

Richard watched his ascent with a small grain of envy. Already Lady Caryn had come to care for him. Richard could see it in her eyes whenever she looked in her husband's direction. 'Twas something to consider, this taking of a bride. Even Odo had made mention of the finding of a woman, of a marriage and the raising of sons.

Richard frowned at the notion. 'Twould be unfair to a woman, should he take her to wife. He had too much to do and too few hours in a day to see it done. Then again, what did it matter? There had been no woman he had found appealing—save for an occasional moment of pleasure—and he had no time in which to seek one out.

Richard grumbled to himself then set the thought away. Crossing the hall, he headed toward the chamber where he worked on his ledgers. Lord Ral needed coin to repay his debt to the moneylenders. 'Twas his duty to see from whence it might come. Then there was the cleaning, which was long overdue, and the stores to see to, and the feast days which must be observed, and the gardening to begin, and—the list went on and on.

Yet he wasn't complaining. He was needed here at Braxston, and he had made the castle his home.

Returning to the heavy wooden table where the ledgers sat open, Richard sat down with a weary sigh and went back to work.

Ral had been gone three days when the boredom—and worry—and Caryn's newly altered status as Lord Ral's accepted wife sent her marching down the stairs.

"I would speak with you, Richard," she called out through his open chamber door.

"Of course, Lady Caryn." He rose from the seat behind his desk, stacked high with ledgers, documents, and petitions. "What is it, my lady?"

She sat down across from him in a high-backed chair fashioned of wood and leather. "Do you think the fighting will go well?"

Richard sat back down at his desk. "The king has strong forces behind him. Not only Lord Ral joins them, but Stephen de Montreale."

Still she was worried about him, more every day. She sighed. "I am tired of this weather."

"As am I," Richard said. He studied her a moment then carefully asked, "What is it, my lady? Is there something you need?"

Caryn forced herself to smile. " 'Tis simple, Richard. Now that I am Lord Ral's wife in truth, I would have you teach me the duties of chatelaine."

A sandy brown brow arched up. "But you hate such tasks. Since you were a child, you have gone out of your way to avoid household duties."

"That is true, and surely 'tis not a job I would choose, but now 'tis my place to see it done. I've plenty of time, and . . ." Soft heat crept into her cheeks.

"And . . . ?"

"And I would please my husband."

He still looked skeptical, his well-formed lips thinning into an uncertain line. "You are sure about this?"

"Am I not a rapid learner? You have known me long and well, Richard. I can read and write; I am tutored in Latin and French. I have learned how to grow corn and how to hunt. I know much of animals and plants, and I'm well-schooled in the care and handling of horses. There is naught I cannot learn, should I decide to accomplish the feat."

For the first time, Richard smiled. There were dimples in his cheeks, she noticed, but he worried so much that she had never seen them.

"What you say is true," he said. "You have always loved learning and have readily mastered your subjects. I will teach you what it is you need to know." He leaned forward on his desk. "God's truth, 'twould be a boon should you decide to take over the task."

They started later that day, Caryn changing into a faded brown linen tunic, braiding her hair, then coiling it into a knot at the nape of her neck.

"In simplest terms," Richard began, " 'tis the chatelaine's duty to see to the running of the hall. There is much to be done here at Braxston. 'Tis well past the time for a cleaning, the rushes must be changed, the walls need whitewashing, and there are keckies and wispies to make."

Keckies were lights made of flax soaked in tallow and stuffed in a hollow reed. Wispies were made of tallow-soaked straw. She had helped her mother make them once, and once she had made them with Marta. She smiled. In this, at least, she would not need his help.

" 'Twould serve the place well should we panel some of the walls," she added, glancing at the stark gray stone interior. "There is an artist in the village, a man named Morcai, who could paint a handsome picture upon the wood. And I saw tapestries in a storeroom. Ral must have brought them here from France."

Richard flushed. "I meant to see them hung, my lady, but there never seemed enough time."

"Do not apologize, Richard. I am the one who has been remiss. But I mean to change things."

He smiled, making him look far younger. It occurred to her he wasn't all that much older than she, yet he had always seemed so. "The tasks are many," he said, "but there are able servants to help you. Still, 'twill require your supervision and the hours will be long. Should you change your mind at any time, do not hesitate—"

"I will not change my mind, Richard."

And she did not.

From daybreak to dusk, Caryn worked beside the servants in the keep. At first, for all her effort, the changes remained obscure. Still, the cleaning kept her mind off her worry for Ral, and as the days turned into weeks the atmosphere in the hall began to change.

"You do your lord husband proud," Marta said, beaming at the tapestry they had just hung on the wall in the master's chamber. "Though 'twould not make him happy to learn how hard you have been working."

"I would have the place ready by the day of his return. Since we cannot know when that day is, I will continue to work as I have been."

Marta grunted. "As much as you have always loathed such tasks, 'tis certain you will eventually come to your senses."

Another week passed and then another. Trestle tables were repaired, linens bleached and mended, and men set to work carving platters and spoons, or plaiting osiers and reeds into baskets or weels for catching fish.

From morning till night, the great hall bustled with activity, involving nearly everyone in some task or other, all save Lynette, who rarely entered the keep. Now that it was well known that Lord Ral slept with his wife, the willowy blonde kept mostly to herself. Caryn wished the woman would leave, but there was no place for her to go, and clearly she had not given up hope of regaining Ral's attentions, a fact that Caryn refused to ponder, except in her chamber in the middle of the night.

Though she had lost a little weight with her efforts and there were smudges beneath her eyes, she continued her long days of labor, until the tasks she had set were finally complete. Which proved to be a boon, since a messenger arrived the following day, bringing word of the lord's return.

"The wardcorne has spotted his banner!" Caryn raced down the stairs to join Marta in the great hall. "Do I look all right? Mayhap I should change the amber tunic for the one of forest green."

Marta chuckled, her thin shoulders quaking, lines crinkling at the corners of her eyes. "The amber suits you, my pet, as does the style of your hair." Left unplaited but bound in a snood of woven amber silk shot with gold. "Lord Ral will be pleased."

Sweet God, she hoped so. She had prepared for weeks for this day, could hardly wait for the look of pleasure she was certain to see on his face when he saw what she had done to the castle.

From top to bottom, Braxston shown like the jewel it was, the soot now gone from the newly whitewashed walls, the tapestries hung, the rushes on the floor strewn with sweet fennel and sage.

She waited out in the bailey, along with the knights who had remained to guard the keep and the servants who waited with anticipation for the arrival of their lord. They watched in silence as the Dark Knight led his men across the drawbridge, traveling with just a small escort, the others remaining in Caanan with the king.

Ral wore his mail, which glinted in the sunlight, but no helmet, and he carried his red and black dragon shield. He must have freshened himself in the stream, for his face was clean-shaven and his hair still looked damp. Sunlight glistened blue-black on the thick wavy strands.

His eyes searched her out as he rode forward, held her fast and did not move away. He halted his huge black destrier in the middle of the bailey, swung a long muscular leg to the ground, and handed his reins to a page. His squire approached, and Ral knelt so the youth could remove his heavy mail and the dusty spurs on his feet, but his eyes remained fixed on Caryn.

In minutes the task was complete and he began to walk toward her. She expected him to pause along the way, to speak to Richard, or mayhap say a word to the priest. Instead he continued his long-legged strides, eating up the distance between them, until he reached the place before her. He flashed a roguish grin, slid a hand around her waist, and scooped her into his arms.

"Sweet Virgin, Ral! What do you?" He only chuckled, bent his dark head, and kissed her with fierce possession. When he ended the kiss, she was trembling, barely aware that he strode through the freshly oiled doors leading into the keep, crossed the great hall without noticing the immaculate linens on the table, and climbed the spotlessly scrubbed stone stairs.

"What of your men?" she asked as he carried her down the newly whitewashed passage. "Surely they are hungry and tired. Surely 'tis sustenance that you need."

"Aye, *ma chere,* that it is." But it didn't appear to be food that he spoke of. He kicked the door open with a booted foot, making a mark on the freshly polished surface, then slammed it closed with an elbow.

"I have thought of nothing but the taking of your sweet body these long weeks past."

He let go of her legs and she slid the length of him, finally coming to rest on her feet.

"I've been so worried," she said.

"The battle is over. The castle has been taken."

"Thank God." Already she could feel his hardened

shaft beneath his tunic, and the strength of his desire made her body grow flushed and damp. His mouth came down hard over hers and the world spun away, leaving her trembling and weak. She found herself gripping his shoulders, opening to the insistence of his tongue, willing his hands to her breasts.

It was almost as if he had heard her, for in seconds he was stripping off her tunic and the chainse she wore beneath, carrying her naked to the edge of the bed. He sat down with her in his lap, kissing her all the while, fumbling with the ties on his chausses and finally freeing himself.

"I have longed for this moment. I've thought of nothing but being inside you." He tore the spun gold snood from her head, drove his hands through the heavy mass, spreading it around her, then lifted her up, parted her legs, and positioned her so that she straddled his hard-muscled thighs.

Caryn clung to his neck and felt his hands on her bottom, cupping them, kneading them, setting her aflame. Shivers raced through her body and a fever roared through her blood. When he slid a finger inside her, Caryn gasped at the feel of it, felt her body tighten around it, then soften to allow him passage.

"As always, you are ready," he said with a voice gone rough. " 'Tis a miracle I thank God for." He kissed her long and deep. "Wrap your legs around me."

"But surely we cannot—"

"Trust me, *cherie,* and I will see us both well pleasured."

It was difficult to move, trembling as she was, but his waist was as lean as his hips, and with his hands to guide her, she soon had accomplished the feat.

His mouth took hers in a very thorough kiss, a hand massaging her breasts, her nipples tightening, aching, pressing feverishly into his palm. Then he was lifting her up and sliding inside her, impaling her to the hilt with a single deep thrust.

Waves of heat washed over her, rippling eddies that tore a whimper of desire from her throat. Her body trembled and flames seared the place between her legs. He was thrusting into her, gripping her and holding her immobile, lifting her and filling her, demanding she respond.

"Ral . . . sweet God . . . Ral." Caryn's head fell back, her hair trailing onto his powerful thighs. He took her mouth savagely, gripping her buttocks as he continued to plunge himself inside her. The world became blurry and distant, then it faded completely away. Fire engulfed her, and waves of mounting desire, until she finally succumbed to the mind-numbing pleasure. She was bathed in sweetness, awash against a blazing crimson sand. She cried out Ral's name as he spilled his seed, following her to that fiery distant shoreline, his movements at last beginning to slow.

Covered in a sheen of perspiration, his head slumped onto her shoulder, his thick black hair curling damply against her throat. Caryn smoothed it back from his face with trembling fingers, feeling the sculpted planes of his cheeks, the sensuous outline of his lips.

As she drifted back to earth, it occurred to her that in his haste, Ral had not bothered to remove his garments. She wanted him to, she realized. She wanted to feel his thick, hair-roughened chest and taut muscular buttocks, the flat washboard ridges of his stomach. She wanted him inside her again, with nothing whatever between them.

Sliding off his thighs, she knelt to remove his soft leather boots and one of his brows arched upward. Then he smiled his approval, correctly guessing her motives. Grabbing the top of his tunic, he jerked it over his head, bent to unlace his garters, but found Caryn's hands already there.

" 'Twould seem you have missed me, too," he said gruffly and her cheeks went even pinker than they were before.

"Aye, my lord, that is so."

"It pleases me—more than you know."

She started to tell him that she and the others had done a great deal more to please him, but already he was taking her mouth, lifting her up and settling her on top of the bed. Once more he was hard and throbbing against her thigh, and she was slick and ready to receive him. How many times they made love, she could not count. She only knew the sun had long faded and nightfall had come, that they slept for a time, woke and began to make love again.

Weariness claimed them sometime late in the night, drawing them into a deep and restful slumber. It was morning when she woke, turned to the place beside her —but found that Ral had gone.

Chapter Thirteen

Caryn dressed quickly and left to search the hall. Her body felt battered and bruised from their wild night of passion, yet she smiled, feeling happy and content.

She stopped at the top of the stairs. "Where is Ral?" she asked of Marta. "I was sleeping so soundly I did not hear him awaken."

"He is gone, my pet."

"Gone? Gone where?"

"He and the men, they have ridden from the castle. Richard saw they received a hearty meal, then they rode out for Caanan. Lord Ral must rejoin his men."

"But the battle is over—King William has won!"

"He said that you were sleeping so soundly he did not wish to awaken you. He said he will return as quickly as he can."

"But he cannot have gone—not after we went to so much trouble! Surely he made mention of the keep and all that we have done."

Marta made a rude sound in her throat.

"What is it? Why do you look that way?" Before the old woman could answer, Caryn whirled around, raced to the top of the stairs, and stared out into the great hall. In the room below, benches were overturned, several of them splintered and broken, and what few linens remained on the tables were stained with wine, spotted with grease, and littered with dried food and bread crumbs. So was the floor, though the hounds had made short work of most of it. Even now they growled at each other over a bone fallen into the rushes.

"I cannot believe it!"

"The men were in high spirits," Marta explained. "They celebrated their triumph and having a night back home."

"High spirits!" Caryn repeated. "Did they not notice the changes we had wrought, how clean was the hall, how spotless the linen? Did they not at least mention how well-prepared was the food?"

Marta shrugged. "Much was made over how tasty were the lampreys in galytyne. 'Twas a favored dish to be sure."

"That is it? They said nothing more? What of Lord Ral? Braxston Keep is his. Surely he noticed the paneling on the walls which has helped to lessen the draughts, the tapestries hung to provide more warmth. Surely he noticed there were fewer musty smells."

"I am afraid he did not say."

"Did he also say nothing of Morcai's beautiful paintings?"

"Nay, my pet."

Caryn thought of the endless, backbreaking hours she had spent preparing the hall. She thought of Leofric and Bretta, of Marta and a dozen others who had worked bent over till their backs were aching and their knees were raw. She thought of dropping into bed in exhaustion only to rise at dawn and start all over again.

"So Lord Ral does not notice." She planted her hands on her hips and surveyed the wreckage in the hall. "Upon his return, he will notice, I vow." She turned to face Marta. " 'Twill be a sight he will never forget!"

* * *

"I beg of you, Lady Caryn. You must end this madness before Lord Ral's return." Richard's sandy brows nearly touched in the middle of his forehead.

"As I have told you, Richard, at least a dozen times, naught will be done but that which is necessary for our own comfort."

"Richard is right, my lady." Geoffrey had also spent hours trying to dissuade her. "You will do naught but earn yourself a beating."

"Mayhap I will. At least Ral will take notice. 'Tis certain he will no longer take me for granted."

For weeks they'd done only the meagerest amount of labor in the great hall, even less in the yard out in the bailey. Richard and Geoffrey had argued against the course she had taken, certain the lord's wrath would fall heavily upon them all. Marta had wrung her aged hands and prayed she would come to her senses. Even the servants had grown skittish and worried, though after their backbreaking efforts, Caryn thought that secretly they might applaud her.

"At least let us clean out the fire pit and replace the rushes," Richard said. "The floors are littered with bones and the droppings of the hawks brought into the hall. And it smells of the hounds you have allowed to sleep indoors."

"We must see the foodstores refilled," Marta begged. "Lord Ral and his men will expect a hearty meal upon their arrival." Less than a week away.

"They received a hearty meal when last they were here. They gave naught of thanks for our labors."

"The linens are badly stained," Richard said, "all but those on the tables we have been using. Let us bleach them, make them at least somewhat presentable."

"Far from it, Richard. On the day of Lord Ral's return, you will see the tables set with the dirtiest linen you can find. There will be no meal prepared and nothing in the larder. The hounds will roam the hall and no fire will be built in the fire pit. Mayhap the next time Lord Ral will not be so eager to trod upon those who work so hard to please him."

"My lady, please—" Geoffrey began, but Caryn's determined glance cut him off.

"And leave off the weeding in the garden, the shoveling of manure from the stables, and the cleaning of the pigpen." She smiled. "In fact, you may tell the servants that until the end of the week, they are to rest and refresh themselves." Caryn smiled with smug satisfaction. With a determined lift of her chin, she turned and walked away.

Her three friends stared after her in silence, knowing full well she was determined to ignore their warnings, though many of their dire predictions would certainly come to pass. She was also fairly certain that the others were facing no danger. Until Ral's return, the lady of the castle was in charge. Her word was law and her husband would know it.

The price of her folly would be hers alone to bear.

Caryn shivered to think of the powerful dark Norman in one of his towering rages. Then she straightened her spine. The battle they were about to wage might be fearsome, but it was one she intended to win.

Eager to be returned to Braxston Keep and, if he were honest, the welcoming arms of his pretty little wife, Ral pushed his men somewhat harder than he should have. The march from Caanan took less than four days and though they were weary, they didn't complain. The men looked forward to hearth and home nearly as much as he did.

"Is it your lands that draw you," Odo asked, riding up beside him, "or thoughts of your little Saxon maid?"

"Do not plague me, Odo. That I crave a tumble with the lusty little wench should come as no surprise. I've been weeks without the comfort of a woman."

"There were wenches in the village at Caanan. You could have had any that you wanted."

"I've yet to have my fill of the one who awaits me at home."

"Mayhap you never will."

Ral grunted. "Do not be a fool."

"You are saying the time will come when you will once more seek out Lynette or some other?"

"I will never fall victim to the power of a woman. You more than any should know me better than that." He thought of Eliana, of how she had betrayed him, and knew Odo's thoughts ran much the same.

The red-haired knight flashed a slightly bitter smile. "I am glad to hear it. It can only come to no good should you give your heart completely."

"Especially to a Saxon. That is what you were thinking, was it not?"

Odo did not answer. But then he did not need to.

"You do not like her, do you?"

"She is a Saxon. I lost a father and a brother to a filthy Saxon traitor. 'Tis a lesson that is bound to make a man wary. But as you say, she is a lusty little baggage. I cannot blame you for wanting to bed her."

Ral clamped hard on his jaw. He and Odo were lifelong friends, yet when he spoke that way of Caryn, it was all Ral could do to keep from dragging him down from his horse and pounding him into the dirt.

It was an odd sensation, one he did not completely understand. Still, he was not concerned. 'Twas true that he desired her, and that her company more than pleased him. But she was only a woman and he had known many. Odds were, he would know many more.

"Do you see it yet, my lord?" That from Aubrey, Ral's squire.

"Braxston lies just around the bend," he said. "If you glance to where the sun peeks through those trees, you can see a corner of the outer wall."

Aubrey craned his neck until he saw the distant gray stone, then settled back in his saddle and smiled. "I will be glad to be home, my lord."

A corner of Ral's mouth curved up. "Aye." He could easily imagine the welcome he would receive: his knights and squires dressed in their finest and waiting in the bailey to greet him, the sumptuous feast served by eager servants, the endless goblets of wine, the laughter and conversation.

Most of all, he could imagine his wife's small arms around his neck, her soft sweet kisses, her building passions, then the tightness of her body as she surrounded his hardness and took the heavy length of him inside her.

Ral's loins clenched at the thought and he worked to stifle a groan.

"Why hasn't the drawbridge been lowered?" Aubrey asked as they drew near the entrance to the castle.

"I do not know. 'Tis certain they received my message." Ral rode forward, called out to the guard at the top of the wall, and the drawbridge was lowered. He led his men across the moat and into the bailey, but stopped dead in his tracks at the sight that met his eyes.

What had once been the neatly ordered yard in front of the stables was now littered with straw and smelled of manure. There were overturned barrels and baskets, and pigs rooted among what appeared to be an upended barrel of garbage. In front of the grainery, hounds had dug great holes and even now fought each other to uncover a half-buried bone.

Ral's astonished gaze flew to the place in front of the stairs leading up to the keep where his vassals would be waiting. If he had expected a glittering welcome from his wife, men-at-arms, and servants, the one he received was as tarnished as a fire-smoked pewter mug.

His men were there, milling nervously about, casting him sheepish, worried glances. His servants were there, their garments unkempt and unwashed, their faces pale and taut. And his wife was there, standing next to Richard at the bottom of the stairs. At least he thought it was his wife—in truth, he wasn't so sure.

He drew rein on his horse, swung himself down, and began striding toward her. The woman up ahead—a small, unkempt creature with dirty auburn hair and a soot-smudged face—saw him and started to smile. She wore a ragged brown tunic, grease-stained and torn in several places, and hadn't bothered with shoes.

"What goes on here?" Ral bellowed, coming to a halt before her, his hands balled tightly into fists.

Caryn merely smiled. "Welcome home, my lord. 'Tis good to have you returned."

Ral glanced around the bailey, taking in the grunting pigs and rotting mounds of garbage, thinking he was certain to awaken at any moment from this terrible, hellish dream.

"You will tell me what has happened," he commanded, keeping his voice as even as he could.

"Naught has happened, my lord. Surely you can see that for yourself."

He worked a muscle in his jaw and then strode past her, taking the stairs two at a time up into the keep, not bothering to close the heavy oaken door.

Caryn followed him in, noting with satisfaction the stunned look on his face as he registered the awful condition of the hall. His neck was red and his mouth had thinned into a furious line. Behind her, Richard and Geoffrey and a number of the men walked into the hall just as Ral turned to face her.

"Why?" he asked with soft menace. "Why have you done this?"

She pretended to look perplexed. "But I have done nothing, my lord. 'Twould seem that is clear."

He took several angry strides in her direction, gripped the top of her arms and dragged her up on her toes.

"You will tell me what this is about. You will explain to me what you have done and why you have done it."

He glanced once more around the hall, noting the refuse on the floors and the unpleasant smell drifting up from the rushes. "Then I will humiliate you as you have done me. I will drag up on the dais in front of the servants and the men, toss up your skirts, and beat you within an inch of your life."

He let her go, stepped back and eyed her with a look of fury that said he meant every word.

Caryn wet her lips. She had known the risks before she started; she wasn't about to back down.

"I am surprised you are displeased, my lord. In fact, I am surprised that you bothered to notice. 'Tis certain you noticed naught of our labors the last time you came home, though all in the castle worked from dawn till dusk to try and please you. Since you cared naught for what we did before, I did not believe you would notice when we did nothing."

Ral's thick black brows drew together in a frown. "The last time I was home, Braxston Keep shone like it never has before."

Caryn's own brow arched up. "You are telling me you saw the work we had done?"

"Of course, I saw it. 'Twould have taken weeks of labor to accomplish such a feat. 'Twas a place a man could be proud of."

"Then why did you not say so? Why did you allow your men to destroy our efforts? Why did you stride in here and take your pleasure then ride away without so much as a 'by your leave'?"

For the first time, Ral looked uneasy. "I did not think much about it. 'Twas selfish, I suppose . . . and thoughtless. I had much on my mind . . . the men back at Caanan, Lord Arnaut, and the king."

"Do you have any idea how much I loath such duties? How much I would rather have been out riding, or visit-

ing the people in the village?'' That was the truth,
though she had discovered her accomplishments could
be surprisingly rewarding. So much so, it had taken a
will of iron not to caste aside her vow of retribution and
set the castle in order again.

He was looking at her strangely. "If you loathed the
task so much then why did you do it?"

Caryn felt the heat rising into her cheeks. She wondered if Ral could see it beneath the smudges of grease.
"Because I wished to please you."

He eyed her cautiously. "And today?"

Caryn straightened her shoulders and her chin came
up. "I would be certain you understand how hard your
people work to please their lord. What better way to
learn than by comparison?"

Ral glanced once more around the hall, and Caryn
held her breath. He surveyed every corner, saw the
beautiful paintings and the tapestries carefully hung,
then saw the barren hearth and dirty linens. The vile
odor of the rushes drifted up, no longer sweetly scented
with dried flowers and herbs.

A corner of his mouth curved up. Lines crinkled at
the corners of his eyes, then Caryn caught a flash of
strong white teeth. The smile became a grin, the grin a
chuckle of laughter that burst into a roar. His hand
slammed down on the table and he laughed even
harder. Behind him Richard chuckled, then Odo, then
Geoffrey. Hugh and Lambert started to guffaw. Aubrey
broke into peals of laughter, and Leo dropped his hand
from his mouth, allowing his giggles to bubble forth.

Chaos broke out in the hall, Bretta laughing, poking
Odo in the ribs. Even Marta chuckled, more with relief,
Caryn guessed, than with humor.

"You are lucky, *ma petite*"—Ral wiped tears of laughter from his eyes—"that I did not wring your lovely little
neck."

Caryn smiled. " 'Twas not for my neck that I feared, my lord."

His mouth curved up. "I presume that you will set things. aright, now that you have made your point."

"Already the servants work to freshen the hall." They had been given instructions beforehand. Even now they labored stripping off the soiled linens and carting out the rushes. The smell of simmering meat had begun to drift in from the kitchen. "By the end of the week, 'twill seem only a very bad dream."

He lifted her chin with his hand. "And what of our chamber? Does it also resemble a very bad dream?"

The flush in her cheeks grew deeper. "Nay, my lord. The rest of the keep has not suffered so. And I held every hope that our problems would be resolved before we retired to our bed."

Ral chuckled softly. "How is it that instead of anger, I find that I am amused. You ever amaze me, little wife."

"And I, my lord husband, find I am more than pleased to see you. If you will allow me to bathe and change, I will give you a proper welcome home."

"Mayhap I will bathe you myself. That way I may be certain the task is properly done."

"Mayhap you should," she teased. "But only if you will let me see you equally well tended."

Ral's eyes swept down her body, his glance both intimate and hungry. Caryn took his hand and he laced his fingers with hers. As the servants worked feverishly to prepare the hall, she led him up the stairs.

Ral awakened well before dawn, uneasy and out of sorts, though his body felt well-sated. Easing himself from his sleeping wife's side, he dressed and returned downstairs. Already the hall had regained some semblance of order. But today instead of a smile, the sight of it made him frown.

It had been images of the hall in disarray and what

had happened there with Caryn that had given him pause this morn and forced him from the comfort of his bed. He kept thinking of the way she had dodged his anger, the way she had charmed him and bent him so easily to her will.

Ral's jaw tightened as he descended the steep stone stairs. No woman he had ever known had dared to gainsay him as his wife had—and she had done so on more than one occasion. He should have punished her for the scene she had caused, justified or no, yet her bravado had only amused him. Just as her passionate lovemaking last eventide had pleased him.

Ral crossed the great hall amidst the snores of sleeping men and headed outside to the bailey. He roused a squire in the stables and ordered his sorrel stallion made ready, then walked to the mews and lifted the great hawk, Caesar, onto a leather-gloved wrist.

"We hunt today, my friend," he said softly. " 'Twill give me the chance I need to think." He rarely rode out on his own. There was danger in the woods, especially for the lord of the castle. And without him, there was danger for his people. Still, today he would risk it. He needed time away from Caryn, time to understand these feelings she stirred and begin to overcome them.

It was a decision he had made sometime in the night, after they had made love and he had held her with such fierce possession. It would not have alarmed him, had she merely been another of his vassals, someone who belonged to him.

What bothered him was this feeling that he also belonged to her.

Ral crossed the drawbridge and rode off into the forest, enjoying the coolness of the shadows and the sound of singing birds. When he came to the meadow, he drew rein on his horse and looked around him. Lifting the small leather hood that covered the hawk's perceptive eyes, he set the great bird free.

Upward, upward it flew, winging its way toward the heavens, yet he knew the bird would return, drawn by some unseen force that existed between them. He had tamed the hawk and now it was his captive. If he did not learn to guard his emotions, he would find himself a captive of Caryn.

Ral watched the hawk spot its prey and begin its descent into the meadow for the kill. For this brief time the bird was in control of its destiny, yet in minutes it would return to his wrist and succumb once more to a life of serving its master.

Ral vowed as he never had before, that he would not succumb to that same fate with Caryn.

"All appears to be in readiness. 'Twill be a fine feast to properly welcome our lord home." Caryn smiled at Richard. Since the day of Ral's return, they had planned this eve. Her husband and his men had received little of their due on the day of their arrival; this night they would celebrate their homecoming at last.

"I believe your husband will be pleased," Richard said.

She and Richard had planned the festivities and worked to set the hall back in order. The night of Ral's return, he had discussed his wife's duties as *chatelaine* and agreed on a compromise. She would see the hall well kept, but do so within limits that would leave time for herself. There was no need, he said, to work from dawn till dusk.

It was a compromise that suited Caryn well, giving her the chance to visit her friends in the village or go for a ride in the woods. Still, she found herself strangely pleased when her woman's tasks were finished and the hall once more well cared for.

"Aye, 'twill be a proper welcome," Caryn said. "But 'twould be far more pleasant should we enjoy it without the company of de Montreale and his men." Lord Stephen had sent word of his arrival. He and his entourage, his personal retainers, mounted knights, and men-at-arms, would be there before the setting of the sun.

"He travels with the king's tax collector. There is little we can do save welcome them with open arms."

"And open coffers. 'Twill increase the burden on the people of the village. Lord Ral already worries what may happen to them next winter."

" 'Tis only King William's due. 'Tis not overly harsh, only that Braxston still bears the cost of building the keep. 'Tis hardly a burden at all for Lord Stephen."

" 'Twould be no burden for Lord Ral had he married Malvern's sister." Caryn flashed Richard a troubled glance. "You know she travels with them."

"Aye."

"How will Ral greet her?"

Richard shook his head. "I know only that they were once betrothed. 'Tis in the past, I am sure, Lady Caryn. You are Lord Ral's wife, not Lady Eliana."

Caryn might be his wife, but she knew little of his feelings. And love had never been mentioned. A shiver passed down her spine. Richard knew naught of the woman from Ral's past. Caryn wished to God he did. For the past few days, Ral had been brooding and distant. Since his return from Caanan, other than the passionate hours they spent in bed, he seemed to avoid her.

Caryn wasn't certain of the cause, but she feared it had something to do with the arrival of Lord Stephen's sister.

"The troubadours will soon be here," she told Richard, determined to keep her mind off Ral and concentrate on the feasting ahead. " 'Tis said they are very entertaining."

"And we've musicians and tumblers—'twill be a night to remember."

She had no doubt of that. Her only doubt lay in how Ral would deal with the woman who had been his betrothed. He had said he had once held feelings for her. If so, why had he refused the marriage?

What feelings did he carry for her still?

Hours into the feasting, Caryn still did not know. Since they had entered the great hall, Ral had been distant and brooding, silent and withdrawn. Lord Stephen and his sister had arrived with Francois de Balmain, the king's tax collector, who now sat beside them on the dais. Caryn had dressed carefully, choosing a deep ruby tunic over a white silk chainse, while Ral wore one of sapphire embroidered with threads of gold.

He was polite to Caryn, as he was to his guests, but his eyes held little warmth. He smiled but there was something odd in his manner, something that dulled the pleasure she should have felt in the evening she had so carefully planned.

Another time she would have been pleased with the lavish meal—the peacock dressed in its own iridescent plummage, the mushroom-stuffed boar, the partridge and plover and herring, the fresh garden vegetables, dried fruit, nuts, and figs. She would have been caught up in the music of lute and zither, of flute and pipe and horn.

The troubadours were as talented as she had been told, entertaining the men with *chansons de geste,* tales of valor and chivalry. Mostly they sang of Charlemagne and his battles with the Basque, of Roland and Oliver, two of his most trusted friends. The tale said Roland was fierce, but Oliver was wise in the war with the Saracens.

Then there was the tale they told of the Dark Knight, himself. Of Raolfe de Gere, a warrior so relentless in battle he was finally given the name. They sang of his courage, of his might against the Saxons on Senlac field, of how Ral had taken the thrust of a saber to save the life of the king.

Though Caryn's people had been defeated, the tale of her husband's fierce bravery filled her with pride and love. *Love.* Aye, 'twas exactly what it was. She'd been a fool not to see it. And now that she did, she yearned for Ral to feel the same.

Instead he remained withdrawn, glancing too often at Eliana, frowning as if her presence somehow plagued him yet drew his reluctant regard. She was a beautiful woman, Caryn saw with more than a little trepidation. Black-haired and blue-eyed, with skin as fair as Lord Stephen's.

And her features were much the same, fine-boned and clearly defined, with a straight nose not as pointed as her brother's. She was tall and well-proportioned, with high, full breasts and ripe ruby lips. When she laughed, the sound drifted musically across the hall, catching nearly every man's attention.

"She is lovely," Caryn said to Ral as they shared a trencher of meat.

"Rest assured her beauty is less than skin deep."

"Lord Stephen seems to find her amusing."

Ral's gaze swept the pair who sat at the far end of the table. "Stephen has been charmed by her since he was a boy."

"Which of them is the elder?"

"Eliana, but only by a summer. 'Tis not her age but her woman's ways that give her power over Malvern. 'Tis possible she is the only person on earth with the talent to wield it."

Caryn heard Lord Stephen's laughter at something his sister had said. His face looked flushed, his eyes bright, and his smile was warmer than any he had ever bestowed. When Caryn glanced at Ral, she saw that he was frowning.

"By God's blood, the woman has the power of a sorceress. She has outlived one husband. I pity the next poor fool who weds her." He pushed back from the table and turned his attention toward Francois de Balmain, the king's tax collector.

The graying man spoke to him in whispered, furtive tones and pointed toward a woman named Tayte, who traveled as his leman. He laughed crudely and Ral laughed with him. Then the two of them left the dais and strode off among the men drinking and gaming in the hall.

Caryn watched them go, feeling a knot in the pit of her stomach. Ral spoke harshly of the Lady Eliana, yet since her arrival, his manner had grown even more withdrawn. He seemed different this eve, aloof from her as he never had been before. She saw the way his eyes ran over de Balmain's leman, a winsome woman with long nut-brown hair. He was blatantly admiring her curves, smiling and laughing at something she said.

A few moments later, he stood beside Odo, who also seemed amused by the tax collector's whore. They laughed together, refilled their goblets and crossed to the fire pit. When Tayte moved away on Francois's arm, Caryn breathed a sigh of relief.

Then Lynette strolled up beside Ral. They began to speak in whispers, and Caryn's stomach grew taut once more.

Sweet God, what goes on? She had never seen him this way, not even before they were married. 'Twas as if she were not there, as if he purposely ignored her. It made her hands tremble and her throat close up. When he left Lynette and crossed the hall to Richard, relief swept over her like a wave.

Do not be a fool, she chided, forcing down her fears. *Ral is your husband now.* She thought of the moments she had spent in his arms, the gentle way he had held her, the passion they had shared. *'Tis only that he chafes at Malvern's presence, and that of the sister. 'Twill be as it was, the moment they are gone.*

Confident once more, Caryn played her role as lady with a smile for one and all. Still, as the evening wore on, she saw little of her husband and finally she grew weary. Eliana had retired and so had Lord Stephen. She sought Ral out and found him near the stairs.

"I would retire, my lord. Most of our guests have already done so. 'Tis certain I will not be missed by the few who yet remain."

Ral merely nodded.

"Will you be long, my lord?"

"I am not certain. 'Tis best you do not wait up."

For a moment she felt uneasy, then he smiled at her, making her insides flutter, and her worry slid away.

"Good night, my lord," but already he was deep in conversation. Walking toward the stairs, Caryn glanced around for Lynette, saw that she was gone from the hall, and gave in to a feeling of relief.

Chapter Fourteen

"Marta, have you seen Lord Ral?" Caryn dressed quickly, though the sun was barely up, carefully choosing a pretty apple green tunic over a soft yellow chainse.

The old woman turned in her direction. Aging, spotted hands went up to Caryn's hair, smoothing it away from her face. "He will return soon, you must not worry, my pet."

The look of concern on Marta's face spiraled Caryn's unease higher. "He did not sleep here last eve. He must have fallen asleep in the solar."

" 'Tis certain that is so," Marta said, but her worried eyes darted away and Caryn's stomach turned over.

"Tell me, Marta. You know all that takes place in the castle. If you know something of my husband, you must tell me."

" 'Tis not my place to carry tales."

"Please," Caryn whispered, clutching the old woman's hand.

Marta's thin shoulders sagged as though she carried some great burden. She wrung her hands and made a sighing sound of despair.

"Marta?"

"I had thought that he was different, that he would not hurt you. I had wrongly believed . . ."

"Tell me!"

"Your husband has returned to his leman."

"No! I do not believe it! Ral would not do such a thing."

"It is the way of men. I had hoped that Lord Ral was different."

"He is different," Caryn said. "He is brave and strong . . . he is gentle." Even as she said the words, a sob caught in her throat. She swayed toward Marta, her eyes beginning to tear, then she whirled toward the door. Her hair still unbound, Caryn lifted her bright green skirts and raced from the room, Marta's thin voice calling out behind her.

Her heart racing wildly, her chest taut with fear, she ran down the stairs past a score of sleeping men. Jerking open the heavy oaken door that led out to the bailey, she ran barefoot down to the muddy yard.

"Come back!" Marta called from the doorway. "You must not do this!" But Caryn only ran faster.

Breathing hard, heedless of the numbing cold biting into her feet, she raced across the bailey to the building next to the stable. Mounting the stairs on trembling legs, she climbed to the room that served as Lynette's sleeping quarters. She grabbed the curtain and jerked it open, then stood frozen in the entry.

Her husband lay sprawled on the bed, a blanket bunched around his lean hips, his massive chest bare, his jaw dark and rough from his night's growth of beard. Lynette lay beside him, her head on his arm, her long blond hair wrapped like talons around his neck.

A whimper caught in Caryn's throat. For a moment she stood transfixed, her heart pounding, her vision blurred, hot tears spilling down her cheeks. She tried to swallow but her throat was too tight, the ache in her chest more painful than any she had ever known. Still, she did not move. Not until her husband stirred, his hand unconsciously brushing Lynette's heavy breasts. He opened his eyes and fixed them on her face.

"Caryn . . ." The word came out on a harsh breath of air.

A sob escaped as her gaze met his and her fingers came up to her trembling lips. She wanted to scream out her anguish. She wanted to collapse on the floor, to pound her fists and cry until she had no more tears. Instead she whirled away from the soul-crushing sight and ran down the stairs, her long hair whipping out behind her.

"Christ's blood," Ral swore, freeing himself from the trap of Lynette's long blond hair, swinging his legs to the floor and reaching for his tunic. He pulled on his chausses and fastened his garters, finding the task more difficult than it should have been, since his hands shook so fiercely.

"Damn." He had never meant for this to happen, never dreamed she would follow him out to the bailey.

He never imagined the look on her face would practically tear him in two.

He glanced at the woman still asleep in the bed. He had taken her quickly, feeling only the briefest moment of pleasure. He had done it with a purpose and a good deal of forethought, determined that in doing so, he would somehow be free of Caryn.

But he didn't feel free, he felt wretched.

And more alone than he had ever felt before.

He came out of the room in long, ground-eating strides, determined to seek out his wife and explain . . .

Explain what? he asked himself, jerking to a halt in front of the stables. That he had done what any lusty man worth his salt would do? That he had done what was his right as lord?

By Christ, he owed her no explanation. He had only done exactly what he had set out to do.

Ral set his jaw and forced his eyes away from the door leading into the keep. This was what he wanted, wasn't it? He had lessened the power his little wife held. He had reclaimed his manhood.

He clenched his fist and felt the slow, dull throbbing of his heart. His chest felt leaden, his throat had closed up, and a slow fire burned in his belly. He could still see his wife's stricken face, the tears in her big brown eyes, and the trail of wetness down her cheeks. He had seen all too clearly the pain she had felt when she had found him in another woman's bed.

If only she hadn't come into the bailey. If only she hadn't seen them. If only she hadn't been so naive as to think he would never want another.

He scoffed at that. He hadn't wanted Lynette, or Tayte, or even Eliana. He had wanted Caryn. He had pretended she lay beneath him, even as he took his whore.

God's wounds, he'd had to do it. He'd had to protect himself. He knew only too well what could happen when a man lost his heart to a woman. He had only to remember the way he had felt when he'd discovered Eliana with her brother. When he had realized how easily he had been duped. When he had uncovered her intention to marry him and see him play the fool.

It was the guilt that was unexpected. And the gut-wrenching pain. Who would have believed the anguish he had caused Caryn would take an ever greater toll on himself?

Caryn cried until she had no more tears, refusing entrance to her room even to Marta. Her throat ached and her eyes burned. She felt numb inside, her heart bruised and broken.

She had loved him so.

And foolishly she had believed he would come to love her.

Sweet God, she thought, *what a naive fool I have been.* She should have known better. He was a man like any other. Like Odo or Francois de Balmain. Not much different from Stephen de Montreale. Even her father had taken other women. She should have been prepared.

By late afternoon, she felt drained and exhausted, her heart heavy and her mind dull. She had missed the midday meal, knowing that her guests would remark on her absence, knowing Lynette would gloat and make certain the others knew the cause. The afternoon passed and yet she remained in her room, pretending illness, still unable to face them.

It wasn't till well after dusk that her Saxon pride resurfaced.

The tall dark Norman might still be her husband, but after what he had done, he no longer owned her heart. She might have been naive, might have been foolish enough to love him, but she would grant him that love no more. She would show him, show them all that she did not care, that if his choice was his leman, then so be it. She would hold her head high and make her Saxon kinfolk proud.

Caryn dressed with great care for the evening meal, using cool cloths to bathe her tear-stained cheeks, finally able to make herself presentable. With guests still in the hall, the troubadours and musicians had remained, the jesters and the jugglers. She would watch them with interest this eve, pray they made her laugh and smile. She would show her husband that he could no longer hurt her.

That she no longer cared.

When Marta knocked, she stood ready, pulling open the door with a pasted-on smile, her auburn hair brushed and gleaming within its silken snood.

Marta nodded her approval. "I had hoped you would not let him defeat you."

"He has defeated himself."

Marta smiled. "There is time to spare before the meal. Lord Ral was late in his return from the hunt."

"Where is he now?" Caryn asked, her voice carefully controlled.

"In the solar. He bathes, as does Lord Stephen and Francois de Balmain. When they are finished they will go down to supper."

Caryn nodded. "I will walk for a time." It would help ease her tension, and she had grown anxious to be away from her chamber. Marta raised a hand to her cheek but said nothing more. Caryn walked past her, heading down the corridor toward the great hall. When she reached the top of the stairs, she paused, seeing that Lynette sat by the fire pit.

Though she tried to will it not to, her bottom lip trembled and tears stung her eyes. Turning she walked back the way she had come, passing her quarters and continuing along the passage until she reached the stairs at the opposite end. These led upward, out onto the parapet, a narrow spot used by archers to protect the keep during siege.

Standing outside the tower, she leaned back against the cold gray stone. A stiff wind blew up along the walls, and made a funny keening through the machicolation, where arrows could be rained on the ground below. It was chilly, though Caryn hardly noticed. She welcomed the breeze to help clear her heart and soul.

She had been there only moments when she heard the latch being lifted on the door. She turned as a young man dressed in the black and white suit of a jester, his face painted in colors to match, stepped through the opening. He jumped when he saw that he wasn't alone.

"I am sorry, lady. I did not know that you were here." His black pointed cap tilted forward, jingling the bell at the end. Around his neck another set of bells made a light jingling sound when he moved.

"How did you know of this place?"

"I discovered it last eve after the feasting. There is a place such as this in most keeps. I like the quiet in such places."

"As do I," Caryn said. There was something about the boy, something of wisdom in his sparkling green eyes and rough yet slightly lilting voice. It made him seem older than his years.

"You look beautiful this eve," he said, "yet I sense that you are sad." He smiled at her, then did a quick little dance, making the bells ring. " 'Tis my job to see that you are happy."

Caryn smiled faintly. "Are you never sad, jester?"

"Aye, lady. There are times I am lonesome for my home, for friends and family I may never see again. But I have face paint to hide my sadness."

"And I have only my strength of will."

The jester reached out and took her hand, giving it a gentle squeeze. Caryn noticed how soft and supple was his skin.

"But strength is something you have a great deal of, I vow." He had finely etched features, his handsome face almost pretty were it not for a pair of small protruding ears. "And there is always tomorrow. Who knows what the future may bring?"

"Who, indeed?" Caryn said, forcing herself to smile. But there was little besides bleakness in the future she foresaw. She might have said that to the jester, since he was a stranger and seemed so willing to listen, but when she turned he was gone.

Caryn's thoughts lingered for a time on the jester, on the youth's soft hands and bright smile, but there was her husband to face in the hall below. By now he would be seated on the dais. So far he had not sent for her and she expected that he would not. He was giving her time to accept what another wife would have known from the start—that a marriage was made for naught but heirs. That a husband took his pleasure, but gave nothing of himself in return.

She needed no more time to accept that. The lesson had been most bitterly taught.

At the top of the stairs she forced a smile. She was dressed as a lady, not one so beautiful as Lynette or Eliana, but pretty enough to turn the heads of the men as she moved between the heavily laden trestle tables. Her husband's gaze was among them, she saw to her surprise. The expression in his blue-gray eyes hit her with the force of a blow, and it took an extra effort to keep her legs moving.

Caryn kept her chin held high and her shoulders squared, smiling to man and maid as she passed, pausing to speak a word here and there. When she reached the dais, Ral stood up and waited while she took her chair.

"I wondered would you join us." There was an odd edge to his voice. "Your serving woman told us you were ill." The look that passed between them said he knew it was not so, that he was surprised she had come, and that he wasn't all that happy about it.

Mayhap he had not wanted to face her any more than she had wanted to face him.

"I hope you are feeling better," said Lord Stephen. "My sister missed your company."

"I am fine now. 'Twas only a passing weakness." She flashed her husband a pointed glance. "I doubt I shall be troubled again."

Beside her Ral frowned.

"Did you enjoy the hunt?" she asked Francois de Balmain. She smiled at him more warmly than she should have, and noticed a muscle bunch in Ral's jaw.

" 'Twas a day to remember, my lady. Your husband was fierce. He brought down a stag with his sword."

She turned in his direction. "Is that so, my lord? After last night's . . . revelry . . . I had feared a little for your strength." Ignoring the dark look he tossed her, she spoke again to de Balmain, then to Lady Eliana.

"I hope you're enjoying your visit."

The black-haired beauty smiled. "I intend to spend the summer at Malvern. Mayhap you could join me for a time."

"My wife will be busy—" Ral broke in.

" 'Twould please me greatly to see some of the country," Caryn countered. "I am certain that my husband can survive for a few days without me."

"We will discuss it when the time comes," Ral said with a dark look of warning, then he changed the subject. "There is someone I would have you meet."

For the first time, Caryn noticed the dark-skinned man who sat at a far end of the table. He stood as Ral looked toward him, and graced her with a bow of his head. It was covered by a flowing length of cloth that reached his shoulders and kept in place by a small circular band.

"Hassan is a surgeon," Ral said. "He once served King William. At the battle of Senlac, he was the man who saved my life."

Caryn had noticed the sword scar between Ral's ribs. It was long but fairly even and not particularly obtrusive. She smiled thinly at the lean dark-skinned man.

"Then I suppose I owe you a debt of gratitude, Hassan. For 'tis certain we would all miss him sorely." She looked down at the trestle tables below the dais and saw the blond-haired head of Lynette. "Some of us far more than others."

"Hassan will be returning to Braxston a few weeks hence," Ral said, ignoring the bite in her words. "Mayhap he can teach you the use of some of his herbs."

"I shall bribe him to do so." She smiled dryly. "Who knows what sort of potions one might learn to brew."

Ral's eyes met hers and he read the bitter taunt there.

Though he muttered an oath beneath his breath, she thought she might have caught a flash of admiration.

The evening progressed and through it they enjoyed the entertainment. At least Caryn prayed that she looked as though she did. She laughed and smiled, and spoke gaily with Lady Eliana. Which in itself, she discovered, was no easy task.

Stephen's sister was different, unsettling in some way, and there was a darkness about her. It shrouded her like a thick night mist, making Caryn even more uneasy, though she did her best to hide it.

Just as she hid her feelings for Ral. But everytime he looked at her, something squeezed inside her. It was all she could do to sit there beside him, all she could do to smile and call him by name.

She didn't want to be there, didn't want to see his handsome face, didn't want to see the smiling face of his whore. She wanted to run from the table, to return to her room and never come out. She wanted to call him every vile name she could think of, to weep and wail and pound her fists against the wall to vent her fury.

Instead she smiled sweetly and laughed at the jester's fare. Remembering their brief meeting out on the parapet, she wondered again about the strangely compelling, fair-haired boy. On the floor below the platform, the lad did his cute little jig, ringing the bells on his hat and around his neck, then began to recite his verses.

> A lover of old in fair Mort
> Had arms that were strong but too short
> When for wenches he reached,
> He was forced to choose each
> From the narrow and spanable sort

The men laughed good-naturedly and called out for more, and the jester readily complied, his face breaking into a half-black, half-white smile.

A wicked young lad from Travatt
With maids would enjoy this and that
A touch and a kiss
Did he mean by his this
You can guess what he meant by his that!

The jester was delightful, holding everyone's attention, teasing and jibbing and calling forth their cheers. For the first time in weeks, the dimples in Richard's cheeks appeared and later in the evening Caryn saw him speaking to the jester near the fire.

She watched them a moment, envious at the laughter they shared, feeling sad and forlorn inside, yet still smiling brightly. It took such concentration, she missed the heavy footsteps that marked her husband's approach behind her.

"You appear uncommonly gay this eve," he said. " 'Twas hardly the mood I expected."

"Because of what happened this morning?"

"Aye. 'Twas tears I saw last on your cheeks."

"The last of their kind you will see, I'll warrant. The tears of a foolish young girl. Tonight I am a woman. One whose eyes have finally been opened."

"I did not mean to hurt you."

" 'Twas hardly your fault that I was such a fool."

For a moment Ral said nothing. Then he took her arm and started for the stairs.

"What are you doing?" Caryn jerked her arm away.

" 'Tis late. 'Tis time that we retired."

Caryn's gaze narrowed on his darkly handsome face. "Since we've guests in the hall this eve, you may walk me up the stairs. If you mean to join me in our chamber, you will find that you are no longer welcome."

Ral clamped his jaw. "You are my wife. 'Tis your duty to accept me in your bed whenever I wish it."

Caryn laughed, the sound unnaturally harsh. "If you believe for one moment, my lord, that what we shared before will be anything like what you will get from me now you are sorely mistaken. You have chosen to sleep with your whore. 'Tis the only place you will find comfort."

She started toward the stairs and felt her husband's presence beside her. By the time they reached their chamber, Caryn's heart was pounding. He could force her; he was certainly strong enough. But she meant what she had said. 'Twould be bitterness he stirred, not passion. He could take his pleasure, but she would feel nothing but icy resentment.

"I will give you some time. Soon you will learn 'tis only a man's way to find ease with a number of women."

For an instant, Caryn faltered, her cool facade slipping away. Pain filled her eyes and with it a glistening film of tears. "I have always learned quickly, my lord. You may be certain this lesson will not soon be forgotten."

Something flashed in Ral's eyes, then it was gone. Caryn turned away from him and went into her chamber, closing the door on her husband and her dreams.

Troubled and unable to sleep, Ral spent a restless night in the solar. And the next night and the next. The tax collector, and his friend Hassan the surgeon, had set off with Stephen for Grennel, Malvern's castle in the south, where he and his men would leave them. It was quiet once more in the great hall, quieter than Ral had ever seen it.

An unsettling quiet, an uncommon quiet. It seemed the very walls were filled with gloom.

Or was it merely a reflection of the gloom that filled his heart?

Ral shifted on his thick fur pallet, working to make himself comfortable. *'Twill lessen*, he told himself. *In time this pain will end.* But he wondered how long it would take, wondered that the loss of his small wife's affections could make him hurt this badly.

Ral swore a savage oath and tossed back the covers. Better to control his feelings now than to let her take control. Seeing Eliana and Stephen had brought that notion home with bitter force.

Still, he had to admit he missed her laughter and companionship, her gentleness and humor, the warmth of her body next to his. He missed the passion they had shared and the soft look in her eyes when he had brought her to fulfillment.

"Enough!" he said out loud. " 'Tis foolishness for a man to be so taken with a woman." In time, he was sure, he would break the hold Caryn had upon his heart. In time, she would accept him once more as her lord and allow him into her bed.

Even now, should he desire it, he could walk down the hall, jerk open her door, and demand she submit to his will. He could do it—'twas certainly within his rights as her husband and lord. But he knew she would fight him and he had never forced a woman.

She was small and he might hurt her.

And though he tried to deny it, he didn't want to lose her any more than he already had.

Ral raked a hand through his sleep-tangled hair. Thoughts of Caryn had left him hard and throbbing. He wanted her more now than he ever had before, but Caryn no longer wanted him.

Ral ignored the thread of fear that had begun to weave its web around his heart.

"What troubles you, Richard? Is there never a time when you smile?" The jester appeared from out of nowhere. His face paint was gone, though a felt cap covered most of his shiny blond hair. Except for his small protruding ears he was an attractive youth, almost pretty. And he had a warm way about him.

"Not lately, Ancil. I worry for Lady Caryn." Why he spoke his thoughts so openly to the jester, Richard could not say, yet he knew without doubt they would not be repeated.

"She laughs gaily, but inside she weeps. She mourns the loss of her husband as if he were dead and buried."

"I am surprised that you know," Richard said. " 'Tis a secret she guards with every heartbeat."

"A jester knows everyone's secrets. Laughter is the potion that releases troubled thoughts."

"And loosens people's tongues?" he asked.

"Aye, but your secrets are safe."

"My secrets?" The jester merely nodded. A breeze blew strands of his hair against his cheek and Richard noticed how smooth was his skin. "Your riddles have clouded your brain. I have no secrets."

"Think you that is so? I know that you labor far too hard, and worry far too often."

"That is no secret. And my labors have lessened since Lady Caryn bears the duties of chatelaine."

"I know that you wish to have children."

Richard's head snapped up. "How . . . how did you know that?" Ancil laughed and Richard found he liked the sound of it.

"I know that you would marry, should you have time to seek out a proper mate."

"I believe you are a sorcerer, existing in the guise of a jester. I have spoken those words to no one." Or had he? The night of the feast, he had been drinking. He had been speaking to the jester, proud of the job he and Lady Caryn had done to make the evening successful. For once he had relaxed and enjoyed himself.

" 'Tis true then, that you wish to marry?"

Richard shrugged. " 'Tis true, I suppose."

"What would you seek in a maid?"

Richard smiled. "That is easy. Gentleness and kindness. Sweetness . . . and that she be a very hard worker.''

The jester made a noise that sounded like a grunt. ''What of fire, Richard? What of passion and love? You speak naught of those things, yet I would think they would be the most important.''

Passion and fire? Richard found himself staring at the jester's well-formed legs. They were long and as shapely as a maid's. Encased in tight hose, they were all but exposed beneath his short tunic. Richard caught himself and jerked his gaze away.

'' 'Twould be an asset, I suppose, should I discover passion in the bargain. Mostly I would wish her to be meek and submissive, that I might swiftly get her to quicken with a son.''

The jester's green eyes narrowed on his face. It was the first time Richard had ever seen Ancil angry.

''Men,'' the boy snapped, his blond brows drawing together, ''you are all a bunch of fools!''

Stunned that his words had affected the young lad so, Richard watched the youth storm away. He watched him longer than he should have, admiring the youth's easy grace. When he realized what he was doing, he hissed in a breath and quickly looked away.

He was hardly the type to go in for pretty young boys. He had simply been too long without a woman. Richard made a mental note to see his needs were tended before the week was through.

Chapter Fifteen

Ral allowed his wife's cool treatment for another two long weeks. She was courteous, though her manner remained aloof, and she never sought him out unless she had to.

Since he had not returned to his leman's bed, Lynette had ceased speaking to him, too, though for that he found himself grateful.

Ral cursed softly as he sat before the fire pit in the great hall. Deep burnished red flames reminded him of the color of Caryn's hair. She sat there now, on the opposite side of the fire pit, across from the young knight, Geoffrey, engrossed in a game of chess. Her gown drew taut over her breasts as she leaned over the board and touched his arm, then Ral heard masculine laughter. When Caryn's soft laughter joined in, a knot balled hard in his stomach.

Sweet Christ, what goes on between the pair? His wife had shown little interest in him of late, but she had no such qualms about the young knight he had once set to guard her. If he thought for a single moment . . . if he had the slightest suspicion that Geoffrey had overstepped his bounds . . . His fingers bit into the arm of his chair as he watched them. There seemed nothing furtive in the young knight's manner, yet seeing them together, a jealous rage welled up inside him.

God's blood, what power did she wield that she could make him feel this way? It made him want to lash out at her, to raise his fist to Geoffrey. It made him more certain than ever that he had done the right thing, and less sure than he had ever been of anything he had done before.

He only knew that she belonged to him and not to Geoffrey. That she belonged once more in his bed. God's wounds, it was his right as her lord and her husband, his right that she submit, that she yield to him and bear him sons!

Ral came up from the chair so swiftly it toppled over behind him, landing with a thud amidst the herb-scented rushes. He rounded the fire pit, bearing down on the two before the chessboard, his mood black and suddenly determined. His hand reached out and encircled Caryn's wrist.

"My lord?" Her head came up from where she had been studying a forward move of her queen.

"Your game is ended. We are for bed."

She stiffened in his hold and glanced across at Geoffrey, making his mood even blacker.

"'Tis certain you would have won," the blond knight said with an even smile.

Caryn looked back at Ral, but did not argue as he had expected. Instead, her chin came up. "As you wish, my lord."

They climbed the stairs in silence, Ral's eyes on the gleam of rushlight on her heavy auburn hair, the seductive sway of her hips. Already he was hard and throbbing, eager to feel himself sheathed inside her.

When they came to the door of their chamber, she paused. "I have done as you wished and returned upstairs. But I would have you know I do not want you in my bed."

A muscle knotted in his jaw. "What you want is no longer important. You are my wife—that is all that counts." He lifted the latch and opened the door, then drew her in beside him.

When he turned her into his arms, she did not fight him, but neither was she soft and responsive.

"I have missed you, Caryn." He caught her chin and tipped her head back, then captured her lips in a kiss. They were cooler than he remembered, stiff and unyielding. He parted them with his tongue and slid it inside, but still he felt none of the heat that usually infused her small body. He ended the kiss but did not move away.

"You intend to deny me?"

" 'Tis your right as husband to take me. I will submit if that is your wish."

His brow arched upward, his temper rising while a cold unease settled heavily in his chest. "Submit but not respond—is that what you intend?"

"If you want me to pretend—"

"Do not bait me, Caryn."

"I do not mean to. 'Tis simply that my feelings for you have changed."

His eyes formed the question without words.

"Once I desired you. Now I do not."

Ral felt a hot surge of anger. "You are a woman of passion. I do not believe you can cool your ardor so easily." He hauled her against him and kissed her again, using his tongue, cupping her breasts, stroking her nipple. He slid his hands down her body, but there was no answering passion. Her heartbeat continued with the same steady rhythm as before.

"You wanted me once," he said, forcing himself away, torn between anger and frustration and a slowly deepening fear. "Now you are saying you feel nothing?" Caryn did not answer. "If you think to bring Geoffrey to your bed, you are mistaken."

"Geoffrey? He is hardly more than a boy."

"He is a man and he is ambitious. He would like nothing better than the power he would gain should he hold the key to your heart."

"I have no yearning for Geoffrey. 'Tis not him nor any other man I want in my bed."

Relief flooded through him, though he worked hard to deny it. "Then what *do* you want?"

Caryn looked at him and did not glance away. "My freedom. 'Tis all I have wanted from the day of our first meeting."

Ral clamped his jaw. "You are my wife. What freedom you have is by my grant of will. 'Tis my right to command you, just as it is my right to bed you."

But instead of forcing her to accept him as he had intended, he found himself turning away, stalking from the room without looking back, slamming the heavy oaken door.

Caryn stared after him and suddenly her knees felt weak. He had not forced her, but he might have—if he had known how hard she worked to hide the passion he stirred inside her. It had taken every ounce of her will, every particle of her determination to ignore the fire that roared through her body. That she had succeeded amazed her. It was a measure of the Saxon pride that also ran through her veins.

She looked once more toward the door. He was gone from her now and part of her felt elated by the victory she had won.

Another secret part wished he had torn off her clothes and carried her over to his big high bed. That he had kissed her until her legs would no longer support her, that he had molded her breasts in his hands and thrust himself inside her. She wished he had spoken soft words in French, that he had held her and caressed her and driven her wild with the feel of his muscular body.

But most of all she wished that he loved her.

The way that she still loved him.

* * *

Ral slept fitfully again that night, imagining Caryn in the arms of the handsome blond knight Geoffrey, seeing her stricken face the morning she had found him naked in his leman's bed. When he awoke, he was bathed in sweat, his insides knotted in a cold hard fist.

He cursed softly, frustration like bile in his throat. Grimacing at the stiffness in his muscles, and the throbbing in a place far lower down, he tossed back the covers and climbed from the bed. *Caryn. Always it was Caryn.* He wanted her with a passion that amazed him and because he did, he refused to give in to his needs and take her.

Instead, he forced his uncertain feelings behind him, forced himself to think of his duties and the day that lay ahead. He dressed as he would for battle, in a short brown tunic and chausses, and pulled on his high soft leather boots. Gathering his sword and shield, he went downstairs. Outside in the bailey, his squire helped him on with his armor and fastened his swordbelt around him, preparing him for a morning of practice with his men.

They were already well underway, armed with sword and shield and wearing their chain mail hauberks. He spotted Odo, speaking to Lambert and Hugh, then noticed the blond knight, Geoffrey, fair and virile and filled with the arrogance of youth.

Ral glanced back toward the high stone walls of the keep, up at the narrow slit of window in what should have been his chamber. Even now, did his wife look down at the knights and men-at-arms in the bailey? Did her eyes seek out the handsome blond knight instead of him? Standing next to Lambert in his padded jerkin and dusty mail, Geoffrey practiced alone, raising his sword then cutting downward in a savage arch, as if he faced a real opponent instead of just his shadow.

Ral smiled with malice and pulled his own heavy sword from its scabbard. He tested the blade with his thumb, saw that his squire had done a good job in honing the edge, then stalked across the yard until he stood before Geoffrey and Odo.

"You're looking fit this morrow, Geoffrey."

" 'Tis exactly how I feel, my lord."

"Your sword arm looks strong. Let us see if your practice has helped hone your skill." Ral pulled on his conical helm and adjusted it till the nasal bar fell into proper position.

Geoffrey smiled. "As you wish, my lord."

They faced each other squarely, raising their shields and then their swords. Around them the men fell silent, enjoying a chance to rest and intent on watching the fray, though none had doubt of the outcome.

Ral stepped closer, goading the younger man with a word or two, waiting with relish for Geoffrey to strike the first blow. When he did, his blade fell squarely, the heavy metal clanking against his own, sending a tremor up his arm.

Ral barely felt it. Memories of the dream pumped through his veins . . . images of Geoffrey with Caryn.

He parried three hard blows, his sword ringing loudly, let another several fall, then countered and went on the offensive. Geoffrey feigned right and lunged left, blocked a heavy blow, then parried, avoiding at first the brunt of Ral's slashing attack. But soon he began to tire.

It didn't take long to spot the younger man's weakness. Ral brought his blade down hard on Geoffrey's left, once, twice, blocked the young knight's feeble efforts to gain control, and continued his vicious assault till the lad went to his knees. Even then Ral continued, casting a ringing blow with the flat of his sword to the side of Geoffrey's helm and another to his mail-covered ribs.

"I yield, lord!" Geoffrey called out but it took a moment more for the words to pierce the haze of his temper. His hands were shaking when he brought his sword back under control, his blood pumping fiercely. As the young knight stood up, he noticed Geoffrey's helm was so badly bent it would take hammer and anvil to straighten it enough to remove it.

Ral felt a twinge of guilt.

He had never seen Geoffrey act aught but with respect to Caryn. It was hardly the young knight's fault his wife found the blond man so attractive.

It was hardly Geoffrey's fault, yet the rage he felt at the knowledge bubbled up inside him, searing his insides and refusing to leave him in peace.

"Richard! Come quickly!"

The steward saw the jester hurrying toward him. Since the night of the feasting, the atmosphere in the hall had been so tense Lord Ral had bade the troubadours remain.

"What is it, Ancil?" Richard caste a worried glance in the younger man's direction.

"Cottars from the village. They have come to see Lord Ral. They say at least half of their cattle are infected with murrain."

Murrain. A disease that destroyed whole herds of cattle and left the people starving in its wake.

"Where are they?" Setting aside the checklist he had been making, Richard hurried in the lad's direction.

"The other side of the drawbridge. The men whose cattle remain well demand Lord Ral lay waste to those that are sick."

"If truly it is murrain, Lord Ral will have no choice. We must destroy the infected to preserve the healthy." Purposeful strides carried Richard out of the hall and across the bailey. Beside him, Ancil hurried along in shorter but equally determined paces. Strangely, Richard found he was glad to have the youth along.

"Over there." Ancil pointed toward the trees.

Richard nodded. He had almost reached the villeins

when he heard a deep voice behind him and the tramp of heavy feet.

"What goes on here, Richard?" Ral caught them in several long strides.

"Murrain, my lord. The cottars say there may be a coming plague of it."

Murrain. Ral took the news like a blow to the stomach. Without the livestock, there would be no butter, no cheese, no meat for the winter. Losing the cattle was the last thing he needed.

He spoke to the men who waited across the drawbridge, then returned to the keep for his horse, choosing the lean sorrel stallion instead of his powerful black. Along with Richard, they followed the cottars back to the village, making a stop at each small wattle and daub hut along the way. At the sight of so many sick animals, Ral grew more and more depressed. The signs of murrain were unmistakable. Worse than that, not half but nearly all of the cattle in the village were infected.

"God's blood," he muttered, "what curse has been set upon us?"

" 'Tis the way of things, my lord," Richard said. "Bad luck seems to swell instead of fade."

" 'Tis truth, my friend, and a more unpleasant one could not be spoken."

" 'Tis certain this will add to the burden of the winter."

"Aye, and then some."

Ral felt weary and defeated by the time they finished their inspection of the village and the surrounding villein's huts. He wished he had someone to talk to, someone who might help lift his mood.

He thought of Caryn, of how it would feel to have her small soft arms around him, of how he might lose himself inside her, forget his troubles for a time. He remembered how, in the past, she would have shared a little of his burden.

"They'll have to be destroyed," he said to Richard.

"Aye, my lord. 'Twill be done in all haste."

"Post a severed head at the crossroads." It was the sign all knew, warning travelers with cattle away. No trade would be allowed for miles around.

Richard nodded. "Aye, my lord."

His mood growing darker by the minute, Ral wheeled his stallion away. When he returned to the bailey, he saw the little jester, standing beside the guard at the drawbridge.

"What do you, lad, out here?"

"Nothing," the jester said. "I merely pass the hours of the day." But it was certain that the lad watched for Richard.

Ral frowned. His seneschal's interest had never seemed to lean in that direction. Still, he didn't know for sure and he had seen the pair speaking together often.

Ral shrugged. What his steward did was his own concern. Still, it would have made him happy to see the man settled with a wife and strong sons.

Caryn spent the day in the village, trying to offer hope when her people felt only bitter despair.

"Lord Ral will not let you starve," she promised Nelda, Leofric's widowed mother. "He has grain put away for just such times. You must trust him to provide for you."

"The lord is far from rich. Even should we survive this winter, what will happen to us the next?"

"My husband will find a way. You must believe that, Nelda."

But even Caryn had her doubts, and they mushroomed when later that eve she found her husband brooding in the solar. He sat before a stout oak table, his elbows propped upon it, his head resting wearily in his hands. Thick black hair pushed through his fingers, catching the light of a candle that guttered in a pool of melting wax. Tension constricted the muscles across his broad shoulders, and Caryn felt an unwelcome pang at the sight.

"Good eventide, my lord," she said softly, pity for him rising though she tried to force it down. "You were missed at supper."

"Was I?" he said, his head coming up. "By whom? You, Caryn?"

Yes, she thought. *I miss you more each day.* "Odo asks after you. Richard and the others."

"With Braxston's animals being slaughtered, I have no appetite for food."

In truth, neither had she. "I have been to the village. I have spoken to the people. I have told them you will not see them starve."

Ral sighed wearily. "Such a plague could not have come at a worse time."

"Will you be able to keep them fed?"

" 'Twill be a close thing. Building the keep was expensive and though I am no pauper, I am not a wealthy man."

"You are still allowed to hunt and there is yet grain in our stores. Mayhap 'twill be enough."

" 'Twill have to be enough." Worry lines marred his forehead. "I would that things were different, that the villeins had not been burdened so heavily. But constructing the keep was all important. It guards the pass from raiders. 'Tis central to William's defenses."

" 'Tis said King William granted you this land because you saved his life."

"That is so."

"You are a man brave in battle. 'Tis only that you face a different battle now."

Ral leaned forward in his chair. "And what of you, Caryn? Do you face that battle with me?" His dark look had shifted, gone from brooding to uncertain. Then she saw the hungry look of his desire.

"Aye, my lord. I would do whatever it takes to help my people." It was not what he meant and she knew it. He wanted her returned to his bed. In a way she wanted it, too, but she knew what danger lay in that direction, and she dared not give her heart to him again.

For a long while Ral said nothing, just watched her in that way of his, making her feel uneasy, bringing back memories of what it had been like to lie in his arms. Then he shoved back his chair and came to his feet, filling the room with his towering frame. When he rounded the table and strode toward her, Caryn took a step away.

"I want you, Caryn." He reached for her, swept her into a fierce embrace. "I need you."

She could feel the strength of him, the power in the muscles that rippled against her breast and thighs. His mouth claimed hers and Caryn felt the heat of it, the incredible sensuous warmth. There was so much passion in his touch, so much yearning, for a moment she gave into it, kissing him back, leaning against his powerful frame.

Then she realized what she was doing, stiffened and pulled away. "I-I beg your leave, my lord." Her hands shook, so she held them against her russet tunic.

"You are my wife," he said. "This has gone on long enough." Stepping toward her, he caught her up in his arms, holding her against his wide chest. Caryn started to protest, but the strength of his hands and the length of his strides told her it would do no good.

Ral kissed her as they moved down the hall toward their chamber, a demanding kiss fraught with heat, then he kicked open the door with a booted-foot and carried her over to his bed. Already she blazed with heat, the fires of passion licking hotly through her veins, yet she knew where this was leading and she'd had time to steel herself.

When he began to remove her clothes, she made no

move to stop him, but neither did she help him. She just stood stiff and unyielding, letting him fumble with the ties, letting him pull the garment off over her head. Ral seemed not to notice, or if he did, he did not care. In minutes, he had stripped off her clothes and his own, and settled her atop his big bed.

"You are a fire in my blood," he said, following her down, his powerful body pressing her into the mattress. "I have never wanted another the way I want you."

He wanted her—just as he had before. And yet he had gone to his leman.

'Twas Lynette you wanted then. Who is it you will want on the morrow? The thought was enough to lessen her ardor, though the heat of his touch seared her skin.

"I beg of you, Ral," she whispered between fiery kisses. "Do not ask me to do this."

His hand went still, then it settled against her heart. "Even now your blood pounds. Do you still deny you want me?"

A soft sound of pain escaped. "My body may desire you but my heart does not."

He swore a savage oath. "Then the plunder of your body will have to be enough." With those harsh words he set to work, laying siege to her flesh as if she were some stalwart castle.

His mouth took hers in a blazing kiss that left her dizzy. His hands cupped her breasts, kneading and molding until each rosy crest grew hard against his palm. She could feel the rasp of the whiskers along her jaw, feel the rough hair on his chest, and the hardness of his manroot.

Though she willed it not to, beneath his skillful touch, her body grew languid and responsive, her heart beating wildly, the blood thick and heavy in her veins. Still, a part of her remained aloof, as if she watched what went on, but did not join in all that happened. She felt safe from this distance, able to accept his fiery caresses with out giving him her soul as she had before.

Ral parted her legs with his knee and his finger slid inside her. He stroked her there until she was wet with desire for him, on fire and blazing with need. Then he settled his hardness against her, eased himself in, and buried himself to the hilt.

"So sweet," he whispered. "How I have missed these times."

Caryn arched against him, taking all of his thick length, feeling the sensual glide, the hot tingling sensations, and his heavy masculine need. In minutes she was arching her body, meeting each of his powerful thrusts, and yet. . . .

It seemed as if something were missing, something elemental that had called out to her before, but this time remained elusive.

"I cannot wait much longer," he said, surging into her hard and deep, urging her onward. "It has been far too long."

Still, he was determined and he pounded into her fiercely. Another time she would have responded, let the wild tide of pleasure carry her off. Another, sweeter time in the past. . . .

As hot and damp as her body was, as much as she shivered with fiery sensations, Caryn did not reach the shimmering plateau. Instead she felt Ral stiffen, felt the spilling of his seed. He lay spent and unmoving atop her, drenched in sweat, his heartbeat only now beginning to slow. When he rolled away, his face looked grim.

Caryn said nothing. For the first time she realized whatever had been missing for her, Ral had been sensing, too.

She felt his withdrawal and wanted to touch him, to give him ease in some way. She did not. "I am sorry if I did not please you."

Ral said nothing. Instead he rose from the bed and

dressed with stiff, uneven motions. When he had finished, he walked to the door without looking back, jerked it open, and stalked out into the hall. She heard his movements next door in the solar, heard him pull the wine cork from its flask and take a drink, and knew she would spend yet another night alone.

Feeling small and forlorn in her husband's big bed, the linens still warm from his body, Caryn touched the place he had lain, empty now and soon to grow cold. And then she started to weep.

"What is it you want, old woman?"

Marta stepped into the solar. "I would have a moment, Lord Ral."

"Can you not see that I am busy? Speak your mind and leave me in peace."

Busy he was not, she knew. He sat in the solar brooding, snapping at the servants, making only rare appearances in the hall.

" 'Tis not like you to be so ill-tempered. Your estrangement from your wife does not appear to suit you."

The Norman's head came up. "What would you know of what suits me?"

"I know that since the night of the feasting you have been unhappy and so has she. I know that you went to your leman. That your Caryn cannot forgive you. I know why you did it."

"You know nothing." But he did not send her away.

Marta moved closer, until she stood in front of the table. "I know the truth of your betrothal."

On the opposite side of the heavy oak planking, Lord Ral straightened in his chair. "What truth?"

"There is only one thing to gain from growing old and feeble. Only one thing, and that is wisdom."

"You speak in riddles like the jester, old woman."

"No one pays attention to one such as me. Our bones

are old and brittle. 'Tis our way to move slowly, to be unobtrusive, to make our way among the shadows.''

"Get to the point," he snapped.

"I know of the unnatural bond between Lord Stephen and his sister. I saw him go into her room."

Lord Ral eyed her coldly. On the surface he appeared calm, but a muscle jumped in his cheek. "What Stephen does means nothing to me."

"Not now, mayhap. But there was a time when it meant a great deal."

The Dark Knight said nothing.

" 'Twas the reason you broke your betrothal." She took a brittle step forward. "You discovered their secret, just as I have. It sickened you . . . and frightened you. You could not imagine a man as strong as Stephen, a man of so much power, being brought to his knees by a woman."

"He has lost his soul."

"At least a dozen times over." Marta assessed him shrewdly, noting the lines of fatigue in the hard planes of his face. "It can happen, as you have seen, but your Caryn is not Eliana. She is not evil, nor does she seek to drain your will. She only means to lend you some of her strength, as any good wife would do."

The Norman pushed back his chair, the sound grating in the emptiness of the room. He strode over to the narrow slit of window. "Bedding my leman is my right. I have done nothing any other man would not do."

"You are not any other man. And she is not any other woman."

Lord Ral shifted uneasily, raking a hand through his thick black hair, driving it back from his forehead. "You do not understand."

"I understand that you have special feelings for her. That you are frightened by those feelings. I also know that there is no need for you to be afraid."

"There is very little I am afraid of."

"That is so, my lord. You are strong and brave. That is why you must seek out your destiny, then be unafraid to claim it."

The tall dark Norman stared a moment out into the bailey. The clash and clank of sword and shield drifted up from the practice yard. He turned away from the sounds and crossed the room to stand before her.

"I will think on what you have said. That is all I can promise. Even then I am not certain that it will matter."

Marta rasped out a slightly grating sound. " 'Tis certain, Lord Ral, that it will matter." She turned and walked away.

Chapter Sixteen

Caryn left the stable and crossed the bailey to the keep. Along with Leo, she had tended the fawn and the kittens, though the kittens had grown big enough to mouse on their own and the fawn had adopted Leo, following the little boy about whenever he went into the stables.

Caryn spent a good deal of time with them. Combined with her duties as chatelaine, it took her mind off the troubles they faced in the village—and the heartbreak she suffered whenever she thought of Ral.

It gave her a chance to forget her foolish dreams.

She was working to do that now as she walked to a storeroom just inside the keep, intending to check on supplies. She opened the door to one of the rooms, then halted as she stepped inside.

"Ancil—what do you in here?"

The jester whirled in her direction. "Lady Caryn!" His hat was gone, his hair, long and golden, hung unbound past his shoulders. One small ear protruded from the side of his head—but the other one lay neatly in place. It was delicate and shell-like and perfectly fit his oval face.

"Sweet Mary! Ancil—you are a woman!" Startled green eyes met hers. The girl made a sound in her throat and sank down in obeisance.

"I beg of you, lady Caryn, you must keep my secret."

The jester's voice was no longer male but decidedly feminine and sweetly lilting. " 'Tis a matter of life and death."

"How did you do that to your ears?" Caryn asked, her gaze still fixed on the uncommon sight of one ear sticking out while the other one did not.

"What? Oh, 'tis merely a hunk of clay." She pulled the clay free, letting the ear fall back in its natural position. "Please, my lady, I beg you not to tell."

She was lovely, Caryn saw, soft and pleasing to the eye. Older than she, mayhap as much as two and twenty.

"Surely the others know your secret, those you travel with on the road."

"My friends do, but no others. I pray you will not tell Lord Ral."

A dozen thoughts buzzed through Caryn's mind. "Does Richard know?"

She shook her head, making her long hair shimmer. Her lips turned down, betraying a moment of sadness. "At times he looks at me oddly and I think that he suspects. I would tell him if I could."

"Then why don't you?"

She chewed her bottom lip, torn by indecision, then she sighed and came up from the floor. "My name is not Ancil. 'Tis Lady Ambra. I am the daughter of Edward of York."

"I have heard of him. I thought your father was dead."

"That is true, my lady. Before I ran away, I lived at Morlon, with my mother's brother, Charles."

"Why did you leave?"

"I was betrothed to Lord Beltar the Fierce. He is rich and powerful, while my mother's brother is poor. Beltar was willing to marry me, though I had only a very small dowery, and my uncle liked the idea of having a wealthy relation."

Caryn thought for a moment. In the back of her mind she remembered something of Beltar . . . something she had heard.

"Aye, now I recall. Lord Beltar claimed you were carried away from your home against your will. He offers a reward for your return." *Sweet Mother Mary, more trouble for Ral should Beltar find her here.*

"He is ugly and mean. Once he tried to force himself on me. I vow it made me sick." She stiffened her spine. "I will not wed him. I swear I will not marry until I can marry for love."

Caryn's insides twisted. " 'Tis a difficult notion in such times, but a noble one all the same."

"Then you will keep my secret?"

Caryn thought of what Ral would do if he found out. "Aye, but do you not miss your home? Are you happy to be traveling as a man?"

"I was happy for a time."

"And now?"

"Now I have met someone. . . ."

Richard. "I will help you, Lady Ambra. Mayhap you will be the one woman who is lucky enough to find love."

Caryn shifted in her chair before the fire pit, where she sat with needle in hand. The delicate embroidery edged the sleeves of a while silk chainse. She pulled the length of thread through the fabric, wondering if Ral would notice her careful work and thinking how the small task helped to ease her troubled mind. In the past she had loathed such duties, now she found the work oddly soothing.

"Why do you not go to him? 'Tis obvious that is what you want."

She glanced up to find Odo beside her, his blue eyes probing, his question stirring unwanted thoughts.

" 'Tis not a matter of what I want but of what he

wants.'' Caryn watched as the lean Norman knight sat down on a stout wooden bench. Flames from the hearth deepened the highlights in his bright red hair. ''For now 'tis me he wants. Who will he want on the morrow or mayhap next week?''

''What happens on the morrow is of no importance. He desires you, as you do him. That is all that matters.''

''If you think that, then you know naught of what is important.''

Odo scoffed. '' 'Tis almost as if you grieve for him.''

Caryn's eyes searched his face. His orange-red brows drew together as he worked to understand. ''Have you never loved, Odo?''

''Nay. Love is for fools.''

''You had a family once. Did you not love your father and mother, your brothers and sisters?''

His tone grew rough. ''Aye, I loved them.''

''And when they died, did you not know pain and grief?''

''Aye, like no other I have known.''

'' 'Tis that same pain when you lose the one that you have given your heart.''

Frustration knotted his brow. ''But you have not lost him. You have only to cross the room and—''

''You will never understand.'' She rose from her chair and set aside her embroidery. She saw that Odo stared at her still, trying to make sense of what she said. '' 'Tis as simple as this, Odo,'' she said with sadness. ''To love someone without pain, they must love you in return.''

Odo watched her walk away, moving slowly, with little of the spirit that had enlivened her before. Though she held her head high, she seemed weighed down with despair. He glanced at Ral, saw his gray eyes locked on her small retreating figure. There was darkness in his gaze, too, and uncertainty, and something else he could not name. It had been there since the night he had gone to his leman.

Odo didn't know what his friend was feeling, but he knew Ral also was in pain.

Odo shoved himself to his feet. He cared little what happened to Caryn for she was naught but a woman, and a Saxon into the bargain, but he worried for his friend.

"You look at her as I have never seen you look at a woman." He approached Ral on the dais. " 'Tis obvious that you want her. Why do you not just take her?"

Ral jerked his gaze from where Caryn had disappeared up the stairs. His chest ached just to think of her, yet he could not seem to stop. " 'Tis only bitter memories the joining brings. There is very little pleasure."

"Because she has not yet learned that she must share you? In time she will accept that you've the need for other women, the same as any other man."

Ral eyed him darkly. "Do I? Why is it I find no other woman pleasing? Why is it I desire her, yet with this wall between us I find no pleasure in the taking?" A weary sound seeped from inside him. "Why is it my wife's pain feels like my own?"

"I cannot answer that. I can only tell you that—"

"Can you tell me why I should continue to deny my feelings when there isn't a man in the keep who cannot see?"

"Do not be a fool. If you give her your heart—"

"What will happen? What terrible misfortune will befall me? I wonder that it could be any worse than that which has befallen me already." Ral gripped the arms of his chair and came to his feet. "I know that you speak what you believe, but only time will tell which of us is the fool in truth." Without a backward glance, he strode away from Odo, leaving his friend to ponder his words.

"God's blood," Ral muttered darkly, tired to his bones of every man jack in the castle giving him advice he did not need.

He took the stairs two at a time then strode with

purpose down the hall. Of all the admonitions he had received, one thing was crystal clear: He wanted Caryn and he had come to believe she still wanted him.

He had seen her watching him this eve as she had on a dozen occasions. He had felt her eyes on his body, seen the heat that rose into her cheeks, the way she unconsciously wet her lips. He had seen that look on a woman's face—God's blood, he wasn't a fool.

Caryn was a creature of passion. She might not admit her desire for him, but he believed it was still somewhere inside her. If she wanted him enough, mayhap she would eventually forgive him. Mayhap she would regain the affection she once held for him. Mayhap she could learn to feel even more.

Ral continued along the corridor past the solar. When he reached the door to his chamber, he knocked then lifted the latch without waiting for permission to go in.

"My lord?" Caryn stood before a flickering candle, wearing only her thin camise, her hair unbound and shimmering like dark auburn flame around her shoulders. Shadows danced on the rough gray walls behind her, reminding him of the shadows from the past that he had come to conquer.

" 'Tis time we settled this trouble between us. 'Tis time once more you warmed my bed."

She stiffened, and he cursed his choice of words, yet his mind was made up, his goal set. He would not falter until the deed was done.

"Does it matter that I do not want you?"

"I do not believe that, else I would not be here."

"I gave in before. This time I will fight you."

He fixed her with a long, determined stare. "You are my wife. Should you try to resist me, I will strip you and tie you to the bed."

Fire glinted for a moment in the depths of her dark brown eyes, then it was gone. "As you wish, my lord.

After all, as you have said, I am your wife, lawfully and truly wedded.''

"That is so, and I am your lord as well as your husband.'' He walked toward her, taking in her soft curves and rounded, upthrusting breasts. He paused at the foot of the bed. "Come here, Caryn."

She hesitated for a long, unsettling moment, then moved forward. There was a tautness in her bearing as she crossed the room, her small frame simmering with careful control and bitter resignation.

Ral cursed inwardly. He would strip it away, he vowed. He would find the chink in her armor, a way to breach her defenses. He would make love to her until she forgot her cool facade, forgot all but the feel of him thrusting his hardness inside her.

She stopped before him, her shoulders proudly set, just as resolute as he, determined she would not lose herself to her passions.

When Ral bent forward and kissed her, he felt her soft lips tremble for an instant, felt their warmth, then a cool reserve infused them. He kissed her again, coaxing her lips apart, nibbling the corners of her mouth, forcing it to soften. Then his tongue slid inside and he tasted the sweetness of her breath, the berry flavor of wine and the seductive essence of woman.

His hands found her breasts and he cupped them through the thin linen fabric. He remembered every sweet curve, remembered how high and lush they were, how rosy they were at the crests. He remembered how it felt to draw them into his mouth, to suckle them until he felt her hands digging into his shoulders. He wanted to do that now, so he lifted off her camise, turned her a little and began to trail warm kisses down her back and along her spine. Her skin felt soft and smooth beneath his lips, and so warm it sent a fresh rush of blood to his groin. Already stiff and throbbing, his shaft rose up and hardened even more.

Still, he could sense her resistance and he meant to set it away.

"Sit down on the edge of the bed."

Caryn's jaw tightened. "As you wish, my lord." She said the words grimly but her voice shook a little, and he believed she was not as immune to his touch as she appeared. She settled herself at the foot of the bed and tossed back her hair, looking calm and collected, but a wash of pink tinged her cheeks at the fact that she was naked, and the warm appreciative look he gave her body.

"I have thought how lovely you are a thousand times."

Caryn said nothing, but her breathing went a little bit shallow. She fixed her gaze on the wall off to his left.

"Open your legs for me. I would see that which you work so hard to deny me." Though the color in her cheeks grew brighter, her legs remained closed. "You are my wife," he reminded her, leaning forward to kiss the hollow of her throat. " 'Tis your duty to obey me."

She slowly eased her legs apart and Ral moved between them, urging her backward on the bed. He leaned forward and kissed her forehead, then her eyes, her nose, her mouth. The kiss he took was searing, his tongue delving in, tasting, coaxing, mating with hers then darting away. All the while his hands caressed her breasts, worked her taut little nipples until they puckered and tightened, turning a darker shade of rose as he took one into his mouth.

Caryn made a sound in her throat, a small odd whimper that might have been fury or pleasure. He opened his mouth to take more of her, used his tongue to tease the rigid peak, then circled it and began to tug gently. For his efforts, he gained another soft moan, one that could not be mistaken.

He trailed his hands lower, through the silky auburn

curls that guarded her sex, a finger spreading the petals, circling them, then easing gently inside her.

"So soft," he whispered as his mouth followed the path his hands had taken, trailing damp warm kisses along her flat belly, his finger still pressing inside her. "So wet." He ran his tongue into her navel, ringed it, then moved lower.

"You were meant for this, Caryn. Can you not see that?" But of course she did not answer, and he felt her draw a little bit away.

He spread her legs wider and knelt between them, kissing the inside of her thighs, continuing to tease and stroke her with his hands.

"Please . . ." he heard her whimper, her palms on his shoulders as if she might push him away.

"Please what, Caryn? Please, Ral, do not make me feel this way? 'Tis my right as your lord to take all that you can give." Several more soft kisses along her tempting flesh, then he found the small pink bud of her desire and settled his mouth over the tiny crease of sensitive skin.

His tongue touched her there and her musky scent enflamed him, sending fire to his loins and making him throb with unspent passion. He was ablaze with wanting, aching and pulsing with every heartbeat. He felt her small body quiver and arch toward him, saw that she thrashed upon the bed, and slid his tongue deep inside her.

Caryn cried out his name and the sound of it drove him on. Even as he laved and tasted, she fought to deny him, fighting herself as well. Then he felt her hands in his hair and her body lifting upward. She moaned softly in her passion, parting her legs a little wider, her breathing swift and ragged.

Still he plundered her sweetness, his hands sliding under her bottom, gripping her buttocks and forcing her to accept each stroke of his tongue. He felt her body stiffen, heard her small sob of defeat, felt the tremors of pleasure engulf her, and knew he had accomplished his goal.

Before she'd had time to spiral down, Ral had stripped off his clothes and returned to the place between her legs. His hardness probed, found entrance, and he plunged himself deeply inside her.

Caryn cried out at the feel of him, the bunching of his muscles as he moved above her, and the rock hard thickness of his shaft.

Dear God, I must not let him win. But even as her mind rebelled, fresh waves of sweetness washed over her, tendrils of heat and incredible pleasure. He was taking her there again, lifting her to that fiery plateau with every hard thrust of his body.

She wanted to deny him, to guard herself from the pain she knew would follow, but this time Ral would not let her. There was nowhere to go, no way to run from his relentless pursuit, no way to save herself from her passions.

She was burning with heat, on fire with pleasure and wanting. She wrapped her legs around him, slid her arms around his neck, and clung to him fiercely. She tried to think of the future, of Lynette and the women he would want, but the moment was the only thought she could conjure. Even that slipped away until there was only Ral's big hard body, only the feel of muscle beneath smooth dark skin, only the feel of him driving inside her.

"Ral . . ." she whispered, "dear God, Ral. . . ." She reached her peak once more, felt him tense and jerk forward, then felt the spilling of his seed.

Even before it was over, tears formed at the corners of her eyes and slipped in salty rivulets down her cheeks. She tried to get up but he would not let her, sliding an arm around her waist and drawing her close against him. She rolled to her side, fighting back sobs, her body shaking with her effort at control and the burden of her failure.

One of Ral's big dark hands smoothed the hair away from her cheeks. "You cry because you think you have been defeated," he said softly. "Can you not see it is you who has won?"

A half-stifled sob was the only sound she made.

Ral gently turned her to face him. In the flickering light of the candle, his eyes looked more blue than gray and a lock of thick black hair fell over his forehead.

"Listen to me, Cara. There is no more need for tears. 'Tis you who have won this battle, not me." He smiled, but weariness shown in his features. "I have made arrangements with the Lord of Pontefact. On the morrow, by the time we leave this room, Lynette will be gone from the castle."

"What?"

"I am sending her away."

"But why?" Caryn searched his face. "Why would you do such a thing?"

"Is it not plain, *cherie?*" A hard male knuckle brushed the wetness from her cheeks. " 'Tis not Lynette that I want. 'Tis you and no other."

Caryn watched the play of shadow against his dark features, the proud, beard-roughened jawline, the steady look in his eyes. Did he mean it? Did she dare to put her faith in him again? "I want to believe you, Ral, but—"

" 'Tis the God's truth, Cara. I have thought of no other since the night I left your bed."

Fresh tears stung her eyes and she had to look away. "Then why did you do it?"

For a moment Ral said nothing, then he sighed. " 'Tis hard for me to say. In part, 'twas because of Stephen and Eliana. Because of the power she holds over him. I have seen what a woman like that can do to a man."

"But I am not like that."

He smiled at her softly. "No, you are not."

"Did you love her?" she asked. *Do you love her still?*

"Mayhap I did . . . once. Now I see her for the greedy, power-hungry female that she is."

"And Stephen?"

For a moment he seemed uncertain. "He loves her as a man loves a woman."

"You do not mean—"

"Aye."

Caryn sucked in a sharp breath of air. " 'Tis the gravest of sins."

"Aye. 'Twill mean God's wrath for sure."

"I still do not see what it has to do with me."

"Do you not, Cara?"

"No, I—"

"Mayhap 'tis better that you do not." He kissed her then, long and deep, and she could feel the steady beating of his heart.

"I have missed you so much," she said softly.

"Nay, my love, not nearly so much as I have missed you."

Caryn closed her eyes and let the warmth of him engulf her. He hadn't said he loved her, had only said he desired her above the rest. Still, it was a beginning, more than she dreamed he would ever concede.

He tightened his hold, raking his fingers through her heavy auburn hair, then pulling her head back to take her mouth in a hot, demanding kiss. She was trembling when he finally released her.

"We are good together, Cara. Can you not see?"

Good for pleasure, for the easing of a physical need, but what of love? she wanted to ask. He had once loved Eliana and he had been hurt badly. Could he learn to love again? 'Twas a question she did not ask. She had not told him of the love she felt for him. She was afraid to. He had run from her once. He might do it again.

The next time, she could not forgive him.

Chapter Seventeen

Worried about the villeins who had lost their cattle to murrain, Richard crossed the bailey toward the pens behind the stable. The animals at Braxston Keep had so far resisted the disease but Richard checked on them daily. Their meat would be crucial this winter.

He started around the building, then on the chance Lady Caryn might be tending her fawn, decided to go inside. It was quiet in the shady interior, dark except for the sunlight slanting in through the windows and doors. It smelled of hay and horses, and as he walked, his tunic stirred dust motes on the hard-packed earthen floor.

At the sound of a voice, and thinking he had found Lady Caryn, Richard turned in that direction. Instead, in a corner of the stable, Ancil said something Richard didn't quite catch then bent over the rim of a barrel.

"What do you in here, little one?" the jester said more clearly, soft laughter floating up, echoing inside the barrel. Richard barely heard the words, his attention fixed instead on the lad's graceful legs. His short brown tunic rode high up on his snug-fitting chausses, revealing a rounded behind.

Firm and curving, it was as lush as any woman's. Too lush for such a youthful, gangly boy. Richard's brows drew together in a frown. He eyed the wriggling bottom and a tightening gripped his loins. This time the masculine thickening did not embarrass him. It only made him more suspicious. For days he had wondered about the jester and his body's strange reaction to the slender youthful boy, the last of the troubadours to remain in the castle.

The rest had returned to their travels, but Lady Caryn had insisted Ancil stay. Now as Richard looked at the lad's shapely hips, he thought of the blond boy's delicate features and at times almost too-gruff voice. Something was wrong and it was time he discovered what it was.

His doubts growing stronger by the moment, Richard walked boldly up to Ancil and whacked him hard on his tempting behind. The boy cracked his head on the inside of the barrel, then shot out so fast that his hat fell off his head.

Silky blond hair tumbled down around the youth's slender shoulders. "Richard!"

The word came out high and more lilting than it ever had before. Except for his ears, Ancil was nothing short of pretty. As pretty as any woman, which it now seemed clear that she was.

"That is my name, you deceitful little wench. Now I would know the truth of yours."

The girl looked frantically around the stable, hoping no one had seen. She reached back into the barrel and dragged out one of Lady Caryn's half-grown kittens, along with her brown felt hat. She slapped the hat on her head and stuffed her shoulder-length blond hair up beneath it. Unfortunately in doing so, she knocked something loose from the back of her ear. The shell-like rim settled perfectly against her head, making her womanliness even more apparent.

Richard reached down and picked up a small chunk of clay. He rolled it around in his fingers. "I believe you're in need of this—you're looking a little lopsided."

She grabbed it out of his hand and pressed it once more behind her ear, forcing the rim to stick out. "Thank you."

"You have lied to us, tricked us, and made us all look like fools." *Especially me,* he thought with some bitterness. "I would know who you really are."

She nervously licked her lips and glanced toward the door as if she meant to bolt at any moment.

Richard took a menacing step in her direction. "You may tell me or you may tell Lord Ral. Neither choice matters to me."

"I beg you, Richard. Please do not tell him."

"Why have you deceived us?" Her slim hand touched his forearm, feeling warm and smooth against his skin. Richard felt a sudden jolt of heat.

"I did not think I would be here overly long. The truth would not have mattered had we not become friends. Since that time, I have regretted my deception every day."

"Why do you pretend to be a boy?"

As briefly as she could, Ancil explained that she was really Lady Ambra, that she was betrothed to Beltar the Fierce, and that in order to avoid the marriage, she had been forced to run away.

"Such a betrothal cannot be broken," he said, feeling an unexpected heaviness in his chest. "You will have to return to your uncle."

Ambra lifted her chin. If he had thought her a graceful appealing lad, now that he knew she was a woman, he found the delicate bones of her face beyond compare.

"Nay," she said. "I have come too far to turn back now. I will not marry a man the likes of Beltar."

"A woman has no say in such matters," Richard said firmly. "If you are destined to be Beltar's wife, then so it must be." He reached for her arm, but she jerked it away.

"I will not do it, Richard. Not you, nor Braxston, nor anyone else can make me. I mean to marry for love."

Richard scoffed. "You speak like a foolish young girl. Your uncle knows what is best for you and you will do as he wishes. Should you be my ward, I would beat you for running away."

"Well, I am not your ward. And I have never seen you so much as raise your voice to another person, let alone your hand."

Richard flushed. He could no more beat her than he could fly. In truth, it was all he could do not to reach out and touch her. He had wanted to, he realized, for a very long time.

"Lord Ral must be told."

"A pox on you, Richard. I thought we were friends."

Friends. It occurred to him that what he wanted from Ambra was far more than friendship. He also knew that she was a lady, wild and unmanageable as she obviously was, and she was betrothed to another.

"Aye, that we are, I suppose."

"Lady Caryn has agreed to help me. Tell me I may count on you, too."

She could, he realized, fighting a fresh rush of desire for her. "You are headstrong and willful. You are certain to lead whatever man you wed upon a merry chase. But, aye, you may count on me."

She threw her arms around his neck and kissed him soundly on the cheek. "Thank you, Richard."

It was all he could do to keep from pulling her against him and kissing her the way a woman should be kissed. Instead he cleared his throat and backed away.

"My first loyalty remains with the Lord of Braxston Keep. You've time to decide what you would do, but I cannot promise your safety forever."

Ambra merely smiled. She did a quick little step, once more Ancil the jester. "I am glad that you know the truth, Richard."

So was he. Decidedly so. At least he was certain now that the desire knifing hotly through his body was for a woman and not for a boy.

Caryn descended the steep stone stairs into the great hall. Since Ral's return to her bed, he had been kind and considerate, loving and gentle, and fiercely passionate in bed.

Yet he seemed wary of letting down his guard completely.

And even more so was she.

As Ral had promised, Lynette had been sent from the castle, but still Caryn did not trust him as she once had, and though each night her body craved his touch, she wasn't sure she ever would again. She avoided him as often as she could, fearful of the power he held over her, determined to protect herself, to keep her heart sealed off from him as much as she was able.

He smiled as she approached, his fathomless gray eyes revealing a moment of hunger before he forced the look away. He waved her over as he stood near the open front door, welcoming the Arab physician, Hassan, back to the castle.

Though Ral spoke to the Arab, his arm went possessively around her waist, drawing her close to his side, making her heartbeat quicken.

" 'Tis good to see you, my friend," he said to the tall, dark-skinned man. "We had little chance to speak when last you were here."

"It is good to be back." He was a quiet man, lean to the point of meat over bone, dark and exotic. His nose was sharp and bent a little in the middle, his eyes black as night yet they seemed to reflect some inward glow.

"Hassan has agreed to remain for at least a fortnight," Ral said, smiling down at her. " 'Twill give us time to renew our acquaintance."

Caryn smiled, too, though she wished Ral would release her and she could move a little bit away. " 'Tis said Arab healers are the finest in the land. Has your friend Hassan also agreed to grant me some time for instruction?"

The Arab's white teeth flashed. "Of course, my lady, if that is your wish." He bent over her hand. "The pleasure will be mine."

Another task to occupy her mind, give her something to do besides think of Ral and worry about the future.

"Ral says you were once physician to the king," Caryn said to Hassan as they made their way inside the keep and across the great hall. They sat down at a table on the dais.

"That is so. I remain in his service even now. It was William who asked me to travel to Grennel. The king will be pleased to know his friend there will live."

"You were with William at Hastings?" Caryn asked.

"That is correct, my lady. It was my good fortune to be attending the injured on the field at Senlac. When your husband's courageous efforts saved the life of the king, I was there to save the life of your husband."

Thinking of Ral injured and bloody made something twist in Caryn's chest.

"You are interested in the art of healing?" he asked.

"My wife is interested in learning," Ral put in. "The subject seems to be of little consequence."

"My mother worked with herbs and healing," Caryn said. "I had no such notion until your last visit. Since then, I have been looking forward to the chance to gain a bit of knowledge."

She had gone to the priest after Ral had returned to her bed, hoping the study would prove a distraction from her fears. "Already I have spoken to the priest. Father Burton acts as physician to those of us at Braxston. He has given me several texts to read in Latin and French."

A sleek dark brow arched up. "A learned woman. It is nearly as unusual in your country as it is in mine."

Caryn flushed. "I hope you do not find it offensive."

"Quite the opposite. It should make my task far more interesting." He steepled his long dark fingers in front of him. "As to the text you have been reading . . . the best of your physicians come from the south of France. Even so, they are no match for our Arab healers."

" 'Tis not idle words, Cara." Ral turned his hand over and laced his fingers through hers, stirring an unwelcome wave of heat. "I know of at least a dozen good knights who would be dead but for Hassan."

"Then I will learn my lessons well," she said, "for 'twould please me greatly to help the people of my village."

And so together, they did. As soon as word reached Braxston village that a great physician was among them, people began arriving at the keep. Old women, sick men, the weak, the blind, the crippled.

Ral had a storeroom cleared and turned into a medicinal. He furnished it with worktables and benches, and Hassan and Caryn used it to care for their patients, though the daily regimen turned out to be far different from what she had expected.

Where the priest prescribed violent purges, bloodletting, and amputations, often convinced the illness was some sort of devine punishment, Hassan's treatments were less severe and most times more effective. A poultice for an abscessed leg, an ointment of docks mixed with lanolin for skin complaints; coltsfoot with honey for coughs; pepper and sulphur for itching; horseradish with tallow for muscle strains and bruises.

Hassan's odd prescriptions didn't sit well with the priest, who was certain the heathen's cures were the work of the devil. When Hassan recommended a change of diet for a woman with a lung condition, Father Burton flew into a rage.

"I cannot believe such a thing," he said. "Why, in France, the head would be shaved, the skull opened up, and the brain removed. 'Tis highly unlikely a change in diet will correct the problem."

Hassan grinned. "It is also highly unlikely that the patient would survive such a surgery."

Caryn grinned, too. She found she liked the exotic, dark-skinned man, and in time she came to admire him. Each day they worked together, she learned more, fascinated by the healing power Hassan found in the simplest of herbs.

Wormwood stimulated the appetite—particularly good for the old and infirm. Mandrake root helped skin infections, or induced the patient to sleep. While the priest prescribed a concoction using the heads of seven fat bats for a spleen infection, a tincture of crickets and ox dung beetles for gallstones, Hassan gathered and worked his herbs, ofttimes heating them in a furnace, or pounding them in a stone mortar.

He showed Caryn his techniques, explaining each one thoroughly, and as always she learned quickly. Though she accepted his skills without question, the rivalry between Hassan and Father Burton grew worse each day. It wouldn't end, she knew, till the Arab was gone, and she had much to learn before then.

She glanced up at the sound of her name.

"Lady Caryn!" Nelda called out. "You must bring the healer and come quickly!" The tall thin woman stood at the door to the infirmary, her hands shaking, her narrow face pale.

"What is it, Nelda? What's happened?"

" 'Tis the young girl, Edmee. Her time is here and the babe will not come. 'Tis breached, Isolda says. She has been unable to turn it, and poor Edmee grows weak. Please, milady, I beg you to come."

"I must find Hassan."

He sat beside Ral in the great hall, leaning back against the stone wall with a casual grace. At Caryn's worried expression, both men came to their feet.

"What is it?" Ral asked, his eyes like steel and suddenly concerned.

"A woman in the village. There is trouble with the birth. They ask if Hassan will help."

The Arab came away from the wall and moved toward her in his graceful way. "Of course. I will get my things."

"I will go with you." Ral's hand rode protectively at her waist and if her heart hadn't lurched with such yearning, she might have been grateful to have him with her.

Gathering the supplies they would need, they ordered their horses readied. It was raining when they left the keep, the wind whipping the branches of overhanging trees, stirring leaves, and bending grasses. The temperature had dropped, and Caryn shivered within the folds of her cloak. When the fabric caught a gust of air and snagged against a tree, Ral rode up and freed it.

"I should have forbidden you to come. 'Tis cold and damp, an unfit night for you to be out."

"I'm grateful for your worry, my lord, but I am fine. Hassan will be leaving soon. 'Tis important that I learn all I can."

Ral grumbled but said nothing more.

They reached the cottar's hut sometime later, a small black shape against the villein's planted fields. Caryn was chilled to the bone, her clothes damp and clinging, but mostly she was anxious for the woman and unborn child struggling for life inside the small thatched cottage.

Hassan stopped her flight toward the door. "It is not believed that cleanliness affects the healing process, yet in my work, I have seen less putrifying of the wound, less infection and death when fresh linens and soap are applied.''

"I have brought them as you requested," Caryn said.

The Arab washed his hands and so did Caryn, then they entered the small, airless room.

" 'Tis too warm in here," the Arab said. "The woman loses too much fluid. Lift the flap on the door."

"But she is bound to catch a chill." The midwife, Isolda, came up from the foot of Edmee's straw pallet. "If the birthing does not kill her, 'tis certain the fever will."

"I have learned that it is best to broach one problem at a time."

"Do as he says," Ral softly commanded. He flashed Caryn a supportive glance, then moved out of the way toward the door. He would wait with Edmee's husband, Tosig, share a flask of wine to ward off the cold and help ease the poor man's fears.

"What do you give her?" Caryn asked Hassan, once Ral had gone. It was amazing how much larger the room seemed without him, yet also it somehow seemed more bleak.

"A potion of rue, savin, southernwood, and iris." He held it to the woman's trembling lips. She was covered in perspiration, her hair clinging wetly to her shoulders. "It will help her to relax."

" 'Tis all right, Edmee," Caryn said to her softly, pressing a damp cloth on her forehead. "Hassan knows what will help you."

"I-I would save the child, if there must be a choice. My husband so badly wants a son."

Caryn's heart turned over. The girl would sacrifice herself for the man she loved. Caryn wondered how far she would go for Ral and knew in that moment, she would do almost anything. It wasn't a comforting thought.

"It is your worry that inhibits the birthing," Hassan said to Edmee. "Please, you must try to relax." He waited for the potion she had drunk to begin its work, then parted her legs and reached inside her. "It is as the midwife says. The child is breached and somehow wedged."

"Can you turn it?"

"I am not sure." But his long arms worked with gentle pressure, moving the fetus around, trying to bring it into position. Every minute dragged, and the small room echoed with the woman's shrieks of pain.

Still, Hassan bent to his task, working until his own body glistened with sweat. Edmee looked so pale Caryn feared she was moments from dying. Finally Hassan looked up.

"Ready the birthing chair. The head is now in position."

"Thank God," Caryn whispered, adding a silent prayer that the babe and its mother would live. Tosig would be wild with joy. Unbidden came the thought: How would Ral feel if she were the woman and the babe were his son?

Hassan mixed two drachms each of the juice of hyssop and dittany, along with two scruples of quicksilver. Edmee drank it as they propped her in the birthing chair. In minutes, the head of the babe slid through. With Hassan's gentle instruction, the shoulders appeared and then the tiny, glistening body.

Isolda took the child from its mother's womb, a wide smile on her face. "You have done it, foreign one. You have succeeded where I would have failed."

"I will show Lady Caryn how to mix the potion and she can show you. Next time you will not fail."

"She is all right?" Tosig asked, walking in behind Ral, searching his wife's closed eyes and pale face as he moved toward her.

"Your wife and son are fine." Isolda set the sleeping

child in the crook of its mother's arm. Edmee slept as soundly as her babe.

"There are not enough words to thank you," Tosig said to Hassan, his eyes bright with unshed tears. "May God grace your goodness in all the years to come." He sat down near the pallet and took his young wife's hand.

It was nearly dawn when they left Edmee's hut, but Caryn had never felt more vitally alert. The air outside seemed less chill, the sky more vast, and the darkness less fearsome.

" 'Twas a wondrous thing we did," she said. "There can be no greater joy." Standing close beside her, Ral cupped her face in his hands. They were massive and powerful yet they could be infinitely gentle.

"Only should the child have been ours," he said and kissed her softly on the lips.

How would it feel to bear Ral's son? she wondered. There would be pain—she had known that all along—but there would also be gladness. The joy of holding their babe, the pleasure of watching him grow through the years. It pleased her to know it was something Ral wanted.

Her glance shifted back to the cottage and her smile began to fade. Inside the hut, the wee babe suckled at its mother's overripe breast. Caryn remembered how cumbersome the young woman had grown in the months before her lying-in, how fat and clumsy. She thought of how Edmee had waddled when she moved, how her heavy weight had left ugly marks upon her skin.

Caryn stared after her husband as he moved off toward the horses. He was tall and handsome, virile and powerfully built. He was every woman's dream and even without his title she didn't doubt he could have his pick. She looked down at her stomach. Her waist remained narrow, but even now his seed might be growing.

What would he think of her when she was as big and cumbersome as Edmee had been? Would the sight of her disgust him? And what of his passions? Would he wait for the arrival of their child? Would Ral remain faithful?

'Twas more likely that he would take another leman.

Caryn's insides churned. He had given up Lynette, but he had not said there would never be another. And he had never spoken of love.

Caryn shivered, feeling a sudden chill.

"You are cold," Ral said, returning to her side. "You will ride home with me."

Caryn did not argue. She needed the warmth of his hard arms around her. She needed to feel wanted and safe.

She wondered how long he would make her feel that way.

Richard absently finished eating, his mind on the night's entertainment ahead.

"Where is the jester?" Lord Ral asked from the seat beside him on the platform. "We have much to celebrate. I would hear a verse to the child of Braxston that Hassan has delivered among us."

Richard shifted uncomfortably, thinking of the girl who would soon come forth to entertain them. Now that he knew that Ancil was a woman, each of her movements drew his eye and fired his blood. What would the other men think should they realize the truth about her? 'Twas indecent for a lady to be dressed so, showing off her shapely limbs beneath the short tunic and making him wonder at the size of her breasts. Was their small size the reason they did not show, or had she disguised them, as she had done to her ears?

Uneasy all through the evening, Richard waited till the meal was ended then approached the girl in the passage at the end of the great hall.

"I would have a word with you, lady."

"Aye, Richard. Why do we not go into my chamber where we will not be seen?" She lifted the curtain to her small private sleeping room.

"We cannot go in there. 'Twould be unseemly to do such a thing."

"No one knows I am a woman." She lifted the flap once more.

"*I* know," he said, firmly jerking the curtain from her hands and letting it fall back in place. "Which is why I seek you out."

She turned to face him more squarely, her expression hidden by her half-black, half-white face paint. "Go on."

" 'Tis unseemly for a woman to display herself as you do. You must tell Lord Ral the truth."

"Nay, you know that I cannot."

"Then at least find a way to end your lewd charade. You are a lady. You cannot continue to behave as you do."

Ambra set her hands on her hips, her tunic sliding in to reveal her tiny waist. "I act the part of jester. There is nothing lewd in that and even if there were, 'tis no concern of yours."

" 'Tis my concern, since you have fallen under my protection."

"I do not need your protection. And I have never behaved as aught but a lady. That I dance and sing does not change that." She ducked beneath the curtain and Richard followed her in.

"Damn but you are vexing." And too beautiful for words. Now that he could see beneath her disguise, his throat went tight just to look at her.

"And you, Richard, are stuffy and prudish. If I displease you so much, then why do you not just leave?"

He bristled, torn between fury and a lust that seemed to swell with every heartbeat. He gave her a courtly, mocking bow. "As you wish, *my lady.*"

"And do not call me that. 'Tis far too dangerous. What if someone should hear you?"

He scoffed at that. "Since when has danger been of any concern to you?" He turned and stalked from the room.

Chapter Eighteen

R al rode his big black destrier at the front of his small band of men, their horses stirring up dust along the trail. They were dressed in full battle gear, chain mail hauberk, sword and shield, patrolling the landscape north of the keep, crossing mountain and valley in search of the Ferret.

Naught had been heard of the outlaw since his disastrous encounter with Malvern—no raids, no travelers assaulted, no caravans lost, yet Ral rode uneasy in the saddle. Instinct and long years of fighting said the Ferret would return, sooner or later, that even now he recruited more men and it wouldn't be long before his villany would once more rain down upon the unwary.

Ral did not intend to let it happen.

"Tracks cross the trail near the river ahead." Odo rode up beside him. "A wagon and travelers afoot. 'Tis unlikely that it is the Ferret."

Ral nodded. "He and his men would needs be traveling horseback. Naught else looks amiss?"

"Nay, my lord."

Just then Geoffrey approached from the rear, riding a big white stallion he called Baron. "Have you found him, my lord? Has Odo discovered the Ferret?"

"Nay, there has been no sign. 'Twould seem that for at least a while longer we are safe from his treachery."

Geoffrey relaxed in his saddle. " 'Tis my fondest hope he does not show his evil face again."

Ral made no comment. In most ways he felt the same, yet the land he would receive for the outlaw's capture remained all important. More so now, with the death of so many cattle. If the Ferret returned, he would rob and pillage and terrorize travelers on the roads. But without him, there would be no grant of land.

Ral glanced at Geoffrey, saw him smiling easily, laughing at something Odo said. He had thought little of Geoffrey since his return to Caryn's bed. Yet thoughts of the handsome young knight crept occasionally into his mind.

Caryn still spoke with affection to Geoffrey, still gamed with him in the great hall, still laughed more readily with Geoffrey than she did with her own husband. What were her feelings toward him? Could he be certain those feelings would not grow?

Ral had known many women. But he had loved only once. *Eliana*. She was a viper clothed in female skin. She was temptation and corruption in the guise of a woman, a vixen who could dupe and betray without the slightest twinge of guilt.

Other women he had known weren't much better. They worked to please him for as long as he would have them, but once he tired of them, they would move on, repeating vows of love and loyalty to the next man and the next.

Still, his mother had been a good woman, faithful even when his father had strayed. She had been kind and loving, tolerating her husband's numerous lemen, always welcoming him back to her bed. And his sisters, so far as he knew, remained ever loyal to their husbands, happily so, it would seem.

But what of Caryn? He knew now that she would not forgive his infidelities, and in truth he had little desire for other women. But what of her desires? Besides her physical need of him, what feelings did she hold for him? How much did she really care?

Each day his own feelings grew deeper. Frighteningly so. Yet he had forced himself to face them. To conquer his fears, to give her his loyalty—and his trust. Each day that trust deepened, reaching farther inside him, gaining a tighter hold on his heart.

It terrified him to think what he was risking.

As he rode back toward the castle, he prayed this time he would not regret it.

"The game is over—Beltar comes!"

Ambra's heart slammed hard against her ribs. She was standing near the drawbridge, enjoying a walk before the midday meal, basking in the bright warming rays of the sun. At the sound of Richard's voice, she spun in his direction.

"Dear God, Richard, say you do not mean it." But his long grim strides continued toward her, and the look on his face said he meant every word.

"A messenger came only this morning. Beltar will arrive on the morrow."

"Surely he cannot know that I am here."

" 'Tis the reason for his journey."

"But how could he have discovered where I am?"

"Lady Caryn knows and so do I. The members of your troupe know. There are bound to be others."

She worked to keep her hands from shaking. "What else did the message say?"

"Beltar accuses Lord Ral of your abduction." Ambra hissed in a breath. "He demands that Braxston give you up. 'Tis hinted the Dark Knight has forced you into his bed, that you are Lord Ral's leman."

"Dear God in heaven. What says Lord Ral?"

A tinge of color crept into Richard's cheeks. "He does not yet know. Thus far I have given the message only to Lady Caryn." He glanced back toward the gray stone walls of the keep. "Even now she seeks him out. Mayhap she can win you his favor."

"He will not be pleased that you did not go to him in the beginning."

"As you said, you and I are friends."

"Aye." But it wasn't his friendship Ambra wanted. Now that she knew she must leave, she discovered what she had suspected all along. She wanted Richard's love.

"Lady Caryn will speak well for you. Mayhap Lord Ral can pursuade Lord Beltar—"

"Nay, I cannot risk it." She started forward, but Richard caught her arm.

"Where do you mean to go?"

"Far and away from here." She took a step, but his grip on her arm grew tighter.

"I cannot let you do that." His eyes came to rest on her face. Reaching out, he eased the hat from her head, letting her shiny blond hair tumble down, then he pulled the clay from the back of her ears. "You are a woman," he said softly, "a young and beautiful one, at that. 'Tis not safe for you to roam the country. If Lord Ral cannot help you, then you must accept the path that lies ahead."

Ambra watched him a moment, her heart thudding softly. Then she steeled herself and shook her head. "I may be a woman, but thus far I have made it on my own. I will continue to do so." She pulled free of his hold and started walking, but Richard caught her in a few quick strides.

He grabbed her arm and spun her around. "You will do as I say, do you hear?"

"I will do as I please." She tried to pull free, but he wouldn't let go.

"You are willful and stubborn. You are reckless and headstrong and totally unmanageable. I pity Lord Beltar, should he take you to wife."

Before she could think, her hand lashed out and

cracked across his face. Ambra sucked in a breath and so did Richard. "I-I am sorry." She chewed her bottom lip as an angry red mark appeared on his cheek. "I did not mean to do that."

Richard said nothing, but a muscle tightened in his jaw. He grabbed her arm and pulled her close, then his mouth came down over hers. She could feel his anger in the tension in his body, but she could also feel his passion. He forced his tongue into her mouth and she thought her legs might give way beneath her. Then his fiery kiss gentled. His hold on her, no longer brutal but no less possessive, slowly began to ease. His lips brushed the corners of her mouth, teasing, tasting, making the heat flow softly through her body. He was shaking when he pulled away.

"I am sorry. I should not have done that."

Ambra touched her kiss-swollen lips. The taste of him still lingered. "I wanted you to kiss me. I have for a very long time."

Richard glanced away. "We are nothing alike, you and I."

"I know. I am stubborn and willful, while you . . . you can be missish and far too set in your ways."

A faint smile curved his lips, then he straightened. "And you are betrothed to another." He gripped her arm and urged her once more toward the keep. "I meant what I said. I will not let you run."

But you will let him have me. As they hadn't in a very long time, tears gathered in her eyes and began to slip down her cheeks.

"I cannot believe you have once more deceived me," Ral said to Caryn, staring at her as if she had somehow failed him. The thought stirred an uneasy feeling in the pit of her stomach.

" 'Tis not a matter of deceit, but of trying to help someone."

"Were you so certain that I would not?"

"Well, I . . ."

"Were you?" They were standing in their chamber, Ral pacing the floor at the foot of their bed, his tunic making jerking movements with each of his powerful strides.

Caryn's chin came up. "When it was your wish to wed me, you did so, whether I desired it or not. 'Tis Beltar's wish to wed Lady Ambra. I cannot believe you would gainsay him in this."

He eyed her for a long, cool moment. "Why have you come to me now, when you did not do so before?"

Caryn stared down at her feet, her soft leather shoes still muddy from her morning trek out to the stables. "Lord Beltar arrives on the morrow."

Ral's hand slammed hard against the bedpost. "Sweet Christ, I cannot believe it! Beltar at Braxston. That is all we need." He raked a hand through his wavy black hair, frustration and anger carving deep lines in his face. "How is it you know?"

"Richard told me. A messenger arrived just this morning."

"Richard? You've involved Richard in this deceit?"

" 'Twas Richard who received the news. He came to me because he cares for Lady Ambra. Have you not seen the way he looks at her?"

"Aye, I have seen it. You are telling me that Richard has also been aware of the jester's ruse?"

" 'Twas only recently that he discovered, though I think his body was certain from the start."

Ral grunted. " 'Twill do neither of them any good. The girl goes back to Beltar on the morrow."

Caryn caught her husband's arm and felt the heavy muscles bunch. "Please, my lord, you cannot mean it. The man is an ogre. Even before the marriage, he tried to ravish her. You cannot mean to let him have her."

"Beltar is her betrothed. There is naught I can do."

"Beltar believes you are to blame. He thinks the girl is your leman. Mayhap if you told him it was so—"

"For God's sake, woman! Beltar is one of the most powerful men in England. He can mount a thousand men, should he desire to. Do you wish me to fight a war to keep one small woman from taking the vows as his wife?"

Caryn took a steadying breath. Put that way, Ral was right. He could hardly endanger his people, mayhap get many of them killed.

"Is there naught that we can do? She is such a lovely girl." But even as she said the words, a thought began to form in her head.

"Nay. I must give her over to Beltar. Let us hope I can convince him I had naught to do with her abduction."

Caryn turned away, the idea growing, taking solid shape in her mind. "As you wish, my lord." She started for the door, but Ral stepped in front of her.

"You give in too readily, my love." He eyed her with shrewd assessment. "What goes on in that wily mind of yours?"

"Very little, unfortunately, my lord."

"Good. In the meantime, just to be safe, the girl will be locked in a room in the keep. I would be certain she is here when her bridegroom arrives on the morrow."

Caryn said nothing more. What she meant to see done had nothing to do with Ambra's running away. She smiled to herself as she walked out the door.

"I would speak with you, Richard." Caryn stuck her head through the door to the room in which he worked. Instead of finding him bent over his desk, as she had expected, he paced back and forth, much as Ral had done upstairs.

"Of course, my lady." He approached her with a brooding expression, searching her face for a sign that her husband's decision might have changed. "They have taken her to a chamber upstairs. Lord Ral sent men-at-arms to be certain she did not run away.''

"I know."

"She weeps, my lady. I have rarely seen her aught but smiling. I find it disturbs me greatly.''

Caryn brightened. "Then you must feel something for her. Is that not so?"

"Of course, I do." He glanced away. "We are friends of a sort.''

"That is all you feel, Richard? Friendship?"

He looked decidedly uncomfortable. "I desire her, if that is what you mean. 'Tis only natural. Ambra is a very beautiful woman.''

"I am glad you noticed."

He sighed. "What does it matter? Lord Ral would see her wed to Beltar.''

"Aye, that is true. 'Tis also true that Ambra could not wed him, if she were already wed to you."

"What!"

"Surely it has occurred to you. You said that you desired her.''

Richard rested an unsteady hand on his desk. "Aye, it has occurred to me. It has also occurred to me how foolish such a notion would be.''

"Why? As you have said, Ambra is a lovely young woman. She would make any man a fine wife."

"Any man but me," he grumbled.

"I do not understand."

"Can you not see? Never were two people less suited. I would choose a quiet, submissive woman for my wife. Someone who would not gainsay me at every turn. Ambra is hardly submissive.''

"No, she is not submissive. She is vibrant and spirited and full of life. The kind of woman who could walk beside you, instead of trailing along in your wake. Surely you would be bored in a fortnight with the kind of woman you describe.''

" 'Tis not a matter of boredom," Richard said. " 'Tis only a matter of behaving as a woman should."

"I have rarely behaved as you believe a woman should," Caryn reminded him, suddenly wondering if that might be the kind of wife Ral had also wanted.

Richard eyed her strangely. "I suppose that is true. I did not mean it exactly as it sounded."

For a moment, Caryn said nothing. Then she sighed. "I am sorry, Richard. I should not have come. 'Twas wrong of me to ask of you something you do not wish to do. 'Twas only that I thought mayhap . . . that I hoped . . ." She moved away from him and started toward the door.

"Wait."

Caryn turned to face him, saw the uncertainty etched on his handsome face.

"Mayhap there is something to what you say." He straightened, looking far too serious for a matter which should have brought him joy. "Mayhap in time she would adjust. Besides 'tis my Christian duty to save her from a man like Beltar."

Christian duty, Caryn thought with a secret smile. 'Twould hardly be duty Richard thought of when he bore the lovely Ambra to his bed. "Mayhap you will learn to adjust a little, too."

He frowned at the notion, but said nothing to dispute it. "You have spoken of this to Ambra? You are certain that she will accept me?"

"I am afraid that discussion must needs be left to you."

A scoffing sound escaped him. "There is a good chance she will refuse me. And there is the matter of the priest. The banns have not been posted. Mayhap he will refuse to perform the marriage."

"Father Burton is treated well here, far better than in other places he might go. He will do whatever it takes to maintain Lord Ral's good will."

"And Lord Ral?"

"Aye, my wayward little wife, what of Lord Ral?"

Caryn tensed at the sound of her husband's deep voice coming from the open doorway.

"I-I . . . I am glad you are here, husband." One black brow arched up. "You see, 'tis Richard's fondest wish to marry Lady Ambra. I have told him you will help see it done."

"Since when did you begin speaking for me?"

Caryn nervously moistened her lips. "I had hoped that you would be pleased, that you would be happy to see Richard wed. Will you help them?"

He surprised her by the faintest of smiles. " 'Tis why I have come. I wished to discover if Richard's intentions were those of an honorable sort."

"Truly, my lord?"

"Aye." He turned to his steward, his tunic swirling with the movement. "What say you, Richard? Is the lady to your liking?"

Richard looked even more uneasy. Then he squared his shoulders. "Aye, my lord."

Ral surveyed him a long moment more, turned and said something to a man who stood behind him. The man nodded briefly and hurried away.

"I have ordered her brought here. We will see what the lady has to say."

Ambra stood in front of Richard's wide desk. "I think you have all gone completely insane!"

Richard's hand shot out and caught her arm. He gave it a firm squeeze of warning. "You forget yourself, lady. These people are your friends. They wish only to see you safe."

"I am sorry, Lord Ral. I did not mean to offend you. 'Tis only that . . ."

"That what?" Ral pressed. "That you would rather

marry Beltar? If that is the case, 'twill go far easier on the lot of us.''

"I wish to marry no man! I wish to be left on my own as I was before."

Caryn approached where Ambra stood trembling, a film of tears glistening in her pretty green eyes. "I thought you cared for Richard," she said. "There was warmth in your gaze whenever you looked at him."

Ambra stiffened. "That was before I knew the way he felt. Now that I do, I would rather marry Beltar."

Richard moved closer, his face drawn in tight lines of tension. "You are the one who has gone insane. Did you not tell me the man is an abuser of women? Can you not imagine what he would do to the woman who has caused him to look such a fool?"

Her bottom lip quivered. "I will not marry a man who does not want me."

Richard swore softly. "What makes you think I do not want you? Even now it is all I can do to keep my hands off you." As if to prove it, he gripped her shoulders. "Were you my wife, I would carry you into my chamber and make love to you for hours on end."

"Richard!"

A blush stole over his skin, from his neck to the sandy brown hair above his forehead. "I am sorry. 'Tis only that you make me so angry. For a moment I forgot where we were."

Ral chuckled softly. "Mayhap 'tis good that you did. What say you now, Lady Ambra? 'Tis obvious my seneschal would be more than pleased to wed you."

He doesn't love me, Ambra thought, *but I love him. And I desire him just as he desires me.* For the present, it would have to do. She looked Richard straight in the eye.

"I am not what you want; I probably never will be. Can you accept me as I am?"

He surveyed her feminine curves, evident even in the

loose-fitting rose linen tunic she now wore. "Aye, that I can."

"Then I will marry you."

Ral smiled. "So be it. I will speak to Father Burton. Make yourselves ready. The sooner the deed is done, the safer your lady will be."

He did not mention the rage they were bound to encounter when Beltar discovered he had been duped. Still, once the girl was wed, he did not think Beltar would raise his might against them.

At least he prayed the man would not. Already Braxston Keep had more problems than he could handle.

The priest awaited them in front of the small alcove that served as the chapel. The last yellow rays of the late afternoon sun brightened the stained glass windows, reflecting the story of Christ's early life, the pictures an uplifting message.

Ambra read them with cool resignation. If only her spirits could be so uplifted. Instead when she glanced at the man who would be her husband, lines of worry marred his forehead. His features had drawn into a taut, unreadable expression.

It took every ounce of her courage to repeat the vows, and only Beltar's menacing arrival commanded her to do so. In minutes the wedding was ended, a blur of images that Ambra would scarcely remember come dawn. A special meal was prepared, and toasts rang out through the hall, knights and servants alike giving the newly wedded couple their blessings.

On a different occasion, Ambra might have enjoyed herself. Instead, each time her glance strayed to her husband, she saw his brooding expression and her heart constricted inside her chest.

"The hour grows late," Richard finally said, maintaining his careful control. "Lord Ral has seen a chamber prepared for us upstairs."

Ambra wet her suddenly dry lips. "Aye, as you say, the

hour grows late.'' The knowledge of Beltar's arrival had kept the celebration subdued and spared them the ritual bedding. Yet by the time they left the hall, her nerves were strung taut as the strings of a lute.

They climbed the stairs in silence and even inside their chamber, neither of them moved to pierce the quiet. Ambra assessed the tension in her husband's wide shoulders. He had said he desired her, yet not a flicker of emotion showed in his face. He had said he wanted her, but taking her body, using it for his pleasure, even should she experience that pleasure too—in these final moments, she realized it was not enough.

"I cannot do this," she said into the stillness, leaning a hand against the bedpost for support. "I will not."

"What are you talking about?" Richard's broad shoulders went even more rigid. "You are my wife. 'Tis too late now for regrets."

"We'll have the priest annul the vows. The marriage has not yet been consummated. 'Tis not impossible for us to—"

"The marriage will be consummated—and soon. You may count on that."

"No!"

"For God's sake, Ambra, we must do this. 'Tis the only way you will be safe."

Tears welled but she blinked them away. "I cannot do it. If I didn't care for you as I do, mayhap I could go through with it. But each time I see the regret in your eyes, it breaks my heart. No, Richard. I will not let it happen."

Richard looked at her in stunned disbelief. "You are willing to marry Beltar because you believe I regret the marriage?"

"All I have left in this world is the person that I am. If the man I love does not value that person—"

Richard caught her arm. "What did you say?"

"Please, Richard. Lord Ral will do as you wish, I know

he will. Tell him you've changed your mind, that you
desire to wed another."

He tipped her chin with his fingers. For the first time,
the lines had left his forehead. "Why would I do such a
thing . . . when it would be a lie."

Her eyes searched his dear handsome face, trying to
comprehend his words.

" 'Tis truth that we are different," he said. "And aye,
it worries me some. But from the moment of our first
meeting, you have stirred me in some way. Since the day
I discovered you were a woman, you have been a fever
in my blood." He pulled her gently into his arms. "If 'tis
truth that you feel love for me as well as friendship, then
I am no longer uncertain." He brushed a tear from her
cheek. "We will make this marriage work—you will see.
We will find a way to be happy."

His kiss took the breath from her lungs and the fear
from her heart. "Do you mean it, Richard?"

"Aye, 'tis a vow I mean to keep." His lips covered
hers once more, a kiss of possession that at last became
tender.

"Are you afraid of what will happen between us this
eve?" he asked softly.

"I have never been afraid of you."

"I promise I will be gentle."

Ambra shook her head. "I do not want gentle. When
you kiss me, a fire rages inside me. 'Tis passion I want
from you, Richard. Mindless blazing heat and kisses
without end."

Richard smiled so broadly deep grooves appeared in
his cheeks. He cradled her face in his hands. "You are
more woman than a man could ever hope for. You believed I regretted this marriage? Had I not wed you, I
would have regretted it all the days of my life."

With a last thorough kiss, Richard carried her to the
bed and began to strip off her clothes. Fresh tears stung
her eyes, but they were not tears of sorrow. Already she

was happy and the night had only begun. With God's will, it would be so for the rest of their lives.

Caryn tossed and turned, caught up in a hazy dream. Ral was lying beside a stately dark woman—Eliana, she saw. He was naked and covered in sweat. They had just made love yet Ral's hand moved over her breast, caressing a nipple, urging her to once more respond.

Willing the image away, Caryn's eyes snapped open. She battled her way to wakefulness with the first dim rays of the sun. Ral lay close beside her, his massive frame enfolding her spoon-fashion, his fingers cupping a breast. He was teasing her nipple, stirring warm languid sensations. His touch had spawned the dream, she realized, feeling his hardness against her bottom. It felt thick and heavy and she knew the pleasure it would bring.

Still, the dark images lingered, vying with the heightened tempo of her heart.

'Tis only a dream and a dream does not matter, she told herself firmly. She was the one Ral wanted, not the beautiful Eliana. She was the one who would take him inside her, the one who would ease his passions, and yet . . .

His lips brushed the nape of her neck. Pushing her heavy mane of hair out of his way, he gently nipped her skin then laved it with his tongue.

"Part your legs, *cherie,*" he whispered, the husky note in his voice sending a shiver of heat through her body. She did as he instructed, the dream faded now, replaced by the flames sweeping hotly through her body. His fingers touched her lightly, probing, teasing, sparking fires, making her achy and damp. She gave herself over to the passions he stirred, the feel of his lips against her throat, the play of muscle as his massive chest rubbed against her back.

When he had readied her enough, he sank himself inside her, huge and hard, and Caryn arched her hips to accept him. He felt rigid and pulsing, hot and thick and demanding. He pulled himself out and sank in again, and fire careened through her body. Caryn moaned at the heat roaring through her, at the overwhelming sensations of sweetness.

He held her hips with his hands, thrusting deeper, harder, touching the far walls of her womb. Each stroke lifted her higher, spiraled her upward, and forced her nearer the edge. Out and then in, out and then in, the steady rhythm hypnotic, the feel of his rock hard flesh against her slick damp skin making white-hot shivers run through her veins.

In minutes she had reached her peak, shattering into fragments of pleasure, then floating, floating, drifting down into a warm, honeyed sea. She felt Ral tense as he reached his own release, then began to drift back down. They lay quiet for a time, arms and legs intertwined, Ral as sated and relaxed as she.

She felt a masculine finger tracing patterns on her shoulder. His softly spoken words moved tendrils of hair beside her cheek. "I wonder was Richard's night half as pleasant as mine."

"I hope they are happy." Caryn settled herself beside him, trying hard not to think of the dream or her uncertain future. For a while those worries had left her. Now they were wont to return. "I would not like to think our interference brought them grief."

"I believe the marriage was Richard's true wish," Ral said. " 'Twas only that by the time he had realized what he wanted, it would have been too late."

Caryn smiled softly, enjoying the feel of having him so near no matter the consequence she might one day face. "I am always amazed at your wisdom, my lord."

Ral scoffed at that. "We will see how wise a decision it was when Beltar arrives."

Lifting her head from a muscular arm, she sat up and

turned to face him. "How shall we proceed, Ral? What do you think is the wisest course?"

Ral sat up, too, pushing heavy black hair from his forehead. "I have thought long on this. I have decided we will welcome the man as a guest. We will prepare a feast, though 'twill have to be a small one, then should things go smoothly, we will make plans for a hunt. 'Tis said the man has a liking for boar. Mayhap the bloody taking of a beast will sooth the loss of his little virgin's blood."

"I hope you are right," Caryn said.

Ral nodded. "My scouts will arrive well before Beltar. We will know how many men we must fight, should my *wisdom* prove wrong."

Chapter Nineteen

As Ral had predicted, word of Beltar the Fierce arrived within the next three hours. A fair-sized army of knights and men-at-arms traveled the road toward Braxston Keep. Ral sent a messenger to welcome them and advise Beltar of the feast they planned in his honor.

Meanwhile Ral continued to lay his plans. With the bulk of Beltar's forces remaining outside the walls, Ral and his knights could defend the keep. Unfortunately, should a siege begin, they would desperately need more men.

With that possibility in mind, Ral sent messengers to lords he could count on for support, and knights who owed him service, asking them to stand at the ready. Still, he remained uneasy.

Beltar arrived just before dusk, a stout, thick-limbed, beetle-browed man with greasy black hair and several days' growth of beard. Behind him, an entourage of advisors, knights, and men-at-arms stirred up dust on the road then came to a halt in the field across from the drawbridge.

With his own knights armed and ready, Ral invited Beltar and his closest advisors inside the wall surrounding the keep, then greeted him out in the bailey. Within the tower itself, archers stood at the long narrow windows and ringed the topmost parapet, ready to rain down arrows from above.

"Greetings, Lord Beltar," Ral called out to him, forcing himself to smile even as he braced his feet apart in a wary stance. "Welcome to Braxston Keep."

"I am surprised to be so well received." Beltar made no move to dismount. He rode a huge blood bay destrier, its nostrils flaring as it tested the wind. "You know why I have come?"

"We received your message. 'Tis clear there has been some mistake."

"How so?" Beltar asked. "The girl is not here?"

"I would have you come inside so that we may discuss it. There is wine and ale, and even now my servants prepare a feast in your honor."

"I asked if the girl is here."

"Lady Ambra resides at Braxston, but I was not the man who brought her. In truth, she came on her own. 'Twas unknown who she was until your messenger arrived. By that time, 'twas too late."

Beltar stiffened in his saddle. Wind ruffled the hem of his short black tunic while the sun glinted fiercely off his armor. "Too late? The girl then is gone?"

"Wed to another, I fear. By the priest here in the castle. The deed is done, my friend. The girl is married to my seneschal, Richard of Pembroke."

"I do not believe you." He nudged the great beast forward until the mail on his leg pressed into Ral's chest. "You've installed the girl in your bed and you mean to see she remains there."

Ral didn't move, just leaned his considerable weight into the horse, forcing it to take a step backward. He started to reply but a murmur rose behind him as Richard stepped from the entry and stood at the top of the stairs leading down to the bailey.

" 'Tis truth Lord Ral speaks, Lord Beltar. The girl is wife to me, Richard of Pembroke. 'Tis also a fact she was never Lord Ral's leman. She was virgin when I took her. And I have done so well and often. Even now she may carry my babe."

Beltar raised a leather-gloved fist and shook it into the air. "All knew of my search for her," he said to Ral. "Why did you allow the wedding?"

" 'Twas not then known who the girl was, since she traveled with a band of troubadours. She was ripe and willing and my steward desired her. The marriage seemed harmless at the time."

"Ripe she was," he grumbled, leaning over to spit into the dirt. "A rare fruit I meant to pluck for myself." He shifted his gaze toward the door of the keep and Ral caught a glimpse of rich dark-auburn hair.

Caryn stood just inside the entry next to Ambra. By Christ, he had told her to stay inside out of danger. She moved a little and her high full bosom came into view. God, but she was a lush little wench. No wonder he never seemed to get enough of her.

He glanced at Beltar, who was staring in her direction with such a lascivious smile it made him want to smash a fist into the man's harsh face.

"Who is the wench with the fire-touched hair?"

"She is my wife," Ral said easily, but it was unease he felt inside. He didn't like Beltar's lecherous expression as he eyed her feminine curves, or the way his hard gaze shifted from Caryn to the archers atop the parapet, as if he sized up Braxston's defenses.

Beltar's gaze swung back to his. "I would see the girl and the priest. I would know for certain you speak the truth."

From atop the wooden stairs, Ambra eased her way toward Richard, who tensed at her appearance, but finally let her pass. The priest stepped out of the shadows along the wall.

"The two are well and truly wedded," Father Burton

said. "As deceitful as she is, you should count yourself lucky."

Some of Beltar's anger swung to the woman with the pale blond hair who faced him across the bailey. "It appears you have duped us all. Mayhap as the priest says, I am fortunate you are wedded to another." He fixed a hard look on Richard. "I advise you take a stick to her, firmly and often. A good sound beating is the only thing a girl of her like understands."

Some of the tension eased from Richard's shoulders. "I will heed your words, my lord. Please accept my humble apologies for any trouble she may have caused. You've my promise the girl will not leave her chamber during the hours of your visit." The ghost of a smile touched his lips. "Ambra, you will await me upstairs."

As Ambra hurried to do her husband's bidding, Ral felt a twinge of amusement. Richard had neglected to mention he would remain in the room along with her. It appeared his role as husband had not been so hard to accept as he had believed.

Ral watched his steward disappear back through the entry. Richard had played his part well and though Beltar still looked disgruntled, the blame for his loss no longer fell on the Lord of Braxston Keep.

"I hope you've a willing wench to take that one's place," Beltar said as he dismounted. "I've imagined driving myself between the girl's sweet thighs for nigh on six months. Just to think of her spreading her legs for your man leaves me hard as a bloody stone."

"We've a comely wench or two inside," Ral said. "They have heard of your prowess and even now await your pleasure." The problem had been expected and Ral had seen it solved. "I will send one of them up to help you bathe. You can enjoy the wench, along with a goblet of wine, then we can proceed with the feast."

Beltar merely grumbled.

They were safe for the moment, at least. Ral glanced

back to where Caryn still stood by the open door. He
had told her to wait inside, and by the mere span of
inches, she had obeyed him. Sweet Christ, the wench
was a handful.

And all the more tantalizing for her stubborn independ-
dence.

He saw her scramble away from the entry as he
started in that direction and made a mental note to see
that she paid dearly for her transgression—tonight in his
bed. He could think of at least a dozen ways.

Ral smiled and then frowned. He would have to make
certain his powerful guest remained occupied and under close-watch in much the same manner.

With his former betrothed out of sight, Beltar seemed to
relax, and the tension in the keep began to ease. He
drank what seemed barrels of wine and insatiably ordered wench after wench to his bed. Fortunately, there
seemed an endless number willing to please him, since
he filled their purses with coin enough to ease his rough
handling and sooth his savage thrusts between their
legs.

Still, his eyes often drifted to Caryn. That he wanted
her in his bed fired Ral's temper. It took a will of iron to
keep from grabbing the man by the throat and squeezing until his lecherous eyes slid closed. Finally after a
long night of wenching, Beltar's thoughts began to turn
in another direction.

"I've had my fill of women," he said the afternoon of
the following day. " 'Tis the boar sport you promised
that intrigues me." Even with his hair freshly scrubbed
and his face scraped clean of whiskers, his smile looked
slightly vicious. "I will bloody my lance at Braxston, one
way or another."

Ral worked to hide a twinge of anger. *Take care,
Beltar, or 'twill be the blood pumping through your
veins that darkens the earth at Braxston Keep.*

They set off at daybreak the following morn, Ral and
en men, Beltar and his ten. The rest remained at the
castle, keeping the uneasy truce.

With the hounds forging ahead, they spotted feral pig
poor several hours into the hills and the dogs picked
up the scent. Both grey- and deerhound bayed into the
watery blue, early morning sky, then feverishly raced
orward, leading the hunters deeper into the forest.

" 'The beast is good-sized," said Beltar, studying the
animal's tracks in the mud.

"Aye, and then some," Ral agreed.

" 'Twill be sport fit for a king."

Ral did not answer. His gaze had moved up ahead,
ollowing the hounds disappearing in the distance. At
he edge of a cluster of oaks they stopped, and the
ound of their frantic baying increased, echoing eerily
off their surroundings.

"They've cornered him at last!" Beltar's voice rang
out. "The great beast has at last turned to fight!"

"Aye . . . so 'twould seem."

They rode in that direction, the men behind them
armed and ready should their lords' arrows fail to stop
he savage boar.

"The beast is even bigger than I imagined." As Beltar
opped the rise, he saw the animal silhouetted against
he thick girth of a tree.

"That he is, and by the look of him, far tougher. Al-
eady he has killed three of Braxston's best hounds."

"Aye," Beltar said, "but they have drawn blood. 'Twill
ncite him to better sport." So saying, he drew an arrow
rom his quiver, notched his bow, took careful aim on
he boar, and let fly. It hit the boar in the hip, spouting
blood and protruding grimly. A terrible squealing
erupted and though the animal still faced them, it
shielded itself between a downed tree trunk and a small
outcropping of boulders.

"We'll have to dismount to take him," Ral said, but

already Beltar climbed down from his horse. Ral did th
same, motioning for Lambert and Geoffrey to join them

Leaving the horses behind, they crept closer to th
wounded boar. It was huge and menacing, bristling with
fury as it stamped its cloven hooves, its vicious tusk
curving up and glinting in the sun as it prepared for
battle to the finish.

The smell of the beast made Ral grimace, the scent o
fear and of blood and of death. He had smelled tha
same odor among men in battle.

"The beast is mine," Beltar vowed, notching a second
arrow into his bowstring. The stout man moved closer
stalking his prey while the huge wild boar stalked him
Ral notched his own arrow, as did Geoffrey and Hugh
and two of Beltar's men, surrounding the boar in the
clearing.

Beltar's arrow sang its death song, flying straight and
swiftly toward the huge boar's side, but instead of strik
ing neatly between the ribs and sinking into the heart a
Beltar intended, it struck a bone and bounced away. The
animal squeeled in fury, then it charged.

Beltar readied another arrow and let it fly, hitting the
animal squarely in the chest. It stumbled and faltered
but didn't go down. Instead it turned a little to the lef
and continued its savage assault. It bore Geoffrey to the
ground even as Ral's arrow sank into its neck.

"Sweet Christ!" Ral swore, tossing his bow aside and
reaching for the hilt of his sword. He raced toward Geof
frey, swinging his blade in a powerful arc, slicing into
the boar and nearly severing the animal's head from it
shoulders.

Before the boar's twitching body had stilled, two o
Beltar's knights raced in to drag the carcass off the mar
lying unconscious in the dirt, his head gashed open and
his shoulder erupting in blood.

"Wrap a cloth around the wound and one around hi

ead to slow the bleeding," Ral commanded. "We've
ot to get him back to the castle."

"What a magnificent specimen." Beltar nudged the
oar with his foot. "A shame about your man, but 'tis
ie danger that makes for good sport."

Ral said nothing. Instead he helped Lambert and
ugh lift Geoffrey onto his horse. They tied him across
ie saddle and Hugh grabbed the reins. Turning the
orses, they started back to Braxston Keep.

Christ's blood, Ral thought, *if only Hassan remained
t the hall.* But the Arab physician had left to rejoin the
ing a few days after the birth of the child in the village.
he priest was there, but Father Burton's healing skills
ere primitive at best.

And then there was Caryn.

His wife had learned much from the Arab healer and
ie was certain to remember. Caryn was the young
night's best chance for survival, as Ral knew only too
ell. Though the priest might not approve, Ral meant to
ee it done.

It would be Caryn who tended to Geoffrey, Caryn
rho saw whether he lived or died. Caryn whose hands
oothed the handsome knight's lean hard body.

Ral's stomach clenched at the thought.

Dear God—Geoffrey!" Caryn rushed toward the men
rho carried the young man into the castle. "What's
appened? He is not . . . he is not dead?"

"Nay," Ral said, "the lad still lives, though his injury is
grave one."

She swallowed the bile that had risen in her throat at
ie sight of Geoffrey's blood, and worked to slow her
ounding heart.

"Bring him in here." Her hands shook as she sur-
eyed his pale face and seemingly lifeless body. The
ien carried their heavy burden into the room that

served as medicinal. Father Burton used it now that Hassan was gone. When she was needed, so did Caryn.

"Be careful of his shoulder." Under her direction, the place had been kept neat and orderly, the bottles and jars she and the Arab had concocted still sat on a wooden table along one wall. "And bring me a pitcher of water."

They laid him on a scrubbed wooden table and hurried to do her bidding as she removed the bloody wrappings from his wounds.

"Mother of God . . ."

"Aye, my lady," Lambert said, " 'twill take God's sweet mercy to save 'im."

Standing beside them, Hugh nervously twisted his hat. " 'Twas as vicious a beast as I've e'er seen, milady."

"Aye, that is clear." Caryn dampened a cloth and began to cleanse the wound with an unsteady hand. "With an injury like this, there is certain to be an infection." She shook her head. "He is pale as death itself. He has lost far too much blood."

" 'Tis a wonder he is not dead already," Ral said, coming up beside her. " 'Twas a difficult journey home."

" 'Twill be a difficult journey to recovery. I only pray that he will survive it."

Ral made no comment, but his eyes searched her face in an uneasy manner and she wondered at his thoughts.

"There is naught you can do but what you have learned," he finally said. " 'Tis as much as anyone can ask." Then he turned and walked away.

For seven long days, Caryn remained at Geoffrey's bedside. She treated his scalp wound with sicklewort to stop the bleeding, wrapped it and changed the dressing often. In time she felt certain it would heal. The wound in his shoulder was another matter entirely.

The boar's tusks had ripped into Geoffrey's skin, leaving the opening torn and ragged, the flesh shades of deep purple and a fiery angry red. She let it bleed for a time, hoping to keep it from festering, but he had lost a great deal of blood already.

Caryn cleansed the wound often, using a solution of mandrake root mixed with lovage, but saw no sign of improvement. Even the poultices she made from Hassan's special fungus could not draw out all the poison.

As Caryn had feared, fever overtook him. He shook with cold, though his skin was burning hot, then threw off the covers as his body raged with heat. Although the priest forbid it, Caryn ordered Geoffrey stripped, then bathed his feverish skin herself, determined to cool him as much as she could. She worried Ral might stop her, but he only stood by mutely, his back stiff, his expression carefully masked as the intimate task was completed.

Though Beltar had left Braxston Keep the day after the hunt and returned to his castle in the north, each time Ral entered the sickroom, he seemed more uneasy than before. Weariness etched new lines in his face, and it was obvious he hadn't been eating. His worry seemed to grow with each passing day, both for Geoffrey and for herself.

" 'Tis time you got some sleep," he said one night as he strode toward her. "I will send Bretta to attend him."

Caryn shook her head. "He grows weaker with every hour. I cannot leave him. 'Tis crucial that I stay."

Ral rubbed his tired eyes, his handsome features marred by the same dark circles she knew marked her own. "What of the priest? Surely he knows enough to tend the boy."

"Geoffrey is my friend. I will not risk his life for a few hours of sleep."

Ral glanced down at the young blond knight whose face looked as pale as alabaster. Geoffrey dragged in rough, uneven, painfully shallow breaths. Watching him,

Ral sighed with weary resignation. "I will see there is a cot set up in here." And he left them once more alone.

During the night Geoffrey awoke her, rambling at first, then ranting and raving in a fit of building anger. He was speaking to his father, she realized, arguing that he would not fail in life as the older man had.

"I will be rich," he whispered, his body thrashing from side to side. "I will take care of Mother as you never have."

" 'Tis all right, Geoffrey." Caryn laid a damp cloth on his forehead. " 'Tis all in the past. You are ill. You must try to get some sleep."

"Mother? Have you come for me, Mother?"

Caryn hesitated only a moment. "Aye, Geoffrey, your mother is here."

"I . . . knew you would come. You have . . . always . . . come when I needed you."

Caryn smoothed beads of perspiration from his brow. "Soon you will feel better."

" 'Tis . . . good . . . to see you . . . Mother. I have . . . missed you."

"I have missed you, too." But already he had lapsed once more into unconsciousness and later that night he grew worse.

"He still burns with fever," Caryn said to Ral, bending over Geoffrey's body to sponge the sweat from his face. " 'Tis the putrifying, I fear. 'Tis sapping the last of his strength."

"You have done the best you could. There is naught else you can do."

Caryn looked into Geoffrey's youthful anguished face. She was afraid of the decision she was about to make, but she knew she must take the risk.

"There is one last chance . . . one more thing we can do." She turned to Ral and in that moment wanted nothing so much as the comfort of his arms around her. Yet she feared should that happen, she might not be able to go on. "Summon Lambert and Hugh. 'Twill take the three of you to hold him."

The expression on his face said he knew what she intended. He left her and shortly returned with the men, who walked uneasily into the room. They discovered the fire had been built up in the brazier and a small sharp knife thrust into the coals.

Caryn stood next to Ral, her heart thudding dully and her chest feeling leaden. "Mayhap I should let Father Burton do the cutting. He has done a good deal of work with a blade while I have only done a few such tasks and watched as the Arab worked."

Ral tipped her chin with his hand. " 'Tis your decision, Cara. You must do that which you believe will be Geoffrey's best chance to live."

She looked into her husband's weary face. "Then I will do it myself. My care of him will be gentler than the priest's, and my will to see him live far greater."

While Ral and the others held him steady, Caryn sliced through muscle and flesh to remove the festering portions of the wound. Then she cauterized the opening to the sound of Geoffrey's screams. She was shaking by the time they were finished.

" 'Tis done now," she said in a voice not much more than a whisper, so tired she swayed unsteadily on her feet. "God alone will decide the outcome." Steeling herself once more, she bandaged the wound and sat down beside him to wait.

Three days later, Geoffrey de Clare, knight in service to the Lord of Braxston Keep, returned to the world of the living.

"How are you feeling?" Caryn asked him from a place by his side. He was pale and somewhat thinner, but still undeniably handsome.

"Just a hair's breadth better than the boar."

Caryn smiled at that, glad to see the light returning to his eyes.

"I'm grateful for all you have done," Geoffrey said, reaching for her hand. As weak as he was, his spirits were high, and with youth and vigor on his side, Caryn believed his recovery would be complete. "I owe you my life, Lady Caryn."

"God and the Arab, more likely," she countered. " 'Tis good to have you returned to us, Geoffrey."

" 'Tis good to be here, my lady."

Still, he required constant care. Caryn was leaning over his bedside, bathing his forehead, when Ral walked silently into the room. He noticed the sheet had slipped immodestly down the young knight's lean body and nestled low on his hips.

Ral tensed as his wife gently bathed Geoffrey's face, then his chest and shoulders. The younger man was sleeping, or so it seemed till he opened his eyes and smiled.

"You are my angel of mercy, Lady Caryn."

She stepped away from him, a blush rising into her cheeks. She reached for the covers then paused and flushed even more as she realized he no longer needed such intimate attention.

" 'Tis certain you are better," she said tartly, but there was warmth in her voice.

Ral pushed away from the wall where he had been standing, causing them both to jump. " 'Tis certain that he is." He took in his wife's rosy features and the lazy smile on Geoffrey's face. "From now on Bretta will attend him. You've duties besides the care of this young buck to see to in the hall."

Caryn did not argue. "Aye, my lord." She glanced back at Geoffrey as she left the room. "The healing will improve with each day," she told him. " 'Twill not be long before you are back on your feet."

And then what? Ral pondered. *What plans have you for my wife then?* He thought of the look on Geoffrey's face when he had called Caryn his angel. What other thoughts did he harbor? What were his intentions? Ral's gaze followed Caryn's retreating figure.

And what of you, sweet wife? Have these long hours with Geoffrey changed your feelings for me? In truth, he wasn't certain what those feelings really were.

Ral clenched his fists, his thoughts still in turmoil as he left the sickroom. He meant to return to the bailey, to practice a few more hours with his men. Instead he turned toward the great hall, his strides long and suddenly determined. He found Caryn with Richard, discussing supplies for the hall and preparations for an upcoming saint's day feast.

"I have need of you, Caryn," he told her. "You will come with me upstairs."

She hurried to his side, her face taut with concern. "What is it, my lord, what is wrong?"

"Naught is wrong," he said, sweeping her into his arms at the top of the landing. "I only just discovered how much I have missed my wife these long days past. I have need of you and I mean to have you."

Caryn sucked in a breath as he kicked open the door to their chamber then slammed it solidly behind them.

" 'Tis the middle of the day, my lord. There is much that needs be done. I must—"

"Are not the needs of your husband more important?"

"Aye, but—" His hard kiss silenced her. She could feel the tension in his body, the muscles that tightened across his chest. They had made love last night, yet his desire for her seemed unabated. What in God's name . . . ?

But the question seemed a moot one as he carried her over to the bed, settled her there, and followed her down on the mattress. Kissing her fiercely, he pulled the combs from her hair and dragged his fingers through it, making her pulse pound with urgency. He found the

laces to her tunic, jerked them loose, pulled the fabric
from her shoulders, and bared her breasts.

"So beautiful," he whispered, his voice husky, the
sound of it sending shivers of heat through her body.
"So high and full . . . and they belong only to me." He
took one into his mouth and began to suckle gently, his
tongue damp and warm as it circled her nipple. Then
his teeth took hold and he bit down just enough to
bring a hot surge of pleasure-pain.

Caryn cried out at the feel of it, arching upward, heat
swirling low in her belly. Beneath his mouth, her breasts
were swelling, tingling, aching with every heartbeat.

"I need you, Cara." His mouth took hers as his hand
shoved up her tunic, his tongue teasing, then plunging
deep inside. His touch was fire, his breath male and
erotic, his hard-muscled body a testament to God's
handiwork.

Sweet Mary, she thought, wondering what drove him
to such frenzy, responding with equal abandon as his
fingers probed the place between her legs. She was wet
and ready, damp and throbbing and on fire. He stroked
her there while his mouth continued its plunder, while
his hardness pressed against her, thick and pulsing and
promising pleasures to come.

A finger slipped inside her, moved deep and with-
drew, slid in and then out yet again. Then he was unty-
ing his chausses, spreading her legs even wider,
positioning himself and driving himself inside.

Pleasure rippled through her, sweet and wildly erotic,
his thick shaft filling her, huge and hot and hard. In
minutes she was writhing beneath him, arching her
back to meet each of his powerful thrusts. Thick bands
of muscle bunched on his shoulders, sinews tightened
across his broad chest. Again and again, he drove into
her, frenzied in a way she'd never seen him, riding her
hard and deep, laying claim to her in a manner that set
her ablaze with fiery need.

"Come with me, *cherie*," he whispered, but it was more command than plea. Caryn's body answered as if it had no choice, obeying his will with shimmering spasms of pleasure, her body contracting, quivering, clenching with wave after wave of delicious heat.

He drew her to the edge of the bed and lifted her legs to his shoulders, positioning them there, burying himself deeper, stirring a second hot spasm of pleasure. Still he drove on.

In seconds she was soaring once more. Upward to that high plateau, riding the crest of her passion, her fingers biting into taut muscle then fisting the covers, her head thrashing back and forth as she cried out his name.

"Aye, 'tis what I had hoped for," he said, though his jaw was clenched for control. "Remember the pleasure, *ma chere*. Remember the man who has made you feel this way."

Four more deep pounding strokes and he reached his own release, his head falling back, the muscles straining in his neck and shoulders, his powerful biceps bulging as he spilled his seed.

Time seemed to still. The room grew dim and then faded away. Caryn barely felt him leave her. She was far too thoroughly pleasured, too sated and content.

Ral bent over and kissed her cheek. " 'Tis rest you need not a riding such as that one. You are not yet fully recovered. I should not have been so demanding." At the soft glow on her face, he smiled roguishly. "Still, I cannot say I am sorry."

Feeling content as he hadn't in days, Ral left his small wife curled among the tousled bed covers, her expression drowsy, her lids half-closed, her beautiful auburn hair a tangled mass around her shoulders.

Far more confident than he had been when he had left Geoffrey's sickroom, he made his way back to the great hall. By supper he was more himself and by the end of the day, he had conquered his uneasy feelings altogether.

What Caryn felt for Geoffrey was nothing more than friendship. It was her husband who commanded her small woman's body. Her husband and no other.

Ral intended it should remain that way.

The winds at Malvern Castle blew fair. The sun shone on the fields and the crops grew robust. Stephen de Montreale surveyed his holdings from an open stained glass window, proud of his vast domain.

His serfs worked long hard hours, the bounty he reaped among the highest in the land. The castle was constructed of the finest Yorkshire stone, its walls and towers considered nearly impregnable. It was furnished in the richest tapestries and most expensive imported furniture. His table was set with silver instead of pewter or wood. His clothes were all as opulent as the royal blue silk tunic he wore, and fashioned in every design and color. They were trimmed with threads of spun silver and gold, and his cloaks were lined with ermine.

But for Stephen it was not enough.

He crossed the room and sat down across from his sister at the carved mahogany table. In a tunic of magenta shot with gold, her hair a gleaming dark mass pulled back from her face, Eliana leaned forward and squeezed his hand.

"Word has come, then?" she asked. "You know when the king's man will pass?"

Stephen smiled with lazy satisfaction. "Aye, I know when de Balmain will come, and where."

"And the Ferret?"

"Has gathered his men and even now awaits my command."

"You are certain you can trust him?"

"I trust no man—especially not that one. 'Tis only that I can supply him with the information he needs, while he"—his lip curled smugly—"he supplies me with half of his bounty. The trade so far has been a good one for both of us."

"He has been raiding far north. Once he attacks the king's men, Braxston will know of his return and once more set out to trap him."

Stephen's expression turned hard. " 'Tis my wish exactly. I will have the king's coin and see Braxston dead not long after. Even now there are those he trusts who would betray him. Once I know his plans, I will put an end to him. Blame will fall on him for the raid on the tax collector and the king's missing silver. Then I will dispense with him and claim all he holds dear."

Eliana arched a fine dark brow. "Including the wench he took to wife?"

"Especially her." He brought his sister's long-fingered hand to his lips. "We will share the bounty, you and I. As for the Lady Caryn . . . you have always been a woman of great imagination. Surely you can think of a way she might pleasure us both."

Eliana's tongue ran over her soft ruby lips. "She is pretty and well-formed, a vibrant young flower that has not yet bent to a man's will—not even her husband's. 'Twill be interesting to sample her nectar before her petals are crushed beneath the heel of your boot."

Stephen's wicked smile lingered. " 'Tis good you are here, Eliana. 'Twill help to sweeten the pleasure of Braxston's defeat."

" 'Tis good to be here, my love. I always knew the day would come you would make Lord Raolfe pay for the insult he dealt me."

"The insult he dealt us both," Stephen corrected. An image of his sister in bed with the huge dark Norman stirred at the back of his mind and pushed its way to the surface.

She had seduced him on purpose, she said, done it to ensure there would be a marriage. The young knight could be easily handled, and they could go on as they were without fear of discovery. She was determined to protect her brother no matter the cost to herself.

She had done so that day in the monastery when he was nine years old. He had gone there to learn, but the learning held a bitter, knife-sharp edge. When Eliana had come with their stepmother for a visit, he had told her what had happened, as he wouldn't have confessed to anyone else. With tears in his eyes, he had told her what the friar had made him do, the ugly, dirty things, and Eliana had held him fiercely while he cried.

She refused to leave him there, though their father's new wife had insisted. Instead, she helped him climb out a window and together they made their escape. It took four long days to reach their home, hungry, dirty, ragged, and so tired they could barely remain on their feet.

It was Eliana who argued with their father, Eliana who convinced him, who saved Stephen from returning to a fate worse than death. She had sheltered him throughout the years, nurtured him in a way no other woman ever had.

Since he had become a man, things had changed and now it was he who protected her, he who guarded their secret.

It was he who loved her.

And Rál de Gere who had sullied her name and played her for a fool.

The Dark Knight had refused to honor their betrothal, humiliating her in front of their father, dishonoring her though he had sampled her charms more than once. It was Stephen who had helped to get rid of her unwanted child, Stephen who had sat at her bedside, fearful at her loss of blood, terrified she might die and certain it was

Ral de Gere's fault instead of his own. It was Stephen
who had vowed revenge.

"Never fear, my sweet." He turned her hand over and
gently kissed the palm. "Braxston will pay and pay
dearly for what he has done."

Chapter Twenty

"There is trouble, Ral." Caryn hurried toward him. "Men come from the village. Even now they are crossing the drawbridge."

Caryn led him toward the huge oaken door and together they descended the stairs down to the bailey. A group of villagers, some armed with wooden shovels, some with iron-tipped hoes, led a huge blond, bearded man, chained both hand and foot, across the bridge and into the bailey.

His clothes hung in tatters. Dried mud clung to his short brown tunic, torn open and hanging off a sun-bronzed, thick-muscled shoulder. His wrists and ankles were bloody where the chains had cut in, his face was a mass of cuts and bruises, his scalp had been sliced open, and his hair was matted with darkened blood.

"What goes on here?" Ral asked as he reached the men. "What has this man done to deserve such treatment?"

"Murder, my lord," said Tosig, husband to the girl whose babe had been born in the village. "He killed a traveler on the road."

The prisoner lifted his head, rattling the chain around his neck that connected his wrists. "I have killed no one."

"Who are you?" Ral stepped closer, coming face-to-face with one of the few men equally as huge and powerfully built as he.

"My name is Gareth. Son of Wulfstan, *thegn* of Valcore."

"I know this man." Caryn moved away from the base of the stairs and hurried to Ral's side. "His father was a powerful Saxon lord. 'Twas said his son was a valiant warrior."

"Gareth of Valcore. I have heard of you," Ral said, a memory of the name finally making its way to the surface. "You fought at Senlac. You were wounded, as was I. 'Twas said that you fought bravely."

Hugh came forward from the group of knights and men-at-arms who had begun to gather round. "I too have heard of him, Lord Ral. 'Twas said he fought with the rebels in sixty-nine. There were rumors he was their leader, but there was no proof. I heard the man was wounded near York—a lance between the ribs." Hugh eyed the golden-haired man who stood even taller than he. "I did not think that you still lived."

The bearded blond knight smiled sardonically, cracking dried blood at the corner of his mouth. "I have cheated death so many times I have lost count. I have fought and I have been wounded. I have killed countless enemies in the name of war, but I have never done murder."

Ral surveyed him cooly, assessing the man's unflinching stare, the way his head remained high, his shoulders straight and proud. Then he turned to the villeins who had brought him in chains to the castle. "'Twould seem he was not a man easy to subdue."

"Nay, my lord," a cottar named Algar said. "He fought like a madman. It took more than a dozen strong men to bring him down."

"What proof do you have of his guilt?"

"He was seen, my lord, plucking the shoes from the

dead man's feet. He stripped the coin from his purse as well.''

''I do not deny I have sunk so low as to scavenge from the dead,'' the big man said. ''But I did not kill him. He was slain when I found him.''

''He ran from us, lord,'' said Tosig. ''When we approached him, he ran.''

''And he fought like a demon,'' said another. ''No innocent man would have tried so hard to escape.''

'' 'Twas not the villeins I ran from, but the Norman overlord I knew I would face should I be captured.'' The glare he threw Ral was heavy with disdain. ''I have tasted Norman cruelty too many times not to know what my sentence would be. Justice is not a word that rides easy on a Norman tongue.''

''Your arrogance will not serve you here,'' Ral said, turning toward Lambert and Hugh. ''Take him to a storeroom below stairs.'' The cellars, granary, and an area for storage sat below the great hall. ''Remove his chains and see to his wounds, then see he's securely locked in.''

''Aye, my lord,'' said Hugh.

''And see he has something to eat. With a bellyful of food, mayhap his mind will dwell less on escape.''

As Hugh, Lambert, and a half-dozen men led the prisoner away, Caryn glanced anxiously up at Ral. Knowing her as he had come to, he slid an arm around her waist and urged her back toward the keep. Once they were inside the great hall, he let her draw him away from the others.

''I wish to have a word with you, my lord.''

''I did not doubt that you would,'' he said with a trace of amusement.

''I do not believe Gareth of Valcore is guilty. I remember hearing tales of him during the war. His skill in battle was legendary. They called him the Griffin. 'Twas said he had the cunning of an eagle and the courage of a lion. He was a knight of honor and bravery. To some he was almost revered."

"Men change, Cara."

"Not that kind of man."

Ral tended to agree. There was something of pride in the huge Saxon's bearing, something that had shone even through the dirt and the rags. Yet war could change the most stalwart of men. Ral had seen it time and again on the battlefield.

"Will his trial be held here at Braxston?" Caryn asked.

"Nay. 'Twill be the royal court that will judge him. Mayhap William himself."

Caryn lightly touched his arm. "Is there nothing you can do to help him?"

For a time Ral did not answer, for strangely he had been wondering that very same thing. "Why is it so important?"

Caryn looked into his face. "Should the Normans have lost the war and you had come to the same end Gareth has, I would hope your deeds of valor would speak to the Saxon lord in your defense. I would hope he would help you because he understood that you were a brave man."

A corner of his mouth curved up. "I will see what I can discover. Mayhap we can find out the truth."

His steps long and urgent, Odo climbed the stairs to the keep and strode into the great hall, his gray cloak billowing out behind him. He had been gone for the past few weeks on a trip to Normandy to visit his cousin. Oliver had sent word of a possible bride.

Odo had returned without one.

"Where is Lord Ral?" he asked Richard, who stood beside Ambra near the dais in a heated discussion of the duties she wished to assume now that she had become his wife.

"We will settle this in our chamber," Richard finished

and his pretty wife scowled. Odo's eyes went wide as Richard bent and kissed the tip of her nose. He was smiling when he turned away. "Welcome home," he said to Odo. " 'Tis good to have you returned." Richard continued to smile, more relaxed than Odo had ever seen him.

" 'Tis good to be here," he said. "Where is Ral?"

"I have not seen him since morning. While you were gone there was a murder on the road leading into the village. A man was seized and brought to the castle. He has been accused of the murder, but Lord Ral is uncertain of his guilt. He looks for more evidence before he turns the man over to the royal courts."

"How long before he's expected?"

" 'Tis hard to say." His face grew more intent. "What is it? What has happened?"

"The Ferret is returned. He has attacked Francois de Balmain, the king's tax collector."

"Balmain is dead?"

"Gravely wounded. 'Tis not known whether or not he will live. Most of his men lie dead or injured and the king's monies are gone. For certain, 'tis the work of the Ferret."

"God's wounds, the man is an ogre."

"Aye, but this time Lord Ral will catch him. The Ferret's days will soon end."

A noise in the entry drew their attention. Odo turned as Ral swept into the room, his dark blue tunic moving with each of his powerful strides.

" 'Tis good to see you, my lord."

"Odo!" For a moment Ral forgot his worries, smiling at Odo and clapping him hard on the back. " 'Tis good to have you returned." He glanced around the hall. "Where is your bride? I am eager to meet her. I will tell Caryn of your arrival and tonight we will—"

"There is no bride, *mon ami*. I have returned as unfettered as the day I left."

"The maid was not comely enough to suit you?"

"Aye, she was comely, and meek, and well-tutored in a woman's wifely duties."

"What then? Her dowry was not enough?"

"Nay, 'twas more than enough."

"But you have searched for a wife these long months past."

Bright color stained Odo's neck above his tunic, nearly matching the red of his hair. " 'Tis only that . . . she did not move me."

"Move you? I do not understand."

He swallowed, looking more than a little uncomfortable. "I looked at her and I felt nothing."

"You did not desire her?"

"Nay, 'twas not exactly that. I could have bedded her, 'twould not have been a hardship. But after that . . ." He sighed and glanced away. " 'Tis hard to explain, but . . . in the weeks since your marriage . . . I have watched you and your lady. I have seen your eyes when you look at her. I have seen the way she looks at you. 'Tis the way I wish to look at a woman."

Ral's brows drew together in a frown. Odo's reminder of his feelings for Caryn brought a tight sensation to his chest. "This time 'tis you who plays the fool."

"Your feelings for her then have changed since I left the castle?"

"Nay, but 'tis far too soon to judge how it will all turn out." Across the hall, Ral caught a glimpse of his little wife's auburn-haired head as she stood in the passage. She was speaking to Ambra, laughing at something the slender girl said. Just the sound of her voice made a hunger sweep over him and a heaviness tug low in his belly.

He shifted uncomfortably, tiny lines creasing his brow. He didn't like these feelings Caryn stirred. He didn't like the possessiveness he felt toward her, or his powerful raging jealousy. He didn't like the times he felt confused and out of control.

His settled his gaze on Odo. " 'Tis best to be practical, as you once said. To wed for heirs and keep your feelings at a distance." There were times he wished he had done so. Now it was too late.

Odo eyed him strangely. He pulled the string on the cloak he still wore and drew it off his shoulders. "I will look further," he said at last. "I am in no hurry. But there is a matter we must discuss that cannot wait."

Ral turned to a serving maid who crossed the hall. "Bring wine, bread, and cheese to the solar." He spoke to Odo. "Come. We will talk there."

As they walked toward the stairs, Caryn appeared through the doorway and hurried in their direction. Wisps of her flame-dark hair had escaped from her heavy braid, her face was flushed from the work she'd been doing, and her breasts rose tantalizingly beneath her simple brown tunic. Ral's groin began to grow heavy.

"Odo—" she said. "I did not know you had returned."

"Aye, my lady."

"Where is your bride?" Caryn turned to survey the hall. "I am eager to meet her."

"Odo remains unmarried," Ral said. " 'Tis a long story, Cara. He can tell you about it later."

Caryn nodded. "How went your search in the village?" she said to Ral. "Have you uncovered the truth of the murder?"

Ral sighed. "Nay, 'twould seem Tosig's story is correct. Gareth was stealing from the dead man and he did his best to escape."

"That does not make him guilty of the murder."

"Nay, and now that the villeins know he is the man they call the Griffin, they seem less certain of his guilt.

Many are grateful I continue the search. Some have even agreed to help me."

Caryn smiled. "I know you will find out the truth. That is all anyone can ask."

Odo's expression looked grim. "This murder of which you speak . . . 'tis possible the guilty man is one of those who rides with the Ferret. 'Tis what I wished to tell you, Ral. The whoreson is returned."

Ral swore an oath beneath his breath. "I vow I am not surprised. 'Twas only a matter of time till he rebuilt his band, and aye, if he is returned, then 'tis all too possible the traveler was killed by one of his murderous men." He urged Odo toward the stairs. "Come, my friend. You can give me the news of your journey and tell me whatever else you know of the Ferret."

They climbed the stairs to the solar and settled themselves comfortably in tall carved wooden chairs. A serving maid brought wine and cheese while Odo spoke of the raid against the king's tax collector, of Francois de Balmain's grave wound, and the loss of King William's tariffs.

"De Balmain has been collecting revenue for weeks," Ral said. "He must have been carrying a small fortune in silver and gold."

"How do you suppose they discovered his route and the date of his travels? Surely 'twas a secret well guarded."

Ral clenched a fist on the arm of his chair. "For coin enough, there are ways to discover most anything."

"I suppose that is true."

"Aye, and you may be certain 'twill work as well for us as it did for the Ferret."

Odo frowned. "I do not see what you mean."

"I mean that for money enough, someone will be willing to tell us what it is we need to know. We will soon find out where the whoreson is camped and when we do, he is a dead man."

Odo smiled with grim satisfaction. "I am glad I a
returned. I would not want to miss the brigand's come
uppance."

" 'Twill happen, my friend, and it will happen soon.

Caryn worked with Ambra in the great hall. The slende
young woman had won her first battle with Richard, an
now kept charge of the stores out in the bailey. Ambr
saw to the granary, the fish pond, and the pigeon house
She oversaw the garden and the drying of fruits an
meats. Richard served Ral, watched over the livestoc
the stables, the manorial court, the crops, and any prob
lems that surfaced among the villeins.

Their lives were busy, but with Caryn acting as chate
laine, managing the kitchen and supplies for the grea
hall, seeing to the housekeeping, to guests, and oversee
ing the servants, Richard and Ambra found time for eac
other.

Caryn smiled at the way things had turned out. Sinc
the day of the boar attack and Geoffrey's successful re
covery, she had been working to heal the sick. Whethe
accident or illness, if Isolda could not help them, the
came to Caryn.

For the first time in her life she felt needed. For th
first time since her childhood, since before the death c
her mother, she felt as if she belonged.

Caryn straightened a small bright tapestry that hun
slightly crooked at one end of the hall. She was proud c
Braxston Keep, proud of what she and Richard, Mart
Bretta, and the others had accomplished. Duties and re
sponsibilities, she had discovered, were not so unpleas
ant as she had imagined. More often than not, the
brought a sense of satisfaction. And the accomplishmer
was its own reward.

"Lady Caryn!" She whirled to see Leofric's small thi
frame racing toward her. "There is news, milady! Impor
tant news!"

For the first time, Caryn noticed a second boy, a dark-haired child named Byrhtnoth she remembered from the village. He was smaller than Leo and several years younger. Everyone called him Briny.

"What is it, Leo?" she asked. "Hello, Briny." She reached for the boy's grubby hand, captured it, and gave it a gentle squeeze.

"Briny seen the murder, milady. The traveler on the road—Briny seen the men who done it."

"What?" She stared down at the olive-skinned boy. He was the bastard son of a Norman knight who had raped his mother. The woman had finally married, but the man had little use for his stepson, and among the other children, the boy never quite fit in. "You saw him, Briny? You saw the man who killed the traveler on the road?"

"He seen 'em, milady," Leo answered for him. "Briny says there was three of 'em."

"Did Briny see the big blond knight the villagers brought in?"

"Aye, milady. Everyone seen 'im."

She bent down next to the boy, squatting at his side so that she could look into his dirt-smudged face. "Was the blond man one of the men who killed the traveler, Briny?"

He shook his head.

"Are you sure?"

" 'E come later," the boy finally said, his eyes cast down, surveying the mud on his bare feet. " 'E scared 'em away, 'e did, just by comin' down the road. The men took the dead man's 'orse and rode away."

"Why didn't you tell someone?" Caryn asked gently.

"He was afraid, milady," Leo broke in. "Briny don't much like people."

Caryn bent over and hugged him. "It's all right, Briny. You don't have to be afraid." She glanced toward the door, wondering when Ral would return. He had gone to Oldham, a small nearby village, in search of information on the murder or any news he might garner of the Ferret and his men. Surely he would be back soon.

Caryn smiled down at the boys. "Why don't you and Briny come with me?" Taking the younger boy's hand, she led them toward the kitchen. "Just this morning, Cook made apple pasties."

The little boy's eyes went wide and he broke into a lopsided grin.

" 'Twas well done of you to speak up," Caryn said to him. "Lord Ral will be pleased with you both."

And he was, joining the children as soon as she told him the story, listening to their tale with interest, asking questions, then smiling with relief that justice would be done.

" 'Twas good that you came forward, Briny. Mayhap, as Leofric has done, we can find a place for you here in the keep."

Briny looked up at him with huge dark eyes in a face alive with awe. When he nodded, Ral reached down and ruffled his hair. He left the children a few minutes later, and Caryn walked beside him into the great hall.

"See the Saxon released from his bonds," he called to Lambert, whose lanky frame leaned against the wall near the stairs. "The man is innocent of the murder."

"Aye, my lord."

"Speak to Bretta on your way out. Tell her to see to a bath and find the man some decent clothes. A knight such as he should not be forced to leave Braxston Keep in rags." As Lambert left to do Ral's bidding, Odo came into the great hall.

"You've discovered the truth of the murder?"

"Aye. 'Twas not one man but three. A boy from the village came forward. He was afraid at first, but from what he has said, there can be no mistake. The traveler was mounted, not afoot as the villeins believed. The brigands were after his horse. Gareth's unexpected ar-

'ival sent them on their way before they could finish
heir plunder.''

"There is still the matter of the traveler's purse," Odo
reminded him.

"I have considered that. When Gareth was taken, the
money was seized then returned. It has been sent to the
murdered man's family."

"It makes him no less guilty."

"These are difficult times, my friend. Especially for
those who have been defeated. 'Tis my feeling a man of
his courage deserves a second chance.''

Standing close to her husband's side, Caryn smiled.
Ral was a good man. Strong, brave, and compassionate.
The Dark Knight might be fearsome in battle but there
was gentleness within him, a belief in justice, and a
fierce sense of honor. Just the sight of him, standing so
tall and proud made her heart go soft and fluttery.

Caryn's bright smile slipped just a little. No matter
her feelings for him, she had no real notion of his. He
had never said he loved her, never promised fidelity,
never said the words which would ensure a happy future. If he pledged these things, she would believe him
without question.

But he had never made such a vow and chances were
he never would.

Caryn looked up at him and a sad smile curved her
lips. That he desired her, she did not doubt; the hunger
in his eyes rarely left him. But could he ever come to
love her? She doubted it. Ral believed a man who loved
was nothing but a fool. He had once loved Eliana and
she had betrayed him with her brother. Ral had seen
what had happened to Malvern, seen the power a
woman could wield. He was determined it would not
happen to him.

Still, she could no longer deny her feelings for him.
Instead she prayed she could make him feel those things

for her. She clung to those hopes and prayed one day
they might come true.

She glanced up as Ral left her, striding off across the
great hall, his features suddenly full of purpose. At the
opposite end, she saw a huge, golden-haired giant of a
man rise to his feet and walk in her husband's direction.
It took a moment for her to realize the huge man was
the Saxon. When she did, her eyes went wide with
astonishment.

Sweet Blessed Virgin. Never in all her years would she
have guessed the man walking toward them with the
perfectly chiseled features, finely arched brows, and
well-formed lips was the ragged, bearded man who had
been locked in the storeroom.

He came to a halt in front of Ral, his bearing erect,
massive shoulders squared, his expression intense.

"You are a free man, Saxon," Ral said with a smile.
"What think you of Norman justice now?"

The huge knight shifted uncomfortably. It was obvious that gratitude was not something that came easy to
him—especially toward a Norman. Still, he lifted his
head and looked Ral straight in the eye.

"You saved my life. 'Tis more than justice you have
done. You sought out the truth. There are few Saxon
lords who would have gone to that much trouble for a
man who was his foe."

"Is that what you are, Gareth? My foe? Will the day
come when I must guard my lands against your rebel
forces?"

"Nay, my lord. Those days are done. William's con-
quest is complete. Only a fool would rise against him
now and I am not a fool."

Ral nodded, seemingly pleased with the Saxon's answer.

"What will you do?" Caryn asked him, walking up
next to her husband.

"I am not yet certain."

"You are welcome here at Braxston," Ral said, "should you wish to swear your fealty and join the ranks of my men. A knight of your valor is always welcome."

"I thank you, Lord Ral, but I cannot stay. I search for my brother . . . and there is a woman. Whatever happens, I must seek my own destiny. I am more than determined to find it."

"Then I wish you godspeed," Ral said.

"As do I," Caryn added.

"I won't forget what you have done." Gareth smiled and deep grooves etched his cheeks, making him look even more handsome. "Mayhap we will one day meet again."

"Mayhap," Ral agreed.

With a nod of farewell to Caryn, the tall knight walked away.

"I wonder what will become of him?" She watched him till he disappeared out the door.

"Hard to say. Once he would have been wealthy. Now . . ." Ral shrugged his massive shoulders. "Who knows? Mayhap one day his luck will change."

Caryn thought of the ragged man who had first been brought to Braxston Keep, of the hard times he must have suffered. It reminded her of the difficult times that lay ahead, of the Ferret and the land they so desperately needed, of the cattle that had died and the winter they must face in the months to come.

She thought of Ral and her uncertain future. Of her love for him that stubbornly continued to grow, of the love from him she so desperately wanted. Gareth's wasn't the only luck she hoped would change.

Chapter Twenty-one

R al rode over the drawbridge, the sorrel's hoofbeats
rattling on the rough heavy timbers, the guard stepping out of the way as he passed. Somewhere in the
distance, thunder rumbled and clouds cast a dismal pall
to the already darkening horizon.

Ral barely noticed, his mind instead on the information he had just received. He was returning from the
village, from a meeting arranged by Tosig with a man
from a neighboring hamlet farther north, a man well-
paid to discover the location of the Ferret.

Ral smiled grimly, even a little bit cynically. *Coin
enough, by Christ, and a man's own mother would
betray him.* Or at least so it seemed. In this case, it was
the Ferret's wench from an alehouse in Camden, a
comely piece who would slit a man's throat for the coin
in his purse.

The Ferret had taken her into his camp, entrusting
her with the secret of his whereabouts, and now he
would pay the price. The outlaw would be surprised by
the woman's betrayal, but Ral was not. He had seen it
too many times.

He rode straight into the stable yard, calling for Aubrey, his squire, to see to his horse, which nickered
softly and switched its long red tail. The youth appeared
from the back of the barn, but so did Caryn, slipping

quietly out from behind a pile of straw, the little spotted fawn trailing silently behind her.

"I am glad you are returned, my lord. I had begun to worry." She looked slightly disheveled, her heavy braid stuck with stems of straw, wisps of dark auburn hair curling softly against her cheeks.

Despite his earlier musings on the nature of women, he found himself smiling as he swung down from the saddle and moved toward her. This wasn't the wench from the tavern. This woman was his wife, and his heart had expanded at the sight of her.

"It pleases me to know that you are concerned," he said, "but I am fine."

"And your meeting . . . it was successful?"

"Aye, 'twas more than I had hoped for."

Footsteps carried through the open stable door as Odo walked in, his expression anxious yet hopeful. "I heard you were returned. News of the Ferret?"

Ral glanced at Caryn, fighting a moment of hesitation. Sweet Christ, she had pledged him her loyalty, the same as Odo had. She cared for him, mayhap even loved him. He had vowed to trust her—against his instincts, against his bitter experience—now he meant to see it done.

"Aye. He camps in the hills near the crossroads at Tevonshire Pass. Some forty men or more. Tonight we make ready. We will move out at dawn."

Odo's freckled face split into a grin. "At last we take the wily bastard. You get your land and the Ferret pays for his sins with the loss of his head."

"Aye, and high time it is." Ral reached for Caryn, slid an arm around her waist, and felt her tremble.

"You are cold. You should not be out without your cloak."

"I am not cold; I am frightened. The Ferret is a blood-thirsty killer. I worry for your safety, husband."

Ral smiled, a thread of warmth gliding through him at

her words. "Have you so little faith in my skills as a warrior?"

"You know that is not the way I feel. There is no finer, braver knight in all of England."

Ral arched a brow, more pleased by her praise than he should have been. "Then you must trust me to dispense with the Ferret and return safely home."

She still looked unsure, her fine dark-auburn brows drawn together in a frown. "I will try, my lord."

Ral tipped her chin up, bent and settled his mouth over hers. Her lips felt incredibly soft, and her breath tasted sweet and womanly. She smelled of soap mingled with the earthy scent of straw. Hearing Odo walk away, he deepened the kiss, then groaned as the blood surged hotly into his groin. He felt like pulling her down on the thick pile of hay, like lifting her skirt and driving himself inside her.

Instead he pulled away. "I am glad that you care, my love." He smiled, his voice a little husky. "I will be busy for the next few hours, but afterward, mayhap you could show me just how much."

The bloom in his pretty wife's cheeks grew a deeper shade of pink. "Aye, my lord, 'twould be my greatest pleasure." With a last warm kiss, she left him and made her way back toward the hall.

Along with Lambert, Hugh, and Odo, Ral worked to ready his men and equipment. He had been preparing for this moment for weeks, gathering the needed supplies, checking and rechecking their weapons, yet the task continued late into the eve.

He wanted the Ferret, and he meant to have him.

This time, he was determined that nothing would go wrong.

Sitting in a chair before the fire pit, Caryn pulled a long scarlet thread through the length of linen spread over her lap. She had spent the evening with Richard, helping him check provisions for her husband's journey. They had finished long ago, and the hall had grown quiet except for a few drowsy servants, but she was too tense and worried to sleep.

Her hand shook a little, the needle slipped, and she pricked a finger. Sweet Jesu, she wished Ral didn't have to go.

"Here, you had better take this." Geoffrey handed her a scrap of cloth. "You will stain your embroidery." She had been so lost in thought, she had missed his approach.

"Thank you." She pressed it against the small drop of blood. " 'Tis only that I am worried."

His other hand came up and she saw that in it he held a goblet of wine. "So I have noticed. Mayhap a little of this will help."

She accepted the wine, though she didn't really want it. "Thank you, Geoffrey."

He sat down on the bench across from her, waiting in silence for her to drink some of the rich dark liquid. Mayhap he was right. 'Twould do no good to sit there all night and worry. She took a long sip, glanced at Geoffrey's concerned expression, took another, and then another.

"Better?" he asked.

She did feel better, warmer inside instead of so empty and cold. The heat spread out, sliding through her limbs, urging her to relax, to put her faith in her husband's skills as he had asked.

"You must not fear, my lady. Whatever Lord Ral intends, he will surely be the victor."

She released a pent up sigh, her heartbeat slowing, throbbing deeply inside her chest. As her worry continued to ease and slip away, so did her surroundings, leaving her in a place of peace and contentment. "The victor?" she repeated, unable to concentrate on the words Geoffrey had spoken.

"Your husband seeks the Ferret, does he not? Surely 'tis discovery of the outlaw's camp that drives him with such vengeance."

Why was Geoffrey asking about the Ferret? Hadn't Ral told his men? But then he might not have. He would be taking no chances that the Ferret might once more escape. She tried to focus on Geoffrey's face, but it blurred in the light of the fire. His skin looked too orange and his eyes reflected the same red color as the low-burning flames.

"Have a little more wine," he urged, pressing the goblet into her hands, tipping it up until she was forced to swallow. "Now . . . what was it you were saying about the Ferret?"

"I . . . I was talking about the Ferret?"

"Aye, you were telling me about Lord Ral's mission." Geoffrey's voice seemed to thrum, his words sounding uneven and strangely far away.

"I was?"

"Aye. Surely, he told you all about it?"

"They . . . have to catch him."

"That we will, my lady. Just as soon as we find him."

She tried to nod, but she could barely hold up her head. Something warned her to say nothing more, that Ral would not be pleased, then the warning grew weak and also began to fade.

"Where is he?" Geoffrey asked so softly she could barely hear him for the odd dull buzzing in her ears.

"He . . . he camps at . . . at the crossroads."

"Which crossroads?"

"N-Near Tevonshire Pass."

His lips curved into a smile, but his teeth seemed to glow and his eyes were ringed by rainbows of color. Then his image became just a faint, soft blur and she could barely hear him.

"Why don't you finish your wine?" he urged. "Mayhap then you will be able to sleep."

She nodded, brought the cup to her lips with an unsteady hand, and took a last drink. As she set it down next to her chair, lay back and closed her eyes, she only vaguely noticed that Geoffrey had walked away.

Ral strode into the great hall, his heavy steps muffled by a chorus of servants' snoring. He started up the stairs, then noticed Caryn asleep in a chair beside the long-dead fire. Smiling at the tender sight she made, he moved in that direction, wondering if she had meant to await him.

He lifted her easily, part of him hoping she would awaken, another part hoping she would not. He nestled her head against his shoulder, her long braid teasing his cheek, stirring places in his body lower down, but she did not wake up.

At the top of the stairs, Marta stepped from the shadows, materializing like a wisp of smoke, rising out of nowhere like the spectre she sometimes seemed.

"She fell asleep before the fire," Marta said. "She has been worried and restless. I did not wish to disturb her. I knew you would come for her soon."

"Go on to bed. I will tend her."

Marta nodded. She started past him, glanced down at Caryn's slightly pale face and frowned. A veined, weathered hand touched her forehead. For a moment Marta paused, then wordlessly she passed on by and slowly descended the stairs.

Ral opened the door to his chamber and carried his small wife inside. Even as he laid her upon the mattress and began to strip off her clothes, she did not stir. He sighed, recalling the moans of passion he had intended to wrest from her, clamping down on the ache that throbbed low in his belly.

He touched her cheek as he drew back the covers. If all went well, he would return before the first of the week. His battle with the Ferret would be ended and the land he so desperately needed would finally be his. There would be new fields to till and the threat of starvation would at last be ended.

Ral smiled. Once Braxston's people were out of danger, he could turn the full force of his considerable will on the woman who shared his bed. In the days of late, he had finally admitted the depth of his feelings and begun to accept them. Now he meant to make Caryn his completely, to bind her to him as she had never been before, to ensure she felt the same hot, roiling, disturbing emotions he felt for her.

Ral tossed aside his sleeping wife's garments, stripped off his own, and joined her naked on the bed. He ached every time he looked at her small sweetly curved body, yet he did not touch her. As hard as he was, it took a good long while to fall asleep and not nearly long enough for the sun to gray the horizon.

Now, he wearily swung his legs to the side of the bed and stood up, hoping the motion would awaken her, hoping he could sink himself inside her one last time before he left her. When she still did not stir, he grumbled an oath, determined that if his wife was that exhausted, 'twas best he let her sleep.

Instead he pulled on his clothes, slid on his boots, and grabbed up his sword. Even his heavy footsteps did not rouse her. Crossing the room to her side, he pressed a hard kiss on her lips, turned and strode out to join his men.

"I cannot believe it, Marta, Ral is gone?"

"The sun shines nearly overhead, my pet. Your husband left well before dawn."

"Why did he not awaken me? I cannot believe I did not hear him go. I waited by the fire and then . . ."

"And then?"

Caryn glanced down at the floor, embarrassed and a

little bit uneasy. "I-I don't know. I suppose I fell asleep. I-I cannot seem to remember."

"How do you feel?" Marta laid a hand on her forehead.

" 'Tis strange to say, but I still feel tired. And my head throbs unbearably. Think you I am ill?"

"Mayhap, my pet. We will have to wait and see."

But by afternoon she felt better. The ache in her head was gone, along with her feelings of fatigue. Still, only snatches of the evening came to mind: Geoffrey fetching a rag when she had pricked her finger, urging her to drink a goblet of wine in the hope it would help her sleep.

Throughout the day, her mind kept returning to the elusive events of the evening, and by nightfall other odd recollections had come to mind: her body growing limp and unwieldy, Geoffrey's face glowing strangely in the red-orange light of the fire.

Geoffrey asking her questions.

Standing at the narrow slit of window in her chamber, searching for the stars but finding only clouds and darkness, Caryn's hand shook where it rested on the cold gray stone. Why had Geoffrey been asking about the Ferret? If he wanted information, why had he not gone to Ral?

Exactly what questions had he asked?

And most fearful of all—what in God's name had she told him?

Sitting atop his big black destrier, his chain mail hauberk rustling slightly as he moved, Ral scanned the foliage in the valley below. The odor of burning turf scented the air and several wispy trails of thin white smoke rose up from distant campfires, wending a path through the thick green leaves.

"This time the whoreson is ours," Ral said to Odo, who smiled with obvious satisfaction.

" 'Tis time our efforts have proven fruitful."

"Aye, though I'll feel better once our scouts are re
turned."

They did so not long after, riding stealthly into the
clearing, the men shed of their armor, traveling light and
fast and making little noise. They had ridden into the
small heart-shaped valley below and returned bringing
word that the outlaw camp was exactly where they had
been told.

"How many men?" Ral asked Girart, who had led the
small expedition.

"Less than you had heard. No more than twenty or
thirty."

"And the Ferret, he is among them?"

"A small, wiry, black-haired man was there. 'Twas obvious he was their leader. 'Tis almost certain he is the
Ferret."

"Were you able to spot the lookouts?"

"Aye, milord. They have already been dispensed
with."

A faint smile curved Ral's lips but it was one of grim
determination. "You have done well, Girart." The tall
knight nodded and returned to his men while Ral spoke
to Odo.

"We will surround the camp, just as we planned, and
once we are in position, I will call for their surrender. I
want no needless bloodshed—but neither will I risk en-
dangering our men."

"And the Ferret?" Odo asked.

"I would have him alive, if it can be done. If not . . .
then it will have to be his head." He tightened his hold
on Satan's reins and the horse danced nervously beneath him. "You take the right flank, I'll take the left.
Once you're in position, we will be ready to move in."

Odo nodded and whirled his horse. Ral nudged Satan
forward, leading his column of men. They moved with
urgency, but not with haste, spacing themselves evenly,

ioving in a wide-open pattern, skirting the valley, then
iowly closing in. In minutes they had completely sur-
ounded the outlaws' camp.

Ral started to call out for his men to move in, but
omething held him back. He commanded eighty men
o the outlaws less than thirty, but instincts honed from
io many years in battle began to flash a silent warning.
ie waited among the trees, scanning the brigands mov-
ig about the campfires, noticing how well they were
rmed . . . and how furtively they seemed to watch
ie forest.

It had always been the Ferret's nature to be wary, and
et . . .

Still, there was no choice but to go forward as they
ad planned. He meant to capture the outlaw. One way
r another, the Ferret's raiding must come to an end.

"Pass word among the men," he said to Lambert.
'Tell them to be wary of a trap." As the lanky knight
ioved silently along the line of men, Ral made a slight
od of his head, a signal for Hugh to proceed.

"You men in the clearing!" Hugh called out in his
ough-edged voice. "The Dark Knight is come! You are
ravely outnumbered and you are surrounded. 'Twill do
io good to fight nor to try and escape. Throw down
our arms and surrender!"

But already the outlaws were bracing for battle, notch-
ig bows and drawing swords, taking cover behind
rates and boxes that suddenly looked all too strategi-
ally positioned. Even as they did so, Ral's men gave a
vild cry of battle and swooped down on the clearing,
ome with couched lance, others gripping a shield in
ne hand, a sword in a leather-gloved fist.

Ral rode among them, broadsword gripped tight, the
tallion obeying commands he gave with his knees, leav-
ig his hands free for battle. They had almost reached
he clearing when savage shouts echoed from behind

them, men and horses, the thunder of hooves, and th
·distinctive clang of armor.

A trap! Ral saw, thankful his warning voice had pre
pared him and praying they wouldn't be too badly ou
numbered.

"Sweet Jesu!" Hugh shouted, riding up beside him
"Knights and men-at-arms—no ragged band of outlaw
these."

A muscle jumped in Ral's cheek. "Nay—'tis Malvern'
men. Again we are betrayed to Stephen de Montreale.

Ral swung his sword at the first knight who emerge
through the trees. Their swords met, clanged, held, the
clanged again. He arced his blade downward, severin
the man's arm at the shoulder, knocking him from hi
horse into the dirt, covering his bright green Malveri
colors with a coat of earth and blood. Two more me
rode forward, one wielding a deadly mace, another
razor-sharp battle-ax.

In his rage, Ral's strength was so great they pose
little problem, though each was well-armed and obv
ously skilled in battle. He dispatched them easily, rur
ning one of them through, decapitating the other
Spatters of blood glittered crimson against his chai
mail, but the fiery heat of anger colored his vision
brighter haze of red.

Who could have done it? Only Odo and Caryn knev
their final destination, or even the hour that they woul
move. Could the wench from Camden have returned t
warn her lover? Even if she had, how had word passe
to Malvern?

He swung his broadsword in a blinding arc tha
stopped a blow from one of the outlaws. The band'
missing men had appeared on horseback, riding into th
valley with Malvern, obviously in league with the devi
who had plagued him for so long.

Where was Stephen? he wondered, beginning t
search among the trees, determined to find him, deter

mined to see him pay for his treachery. All the while his mind ran over the person or persons who might have betrayed him.

Through a break in the forest, he saw Odo, fighting valiantly against two of Malvern's men. No traitor there, as he knew there would not be.

Even as he parried one of Malvern's lancers, Caryn's lovely image came to mind. Caryn and Stephen? His stomach clenched at the thought. No, she detested the man nearly as much as he did. Why then, would she have done it? What could she possibly have to gain?

Ral fought his way through a small group of stubbornly fighting outlaws. His men were holding their own, he saw, though the odds were distinctly in Malvern's favor. 'Twas loyalty, he knew, that kept them fighting so hard, while Malvern's men felt little or naught for their leader. Only the promise of gain drove them on.

And his men had received far better training. Hours of it, endless and grueling, honing their skills to a razor-sharp edge, placing Braxston's knights among the finest in the land.

"Malvern!" Hugh pointed frantically northward, knowing Ral would be searching, determined to see the bastard suffer the sharp cold thrust of his blade.

Ral rode hard in that direction, the stallion darting among the trees, dodging men in battle, the big horse far more agile than it appeared. Ral saw Stephen ride off to the right, turned Satan in that direction, and was almost upon him when two mail-clad men, mounted and wielding bloody swords, swooped out from behind a copse of trees.

Ral swore a vicious oath as Malvern rode safely away, and a fresh rush of anger broke over him. The first man took a blade thrust in the shoulder but kept on fighting, distracting him long enough for the other man's sword to pierce his thigh. He grunted in pain as Satan reared, his hooves lashing out, coming down hard on a knight on foot who raced toward him across the muddy earth. Two more ringing blows ended the first man's life. Ral spun the big black, avoiding the second man's blade, felt the animal stumble and begin to go down, leaned to the side and jumped clear of the saddle just as the huge horse crashed to the earth.

Satan rolled to his feet, shaking himself and apparently unharmed, while Ral came up swinging his blade. Slicing into the taller man, hearing his wild shriek of pain, he turned to see two more men bearing down on him. Footsteps behind him signaled the approach of a third man. Ral tried to turn, to position himself to defend against all three, but his strength had begun to fail, and his leg was oozing a thick stream of blood.

He could almost feel the blade's sharp teeth sinking into his back when he caught a flash of Braxston red and black from the corner of his eye. He saw Geoffrey's tall lean frame, saw the blond knight wield his sword against the man approaching Ral from behind, heard metal clang against metal and the man's grunt of pain. Ral landed several clanging blows against his two attackers, thrust into one, sliced into the other, and turned to see Geoffrey take a blade thrust high between his ribs.

A mortal one, it appeared to Ral, who stiffened at the needless death of one of his own, especially one so young.

Around him the battle still raged. He dispensed with the knight who had wounded Geoffrey, searched for other possible attackers but saw none. As he scanned the campsite and the forest around him, he discovered Malvern's men had begun to retreat, that some of his own men gave chase, and that the others were dealing with what remained of the outlaw band.

Knowing Malvern would be long gone, he turned his attention to Geoffrey and saw that Odo also moved toward him. At the same moment, the two of them

reached the man who lay on the ground in a spreading
pool of blood.

Ral knelt beside him. "Rest easy, lad. The battle is
nearly won."

"Malvern . . . he is . . . dead?"

Ral clenched his jaw. "Fled, I fear. The man has no
stomach for defeat."

"W-What of the Ferret?"

Ral glanced at Odo, certain he would not have left his
men without having the outlaw in hand.

"Captured," his red-haired friend confirmed. "He can
speak to the king of his pact with the devil."

"How many men . . . did we lose?"

Again Odo spoke. "Twenty dead so far." He glanced
down at the blood seeping from Ral's thigh to darken
his tunic. "Another twenty wounded. We are lucky the
number was not greater."

A tight sob came from Geoffrey's throat, followed by
a jagged fit of coughing. Tears welled in his eyes and
began to slide down his cheeks. "My fault," he said,
gasping as he fought to drag in short breaths of air. "I
believed . . . Lord Stephen meant only to capture the
Ferret. He wanted . . . to win the king's favor, he
said."

Ral's chest went tight. Already his mind was spinning,
moving forward to the logical conclusion, fighting that
painful truth, denying it with every beat of his heart.

"He . . . he promised to give me the land," Geoffrey
was saying. "He didn't need it . . . and I did."

"How?" Ral asked, though every fiber of his body
begged him not to. "How did you know where we were
headed?"

Geoffrey coughed harder, his body shaking, wheezing
as he spit up a lungful of blood. "You . . . you must
not blame her. My . . . fault, not hers." The coughing
expanded into deep wracking spasms. My . . .
fault . . ." and then he was gone.

Ral stared down at him, cold hard fury pumping wildly through his veins, rough leather cutting into his palm as he clenched a gauntleted fist.

Not her fault—yours, Geoffrey. For being so young and handsome, for wooing her as I tried to do but failed. For convincing her to use her passion to get what she wanted, to pretend she had feelings . . .

For convincing her to betray me.

A fresh wave of fury rolled over him. Christ's blood, what a fool he had been! The rage welled and grew, blotting his surroundings, blinding him to all but the knowledge that everything he had come to believe in, all of his dreams for the future, had just shriveled up and blown away.

He clamped his jaw against the insane urge to howl out his anger like a deerhound baying at the moon. His voice shook with rage and he fought to control it then found that he no longer cared.

"Find Lambert," he said to Hugh. "Pick twenty men and see that the Ferret and what's left of his men are turned over to King William. Tell him what has happened. 'Tis for him to decide what must be done with Malvern."

"Aye, my lord. We leave in all haste."

"And keep an eye out for Stephen, though 'tis nearly certain he'll continue his retreat. His forces were badly defeated. I do not think he will attack again."

Hugh just nodded.

"The rest of us return then to Braxston?" Odo asked.

"Aye. We must see to the injured." His jaw clamped until he could barely speak. "And there is the business of the traitor."

"You do not mean Lady Caryn?"

" 'Twas she Geoffrey spoke of, was it not?"

"You cannot be certain. He did not say her name."

"Besides the two of us, she is the only one who knew of our mission. You must know it can be no other."

Still, Odo's words had raised a thread of hope. He would cling to that hope through the hours of his return and pray there was some other answer.

In his heart, he knew that there was none.

Chapter Twenty-two

Bretta raced up the stairs to the keep, bursting through the heavy oaken door and running into the great hall. "Lady Caryn! The wardcorne just called out 'E comes, milady. Ye lord husband and his men return home!"

A wave of relief rolled over her. "Can he see them yet? He is certain Lord Ral is among them?"

" 'E seen the banner, 'e did—the lord's black dragon on a field o' bloodred. There was naught else 'e could make out."

Caryn glanced toward the door, suddenly uneasy, her stomach beginning to churn. What if something had happened? What if Ral were injured? What if he were maimed or mayhap even . . . ? No! She would not think the unthinkable. He was safe and he was well. Geoffrey had only been curious, and the questions she had answered . . . dear God, the trust she had broken . . . it amounted to naught but a young knight's eager thirst for battle.

The men were returned and nothing untoward had happened. She would speak to Geoffrey, learn the truth of what had occurred that last eve.

She vaguely heard Bretta's frantic urgings. "Ye'd best hurry, milady. 'E'll be here soon, 'e will. Ye want t' look ye best fer him." They had been working together in the

toreroom all morning, anything to keep her mind off
Ral and the dangers he faced in his battle with the Ferret
nd his men.

"Hurry, milady!"

Caryn looked down at her tunic. It was old and faded,
nd her hair—sweet Mary, she looked like an urchin!
Lifting her gown up out of the way, she whirled around
nd raced for the stairs. In minutes, she returned,
dressed in her forest green tunic with a buttercup
chainse, her hair neatly brushed and pulled back with
tortoiseshell combs, just the way Ral liked it.

At the door to the bailey, she took a long calming
breath, then started down the stairs. She stopped before
she reached the bottom, noticing the servants no longer
looked excited, their expression now solemn, some of
the women close to tears.

"Sweet God, what is it?"

"A man from the village has run ahead of the others,"
someone said. "Only half the men return. There are
many wounded. The rest are feared dead."

Caryn reeled as if she'd been struck by a fist. "What
. . what of Lord Ral?"

" 'Tis was naught but bits and pieces, I heard. The
man spoke to your steward."

With eyes that seemed oddly out of focus, Caryn
searched for Richard. He was standing among a group of
peasants, Ambra at his side, staring toward the drawbridge. Woodenly, she made her way toward them.

"I would know, Richard, what . . . what news it is
the villein has brought."

He turned in her direction. "Lady Caryn. I was about
to seek you out." He steeled himself then told her much
the same story the villein had, adding, "The Ferret has
been captured. 'Tis said that a group of Braxston knights
travel with Lambert and Hugh to King William. They
mean to claim the king's reward."

"And Lord Ral?"

"Injured, I fear, though 'tis said the wound is not a grave one."

Caryn swayed on her feet, and Richard's arm shot out to steady her. "You must not fear, my lady."

"I am sorry, Richard." She forced some stiffness into her spine and prayed with every ounce of her will that Ral was truly all right and that whatever had happened the night she spoke to Geoffrey had nothing to do with the death of his men.

Richard said nothing further and neither did she. They just stood gazing toward the drawbridge, watching the black dragon pennant as it occasionally bobbed above the castle wall, signaling the Dark Knight's arrival and what was left of his men.

By now the bailey was filled with servants, all of them watching and waiting, praying for friends and husbands they loved.

Caryn's breath caught as Satan crossed the draw bridge, Ral sitting straight in the saddle, his shoulders erect though his black hair was mussed by the breeze and his face looked incredibly weary. He rode with his shield hanging down from his saddle, his conical helm clamped under a powerful arm.

Ral drew rein on Satan, and Caryn found herself hurriedly moving toward him. There was blood on his mail and where his tunic rode high on one leg she could see a length of cloth had been tied around his thigh. It too was darkened with blood.

Caryn made a sound in her throat and stepped forward as her husband dismounted. She stopped when she saw his face. Mother of God, it appeared carved in stone. His jaw was clamped, the muscles drawn taut across his cheeks, his eyes the palest, iciest gray she had ever seen. Several days' growth of beard made him look like the name he once carried—the Dark Knight, Ral the Relentless.

Her stomach clenched as he strode toward her, his

xpression deadly, not an ounce of warmth in his face.
antically, she looked behind him, searching for Geof-
ey, praying the truth being shouted in her head was
mehow wrong.

"If you search for your lover, he is dead." The words
acked harshly across the bailey. "Along with twenty
her good men."

Lover? Geoffrey wasn't her lover. "I-I do not under-
and."

"Do you not? I think that you do." He cast his helm to
s squire and stepped in front of her, his eyes piercing
she had never seen them, slicing into her, accusing
er without the need for words. "I think that you have
onspired with Geoffrey, that your words have caused
ath and injury to my men. I think that once more you
ave betrayed me."

"No!" But even as she said the words, Caryn knew, at
ast in part, it was the truth. Tears stung, welled in her
es and blurred her vision.

"You deny that you broke my trust? That you told
eoffrey about the Ferret?"

How could she deny it? Ral had trusted her and she
d betrayed that trust. She hadn't meant to—dear God,
e would never do anything to hurt him. Yet twenty
ave men were dead, and even now her husband's
ood dripped onto the earth.

"I would hear you say it." The slash of his blade could
ot have cut deeper than the bitterness in his voice.
id you speak to Geoffrey? Did you reveal my plans for
e Ferret?"

"I-I did not mean to, I—"

"Did you tell him!"

She blinked and the tears began to trinkle down her
eeks. "Aye. I am the one who told him."

He struck her such a blow that she reeled and
ammed into the dirt. The salty taste of blood filled her

mouth but Caryn welcomed it. She wished for its like
and more, for in truth, she knew she deserved it.

She struggled to her feet and forced herself to look a
him, certain he would strike her again, hoping in a way
that he would. Instead, she saw a face contorted with
the same pain she was feeling, a man stricken with such
conflicting emotions it was tearing him in two. She
wanted to reach out to him, to comfort him and give
him ease. She wanted to fall onto her knees and beg hi
forgiveness.

Instead she did nothing.

One look in those cold unfeeling eyes and she knew
there was no forgiveness there.

Ral had steeled himself against her. The expression he
now wore was the same one he had ridden in with
anger, disillusionment, and bitter despair. Even those
emotions were soon banished, leaving nothing but emp
tiness and cold determination.

"Is there aught you wish to say?" he asked.

So much and so little. She could do naught but shake
her head.

"Since the day of our betrothal you have implored me
for your freedom. You have sought it above all else
From this day forward, Caryn of Ivesham, you shall have
it."

Caryn said nothing. Her throat had closed up and
tears streamed hotly down her cheeks. Her chest ached
until she could barely breathe, and her heart hurt as if i
had been cleaved in two.

Towering above her, Ral's lips curved into a hard, un
forgiving line that made him look even more fearsome
"For some months now, Lynette has made her home a
Pontefact. My friends there will also take you in. You
may join the ranks of my lemen . . . or you may return
to the convent. The choice is yours. Which is it to be?"

The decision was not a difficult one to make. Free
dom, the gift she had once craved above all else, mean

othing to her now. Nothing without Ral and the home
he had come to love.

"I would return to the sisters." Mayhap she would
nd peace of a sort there, discover a way to forgive
erself for the deaths of Ral's men.

He frowned at that, surprised a little by her choice.
You are certain that is your wish?"

"Aye, my lord."

He stiffened. "Then so be it. Pack your things and
ake yourself ready to leave. Girart will see you safely to
he convent." He turned away from her then, his back
rect, ignoring his cut and bleeding leg as he walked off
oward his men.

She watched his tall frame striding away from her, his
road shoulders straight though he was obviously so
eary, and knew more love for him in that moment
an she had ever felt before.

"Ral . . ." He stopped, his back going even more
gid, but he did not turn around. "Your leg . . . I . . .
lease . . . you must let someone tend it. Isolda
an—" But he only started walking, his long tired
rides carrying him farther away.

She wasn't sure how long she stood there. Seconds
at seemed hours. Minutes that seemed an eternity.

"Come, my pet. We must make ready." Marta's bony
ands bit into her shoulders, forcing her to move, forc-
g her to place one foot in front of the other. Caryn
id nothing, just let the old woman guide her upstairs,
en stood at the window while Marta packed a handful
f her belongings. She would need little at the convent.

What she needed most in the world she had already
ost.

Vith Girart and two of Ral's men to lead the way, Caryn
ode her small gray palfry along the road to the convent.
he remembered little of the journey, seeing the land-

scape through a film of tears, crying in silence, her hea
breaking into smaller and smaller pieces.

Marta had tried to console her, to convince her tha
somehow things would work out. Caryn had only stare
at her and said things would never work out for he
again.

Men were dead because of her. Her husband ha
been wounded. He had trusted her with his life an
those of his people, and she had failed him.

Just as she had failed herself.

"Will you be all right, my lady?" Girart stood at th
convent door, the other two men behind him. He ha
ever been kind to her and she had liked him. She wa
surprised at his kindness now.

"She will be fine," said Mother Terese, the stern-face
abbess of the Convent of the Holy Cross. "Her siste
Gweneth, is here and there are others who are he
friends. This place was once her home."

Home? Caryn thought vaguely. The only home sh
had known in years had been at Braxston Keep. Th
only place she had felt needed . . . the only place sh
had ever really belonged.

"Come, Caryn. We must see to your garments."

Still she said nothing. She didn't deserve the beautifu
forest green tunic she still wore. Sackcloth and ashe
and hours on her knees in prayer. Even that wasn't pu
ishment enough.

"You will feel better once you are settled," the abbes
was saying. "God will forgive your sins, even if you
husband does not." They traveled the dreary corridor
even more loathsome than she remembered. Mayhap b
cause this time she knew she would never escape then

"In a way your arrival is a blessing. In return for ou
care of you, Lord Raolfe has been generous. 'Twoul
seem he is a good man and fair. 'Tis a shame you faile
him so completely."

It went unsaid 'twas what the abbess had expected a

long. Caryn had been a misfit in the convent, had plagued them all with her misadventures. She had been a miscreant and a troublemaker. She deserved exactly what she got.

She followed the tall thin abbess into a long narrow cell with a corn husk mattress at one end. This would be her home from now till the end of her years.

Caryn felt rough hands on her forest green tunic, felt the combs being drawn from her hair. Several of the sisters, one she recognized as the hateful Sister Agnes, helped her to pull on a coarse linen shift. A brown woolen tunic followed, then she was once more left alone.

Caryn sank down on the lumpy corn husk mattress. She touched the damp stone wall, rested her cheek against it. It felt damp and cold, just like her heart. Tears leaked from beneath her lashes as she curled up and closed her eyes.

Ral, I love you so. I am sorry that I failed you. She sobbed against the rough gray stone, wondering how everything could have gone so wrong.

Ral lifted his head from the table. Around him several knights snored while other men's ribald laughter echoed against the castle walls.

" 'Tis getting late, my lord." Richard nudged his shoulder. "Mayhap 'tis time you went to bed."

Ral's arm snaked out across the table, scattering platters of leftover food, empty wine goblets, and overturned drinking horns. He reached for one of the latter, held it upright and extended it to Richard. "See it filled for me."

Richard hesitated a moment, then motioned toward the page half-dozing in a corner. "Bring the wineskin. Lord Ral would have more."

Leo scurried forward, filled the horn, then backed

away. Ral downed the contents and held out the hor
for more, which Leo reluctantly poured.

"He is ever like this since Lady Caryn is gone," Le
whispered to Richard.

"Aye," he agreed with a grimace. "Soon he will slee
as soundly as the others and I will have some of the me
see him up to his bed."

"I do not believe what they say of Lady Caryn. I d
not believe she would ever betray her husband."

Neither did Richard nor Ambra nor at least a hal
dozen others, yet Caryn herself had said it was so. Ricl
ard turned away from the pitiful sight Lord Ral made, h
dark head lying once more among the litter on the tabl
Standing in the shadows a few feet away, Marta watche
him and worriedly shook her head.

For six full days he had been drinking, his movement
jerky and out of control, his voice slurred, his com
mands barely coherent.

The pain was too great, Richard knew, the hurt to
deep, too raw for him to bear. Richard understood tha
pain as no one else in the castle. If the woman had bee
Ambra, if she had turned to another, if she had betraye
him—he was not certain that he could go on.

"I will see he gets upstairs." That from Odo, wh
looked as grim-faced and worried as he and the other
Along with Girart and several of the men, they lifted th
huge man who was their lord and carried him up th
steep stone stairs.

It was no small task that was fast becoming a nightl
chore.

Richard watched the men until they disappeare
down the passage, then wearily set out for his chambe
He would find succor in his young wife's welcomin
arms. Lord Ral would find only an empty bed and
hellish night of bitter memories.

Richard wondered if Caryn's nights passed anywher
near the same.

* * *

For the first few days they left her alone. To meditate, they said, to pray for God's forgiveness. She had spent the time in bitter isolation, unwilling to leave her cell, sick inside and unable to swallow a mouthful of the dismal convent food.

Then early one morning, her tortured sleep was ended by the sound of someone entering her cell. Fatigued from her fitful rest, Caryn slowly opened her eyes, her heart beating dully.

At the foot of her pallet, she recognized the outline of a girl in a tunic the same brown woolen as her own and knew in an instant that the girl was her sister. Caryn sat up rubbing the sleep from her eyes.

"Hello, Gweneth," she said softly. Even in the darkness, she could see her sister smile. The black-haired girl knelt beside her and Caryn took her hand. "You should not be up so early." But there was no censure in her voice.

She had avoided her sister on purpose, been unable to look into those guileless blue eyes for fear of what her sister would see in her own.

Gweneth did not understand that Caryn was her sister, yet there was a sense of recognition, a glow of warmth for someone she knew as a friend. Though she had not spoken since the day of her accident, she felt great empathy for the people around her, sharing their joy, their pain, their happiness, or their sorrow. Gweneth seemed to blossom with goodness, so much so there wasn't room for anything else.

In the shadows above them, sunlight crested the high barred window in the small narrow room, slanting down, warming the lumpy pallet Caryn sat on.

"The sun comes up," she said needlessly, for already Gweneth tugged her hand, urging her up from the floor. Pulling on her woolen tunic, she followed her sister's lead, letting Gweneth guide her down the hall and out the door. The lovely girl led her to the garden where she had planted a patch of marigolds. Gweneth pointed to the sun and then to the beautiful yellow flowers.

"Aye, they are like tiny suns," Caryn said. Plucking one, she slid the stem behind Gweneth's ear. In back of them a familiar voice called out her name and Caryn turned to see her friend, Sister Beatrice, smiling and waving in their direction. Caryn and Gweneth waved, too. Lifting her skirts up out of the way, her sister raced back toward their friend at the door of the convent, but Caryn did not follow.

Instead she glanced down at the patch of bright yellow flowers. She was glad the marigolds brought sunshine and joy to her sister. For herself, the sun had gone out of her life the instant that she had lost Ral. From that moment on, though the warm yellow rays continued to beat down, her insides felt cold and she seemed to exist in darkness.

She wondered if ever the sun would warm her again.

"I tell you something is wrong!" Odo paced in front of the desk in the solar while Ral poured over the Braxston ledgers.

"What? What could be wrong? 'Tis not as though she has denied it."

"It matters not what she has or has not said. I still say something is not as it seems."

"Leave off, Odo. I tire of this foolishness. You make me wish to forget we are friends." Ral had finally roused himself from his week-long drunken stupor. It had helped him dodge the pain for a time, but unless he climbed into the wine flagon, he could not avoid it forever.

" 'Tis because we are friends that I speak to you thus. I implore you to discover the truth."

Ral slammed his hand down onto the table. "You want the truth? The bitter truth is that my wife was in love with another man. He was greedy and ambitious. He used her to get what he wanted, but got himself killed in the bargain. That, my friend, is the truth!"

"Your wife was in love with you, not Geoffrey. If she told him your plans for the Ferret, she must have had a reason."

"I cannot believe you defend her. You, who did not even like her."

"That was true . . . in the beginning. Then I saw her care of you, how happy she made you. I saw the way she looked at you when you no more than walked into the room. I saw the way you looked at her."

"You talk nonsense. The woman was in love with Geoffrey."

"She was in love with you!"

Ral sighed wearily. There wasn't a particle of his being that believed it. "Even were that the truth, the woman betrayed me. I cannot live with a wife I cannot trust."

"I do not believe she would purposely betray you. You meant too much to her."

"Enough of this! Why do you insist she cared for me? Nay, even loved me? Never once did she say those words to me."

"Did e're you say them to her?"

"Nay, but—"

"Once she spoke of the love she felt for you," he said softly. "Never have I seen such a look on a woman's face. A man would forfeit a kingdom for a woman who looked at him that way."

Ral's insides churned. Every moment of his day was plagued with loss and pain. No matter how hard he worked to ignore it, it was always there with him, making him ache inside. Now Odo had come, adding to his burden, stirring the memories, the doubt that never quite left him, making him wish for things that could never be.

"Get out," he said with soft menace. "Get out and do not return."

Odo stiffened. "I am sorry. I did not mean to pain you." He stopped when he reached the door. "Yet even that I give you grief cannot make me regret my words."

Ral slammed the ledger closed as Odo shut the door.

"He has gone mad," he grumbled to Marta, who stood just outside the door. The old woman said nothing, but her shoulders seemed to slump with the weight of his words as she turned and walked down the hall.

Caryn sat on the knoll among the soft grass and flowers. She went there whenever her endless hours of toil in the convent were ended, just to sit and remember.

At first she had tried to block the past, to forget it and make it disappear. Then she discovered that it was the past that offered her solace, the past that provided her only refuge from the pain.

Though her days were filled with backbreaking toil, of scant meals, stifling confinement, and days upon end of guilty reflection, the moments that she spent in the past, the hours she relived her time with Ral, brought peace as nothing else could.

It was easy enough to remember. In the eye of her mind, his face was as darkly handsome as the day that she had first seen him astride his big black stallion in the meadow. She could imagine every line, every curve of his sensuous lips. She could see the teasing light that changed his eyes from gray to blue, or the deeper tantalizing shade that signaled his desire for her.

She could remember his powerful hands and the way they had felt when he touched her, the gentleness and the strength. She remembered the sensuous way they aroused her, the way they had held her when she cried, the way they had soothed her and helped to ease her pain.

She thought of the wolves and the way he had risked

is life to save her. She thought of the way he'd helped
eo, the justice he had sought for the huge blond Saxon
warrior. She thought of Ral, and as much as her heart
ched for him, she rejoiced in those times as she never
ad before, as she knew she never would again.

Mostly she thought of just being with him, of the
ound of his deep compelling voice, of the way his lips
urved up when he smiled, at the laughter they had
hared . . . and the worries. Who shared his burdens
ow? she wondered. Who did he have to turn to? He
ad needed her and she had let him down.

Caryn glanced up and was surprised to see her sister
tanding beside her, the shadow of Gweneth's perfect
rofile falling across her face. She looked down at Caryn
n silence, then Gweneth knelt beside her, her fingers
lutching a small bouquet of posies. She held them out,
hen pressed them into Caryn's hand. Caryn's own
ands trembled as she accepted them, the ache inside
er swelling, the pain increasing, threatening to tear her
part.

She reached toward Gweneth and for the first time
oticed there were tears in her sister's blue eyes, a well
f sorrow that overflowed and made a path down her
heeks. There was pain on her face, a sadness as deep
nd profound as her own. A lump rose in her throat to
ee her sister thus, for she had rarely seen her cry, rarely
nown her to be so unhappy.

It came to her then, that Gweneth's tears were a re-
ection of her own, that she felt the pain Caryn was
eeling, the heartbreak and loss that must be evident on
er face. Seeing Caryn on the knoll, her emotions un-
uarded, Gweneth had sensed her sorrow, her terrible
eelings of grief.

Caryn brought the flowers to her nose with unsteady
ands, inhaling the light sweet fragrance. She glanced
nce more at Gweneth and forced a smile to her face.

Leaning forward, she brushed the tears from her sister's pretty cheeks, then wiped at those on her own.

"You mustn't cry," she said with false brightness. " 'Tis beautiful here, is it not?" She continued to smile for long heartbreaking moments, forcing away thoughts of home, thoughts of Ral and love and her loneliness until finally Gweneth's soft red lips began to curl upward.

Caryn reached toward a small stand of bluebells, plucked one and handed it to Gweneth. "See how pretty? The same shade as your eyes." Her sister was smiling in earnest now, nodding eagerly, searching the ground for more of the precious blue flowers. She spotted a patch some distance away and wandered in that direction. Caryn watched her go, knowing Gweneth's sadness was forgotten, the pain as fleeting as the butterfly she had started to pursue.

Caryn's own pain had not altered, searing in its intensity, burning a hole in her heart. For the first time in her life, she felt no joy in her surroundings, no joy in the sunshine, or the blueness of the sky. For the first time ever, she envied her older sister the oblivion of the far off world in which she lived.

Chapter Twenty-three

Ral glanced toward the big empty bed and the pain in his heart stabbed fiercely. It never left him now, not since the night he had argued with Odo. In truth, it had worsened each day since the doubt had crept in.

He ached for Caryn, thought of her moment by moment as he had from the beginning, only now the ache was dulled neither by an outpouring of spirits nor the blinding haze of his rage.

Sometimes he hated Odo for what he had done, stirring up his anguish, rousing his uncertainties. From dawn of one day to dusk of the next, the doubts never left him, springing up at the oddest times, memories of little things his wife had done or said, things that spoke of her care of him . . . things Odo would say spoke of love.

He remembered every detail of the time they had spent together, the way in the beginning she had run to escape their marriage then faced his wrath with such courage; the way afterward he had held her and she had cried against his chest. He remembered the way she had stood beside him, risking her life as she faced the wolves, determined not to leave him. She had braved his anger for Leo, protecting the boy at no small risk to herself. In doing so she had won his admiration, and his respect.

His mouth curved up as he remembered her care o
the hall—then her flagrant disregard of it. What courag
it had taken to defy him, but in the end she had won th
servants' loyalty and no small amount of his own. H
thought of Lynette and how much his taking of th
woman had hurt her. Why had she felt such pain if sh
did not care?

Or mayhap it was the pain he had inflicted that ha
driven her away from him.

Ral sat down in his chair, his elbows propped on th
table, his head bent forward, his fingers laced in his hai
How many times would he think of her, remember th
feel of her soft woman's body? How many times woul
he dream of her smile, imagine her laughter, or simpl
the sound of her voice?

How could he feel such despair over the loss of
woman who would betray him?

He sighed into the darkness of the room, lit only by
single, guttering candle. He thought of Eliana, tried t
remember the hurt he had felt when he had discovere
her evil liaison with her brother. There had been pai
then, too. The pain of being duped, of feeling used, o
losing something destined to be yours.

But there was none of the anguish he had felt since h
had lost Caryn.

And because his feelings were so very different th
time, the doubts continued to plague him. He aske
himself, would he feel so much grief for a woman cap
ble of such pretense, a woman of so few morals sh
would take a lover behind his back, dupe him, deceiv
him, and use him to gain her own ends?

Would he hurt so for a woman such as that? Were h
instincts so dulled by his passions that she had led hi
that far astray?

He heard a slight shuffling sound and lifted his hea
to see Marta standing in front of the stout wooden tabl

"You have suffered much, my lord, but so has she. Are you ready yet to hear the truth?"

His heart skipped at her words then began thudding softly, yet there was wariness in him, too. "What truth?"

"The truth of what happened the night your Caryn betrayed you."

"She is no longer my—"

"Is she not? Then why is it you grieve so?"

"If you've something to say, old woman, then say it or leave me in peace."

Marta pulled an empty goblet from the folds of her gray linen tunic and set it upon the table. " 'Tis the same one your lady wife drank from the eve of your search for the Ferret."

"If you are saying she was drunk, it matters not. If she cannot be trusted—"

"She was not drunk. She had only but this one goblet. I am saying that she was drugged."

"Drugged?" He tried to bury the small surge of hope, the indefinable pulse that had not beat in so long, but it would not be still. "You are saying that Geoffrey put something in her wine?"

" 'Tis called verosa. Far more than just something. The juice of the plant is dried into small brown cakes and used to deaden pain. When the dose is too strong, it can make a person see things . . . do things he would not do."

"You expect me to believe such a tale? What proof have you—and why did you not speak out sooner?"

"Is there a time you would have listened?"

Nay, he knew that there was not. His rage had been too great, the pain too strong. "Tell me your tale, then I would see your proof. If there is none, our conversation is ended." Yet his insides fairly quaked with the hope the old woman had unleashed. He found himself praying she would not turn to leave.

She did not disappoint him. Instead she began her

story, starting with the odd pallor of Caryn's skin that
she had noticed that night on the stairs. Because of her
worry, she had returned to the hall and there discovered
the goblet, which still smelled of traces of the drug. She
had gone from the hall to the medicinal, had found that
Hassan's jar of the dried narcotic had been disturbed,
seen bits of the powdery substance still left in the bottom of the mortar. Though she hoped it meant naught,
she had secretly questioned the servants.

When Ral remained unconvinced, Marta paused and
shuffled to the door. She pulled it open and one of the
serving women walked in, her eyes darting nervously in
his direction.

"Do not be afraid," Marta said. "You must tell Lord
Ral what you saw that night as you passed by the medicinal."

Her name was Elda, he remembered, a young girl not
much older than Caryn.

" 'Twas Geoffrey, milord. I wondered what he might
be doing in there so late, but 'twas not my concern and
so I did not ask."

"What did he in there?" Marta asked.

"He ground something in the mortar. He was in a
hurry, to be sure, for he left a few moments later."

"How would Geoffrey know of such a potion?" Ral
asked, but the beating of his heart had grown stronger,
the hope expanding, growing into something that
swelled and urged the heaviness to lift from his chest.

"You forget he spent a good deal of time in there.
Lady Caryn used a tiny bit of the drug to ease his pain.
Make no mistake, my lord. Geoffrey de Clare knew ex-
actly what he was about."

"There is still the chance that you are wrong. I know
the feelings you carry for your mistress. It is possible
you only wish—"

"Think you back to that night, my lord. Do you not
remember how it was that your lady wife slept? No

even did she waken to wish you godspeed on your journey. She was much overwrought when she awoke to discover you had gone."

He recalled carrying her up to their room. Even his heavy movements could not rouse her. She slept as if she had been . . . drugged.

His hands clenched into fists atop the table. "If this happened as you say, why did she not try to explain? Why did she say naught in her defense?"

"Your Caryn believes herself guilty. Your men are dead and the fault is her own. You bestowed a trust in her and she failed you. She will punish herself for it all the days of her life."

"Sweet Christ, I cannot believe this." But suddenly he did. Every sweet, life-breathing word of it. He wanted to shout from the rooftops, he wanted to pound his fists and grind his teeth for not being able to see it before.

Something is wrong, Odo had said, but in his pain, in his anguish he could not see.

"I must go to her."

" 'Tis too late to begin such a journey. 'Tis dark outside with only a sliver of moon to guide you."

He smiled, joy rushing through him, his blood pumping, his spirit coming alive. " 'Tis more light than has lit my way in weeks." Long strides carried him toward the door. He shouted for Odo, roused half the servants, and began to call out instructions.

Behind him, Marta smiled softly and brushed a tear from her cheek.

Ral took ten men and set off for the Convent of the Holy Cross. He rode hard that night, slept only a few hours, then set off again before dawn. As tired as he was, he felt alive as he hadn't in days, as he had feared he never would again.

His purpose was set, yet as he drew near, his unease began to grow. What would he say to her? What would she say to him? In a different way he was just as guilty of betrayal as Caryn believed herself to be. If he'd had more faith in her, if he had but listened to his instinct instead of his anger, he would have discovered the truth.

Even Odo had been able to see it. But not the man who was her husband. Not the man who was entrusted with her care.

His stomach twisted to think of the brutal way he had struck her. In his anguish he had lashed out, though the pain she had suffered had ripped through him as viciously as it had her. He wondered if she would forgive him. Mostly he wondered if she was happy there in the convent. She had wanted to be free of him, to live a life unfettered by duty and responsibility.

He worried if, after all that had happened, his Caryn would come home.

"Lord Raolfe!" The abbess stepped back to allow him in. "I am sorry . . . we received no word of your arrival."

He barely paused to greet her. "I have come to see my wife. Where is she?"

The abbess smiled a bit stiffly. "Outside, as she prefers. 'Twould do her far more good should she spend the hours on her knees, praying for her soul." The tall, thin woman walked to an inner door and pulled it open. "If you will follow me to the end of the hall, Sister Beatrice can show you the way."

While his men-at-arms waited out in front, Ral followed the woman down the barren, dimly lit corridor. It was dank and dark and dreary. His jaw clamped to imagine Caryn living in such a place, and guilt washed over him like a wave. At the end of the corridor, the abbess handed him over to a slender young nun he remembered was Caryn's friend.

"If there is aught you need," the abbess said, "Sister Beatrice will see it done." Turning away, she left them

"You have come to see your wife, my lord?" the little nun asked.

"Aye. How does she fair?"

"Not well, my lord, I fear. For days she has hidden herself away. 'Tis like watching a beautiful blossom wilt and fade. She does not belong here, my lord."

Ral cleared his throat, but his voice still came out husky. " 'Tis plain to see that is so. I only hope she feels the same."

Beatrice pulled open a heavy wooden door with rusty hinges. It creaked eerily as they passed through and she led him outside.

"There, my lord." She pointed to a gently rising hill across a meadow. "She sits in the sun whenever the sisters allow it, though it never seems to warm her."

"Aye. Too well I know the feeling."

Beatrice left him there and he stood for a moment, gathering his courage, praying the right words would come. Then he crossed the rolling field toward the small seated figure in the distance.

Caryn sat atop the knoll, staring out at the horizon. There was much to do within the halls of the convent; the tasks often seemed without end. Yet in the past few days, she had been allowed these times alone. She wondered if it was the money Ral had paid for her care . . . or if it was the sadness they saw in her eyes, the sorrow that reached the depths of her very soul.

She looked out over the meadow, seeing little of the beauty, barely feeling the sun. She wasn't sure how long she sat there, but the fiery yellow ball had passed some distance closer to the horizon. It was the shadow that fell over her, the pair of knee-high, soft leather boots encasing a man's long legs that drew her from her musings and made her glance upward. Shielding her eyes, she recognized the tall man outlined by the sun's bright rays.

"Ral . . ." it was the softest of whispers, yet he smiled when he heard it. She had never thought to see that smile again.

" 'Tis good to see you, Cara."

She swallowed the pain he caused by using what was once an endearment, and the yearning that tore through her at the sound of his voice. She came to her feet as hurriedly as she could, brushing blades of grass from her coarse brown tunic. All the while, her eyes drank in the sight of him, of how tall and splendid he looked, of the dark masculine beauty of his face. He was thinner, she saw, his body leaner, even more solid, if such a thing could be.

"Y-You are well, my lord? Your thigh is healing as it should?" Why had he come? She couldn't imagine a single solitary reason.

"The wound was minor. I am fine." He stood in front of her, looking oddly ill at ease. "And you, Cara? You are also fine?"

Why did he keep calling her that? Saying the word so softly, almost caressingly. It made tears burn the back of her eyes and a lump rise in her throat. She forced herself to smile and prayed it didn't look far too bright.

"Aye, my lord, the sisters treat me well. And Gweneth is here. It pleases me to see how happy she is."

Ral glanced off toward the horizon, his gaze fixed somewhere in the distance, much as hers had been. She memorized his powerful jawline, the sensuous curve of his lips. He shoulders were so broad they blocked the sun, until he turned and looked once more into her face.

" 'Tis pleasant out here. Walk with me for a time?"

"As you wish, my lord." But she really didn't want to. The pain he stirred was too great, the agony of her loss nearly unbearable. Yet she shouldn't have been surprised by his arrival. It was like him to check on her welfare. She was still his wife, after all. Or mayhap that was the reason for his visit.

Caryn's insides squeezed into a hard tight ball. It should have occurred to her that he would want to end their marriage. There was the matter of children, of heirs for Braxston Keep and its lands. She bit down hard on the inside of her cheek to keep the tears from welling in her eyes.

"How is Marta?" she asked as they moved farther away from the convent, the soft grass bending beneath their feet.

"Well. She worries overly for you. So does Ambra."

"You must tell them that I am fine. That . . . that I am pleased to be returned to what was once my home." She could have sworn his body tightened. At the bottom of the knoll, he paused and the breeze rippled gently through his wavy black hair.

"I have come this day for a reason," he said. "There are questions I must ask you, things I must know."

"Questions, my lord?"

"About the night you spoke with Geoffrey."

She swayed a little on her feet, the pain was so great, and Ral reached out to steady her. Just the touch of his hand sent a fissure of longing through her body.

"You are all right?"

" 'Tis only that . . . that I would rather not remember. 'Tis painful for me. I—"

"I too would rather not recall, but I must know why it was that you told Geoffrey about the Ferret."

A hard ache rose in her throat. He was making her remember when she tried so hard to forget. "I did not mean to." She swallowed, wishing it was not so difficult to speak. " 'Twas the wine, I suppose. It made me see things, say things. . . . Often I have wondered why he did it . . . what was it that he had to gain."

"He wanted the land. Malvern promised the king's bounty in exchange for information."

Caryn nodded absently. The reason no longer seemed important. "During the time of his illness, he spoke of his mother, of caring for her as his father never had. You once told me that he was ambitious. Too late, I discovered 'twas the truth."

"Then he was not your lover."

She shook her head and smiled forlornly. "Nay, my lord. I was ever faithful to you."

Ral's jaw went taut. "You are saying that you did not love him."

"Geoffrey? He was little more than a boy. I felt naught but friendship for Geoffrey."

For the longest time Ral said nothing. When he did, his voice sounded oddly strained. "I should have asked you to explain. I am bitterly sorry."

"Explain, my lord? There is naught to explain. Your men are dead because of me. You entrusted me with your secret and I revealed it. Once again I betrayed you. 'Tis I who am sorry, my lord."

Ral turned and gripped her shoulders, his fingers biting in, forcing her attention to his face. "You did not betray me! Think you that had Geoffrey gained the knowledge from Odo in such a manner I would have banned him from the castle?" *Banned him from my life? From my heart?* "Think you I would not have seen the fault was Geoffrey's, that he alone was to blame?"

"I-I do not understand."

"We all make mistakes, Cara. The mistake you made was in trusting Geoffrey. 'Tis your nature to place your faith in others and 'tis not something I would have you change. 'Twas never my intention to punish you for making a misjudgment, for certainly I have made mistakes myself."

"You, my lord?"

"Aye. I made a terrible mistake the night I sought out Lynette. 'Twas a deed I regret most sorely."

"Your men are dead, my lord, because of me. There is aught that can change that."

"My men are dead because of Geoffrey!"

Caryn said nothing more, just stared at him as if she tied to grasp his words. He raked a hand through his air and looked down at her, uncertain what more to ay, fighting an urge to touch her, knowing if he did he 'ould crush her against him.

"There is a favor I would ask you, Cara."

"Aye, my lord. But first I would ask a favor of you."

He arched a brow. "You wish a boon of me?"

"Aye."

"What is it?"

"I would ask that from this day forward you do not :turn to this place. You have seen that I am well. If you 'ish to set aside our marriage, I ask that it be another 'ho carries the news."

Ral fought the tightness in his chest. "Why?"

She gave him a sad little smile and he noticed there 'ere tears in her eyes. "I do not wish to see you . . . ecause it hurts my heart . . . too much." Uncon- :iously her hand came up to the spot and Ral felt as if a lade sank into his own.

"I beg you, *cherie,* you are killing me with every 'ord. Do not say more until you have heard the favor I 'ould ask."

She merely nodded and dashed the wetness from her heeks.

Ral took a deep, steadying breath. "During our time ogether, I have come to know how highly you value our freedom. I know how much you loath being tied own by duties and responsibilities, but I would ask if ou might consider . . . returning home."

Lines furrowed her brow. "Home, my lord? You do ot mean that I should return to the castle?"

"You are needed there sorely. Marta is old and frail, nd there is Leo to consider. Ambra and Richard need

help with the hall and . . . more than the rest . . .
need you, Cara."

She stared at him for long uncertain moments, then
tears began to trickle down her cheeks. "You would
forgive me?"

"I told you, *ma chere*, 'twas naught but a mistake that
you made. I am the one who should seek forgiveness. I
should have believed in you, trusted you." He reached
for her then, his arms going around her, drawing her
against him with infinite care, holding her so close she
felt the beating of his heart. Bending his head, he kissed
her, a tender, yearning kiss that changed to one of blazing heat and such fierce possession Caryn trembled.

"I love you," she whispered when the fiery kiss had
ended. "Mayhap I have loved you from the moment I
first saw you."

Ral crushed her against him. His smile was so bright it
seemed the world had suddenly blossomed anew. "If
that is so, then say that you will come home."

Her answering smile came from deep inside her, the
dawning of the sun after endless darkness and storm.
" 'Twould please me more than anything on this earth."

He kissed her again, molding her against him, claiming her in a way he hadn't before, saying without words
exactly how much he cared. With hands a little unsteady, he brushed back strands of her hair.

"We will leave as soon as you are ready. I would see
you once more naked upon our bed. I would hold you
and kiss you and make love to you for hours on end.
Were we not now standing on the grounds of the Holy
Cross, I would take you right here."

Ral kissed her one last time, so thoroughly her knees
nearly buckled beneath her. Then he was lifting her into
his arms, striding across the grass toward the doors to
the convent. He paused inside the bleak stone corridor
just long enough to tell the abbess to have his wife's
possessions readied and given to one of his men.

At the front door, he set her upon her feet. "You would say farewell to your sister?"

"Aye, my lord."

"Then do so, for I long to take you from here." Even as he said the words, Sister Beatrice hurried toward them, tugging Gweneth along by the hand.

"Ever have you been a friend, Beatrice." Caryn leaned forward and hugged her, then turned and hugged her sister. Her smile must have been radiant, for Gweneth's seemed to light the very corners of the room.

"I shall return soon for a visit," Caryn promised. She clasped Gweneth's hand and her sister leaned forward and kissed her cheek. Caryn hugged her one last time, then turned and walked outside to join Ral and his men.

"Be happy," Sister Beatrice called out behind her. But she needn't have bothered, for Caryn already was.

She found Ral waiting just beyond the heavy oaken doors, his eyes a brilliant shade of blue, his smile so warm it made her heart turn over.

"We are for home?" she asked.

"Aye, my love. We are for home."

Home. How precious was the word. She smiled as Ral lifted her up on his saddle then swung up behind her. He slid his arms around her waist and she leaned into the hard wall of his chest.

They traveled swiftly, Ral as eager to be returned to Braxston Keep as she. During the night, Caryn slept close beside him, feeling his desire for her, the rock hard evidence making him groan with discomfort. And yet he did not take her. She knew it was his way of showing his care of her, his regret of all that had occurred.

The following day, she rode the little gray palfrey Ral had brought for her return, though he stayed close by her side and smiled at her warmly and often. Their spirits were high as they neared the castle, so much so that mayhap Ral might have relaxed his guard.

By the time they heard the thunder of hoofbeats, their attackers were upon them, broadswords flashing as they bore down on the handful of Braxston men.

" 'Tis Malvern!" Ral shouted, working to keep his sorrel in front of Caryn's palfry while his men bravely fought the men attacking them from the rear. Still, they were badly outnumbered. Braxston's ranks were soon broken, Lord Stephen's knights riding in, cutting Caryn off from her valiantly fighting husband.

"Ral!" she screamed as one of Malvern's men came at him from the left, a blade arcing downward toward his head. Ral thrust his shield upward, deflecting the blow, but two more men pressed in behind him.

"Ride for the keep!" he called out, and for the first time, Caryn realized it was she the men were after.

She whirled her horse and dug in her heels, but already it was too late. As she frantically turned her palfry one way and then another, a tall knight leaned forward, bent and swept her from the saddle. Though she tried to fight him, he forced her down across the withers of his horse, turned the animal and pounded away. The rest of the men continued their attack on Ral and his men wounding several and preventing them from pursuit until Caryn had been carried far into the forest.

Ral swung his broadsword, the fury of seeing his wife slung over his enemy's horse driving him on. He fought until a lance wound brought the sorrel down beneath him, fought until he and four of his men were the only ones still able to wield their swords. At the sound of a high, shrill whistle, Malvern's remaining knights stopped fighting and to Ral's surprise began to back away. They whirled their mounts, sheathed their blades and rode off into the forest, following the men who had taken Caryn.

"Why have they left us alive?" Girart gazed blankly after them, the dust of their departure still marking the trail. "I do not understand."

Ral's fingers tightened on the handle of his bloody sword. "We are alive because Stephen wished it. 'Twas exactly what he planned."

"But why, my lord?"

"He means to demand a ransom." Ral swore a savage oath. "He means to bring me to ruin one way or another." Ral glanced around him then strode toward a loose horse grazing among the trees. The long-legged bay had belonged to one of Malvern's fallen men.

"How fare the others?" Ral asked, leading the bay horse forward.

"Two dead. Four injured."

"Are the wounded able to ride?"

"Aye. Even now they gather their horses."

"Good, then we are away." The sooner they reached the keep, the sooner he could gather what remained of his forces and send word to his supporters that he would need more men. He didn't allow himself to think of Caryn, of what vengeance Malvern might seek against her solely for being his wife.

He only knew one thing for certain—this time he would not fail her.

Chapter Twenty-four

Caryn winced as the horse stepped into a rut, jarring her stomach against the hard ridge at its withers. She was bruised and battered from her journey through the forest and the tall knight's brutal treatment. She was thirsty and tired and afraid.

What had happened to Ral? Had he been injured, mayhap even killed? She had worried every step of the way, yet she believed with all her heart that he still lived. She would know, something told her, if aught untoward had occurred.

At present, another worry loomed before her, for as she turned her head, she saw Malvern's green and white colors, then the appearance of a huge green silk tent. The tall knight pulled rein on his horse, and she felt rough hands lifting her down. As her feet touched the earth, one of them shoved her toward the tent. When she reached it, the flap was lifted and she was thrust inside.

At the sound of coarse laughter, Caryn turned, but it was not Lord Stephen that she saw. Instead it was Beltan the Fierce, his greasy black hair and beetle-browed face just as harsh as she remembered.

Malvern sat beside him. "Welcome, my lady," he said, as though she had merely strolled in for a visit. " 'Tis kind of you to join us."

"Kind? That is what you call your vicious abduction?" Though she addressed herself to Malvern, she surveyed the interior of the tent, noticing the riches, the lustrous silks, heavy tapestries, and exotic furs. Her eyes widened as they returned to Beltar, for she suddenly noticed the slender blond woman, gagged and bound hand and foot on the thick Persian carpet at his feet. "Ambra!"

Beltar chuckled gruffly, and Caryn tensed. "What does she here? And why do you so mistreat her?"

"I am afraid your friend was not nearly as reasonable as you, my lady. Mayhap you can convince her 'tis in her best interest to cause us no more trouble. If not, she will remain just as she is."

Caryn hurried to her friend's side. There were bruises on her cheeks, and dried blood marked her lip. "H-How did she come to be here?"

He chuckled again. " 'Twas simple, really. A message was sent that she was needed in the village. My only mistake was in sending just two of my men to fetch her. They look nearly as battered as she."

Caryn smiled with a hint of satisfaction. Reaching down, she clasped Ambra's hand and gave it a reassuring squeeze. "Will you agree to cause no more trouble?"

Ambra nodded.

"She will do as you wish."

Beltar made a motion and the ropes were cut from Ambra's hands and feet. Caryn removed the gag.

"You are all right?"

"I am fine—no thanks to them." Ambra rubbed her chafed wrists while Caryn turned a hard look on Stephen.

"What is it you want from us?"

" 'Tis not what I want from you, Lady Caryn . . . although at a later time, once my sister arrives, you may be certain there will be much that I will demand. At

present, what I want is the ransom I mean to colle
from your husband."

"And Ambra? Is she also to be ransomed?"

"Nay," Beltar said with a smugly lecherous grin. "Tl
wench belongs to me."

Ambra opened her mouth to argue, but Cary
clamped hard on her arm.

"I am hungry," Caryn said. "I am also thirsty ar
tired. 'Tis certain Lady Ambra feels the same. Unless yo
intend to inflict further cruelty upon us, I ask that we I
allowed to refresh ourselves."

Beltar started to object, but Stephen's raised har
gave him pause. "Take them to the smaller tent. Se
they are fed and allowed to tend their needs. Then t
them up and leave them until they are summoned."

Beltar relaxed against his high-backed chair. "You ma
be certain that you will be called," he said to Ambra.
intend to enjoy your charms before this night is ende
'Tis my plan that you provide the evening's entertai
ment."

Ambra bristled, but Caryn propelled her forward. "D
not be foolish," she warned. "We are naught b
women. There is little that we can do."

"Naught but women!" Ambra fumed but the man b
hind her merely shoved them out the door. Caryn hear
Beltar's rumble of laughter as they were marched acro
the camp toward a smaller tent at the rear.

"How can you let them—"

"Do not waste your strength when you are so bad
outnumbered. Let them believe we will not fight ther
In the meantime, take stock of what you see, wh
might be of use to us later."

Ambra smiled with understanding, but her smile w
gone by the time they reached the second tent.

"There are forces enough here to wage a small war
she whispered. "Far more than would be needed we
ransom their only purpose."

"Aye," Caryn said, disheartened. " 'Tis a siege they intend. 'Tis obvious they mean to take the castle, and I fear it is not far away."

Both women said nothing more. Even was Ral yet alive and unharmed, there was no way he could defend against such a force as Stephen and Beltar had assembled.

"We must find a way to warn them," Caryn whispered as the men thrust them through the small tent opening and lowered the flap. One knight took up a position out front while the sound of footsteps meant the other man stood at the rear.

"How can we warn them? They are certain to watch us closely. Beltar has . . . plans . . . for me, and there is no telling what Malvern intends for you."

Caryn shivered. She had seen Lord Stephen's cruelty the night he had taken the novices from the convent. He would see her pay doubly for having escaped him . . . and because she now belonged to Ral.

"If we are careful, we may yet find a way. Do not be discouraged." But even as she said the words, her pulse beat dully. Sweet Blessed Virgin, how could they possibly escape?

Ral saw the heavily guarded walls of Braxston Keep and knew that in his absence, Odo had discovered Malvern's presence. He hailed the wardcorne, who called for the bridge to be lowered, then motioned for his men to follow him in.

It hadn't taken long to reach the castle. They had been close to home when Stephen's men had attacked them, which meant Malvern and his men were far too close at hand. Odo met him in the bailey, Richard beside him, both men's faces lined with worry.

"We feared for your safety, my lord," Odo told him. "I am glad you are returned." He took in the four injured men being helped from their horses. "Malvern?"

"Aye. He fell upon us near the crossroads. Two men are dead and they have taken Caryn."

"Sweet Jesu!"

"Ambra has also been taken," Richard said. "In our search for her, we discovered Stephen's men. There were too many for us to fight so we were forced to return."

"I had hoped we had seen the last of him," Ral said bitterly. "Were it not for William's friendship with his father, he would have tasted the thrust of my sword."

"There is more, *mon ami*," Odo said. "I fear Lord Stephen is not alone. He has joined forces with Beltar. 'Tis a virtual army we face outside these walls."

"And they have our women," Richard added.

Ral's jaw clamped. "Aye, that they have." He turned and started striding toward the stable. "They will start by demanding a ransom, but I fear 'tis Braxston Keep that they are truly after."

"I believe you are right," Odo said.

"We must get word to William. His support in this is crucial, though against such forces as Malvern has assembled, his help may come too late." Ral turned to his squire, who followed along in his wake. "Ready Satan for me. 'Twill soon be dark. I would see for myself what we must face."

"Aye, milord." As the young lad hurried away, Richard walked up beside him.

"This time I would go with you."

Ral started to deny him, to tell him he would better serve by staying in the castle. But he knew the twisting fear he felt with Caryn in the hands of his foe, and that unless he was bound in chains, there was no one who could stop him from going after her.

He nodded. "Make yourself ready. We travel by cover of night, taking only a handful of men. Odo will stay here and see to the keep's defenses."

"I intend to return with my wife," Richard said with

some defiance, his eyes fixed firmly on Ral's face.
" 'Twas my intention to do so long before this."

Ral smiled with soft menace. "You may be certain my
intentions are the same."

"I can hardly force down a single bite," Ambra com-
plained as they stood beside the table in the small tent
at the rear of the camp. A few feet away, scarlet silk
cushions rested on a thick Persian carpet. In one corner
sat a screen inlaid with mother-of-pearl, and sleeping
pallets had been fashioned on the floor.

"We must eat," Caryn said. "We will need to keep up
our strength." A tray of roasted wild duckling had just
been brought in, along with a flagon of wine.

"Aye, but I am too worried to eat. Besides, 'tis stringy
and tough and—"

"Aye," Caryn agreed, her head coming up, her eyes
alight with the first uncertain stirrings of a plan, "that it
is." She leaned closer to Ambra. "What say you we pretend that you are choking? When the guard comes in, I
will hit him over the head with the flagon of wine and
we will escape."

Ambra smiled and thrust a duck leg into Caryn's hand.
"I am bigger than you. You pretend to choke and I will
hit the guard over the head."

"With your months in the troupe, you are far better
suited to acting. You—"

"I tell you I am bigger!"

Caryn sighed as Ambra picked up the wine flagon and
moved it into position atop the table. "All right," Ambra
said, "pretend that you are choking."

Biting into the greasy duck leg, it wasn't that hard to
pretend. As Caryn started to sputter, Ambra pounded
her on the back and began to worry aloud for her safety.
All the while, Caryn continued to cough and wheeze.

"Help us! Someone help us!" Ambra ran to the tent
flap and jerked it open. "She is choking. The Lady Caryn

chokes to death on a duck bone. Please, you must help us!''

Unfortunately, both men rushed into the tent. While Caryn rolled her eyes and clutched her throat, gagging and wheezing and teetering forward, the men looked anxiously on. With a final sputtering gasp, she sucked in a great gulp of air and collapsed to the floor of the tent.

"I must go for help," the first man said, but as he turned, Ambra swung the wine flagon, smashing the heavy jug over his head. When the second guard spun toward the sound, Caryn scrambled up from the floor, grabbed the pewter tray filled with roast duck, and slammed the heavy metal against the side of his face.

"Bitch!" He swayed on his feet, but did not go down, just began an ominous move in their direction.

"What do we do now?" Ambra asked.

"I-I am not certain." He was blocking the entrance and even should they try to run he would signal the others before they could get away.

"A few well-deserved bruises should not matter to Lord Stephen," the man said with undisguised malice, balling his hands into fists as he moved toward them.

Above the hammering of her heart, Caryn heard a faint buzz somewhere behind them and turned to see the blade of a knife zipping upward through the tent. The guard saw it too but before he could reach the spot, a huge bare-chested figure appeared through the opening. A powerful arm snaked out, wrapping around the guard's throat. He squeezed then twisted, and the guard slumped unconscious onto the floor of the tent.

" 'Tis Gareth!'' Caryn said excitedly to Ambra. "The Saxon warrior the villeins brought to the keep.'' She turned to the huge golden-haired knight with a smile. "I am more than glad to see you, Lord Gareth, but how did you know we were here?''

A grim smile darkened his features. "I have been watching since Malvern's arrival. Think you I do not

ow who he is? There is not a Saxon warrior for three
ndred miles who does not know of Malvern's cruelty
ind despise him for it." He motioned toward the hole
the tent. "There isn't much time. We can talk of this
er."

Her heart still beating wildly, Caryn followed him
m the tent, Ambra hurrying along behind them. In
nutes, they were swallowed up by the thick trees and
shes surrounding the camp, but still they pressed on.
the darkness it was difficult to find sure footing. More
in once, Caryn winced as a sharp branch dug into an
n or leg, or her ankle twisted in a hole.

'We dare not stop," Gareth said quietly. "Too soon
y will discover you are missing."

Caryn nodded. Ignoring the cuts and abrasions the
nse growth inflicted, she and Ambra followed Gareth
ng, making their way toward Braxston Keep. When
y came to a clearing, they paused, Gareth's tall frame
ldenly going alert.

"Stay here," he whispered, indicating a place in the
rubbery as he moved stealthily off into the woods.
ryn crouched low beside Ambra, clutching her
end's slender hand. When a twig snapped beside her,
ryn nearly leapt out of her skin.

" 'Twould seem that much of our worry has been for
ught—would you not say so, Richard?"

"Ral!" Caryn came to her feet and he swept her into
arms. "How did you find us?" she asked. "How did
u know we were here?"

He tightened his hold protectively around her.
Twas Gareth. He spied us coming through the forest."

" 'Twas Gareth who helped us escape," Caryn said.

Richard smiled, Ambra snug in his arms. "Gareth says
vas mostly that you helped yourselves. He said 'twas
ur courage that saved the day." He touched Ambra's
eek, saw the purple bruise there, and anger suffused
features. "Other women would have acted no more

than frightened lambs led to the slaughter. Once
thought I wanted such a woman. I was wrong."
kissed his wife's cheek. "And I am proud of you botl

Caryn looked up at Ral. "Malvern means to take Br
ston Keep. He has gathered a sizeable army."

"Aye. Gareth has shown us."

"Where is he?"

"Somewhere in the forest. He will help us if he ca

"And Malvern?"

"Our only chance is in holding the keep until m
loyal to me can arrive."

Caryn nodded, shivering inside to think of the dea
and destruction the siege would bring—and wonderi
what would happen to them all should help not arri
in time.

Chapter Twenty-five

Ral spent the next two days fortifying the castle. With food supplies short and Malvern's forces cutting off the village, he was uncertain how long they would stave off their attackers. Still, he intended to hold his ground for as long as he possibly could.

Though he said naught to Caryn, he knew that should help not reach them in time, Stephen would give no quarter. It would be certain death for him—and an even worse fate for Caryn.

On the third day of their return, the guard signaled movement outside the walls of the castle. Climbing the steep stone stairs to the battlements above the keep, Ral watched in grim fascination as Malvern's men swept into the field across from the drawbridge, his green and white pennants flying, lines of armor flashing in the sun. Behind him, Beltar's forces moved into position around the castle.

Ral's hands unconsciously fisted. All too soon, the siege would begin. He shuddered to think of the dismal conditions they would be forced to endure, the hunger and disease, the violent deaths his people would suffer, not only here, but also in the village.

He remembered such battles in his past, remembered men walking over the bodies of their fallen comrades, piled into the moat to form a bridge. He remembered

boiling oil rained down through the brattice, remem
bered men screaming in agony as they suffered a fier
death worse than hell itself.

He remembered only too well and yet there was noth
ing he could do.

Only time could save them. Time for the knights h
had summoned to arrive. Time for support from th
king.

From his place atop the parapet, Ral watched his en
emy's army assemble. With Braxston's archers and mer
at-arms at the ready, with their arrows notched an
shields in place, with good men manning the walls, the
awaited the first assault. Hearing movement behind him
he turned to see Caryn pull open the door that led ou
side, step out on the parapet and walk toward him
Worry tightened her features and uncertainty darkene
her eyes. When she reached his side, she leaned towar
him, and he drew her against his chest.

"I am glad that you have come," he said softly.

She glanced out at the army in the field. "I was lonely
I missed you and the uncertainty is torture. At times,
think that the waiting is the worst part."

"Nay, *cherie*, it only seems so until the fighting be
gins."

"Can we hold them?"

"For a time. After that, 'twill rest in the hands o
God." He looked out at the hundreds of men in th
assembled army, at the siege tower and the catapult be
ing shoved into position. A battering ram waited in th
distance beside a giant, metal-plated tortoise that woul
serve as cover while the men worked to construct
makeshift bridge.

Stephen is well-prepared, Ral thought bitterly, h
stomach twisting at the thought of what lay ahead.

He glanced down at Caryn, felt her soft body agains
him, and for a moment forgot the hellish days they mus
endure. Instead, he noticed the sunlight reflecting o

ıer flame-dark hair, the way it glistened and shimmered. Ie recalled the silky feel of it as he had taken her last ıight in their bed. He had needed her fiercely, and she ıad filled that need again and again, her feminine curves :nticing him, her body responding, becoming so much ı part of him they had seemed almost one.

He touched her cheek, tilted her chin with his hand. 'There is something I would say to you. Something I ;hould have told you long before this.'' Her fine dark ıuburn brow arched up and he smoothed it with his ınger.

"What is it, Ral?"

" 'Tis not a thing easy for me to say. In truth, for a ime, I did not believe such a feeling existed. Since I ıave met you . . . since you have become my wife . . I have discovered it does most surely exist, and I ım the most fortunate of men to have known it.'' He ;miled at her with all the tenderness he felt in his heart. 'I love you, Cara. I have known it for some time, but I :ould not say the words. I love you and for me there can)e no other woman. Not now. Not ever.''

Tears filled her eyes and she spoke his name softly, ıer hand coming up to his cheek. "I never thought to ıear you say it. I prayed for a day such as this, but in my ıeart, I did not believe it would happen.''

"I should have told you sooner. Mayhap if I had there would have been less hurt between us.''

" 'Twas I who should have spoken, but I was afraid of osing you. You are the husband of my heart and I will ove you forever.''

"Cara . . .'' Ral bent his head and kissed her, a :ender, gentle kiss to show her the love in his heart. When he finished, he held her against him, looking over ıer head toward the field that would soon erupt in bat-le. Death surrounded them, yet he felt content as he ıever had before. Caryn leaned into him and he tight-

ened his arms around her, holding her for long, achingl
tender moments.

If only he could be certain of her safety, what hap
pened on the morrow would not matter. Ral stared a
the mighty forces they faced, at the death and destruc
tion just beyond the walls, and knew he could be cel
tain of naught.

The wind blew bitterly across the parapet, tugging a
Caryn's braided hair. For a while she had been able t
escape the harsh reality of men about to make war, c
lives to be lost, of the horror about to begin.

"They have been ready for some time," she finall
said, breaking into the silence. "Why do they not a
tack?"

Ral shook his head. "I do not know."

"Our men seem more than ready. 'Tis a comfort t
know you have trained them so well."

"Aye. 'Tis an advantage we will need, to be sure."

They watched and waited a good while longer, till
man on the tower shouted down to Ral and pointe
wildly toward the field. In an instant she saw the reasor
for behind Stephen's army, another group of armore
men and horses appeared.

"Dear God," she whispered, her stomach going ho
low, "he has enlisted even yet more men."

Tense and strained, Ral stepped toward the edge c
the parapet, then to her surprise, he smiled. "Nay, m
love. 'Tis King William's army, no other."

"William? If that is so, why does Beltar ride wit
him?" 'Twas for certain that he did. Through the cente
of the encampment next to William, who sat tall an
proud, stout and aloof in the saddle. The king rod
toward them, Beltar to one side, Stephen on the other. /
meeting of some sort had occurred, it would seem, fo
as they drew near, it was obvious Beltar bowed to Wi
liam's command—and Stephen was bound in chains.

"Come," Ral said. "With William arrived, we are safe." His hand rode at her waist as he guided her back inside the keep.

She could feel his relief in every powerful stride, and her own relief grew with each step they took down the stairs. Recalling the words of love he had spoken, her own love soared. He had pledged his heart and committed himself to their future. With the king's arrival, and an end to Malvern's treachery, that future had only begun.

They made their way down the stairs and across the great hall, then down the wooden stairs leading out to the bailey.

"Wait for me here," Ral said with a reassuring smile and a quick kiss on the lips.

Anticipating his needs, his squire had Satan saddled and ready, the huge black destrier prancing and pawing the earth. Ral swung effortlessly up on the horse's back, though he wore his heavy chain mail, and Aubrey handed him his conical helmet. As Ral pulled it on, Odo and Girart and twenty mounted knights rode toward him across the bailey.

Calling for the drawbridge to be lowered, Ral nudged the black horse forward. The stallion clattered across the heavy timbers then they reached the opposite side, the men making a well-formed column behind them. As the last of the knights crossed the bridge, Caryn raced toward the gatehouse, arriving at the same time Ambra did.

" 'Tis Lambert and Hugh," the slender girl said, pointing excitedly toward the men in the field. "I could see them from my window. William must have set out for Malvern the moment he received news of Lord Stephen's betrayal."

"Thank the Blessed Virgin. I had not dared to hope for such a thing."

"What think you of Beltar? He seems to have sided with the king."

"The man may be ruthless, but he is no fool. I do not believe he ever intended to incur King William's disfavor. He has far too much to lose. Once William learned of Stephen's alignment with the Ferret and the part he must have played in the attack on his tax collector, Beltar was forced to withdraw his support."

"And without it and against such odds," Ambra said, "Stephen's own men would surely turn against him."

Caryn smiled. "Aye. 'Tis certain that is what happened."

They reached the top of the stairs, Caryn's heart pounding with excitement, and looked out across the field toward the armies of armored men. Close to the front, the king and his lords were talking, arguing heatedly, it seemed. Oddly, when they had finished, Ral dismounted and so did Lord Stephen. Someone cut Malvern's bonds and to Caryn's horror handed him a sword.

"Sweet God in heaven," she whispered as Ral pulled his own sword from its scabbard.

"They mean to fight," Ambra said.

"Aye." The word came out brittle and shaky. No matter that Ral was the finest warrior in the land, no matter that his body was honed to perfection, Stephen de Montreale was no coward. He was tough and strong and he was desperate. God only knew what he would gain should Ral be defeated.

Her fingers trembled against the wooden support beneath the roof of the gatehouse. *Blessed Virgin, please let him win.*

The men raised their blades and the ring of metal against metal echoed across the field with each clanging blow. Caryn shivered at the sound, desperately afraid for her husband, willing him not to lose. Stephen's thrusts were clean and fiercely delivered, yet they were sporadic, as if the events of the day had somehow dulled his senses. Still, he fought like a madman. Had Ral not met each of his blows with cool control, the man would have seen him dead.

As it was, Malvern soon began to tire and Ral's heavy blows began to take their toll. Blood appeared on Stephen's tunic, a streak of bright red visible even from the distance.

A blow sliced into his thigh and he went down on one knee then came back with a vicious arc of his blade that nearly caught Ral full force. He blocked the blow, but in doing so, left himself open. Caryn held her breath, her knuckles white as Stephen lunged toward him, sure his blade would connect with Ral's chest. Instead, Ral stepped backward and at the same time thrust his blade forward, the tip sinking in, driving deep into Stephen's malevolent heart.

For a moment the handsome blond lord just stood there, unable to respond, unwilling to believe that in an instant he would be dead. Then he toppled over, falling like a broken twig sailing toward the earth.

Caryn released a small sob of relief, her hand going up to her throat, tears burning the backs of her eyes.

"He is all right, my lady," Ambra said, smiling and gripping her hand.

"Aye. Thank God he is safe."

Even before Stephen's body was dragged away, Beltar signaled to his men and they began to pull back from their positions. The king said something to Ral then turned to his knights and continued to call out orders. Mounting Satan, Ral motioned to his men and they rode back toward the castle, giving Caryn a chance to climb down from the platform and make her way across the bailey to await his return.

With her heart pounding nearly as fast as her feet, she reached the base of the wooden stairs leading inside the keep and turned to look for Ral. She smiled as she

watched him riding forward, sitting his huge black horse
so straight and proud. In minutes, he stood before her, a
radiant smile on his face.

"The fighting is ended," he said, "even before it has
begun."

"Aye. 'Twould seem God has answered our prayers."

"Stephen is dead. His lands and those of his sister
have been confiscated by the king. We are safe from his
villany at last."

"What of the villagers?" she asked. "Their homes sat
in his path. Have they suffered greatly from Malvern's
mistreatment?"

"There was a good deal of raiding, but no one was
hurt. The king has agreed to replace the villeins stores
from the riches at Malvern."

"And the bounty?"

"Is ours. Braxston's people will at last have the land
they deserve."

Caryn went into his arms and he held her against his
mail-clad chest. "I love you, Ral."

He smiled, his eyes alight with joy, his hold one of
fierce possession. " 'Twould please me greatly should
you come with me upstairs and show me just how
much."

"But the king—"

"William will not arrive before supper. Richard can
see that the hall is made ready."

Caryn smiled, leaned forward, and kissed him on the
lips. "Then 'twould be a pleasure to accompany you, my
lord."

Ral tipped her chin with his fingers, bent his head and
kissed her, long and deep. "I love you, wife of my
heart," he said softly. Sweeping her into his arms, he
smiled as he headed for the stairs.

London, England, 1809

Cat and mouse. Damien scoffed. *More like seasoned panther and wary young doe.* He watched her through the French doors leading into the main salon of Lord Dorring's townhouse. Gowned in emerald silk the same shade as her eyes, laughing softly with one of her beaux, she led the man onto the dance floor.

It was crowded in the sumptuous high-ceilinged room, a crush of London's finest. Men in tail coats and brocade waistcoats, ladies in silks and satins, some of them more richly gowned than the woman he watched, but none of them nearly as lovely. She crossed the inlaid marble floor, all elegance and grace, a slender, white-gloved hand resting lightly on her suitor's arm. For an instant, her glance strayed toward the terrace.

She knew he was out there.

Just as he had been watching her, she had been watching him.

Damien Falon, sixth earl of the same name, propped one wide shoulder against a rough brick wall of the townhouse. He had made it a point to discover the balls and soirees, house parties and musicales the young woman would be attending. The Season had begun and the fashionable elite had arrived in London—Alexa Garrick among them.

She danced a roundel, her pretty face glowing with exertion, fiery auburn hair shimmering softly at her cheeks. Then she and her partner left the dance floor. The young Duke of Roxbury pressed her to continue, but Alexa shook her head. The duke bowed somewhat stiffly and left her near the door.

Damien raised the snifter he cradled in a dark, long-fingered hand and took a sip of his brandy. Alexa was walking toward the terrace, tall and regal, looking neither right nor left, making her way through the French doors. Careful to avoid the place where he stood in the shadows, she crossed the terrace and paused at the opposite end, her gaze going out to the garden. The faint glow of torches lit the manicured oyster-shell paths, and moonlight glistened on bubbling fountains of water.

Smiling faintly, Damien set his brandy glass down on a small ornate pedestal and made his way across the brickwork to the woman at the opposite end.

She turned at his approach and something flickered in her eyes. He couldn't decide if it was interest—or anger. It didn't really matter. Already he had achieved his first objective.

"Good evening . . . Alexa."

She looked surprised, taking in the fashionable cut of his black tail coat and white cravat, seeming to approve, though the use of her name had caught her a little off-balance.

"I'm sorry," she said. "I don't believe we have been introduced."

"We haven't. But I know who you are . . . and I think you know who I am."

Her head came up. She wasn't used to a man who challenged her. It was the key, he had discovered, the way to intrigue the lady, capture her attention, and draw her into his web.

"You're Falon," she said, her tone telling him she had

ard the stories about him, most of which were true.
only hoped she didn't know too much.

"Damien," he corrected, moving closer. Another
oman might have walked away. He was betting Alexa
ould not.

"You've been watching me. I saw you last week and
e week before that. What is it you want?"

"Nothing every other man here doesn't want. You're
beautiful woman, Alexa." He stood close enough to
ell her perfume, the soft scent of lilac, to see the
all black pupils in her pretty green eyes. "The truth
you intrigue me." The tiny circles flared for an in-
nt. "That hasn't happened to me in a very long time."

"I'm sorry, Lord Falon, I don't know what it is you
pect from me, but I assure you it isn't worth all of this
uble."

A corner of his mouth curved up. "No? Perhaps it will
. . . if you let it."

She glanced out into the shadows and nervously
oistened her lips. "I-It's late," she said with a slight
sitation. "They'll be looking for me soon. I had better
going back in."

He could ruffle her a little. Good. From what he had
en, it wasn't that easy to do. "Why would you want to
in when it's far more pleasant out here?"

She straightened a little, throwing the lines of her face
to shadow. "And far more dangerous, I should think. I
ow who you are, Lord Falon. I know you're a rouge
th a despicable reputation. I know you're a rake of
e very worst sort."

He smiled. "So you've been asking about me. I sup-
se that's a start." A delicate indentation marked her
in, he saw, as she thrust it forward.

"You flatter yourself, my lord."

"What else have you heard?"

"Not much. You aren't exactly dinner conversation."

"But the consensus is that I'm off limits to innocent
ung girls."

"You're very well aware that it is."

"You don't think a man like me could change?"

Her eyes surveyed his face. There was nothing tim[ ] in that look, nothing shy or demure. He hadn't expect[ ] there would be.

"I didn't say that. How could I? My brother was [ ] even worse rogue than you—if that's possible. Now h[ ] a happily married man."

"So you see, there's hope for me yet."

She said nothing for a moment, sizing him up aga[ ] studying him from beneath her thick dark lashes. [ ] really have to go." She turned and started walking.

"Will you be at the soiree at Lady Bingham's on Sat[ ] day next?"

She paused but did not turn. Beneath the torches, h[ ] burnished red hair seemed to blaze brighter than t[ ] flickering flames. "I'll be there," she said, and then s[ ] was gone.

Damien smiled into the darkness, but his hands ball[ ] into fists. How easily she could make a man's blood he[ ] up, his loins grow thick and heavy. Half the young buc[ ] in London had begged for her hand, but she had refus[ ] them. Instead she merely toyed with their affection[ ] leading them on, flirting outrageously, moving from o[ ] poor besotted fool to the next.

A dozen had offered her marriage.

She should have accepted when she had the chanc[ ]

"Alexa! We've been looking all over for you. Where [ ] earth have you been?" Lady Jane Thornhill, a sma[ ] round-faced girl of two and twenty, walked toward h[ ] Gowned in a tunic dress of aqua silk heavily embr[ ] dered in gold, Jane was the daughter of the Duke [ ] Dandridge. She was also Alexa's best friend.

"I was just out on the terrace." Alexa plucked at [ ] button on her long white glove. "It's so very warm [ ] here."

"The terrace? But surely you haven't forgotten Lo[ ]

Perry? Faith, he's one of the most eligible bachelors in London. And so handsome. . . ."

"Lord Perry, yes. . . . I'm sorry, Jane. As I said, it was just so warm."

Her friend eyed her shrewdly, soft brown eyes taking in the heightened color in her cheeks. She glanced toward the French doors leading out to the terrace, just as Lord Falon walked in.

"Dear God, Alexa, surely you weren't out there with *him*!"

Alexa shrugged. "We spoke briefly, that was all."

"But he's . . . he's . . . why, you haven't even been introduced."

"No, and we probably never will be."

"You've the right of it there. Your brother would have a fit if he knew that man was anywhere near you."

"I don't see what's so awful about him. Lots of men have affairs with married women."

"There aren't many who've killed three husbands fighting duels over them."

"My brother has certainly fought duels. And it's hardly a secret that Rayne carried on with Lady Campden. Why, he was—"

"Rayne is reformed. Lord Falon is not, and probably never will be."

She toyed with a strand of her hair. "I don't remember seeing him before, not until this Season."

"He's been out of the country for the past several years. Italy, I believe, or perhaps it was Spain." She glanced back toward the earl. "At any rate, he isn't much for Society. And they aren't much for him."

"Then why do you suppose he's here?"

"I can't imagine." They watched him cross the main salon, turning more than one head as he passed, moving gracefully toward the ornate doors leading out to the street. He was taller than most of the men in the room, lean but broad-shouldered, with wavy black hair and dark skin, high carved cheekbones and incredible bright blue eyes. In a word, he was one of the handsomest men Alexa had ever seen.

"Do you think he's a fortune hunter?" she asked, almost reluctant to hear the answer. She was at present unmarried, and one of the wealthiest young heiresses in London.

"To be honest, I don't think so. From what I've heard, his estate has dwindled, but he isn't really poor—and he isn't in the marriage mart. If he were, there are at least a dozen wealthy young ladies who would marry him and gladly. To say nothing of a number of the eligible widows who are his usual cup of tea."

"What else do you know about him?"

"Not much, really. He lives in some musty old castle on the coast. At one time there were rumors that he was mixed up in smuggling. Another time there was gossip that he was sympathetic to the French."

"The French!"

"He's part French on his mother's side. That's where he gets those dark good looks."

Alexa sighed. "A womanizer, a smuggler—perhaps even worse. There isn't much to recommend him." She frowned at the thought, a little uncertain why the dark earl so intrigued her. Then she smiled more brightly than she had in a very long time. "Still, he *is* incredibly handsome. And those eyes—as blue as the sea after a storm."

"Yes, and just as unfathomable. You may rest assured that man means nothing but trouble."

Alexa merely shrugged. Already she was counting the days until Saturday next . . . .

DEVIL'S PRIZE—THE NEXT STUNNING HISTORICAL ROMANCE BY BESTSELLING AUTHOR KAT MARTIN— ON SALE IN 1995 FROM ST. MARTIN'S PAPERBACKS

KAT MARTIN

Award-winning author of *Creole Fires*

GYPSY LORD
_____ 92878-5 $6.50 U.S./$8.50 Can.

SWEET VENGEANCE
_____ 95095-0 $6.50 U.S./$8.50 Can.

BOLD ANGEL
_____ 95303-8 $6.50 U.S./$8.50 Can.

DEVIL'S PRIZE
_____ 95478-6 $5.99 U.S./$6.99 Can.

MIDNIGHT RIDER
_____ 95774-2 $5.99 U.S./$6.99 Can.

Royd Camden is a prisoner of his own "respectability." But when he sees beautiful Moriah Lane—condemned by society and sentenced to prison for a crime she didn't commit—he cannot ignore her innocence that shines through dark despair. He swears to reach the woman behind the haunted eyes, never dreaming that his vow will launch them both on a perilous journey that will test her faith and shake his carefully-wrought world to its foundation. But can they free each other from their pasts and trust their hearts to love?

Evergreen

by Delia Parr

"A UNIQUELY FRESH BOOK WITH ENGAGINGLY HONEST CHARACTERS WHO WILL STEAL THEIR WAY INTO YOUR HEART."
–PATRICIA POTTER